D0952375

THE GODS OF
HEAVENLY
PUNISHMENT

THE GODS OF HEAVENLY PUNISHMENT

Jennifer Cody Epstein

W. W. NORTON & COMPANY

New York • London

Excerpt from *The Letters of D. H. Lawrence, Volume 2: 1913–16*, published by Cambridge University Press, reproduced by permission of Pollinger Limited and the Estate of Frieda Lawrence Ravagli.

For information about permission to reproduce selections from this book, write to Permissions, W. W. Norton & Company, Inc., 500 Fifth Avenue, New York, NY 10110

For information about special discounts for bulk purchases, please contact W. W. Norton Special Sales at specialsales@wwnorton.com or 800-233-4830

Manufacturing by Courier Westford
Book design by Chris Welch
Production manager: Julia Druskin

ISBN 978-0-393-07157-3

W. W. Norton & Company, Inc.
500 Fifth Avenue, New York, N.Y. 10110
www.wwnorton.com

W. W. Norton & Company Ltd.
Castle House, 75/76 Wells Street, London W1T 3QT

1 2 3 4 5 6 7 8 9 0

Dedicated to Katie and Hannah,
my two goddesses of light, inspiration and perspective

Though *The Gods of Heavenly Punishment* is based on a true event (the 1945 firebombing of Tokyo) and contains characters who are either based on or inspired by true historical figures, it is in the end a work of fiction. As such, all interactions, thoughts and dialogue within its pages are purely products of the author's imagination and are not intended as statements of historical record.

The war is dreadful. It is the business of the artist to
follow it home to the heart of the individual fighters—not
to talk in armies and nations and numbers—
but to track it home.

—D. H. LAWRENCE

Tadahiko Hayashi

Contents

I. *Hamburg, New York*

THE CLIMB FELT ALMOST ARDUOUS, THE ENGINE JUDDERING AND restarting four times during the creaking ascent up. But when they reached the top it was worth it, as it had always been worth it: they were so far above the ground that the poor, patched and battered world seemed as small and harmless as a toy train set.

It was as close a thing to flying as he could imagine.

"Is it broken?" Lacy Robertson asked, beside him. "Why did it stop like that?"

Cam shrugged. "Maybe they had to oil the gears or something."

He stretched his arms up, luxuriating in the feeling of isolation and quietude, the oddly omniscient power the Ferris wheel had always given him. The Hamburg Fairgrounds stretched out below them, the green grass taking on its first tawny tinges of autumn, the exhibition tents billowing like landlocked sails. Small boys with crew cuts and girls with corkscrew curls buzzed, manic and intent, from stand to game to stall. Their parents meandered behind them, dressed in their shabby Sunday best, pausing briefly before the Strongman exhibit, the pickle contest, the Dress Sewing Revue, exchanging pleasantries but rarely staying anywhere long enough to make a purchase. No one really had any money.

A few fairgoers trickled out past the tents towards the make-shift airstrip on East Field, where wing walkers had been advertised earlier. Now, though, there was no sign of sequined women on the planes' bluntly shining wings, and the gleaming birds were flying upside down, easing along against the darkening cloudline together.

God, Cam thought, *someday I will know what that feels like.*

"Will you look at that," Lacy was saying. "I can't imagine the poor fellows eat much before climbing into that tin can. If it were me, it'd all just come right back up again."

Her voice, normally deep and slightly husky for a girl, now sounded high and strangely brittle. When Cam turned towards her he saw she'd gone pale—as pale as the shawl collar of her white cardigan.

"Are you all right?"

"I get a little scared of heights, is all," she said, and smiled a little as though to say *Oh it's nothing.* But her lips were pressed together so tightly they looked almost colorless.

"You are? But—wait. Weren't *you* the one who said you wanted to take this ride?"

She nodded emphatically. "Yes, sir. That I did."

As though to underscore the point their car lurched forward another foot. Then it wheezed to a stop, as though it'd finally run out of gas. The motion made their car swing, and Lacy grabbed onto the side of the door, squeezing her eyes shut. She had impossibly long, thick eyelashes; the kind of lashes you saw on girls in makeup advertisements. Her lashes in particular fascinated Cam. Not just because they were so girly and graceful and pretty, but because his own lashes were as far from that as was possible: so blond and fine that in certain lights Cam—like his brother and their father too—appeared like lizards, almost lashless.

"I don't get it," he said, taking her hand without thinking (which was funny, since on their last date it was *all* he'd thought about, but he somehow hadn't dared to do it). "Why ride something that makes you scared?"

She opened her eyes, looking down at their meshed fingers and looking up again with that same wry look that had caught his attention last week. A look that took him in and turned him over like a toy plucked casually from a shelf, and seemed both indulgent and somehow amused.

"Well, for one thing," she said, "I figured getting really scared in front of you was one way to get you to hold my hand."

Cam felt his ears and cheeks redden. He almost dropped her fingers again, but Lacy Robertson squeezed his palm so tightly that her ring bit painfully into his knuckle.

"Don't even think about it," she said.

Cam cleared his throat. *Breathe*, he instructed himself. "So you're not really scared, then?"

"Oh, I am," she said. "I'm downright terrified."

He gave a short laugh. "And it was worth it to scare the bejeezus out of yourself simply to get some guy to take your hand?"

"Not just *some guy*," she said, in a tone that made him blush all over again. "And it's not just that." She grimaced as the car took another jolt forward, then squeezed his hand again. "It's something my dad always told me."

"And what's that?"

"That the best way to fight fear is to just try to do whatever it is that really scares you."

"I suppose that makes sense."

"Doesn't it? It's why he signed up to fight in the Philippines in '01."

He looked at her sidelong. "Because he was afraid of Filipinos?"

She punched him in the arm with her free hand. "No, you big

dolt. He was afraid of fighting. He'd been bullied in school. You probably don't know anything about that, though, do you?"

More than you know, he thought. But he kept his mouth shut—that was always the safest option.

She looked out at the sky. "Well, at least we seem to have stopped moving. For the time being." She gave him a sly look. "I can take my hand back now, if you want."

He pulled it towards him protectively. "Don't even think about it."

"Don't worry," she said lightly. "It'll be back."

Gently disentangling her fingers from his, she picked her purse up from her lap and opened it. Cam watched her, slightly awed. *She just did it again,* he thought; though he wasn't certain what "it" meant. It had something to do with the absolute ease she evoked in him, something he'd never experienced with anyone besides Mike and his mother. But it was also the way that, over the course of their two-and-counting dates so far, she had cut effortlessly through to the truth of things. Or at least, something very akin to *his* truth of things. What he was certain of was that he liked it.

"I've always thought the same thing," he said, leaning back.

"About what?" She was rummaging in her purse, the oversized ring he'd felt digging into his knuckle the same color as her eyes gleaming in the slanting afternoon sunlight. Her face was looking pretty green too, and Cam hoped she wasn't searching for a sack or something to be sick in. To his relief, she only pulled out a silver lipstick tube, and a matching silver-dollar-sized compact.

"About fear," he said.

She frowned at herself, applying color to her lips fiercely, as though doing this might somehow avert disaster. "Really? You don't strike me as the easily-scared sort."

Ha, he thought. "Everyone's scared of something, right?"

She was puckering her mouth, and he wondered again what it

would be like to kiss her. He'd thought about it last week too, after they saw *China Seas* together. He'd even told himself he'd do it when the date was over. But at the very last minute, standing there on her walkway, he'd found himself chickening out, because it had all rushed back to him: the mortifying terror of his old stutter.

"So what is it that scares you, Mr. Cameron Richards Junior? Lightning? Huns? Sharks?"

He forced himself to shrug. "Not that kind of stuff, really. I'm more scared of—I don't know. Smaller things."

"Like what?"

Like asking a girl to a dance and having it take five minutes, only to have her laugh in your face. Like having the teacher roll his eyes every time you raise your hand. Like having your father introduce you to strangers by saying, "This is my son Cameron Junior. He don't talk very well."

"Making an idiot of myself, I guess," he said, carefully.

She arched a brow over her mirror. "You?"

He nodded, feeling his face flush again despite himself, and despite that cool green gaze of hers that made him feel like he was floating in a mint-tinged sea.

"Well, that beats all," she said, snapping her mirror shut and laughing her hearty, unapologetic laugh—another thing he liked about her.

"What does?"

"You." She shook her head. "You really have no idea, do you?"

"No idea about what?"

"About *yourself*, silly. The girls in my dorm gave you a top grade, you know."

"Top grade for *what*?"

"You know. On the date-rate scale."

He still didn't get it, so she gave him a little lecture, drawing each letter in the air with her lipstick tube. "It goes A through D. An A means you're smooth, a B that you're OK. A C means you pass in a crowd."

"How far down does it go?"

"Just to E." Her hands were no longer shaking, an observation that left him slightly pleased with himself. As though he had set out specifically with the goal of easing her terror and was now witnessing the fruit of his efforts.

"An E means you're a spook," she went on. "A D's only a little better."

"What's a D?"

"Semigoon." She grinned, tucking the lipstick back. "But you don't have to worry. As far as my girlfriends are concerned you're an A. Real BMOC material."

He had no idea what that meant either, but he wasn't about to ask her. "So why were you laughing, then?"

"Because you aren't at all like that, are you. You don't even try to play the Big Man."

He couldn't tell if she was mocking him or not. "Well, should I?"

She studied him a moment. Then she leaned forward until her nose was barely a hairsbreadth away from his. "Should you what?" she murmured.

He inhaled sharply, tasting rather than smelling the musky sweetness of her perfume. It took every ounce of willpower he had not to jerk back, and in that moment he saw it happening all over again: opening his mouth and having his thoughts lodge there like bits of suet behind his tongue. Stuttering *puh-puh-puh* like a dry engine while her smile inverted to that familiar frown of revulsion.

"Cat got your tongue?" she whispered. "Should you *what*?"

Just breathe, he told himself. *Just breathe, and say it slowly. You know how to handle this now.* And he did. He'd spent his last summer before college mostly alone in his room, in a straight-backed chair in front of his mirror, *Self-Treatment Methodology for the Chronic Stammerer* (Third Edition) in his lap. Eyes trained upon his own lips, jaw and tongue, he had followed the steps prescribed with religious fervor: retraining himself to keep his hands and face relaxed while he spoke. Breathing from his diaphragm like an opera singer. Deliberately increasing his use of "trigger" words like *stop* and *catch* and *play* so he'd stop avoiding them out of reflex when he spoke. He hadn't completely lost his stutter by the time September came, but he'd managed to contain it for the most part. He'd kept it stuffed in the back of both his esophagus and his mind, and there it usually remained hidden—unless he let his guard down.

Or got nervous. Or scared.

Just breathe, he told himself now, *and say it slowly to her.* "P-play the Big Man."

He winced at the chipped way that first word came out, but if Lacy picked up on it she gave no sign. "No," she breathed. "You want to know why?"

He nodded, not trusting himself to speak.

"Because I don't want anyone else on campus to get you."

She leaned forward, and for a frozen moment he thought she was going to kiss him full on the lips. Instead she kissed him on the cheek: sweetly.

When she leaned back they locked gazes for a moment. Then, not giving himself time to think, he leaned forward and kissed her back on the mouth. Feeling her lips soft and warm and giving, feeling the scratch of her sweater. The subtle sculpture of her clavicle. He felt his heart flip in his chest like a skybound biplane, and felt himself a hundred feet above his own body—as if he'd climbed another, invisible Ferris wheel and was looking down at himself: a tiny Cam Richards kissing a tiny Lacy Robertson, in the little toy train station the Hamburg Fairgrounds had become.

They kissed until he could almost no longer tell where her smell and lips and skin ended and his started. She showed no sign of slowing down, and Cam was just starting to wonder whether he might slip a hand under her sweater when the car gave another shivering lurch and she finally pulled away, her mouth smeared with red lipstick. There was a brief, toe-tingling sense of falling, though whether it was from the kiss or the carriage dropping he wasn't sure. Then he got his bearings and realized they were halfway to the ground already. He gave a laugh: mingled joy, disbelief.

"What?" Lacy asked, dabbing at her mouth's corner with a pinkie finger, sounding faintly indignant.

He ran a hand through his hair and across the side of his neck. His skin still felt warm from her touch there. "I—I guess I wasn't expecting that."

"The bump?"

He laughed. "No. The—uh, kiss."

She glanced at him sidelong. "I was. I've been wanting to do it for a while."

He shook his head, still reeling. *What a girl.* She was studying him again. "Tell me what you're thinking," she said, very seriously. "Right this minute."

He shut his eyes, still faintly dizzy. "Ah—I guess I am thinking that most girls I know would be scared to do what you just did."

She pursed her lips in again. Then she leaned forward and kissed him once more—a brief kiss this time, a mere brush of the lips. Afterwards she sat back and gazed complacently out towards the clouds, where the planes were now spelling out the words *Get a Lift from a Camel* against the sky in white smoke.

"All the more reason," she said.

THE DAY DARKENED towards sunset and the tent shadows grew longer, and by mutual agreement they were done with rides and games. They wandered the fairgrounds slowly, their fingers laced together and their hands swinging in what seemed to Lacy a completely effortless and natural rhythm. She liked the feel of him just as much as she'd liked the look of him; the way his fingers were thin but strong, his palms warm but dry. The way his pale cheeks—which had blushed blood-beet red back on the Ferris wheel—were as smooth as a baby's, even at 5 p.m. She wondered how often he shaved, then tried to picture what he looked like when he did it. Naked from the waist up, a towel wrapped around his slim hips. Something inside her softened slightly.

"Where to next?" he asked her.

She shrugged. "Wherever you choose to lead."

"All right, then," he said, with that slow, quiet confidence he had. He was so unlike anyone else she'd dated at U of B, or in high school or even junior high. He was handsomer, for one thing. He had the blond-haired, blue-eyed good looks of a Swedish athlete or a movie star. Then again, looks had never meant much to her. Lacy generally found that the better-looking the man, the less work he put into charming her.

But this Cameron Richards Junior was different. He didn't *act* like a handsome man. In fact, he acted as though he were the exact opposite of that. It was hard to put her finger on it, but there was a timidity about him that was strangely—though not unappealingly—coupled with a fierce deliberation, both in the way he listened and in the way he spoke. It lent him a kind of strength that was devoid of arrogance. Or maybe it was forcefulness, softened by self-doubt. Whatever it was, she'd felt it right away that first day she saw him in English literature class, when she had (by complete accident, though her dorm mates didn't believe that) dropped her notebook on his scuffed leather shoes.

"Oh my," she'd said. She was about to say something else, some typically flippant comment about his big feet or her buttery fingers. But when she looked at him he was staring at her with such startled concentration, and such open-sky blue eyes, that the words stuck in her throat.

"Are you all right?" she asked instead.

He blinked, licked his lips. For a moment she thought he wouldn't answer. But then he smiled, and took a noticeably deep breath. "Yeah," he said, very slowly. "Thanks. I'm fine."

After class he'd waited outside in the hall for her, and—still with that same tentative-yet-forceful manner—asked her whether she would like to go to the movies. And while she knew that she wasn't supposed to say "yes" the first time (all the magazines said so, and her girlfriends too), Lacy told him that she'd love to, that she'd been dying to see Jean Harlow and Clark Gable in *China Seas* and could he pick her up this Friday at seven-thirty.

Throughout the movie she'd kept her hand slightly open on her armrest, like a fisherman dangling bait in a dark flickering sea. Their fingers brushed when he shared her popcorn, and again during the scene where Clark Gable had to fight off Malay pirates. At the explosion of the ship's cannon, they both jumped and their arms bumped. Beyond that, though, he'd made no move to hold her hand or touch her, and to her disappointment that didn't change when they went to McKinsey's after for coffee.

But at McKinsey's, at least, he'd finally opened up and talked. He talked about his father's farm, how it had been the biggest one in the county and so escaped failure and foreclosure when the economy soured. About how lucky he was that there was money for college for him, and that his father—who had initially talked about Cam working after high school ("He never thought I was all that bright")—had let him go. Not because that was what Cam wanted, but because there were no jobs to be had anywhere and hadn't been for a very long time.

For every question she asked him he asked her one about herself—again, so unlike your average dreamboat. Lacy had always been a talker, but she found herself talking especially easily with him, the words flowing fast and fluently as though it were her role to fill in all that space his slow speech left open. She told him about her job at the Aid Office, where she worked part-time issuing food vouchers to poor people who seemed less grateful for the help than embarrassed at needing it. She told him about her dream of living in California, and of seeing the Orient someday. "You should come with me," she told him. "You can be like Jean Harlow, with that platinum blond hair of yours. We can ride a trading ship through the China Seas."

He tilted his head and considered this, as though she'd just extended a formal offer. "I'm not much on water," he said, slowly.

"Really? Then how would you get to Peking?"

He'd smiled. "Why, I'd fly there, of course."

And that was when he told her of his childhood fascination with airplanes. It was what had led him, initially, to his major in aeronautical engineering at Buffalo. Lately, though, he'd come to realize that what he really wanted was to *fly* planes, not build them. He was thinking about signing up with the Army Air Corps after he graduated, something that both impressed Lacy and frightened her a little, though she wasn't sure if this was due to her long-standing fear of heights or a premature fear that he'd fly away from her.

At the end of the date he still hadn't touched her with more than his pale blue eyes, and when they parted ways she was again disappointed.

Now he was standing with his head back, staring up at the stunt planes that were still doing their stomach-roiling numbers in the sky. Lacy gave his hand another squeeze. "What are you thinking," she teased him, "with that dreamy look on your face?"

He gave her his sleepy smile. "I was just thinking about one of the other times I came to this fair."

"With another girl?"

"With my father and brother. I was seven."

"You have a brother?"

"Mike. He's two years younger than I am."

"That must've been nice. I always wanted a sister." She herself had been born when her mother was in her forties—a so-called "lucky surprise."

He shrugged. "It was all right, I guess."

"When I have kids, I'm definitely going to want two," she added, though this was another subject dating columns and her girlfriends warned against bringing up. "Being an only child can get awfully lonely."

He gave her a strange look. "Being a brother can be lonely too."

Their hands had parted briefly, and reaching for his once more she squeezed it. He smiled, bringing her fingers up to his lips. Giving them a kiss that was sweet and brief and tentative—as though after all that he still expected her to say "no."

He touched her mother's ring lightly. "Where's this from?"

Lacy pulled it off and gave it to him. "My mother calls it the 'come home to me safely' ring."

"That's a long name for a little piece of jewelry."

"Isn't it? There's a not-so-long story that goes with it."

"So tell me." He smiled.

She smiled back. "The ring belonged to my mother, and her mother before that. She gave it to my father when he went off to fight with MacArthur. She told him to bring it back from the Philippine Islands safely, or she'd kill him."

Cam laughed. "Your mother sounds like you."

She shrugged. "People say that a lot."

They were passing the House of Marvels, and the conversation hit a brief lull as a turbaned barker tried to hawk them their futures. "Only a nickel," he called to Cam. "That's all it takes to know what your life has in store! Find out now! Be prepared for later!"

Cam nodded at him but kept on walking.

"You don't believe in fortune-telling?" Lacy asked him.

"More like I'd rather just not know," he said. "That way if it's something good coming it can still be a surprise."

"And if it's not?"

He shrugged. "At least I can't worry about it before it happens."

He handed the ring back, watching thoughtfully as she pushed it back onto her ring finger. "So your dad did come back?" he asked. "From the war?"

Lacy nodded, tracing the jewelry's ornate silver scrollwork lightly before pushing it back onto her finger. She'd never told her mother this, but she'd always found it slightly ominous. The smoky green of the polished stone had reminded her of poison for some reason. Though she'd never actually seen any green poison.

"And it was the ring that did the trick?"

He asked it so seriously, as though he really believed it might be true, and Lacy felt a wave of tenderness wash over her. *I might fall in love with this one*, she thought, and the realization surprised her enough that she had a rare moment of being unable to say anything.

"I mean," he said quickly, misinterpreting her silence, "your parents thought it was because of the ring?"

She shrugged, her heart still racing from her epiphany. "My mother never said as much. But after that she wore it every day until I was sixteen. Then she gave it to me."

"Why at sixteen?"

"That's when I started to date boys."

He gave another easy laugh—something else she liked about him. Other men laughed too loudly, or unnecessarily, or sometimes not enough. "Let me guess," he said. "She wanted you to come home to her safely?"

His eyes were back on the planes again, and she wondered how he could even stomach the thought of being in one. "Yes," she said simply. "She did."

But in her mind she was thinking something entirely different. *You're a brave one, Cam Richards,* she imagined telling him. *You're the real thing. You are a keeper.*

Which was doubtlessly yet *another* thing she wasn't supposed to consider on a second date. Then again—and as her roommates and parents were always reminding her—she'd never been a big follower of rules.

II.   *Karuizawa, Japan*

MAY 1935

IT WAS MAGIC HOUR. THE SKY WAS A DUSKY PINK AND THE CLOUDS rose-hued and silver-edged, and the setting sun repainted their brown summer house crimson. Billy Reynolds sat beside the girl Indian-style in the long grass, his new Brownie hanging from his thin and freckled neck as it had hung for nearly every waking hour these past weeks.

His mother had given the camera to him at breakfast on his birthday last month, after a Belgian waffle with twelve candles that Billy only managed to half blow out before plunging into a coughing fit. After he'd quieted down and had some water she'd handed him the shiny device. Just like that: no wrapping paper, no card. As she washed up the breakfast dishes she told him matter-of-factly that she'd seen him studying *National Geographic* photographs and thought he might enjoy taking some himself. "Document your life as it is now," she suggested. "It's a remarkable place you are living. And we won't be in Japan forever."

And then she had kissed his red head and handed him his lunch for school.

By the end of that day Billy had shot a whole roll of film and made a list for the developing materials he'd need to turn his closet into a darkroom. He'd lain on his bed, staring up at the poster of Yukiko Ono he'd tacked to the ceiling, the comforting bulk of the Brownie resting on his chest and his dog Rasputin's chin resting on his upper thigh. He'd imagined exhibitions across the world where he'd be acknowledged a visionary, the dashing assistants who'd keep his myriad lenses polished and ready for his next masterpiece. In short, he'd imagined everything finally making sense for him. All in all it was a pretty terrific birthday—much better than last year's, when his father took him to see the Yomiuri Giants for some "man time" and barely spoke a word to him the whole game.

After he turned out the light, though, he'd heard them—his parents, arguing again in the kitchen. "You could at least have consulted me," his father fumed, his Czech accent thickening as it always did when he was agitated. "Do you have any idea at all what a thread we live on—with your craft classes and the boy's school and the jobs slowing down by the month since this whole China nonsense started?"

"It really wasn't that expensive," Billy's mother responded calmly, her own French accent neatly in check as always. "And it will give him a channel for his imagination. A purpose. He needs a *hobby*, Anton."

His father snorted. "What he needs are friends."

"With a hobby friends will follow," replied Billy's mother crisply. "Though of course, if *you* spent more time with him I'm sure he'd appreciate the company just as much."

During the pause that followed Billy's heart pounded, whether from fear of losing the camera or of spending time with his father he wasn't sure. But when he heard the ice clinking in his father's glass and Anton muttering to himself in Czech he knew that the Brownie was to remain in his life. Once again, his mother had won.

Now, leaning back on his elbows, Billy studied the child next to him. She was lying flat on her back, and had lifted her short legs to be nearly perpendicular with the sky. She was frowning. Someone had painted her toes scarlet. Nail varnish aside, though, they were very sweet feet; pudgy. Almost perfect. He'd already shot them twice, once flat against the grass and once pointed up and splayed apart, the summer house in the distance between them. He'd regretted that there was no way to capture the exact colors and contrasts: hard red paint. Fringed green blades bending beneath the unmarred heels. The soft pink flesh; its grubby coat of dirt and grass-stain.

"You'll have to wash those before you go home," he told her, in Japanese. "Your feet, I mean. Otherwise you'll get your house dirty."

She just gazed up at him with enormous dark eyes that reminded him of Princess Rose Red from Grimm. She wasn't, he'd noticed, much of a talker. In fact, so far this evening she'd spoken just two words: *"Nani?"* (What is that?) and *"Misette?"* (Can you show me?), both times pointing to the Brownie. Billy answered both times in Japanese, though according to his mother Yoshi understood English and a little French as well. Maybe *that* was why she was so quiet. Three languages were a lot for a six-year-old. He knew that from experience.

"Totte," Yoshi said fiercely, as though hearing the thought. *Take one.* She was pointing a chubby finger skyward. Obediently, Billy tipped his head back and lifted his lens, though he initially had no intention of wasting film on a square of empty space. But then a gilded motion over to the lower left caught his eye, and he shifted to see a brown hawk circling the woods below them. It was both very near and very large. The wingspan alone had to have been six feet.

Letting out a low whistle, Billy tightened his focus until the tawn of the underbelly came into finer detail. Then, finger crooked for the shot, he followed the bird's lazy arc. He didn't quite know what he was waiting for until he saw it: the black shadow of the predator cast against the canvas of the green treetops of the little glade at the bottom of the hill.

He pressed the shutter release: *click.* It was a sound and a sensation he'd loved from the first moment he'd felt it; the metallic snick of time stopping. The magic shutter that could capture life, render it examinable and perhaps even solvable.

"To'tta no?" Yoshi asked.

"I did, thanks." He tried saying it in English this time. "Maybe I'll give my dad a copy to give your dad."

She looked at him blankly, then climbed to her bare feet. *"O-shiko,"* she announced. *I have to pee.*

"Oh, OK," Billy answered uncomfortably. Was he supposed to bring her to the washroom as well? What if they expected him to help her *go?* The thought of being so near a girl's privates—even a little girl's, like this one—filled him with a sickening panic. Still, he pushed himself to his feet, extending his hand towards her. "Well, then, let's go."

But Yoshi had already set off towards the house below, racing down the hill with her red skirt fluttering like a flag. Billy loped after her, clutching the Brownie to his chest and stumbling twice on molehills before catching up with her on the patio, with the grownups.

His parents had been known to entertain up to a hundred guests at their vacation home, but there were only four at this particular dinner party. There were Yoshi's mother and father, both of whom were Japanese. The father helped Billy's father build his buildings. And Mr. and Mrs. Yamashita, who despite the Japanese name were actually first-generation American. Mr. Yamashita was one of the top draftsmen at Billy's father's Aoyama office.

Panting slightly, Yoshi hurled herself at her pretty mother, who cried out laughingly in English: "Oh my gracious, Lady Yoshi! Where's the fire?"

But even as she said it she was wrapping her daughter in her white arms, was holding her tightly and rocking her slightly and kissing the top of her dark head as Yoshi whispered something into her ear. On an impulse, Billy lifted the Brownie and framed the two of them. Seeing his father frown at him, he dropped it again.

"Why can't you go yourself?" Mrs. Kobayashi was asking, in French. "You're a big girl. I'm sure you can manage it." She pointed towards the open door. "Look. You just go straight through—wipe those feet first—and you'll see the water closet door around the corner."

Yoshi gazed up at her, her rosebud lips pursed. "*Oui*," she pronounced gravely, "*je peux.*"

Scrambling off her mother's lap again, she sidled towards the house cautiously, as though approaching a dragon's lair. She looked back for encouragement, and upon Hana's firm nod scurried off into the cool darkness.

"So impressive," said Billy's mother in Japanese. "Only six years old! And three languages!"

"Hard to believe, isn't it," Kenji Kobayashi grinned, his gold tooth flashing in the late sun. "Here I can barely speak Japanese properly, and I'm all but raising the League of Nations."

"You're not planning on withdrawing from it, are you?" George Yamashita asked dryly.

Kenji gave him the kind of look Billy had sometimes seen native Japanese give to American-born Japanese counterparts—slightly intrigued, slightly baffled. "Only if England and America behave rudely," he said.

He turned back to his wife. "*Oi, Omae*, shouldn't you go with her?"

"Shouldn't you?" she replied archly.

Kenji, already flushed from his two Kirin beers, seemed to Billy to flush a little deeper. "It's the mother's job."

Sighing, Hana Kobayashi set down her drink and stood, smoothing her skirt around her thighs. "Let's hope it's not another false alarm. It's all still rather new to her, this toilet business."

Turning on her high heel, she took a step towards the house. Then, however, she turned back.

"William-*san*," she asked, "had you wanted to take a picture?"

Billy flushed. "No—no," he stammered. "That's OK."

"Oh, come!" Béryl interceded warmly. "You *should!*" Turning to Hana, she explained: "We just gave him the camera for his birthday . . ."

"Cleaning out the bank in the process," muttered Anton.

His wife waved him off. "Oh, enough already. I told you it's a cheap one." She turned back to Hana: "You see, he's documenting his life in Japan so he can show his children what it was like to grow up here."

My children? Billy thought. They hadn't discussed that part.

"What a marvelous idea," Mrs. Kobayashi beamed. "Children *should* have creative hobbies and exposure to culture. I myself teach Yoshi French on Tuesdays and English Thursdays. And she's been taking piano for three years now." She looked at Billy thoughtfully, then looked back at Anton, rubbing the corner of her red mouth with a manicured finger. "Where would you like me to stand, Billy-*san?*"

Billy fiddled with his shutter speed, battling an extreme wave of shyness. Lifting the camera between them, he pointed to a spot by the door. "Uh, maybe right there. No, wait. Maybe a little closer to the entrance? The light's better . . ."

He followed her with his viewfinder as she stepped back and to the side. "Ready?"

"Oh heavens, no. Wait a moment," she said, snapping open her purse. "Let me fix my face."

It seemed an odd turn of phrase, particularly coming from some-one whose face, to his eye anyway, needed less "fixing" than anyone's he'd ever seen. Certainly compared to his own (freckle-splattered, cartoonishly long, framed by that wild mop of red hair), it was almost flawless. *A real looker,* his classmates at St. John's might have said. *Hot stuff.*

For his part, Billy didn't take much notice of female charms—not that he had much opportunity at his all-boys school. But in Mrs. Kobayashi's case they were hard to miss, if only from an aesthetic point of view. She dressed and carried herself with an erect elegance that seemed fully at odds with normal beauty standards here. Japanese beauty—at least, so far as Billy had surmised—involved wrapping women up like spider victims in layers and layers of silk, and then having them pretend to be more or less invisible. Mrs. Kobayashi, by contrast, was anything but invisible. In fact, she seemed *determined* to have people notice her. She was certainly not what he would have expected as the wife of Kobayashi-*san*, who Billy had seen on his father's sites shirtless, with a towel wrapped around his head and his *monpe* stained by sweat and turpentine.

"All right," she said cheerily. "All set."

When he framed her this time she'd not only powdered her nose and reapplied her lipstick, but had inserted a fresh Winston into her long cigarette holder. The latter she held languidly in the air, like a conductor between movements.

"Oh, aren't you *glamorous*," sighed Mary Yamashita. "Like a Japanese Rita Hayworth." In Japanese, she added: "You're a lucky man, Kobayashi-*katcho*."

"I am that," Kenji conceded, though the way he was studying his wife struck Billy as not all that unlike the way he'd studied George Yamashita earlier: intrigued. Baffled.

"OK," said Billy. "Smile."

She did, dazzlingly. A real movie-star smile. *Click*. He was going to thank her and perhaps ask for a backup shot when a clatter and a wail came from inside. Behind them, Kenji Kobayashi jerked to attention.

"I *told* you to go with her," he snapped at his wife, the beer in his hand sloshing slightly over the glass's rim.

"*Ara!*" Hana exclaimed, making a wry face. "*Quelle catastrophe!*" But she still sprang into the house with surprising alacrity, given her heels. *"Anata,"* she called out. "Sweetheart. What happened?"

"Quite the drama," noted Billy's father, shaking the cubes in his empty glass.

"I hope the baby's all right," said Mary worriedly.

"Alors, she's fine," said Béryl. "Children fall."

And sure enough, within moments the crying had stopped, and shortly after that Yoshi herself skipped out, her face still tear-streaked but lit by a proud grin. "Papa!" she cried, running over to him. "I did it! I found the bathroom and went pee-pee and washed my hands like a big girl!"

"Well, now," he said, standing and picking her up in a bear hug, then sitting down with her in his lap. "Is *that* what all that loud noise was? You washing your hands?"

"No, *otoo-san,*" she told him, pinching his nose. *"That* was the door. I hit my finger with it."

She held up her index finger, which Kenji took between his own callused thumb and forefinger and studied somberly for a moment. "I think you'll survive," he said, and touched it gently to his lips. "Where's your mama now?"

"She had to go pee-pee," Yoshi announced authoritatively, and the patio erupted in laughter.

All, that is, but Billy. Watching father and daughter together, he felt something like sadness tighten the cords in his throat, and without really realizing it he lifted the Brownie again. He felt his father's eyes on him without having to see them, and knew they were disapproving as usual. But this time, he decided to ignore them.

THE DOWNSTAIRS WASHROOM in which Hana Kobayashi was standing was as modern, airy and painstakingly detailed as the hallway leading up to it. The main material was wood, but there was also steel and sparkling glass. Between the arching ceiling and slanting skylight the feel was somewhere between a Swedish sauna and a seventeenth-century Kyoto temple. Standing behind her daughter, Hana studied these and other details in the teak-framed mirror that was clearly hand-carved and imported from somewhere at great expense.

She was holding Yoshi's index finger beneath the custom-sculpted steel tap, though she had no idea whether applying tepid water would have any practical effect at all on the injury. It had clearly had an emotional one, though: after five minutes on a stepstool with Hana's arms around her, Yoshi's wails had reduced themselves to gulps and then sniffles, which then turned into reflective silence. This, in turn, led to a typically unanswerable question: "Who invented water?"

"Who invented water?" Hana repeated in English (she liked to use all three languages with her daughter, if only for the thrill of how quickly Yoshi seemed to learn them). "I don't know who invented it. Someone very smart indeed. Because—look!" She held Yoshi's finger up to the mirror. "It's all better, *desho!*"

In fact, with its tiny white sickle-moon-topped nail, the finger looked exactly the same as it had when Hana had raced inside earlier, not even stopping to take off her shoes. She'd found Yoshi crouched outside the bathroom, weeping down at her left hand as though it had been sliced right off. Now, however, the girl gazed at the sun-sparkled stream of Karuizawa water, curling and uncurling her chubby fist.

"Water helping," she agreed, meeting her mother's eye in the mirror.

"Yes, *the* water *is* helping," said Hana. Thinking: *She is so lovely.* Because she was. Just lovely. Beautiful, really—if not in the broad-browed, sloe-eyed fashion depicted in the old scrolls and paintings. Yoshi's was a sharper beauty; the dark-etched brows, the delicate chin. It was a shame that she frowned so much. Even at six she seemed to ponder the world's weight; as though she knew already that childhood was merely a brief lead-in to the far more devastating business of adulthood.

"You're darker than me now," Yoshi observed, in Japanese again. She was looking at Hana's forearm, which intersected Yoshi's at the wrist.

"You're right," Hana conceded. "I lay outside on Thursday."

"In your swimsuit?"

"*Nn.*"

"On the roof?"

Hana nodded again: "*Nn.*" Kenji didn't approve of that either—the way she'd slip up to the tiled rooftop with her sunglasses and her book and spend an afternoon there on the embankment, Honjo-ku's backyard industries and workshops grinding out their metallic rhythms below her, and above her the fume-screened Tokyo sky. She always brought the same book: the D. H. Lawrence Andrew had given her after their fourth lesson together. Though she'd read it so many times now—a hundred? A thousand?—that she didn't need to open it. The words were engraved on her mind as clearly as her daughter's perfect face: *She was old, millions of years old, she felt. And at last, she could bear the burden of herself no more. She was to be had for the taking. To be had for the taking . . .*

This is how I see you, Andrew had said. *It just seemed so clear, when I reread it last night.* And while she had been shocked by both the gift and by the comment—the book was mythical in its perversity, and it should have been so obvious what it meant—he had seemed so tender and intent, and so understanding of her dilemma that it had actually brought her to tears, right there. Right in front of him. Which, in turn, had brought her into his arms.

"Eh! what it is to touch thee!" he said, *as his finger caressed the delicate, warm, secret skin of her waist and hips. He put his face down and rubbed his cheek against her belly and against her thighs again and again . . .* It had happened first

that Tuesday and then that Thursday, and then every Tuesday and Thursday after that, for two years. Two years. Two days between visits; two days to regroup. Five days to miss him so badly that his absence felt as palpable as his pale, lean body. Then she'd hurry up the embassy steps, past the stone-faced Japanese guards and into his windowless office, her smart English heels tapping against the slate and her plain black notebook tucked into her purse. The guards would bow and say *Ohayo Gozaimasu Sumimoto-sensei* and Andrew's secretary would press a button and say *Mr. Greensborough, your tutor is here.*

For a while they'd made a pretense of continuing his studies, taking out their respective dictionaries and laying them side by side above whatever *Asahi* article or Okada essay Hana had chosen to pretend to work on. But soon enough they stopped bothering with these scholarly rituals. He would lock the door and push her down to the couch or the carpeted floor or (once) across his marble-topped desk, and during these sessions, it was he who had taught her. Showing her what to do and where to touch, when to tighten. When to quicken and when to slow. Covering her skin with his, inch by soft inch. When he'd told her *I will marry you* he had seemed to truly mean it, and so she had chosen to believe him.

Remembering, she gave a snort. She'd *believed* him! *She*, who had so long ago learned to believe in no one at all: not in the parents who'd dragged her as a child to that stiff pale city "across the Pond" (such a lie, that term: it was a universe, an empty aching black hole) and left her there alone for a decade. Not in the teachers at her Highgate boarding school, who'd professed publicly to find her "charming" and "exotic" but whom she'd also heard whispering withering phrases like "yellow savage" and "little geisha" when they thought she couldn't hear them. And certainly in neither of the two countries she had once called "home," only to find—far too late—that neither of them wanted her. That she was too strange and foreign to find welcome in either one, and that this was something that no amount of apologizing or prostrating would change.

Home was a place you lived in, love was a thing you didn't fool yourself about, joy was a word you applied to a good Charleston, happiness was a term of hypocrisy used to bluff other people . . .

She'd believed him.

"Mama?"

The small voice wove itself into her awareness, a bright thread against a dark and tattered backdrop. Hana blinked, realizing that once again she'd slipped away in full view. It was happening more and more often these days.

"Daddy says the sun will make you dark like a Filippino or an Indian," her daughter said sternly.

Hana shut her eyes, tried to smile. "Isn't your father the one who taught you that every Japanese has a little bit of the sun *in* them?" she asked, lifting her daughter off the stool. "How does that go? Can you tell me?"

"It's because of Amaterasu," Yoshi piped up immediately. "The sun goddess. She was Ninigi's grandmother. And Ninigi was the great-great-grandfather of *Jinmu-Tenno*, the first emperor."

Hana nodded, though of course she didn't believe any of this nonsense, which was now being taught in the schools as methodically as science class. "So you see," she said, forcing a laugh (it felt like all her laughter was forced these days), "since we are all the Emperor's children we must have some sunshine inside us. But sometimes I feel like my—like my sunshine is flickering out. And so I lie under the sun to light it up again." *Where had that come from?*

Yoshi frowned up at her, chewing her bottom lip. "Maybe I could light it for you," she said at last.

The words seemed to stop Hana's heart. "You do," she told her, smoothing Yoshi's white collar. Then, surprising both of them, she pulled the child into her arms, hugging her so fiercely that Yoshi squealed and squirmed. Hana didn't release her for a full three breaths: three magical breaths full of grass and dirt and sunshine. Of sweet, peat-tinged childish sweat. When she finally set her down it was with the irrational but also unspeakably fearsome feeling that one day soon, even very soon, she'd reach for this child and embrace nothing but air.

It's not real, she told herself, which she knew to be true. Dr. Fuku-yama had told her as much last month after Hana had spent three days in bed with no apparent ailment beyond a terror that if she left the house she'd somehow disappear. *You must strive to remain calm, Mrs. Kobayashi,* the family physician had commanded, writing her a pre-scription for a Chinese herb. *Quiet your mind. Think of good things. Easeful things: the twinkling ocean on a summer day. The steam and peace of a northern hot spring . . .* Though of course, she hated the ocean—all that lonely gray water. And she could no more step into an *onsen* than balance on her nose. Especially not naked. All those years in London had left their prudish taint.

"Mama?" Yoshi was standing by the doorway, her black eyes fixed on Hana's face. "Are we going outside now?"

Oh god, Hana thought, thinking of Kenji's red face, his redden-ing eyes, which were sure to turn on her with accusation again. "Of course. But Mama—Mama has to go pee-pee too. Why don't you go tell Papa what a big girl you were."

Nodding, the child turned on her grass-stained heel. She looked back at Hana one more time. Then—as quietly as a cat—she raced off down the hallway.

Just as quietly, Hana closed the door behind her. She splashed her face with cold water, then sank down onto the stepstool that had just been graced by Yoshi's perfect but appallingly dirty feet. Her husband, she knew, would find as much fault with her letting their daughter go out alone as he had with allowing Yoshi inside on her own. Her husband: her gamekeeper. Her husband: her burly savior.

You should feel lucky, her mother had whispered during their initial *omiae* meeting, a year after Andrew's departure. By that point they'd met with a half-dozen candidates, all of whom (the matchmaker regretfully informed them afterwards) politely declined a second meeting. But Kenji—an Osaka builder with working-class origins and a staunch determination to grow beyond them—had clearly been enamored from the start; watching her sip her tea and light her cigarette and use her fork and knife, all with the same sort of fascination a child watches a paper lantern show. For most of the meeting he'd seemed too shy to address her. But as they paid the bill he finally mustered the courage: hadn't she found living amid all those Westerners dirty, and a little smelly? Or had she just gotten used to it after a few years?

At first she thought he was joking. When she realized he wasn't she reminded him that he worked with foreigners too, and asked him the same question right back. Beaming, he shook his head. "It's usually only a few," he said. "And outside, for the most part. The fresh air helps." His wink had felt like a slap on the face. *I know all about you,* it seemed to say. *I know that you don't have a choice in this matter.*

"I don't like him," she'd told her mother moments later, in the Imperial's ladies' room. "He's crass. He's uneducated. He's—"

"He's a good man," her mother snapped. "As good as someone like you will likely ever get, with all the rumors and stories going around."

There had been such unmitigated and unexpected rage in Tat-suko Sumimoto's voice that Hana stared at her in shock. Perhaps due to her expression, her mother softened slightly. "Be sensible, Hana-*chan.* You need a husband. You can't live with us forever. And he can protect you after your father and I have passed on."

Six years later, the memory still made her smile bitterly. As though her mother had ever tried to protect her! As though aristocratic Madame Sumimoto had even *acknowledged* the pleas; the pained and lonely letters that crossed the ocean in those first four or five years of Hana's exile to England. Each one had been answered only by a neatly scripted and mercilessly upbeat page or two that completely ignored Hana's heartfelt plea to come home.

And yet, as the engagement progressed, the contracts were signed and the gifts exchanged, it gradually became clear that her mother was also cringing, if inwardly. Her daughter! Grandaughter of a Samurai! Marrying a lowly *carpenter*—a man who proudly acknowledged having helped to build the very hotel in which they were to be wed! Still she had pushed her forward, and planned the wedding dresses and the wedding and the brief week away together in Hokkaido. And Hana had mutely followed her direction; standing dutifully for the fittings, expressionlessly approving invitations. Tricking herself out of bed each morning by allowing herself to think of the marriage as a temporary measure; one that would hold her over until Andrew returned to his senses and returned to Tokyo, or else sent for her.

Andrew. *Don't think about him.*

Sighing, Hana set her cigarette holder down and smoothed her hair with both hands. These days, with his business flourishing and his travel schedule ever expanding, her husband no longer seemed quite so enamored of her. And yet he was a good man. He treated her well, at least in the ways that really mattered. *She was his wife, a higher being, and he worshipped her with a queer, craven idolatry, like a savage, a worship based on enormous fear, and even hate of the power of the idol, the dread idol . . .* He brought her jewelry and coffee and other delicacies from his travels. He built her a Western-style bathroom with indoor plumbing; a Western-style closet with a rack and hangers. A Western-style shoe tree for her beloved Italian and English shoes, which she still refused to leave in the *genkan* like an ordinary housewife because she didn't trust their visitors not to take them. About all of this he made no comment, just as he made no comment about her limited literacy in her own language, or the fact that she bowed awkwardly and occasionally dropped without thinking into man's speech. Sometimes Hana would catch him staring at her with a combination of adoration and confusion, as though he still didn't quite know what she was or how she'd come to be his. Sometimes she disdained him for this. And yet sometimes it also moved her, as did many of his rugged and manly mannerisms; his way of shoveling rice into his gobbling mouth like a child with his chopsticks; of drinking warm Kirin beer with his breakfast. Of praying to his ancestors in a deep and guttural chant that she found strangely soothing, though she didn't really understand it: *nam amidabutsu nam amidabutsu nam amidabutsu . . .*

Because of these things, Hana tried to be kind. She did her best to behave "normally" around friends and colleagues, like the odd bunch he'd brought her to meet tonight (an American-Japanese couple with half a personality between them; a mannish Frenchwoman who kept ordering them all around; that wiry little architect with piercing eyes that he kept turning on Hana, like a hungry bird of prey). She'd given Kenji gifts on their anniversaries, on his birthday and New Year's. She'd even sewn him a silken cravat on one occasion, since he'd admired one they'd seen together when they went to see Clark Gable in *Sporting Blood.* She had done all this to express gratitude for the fact that he protected her, and—even more importantly—had given her Yoshi; which meant that for all his roughness, he had delicacy and fineness within him too. For she was so *perfect*, this child. So miraculously perfect—the one good thing to come out of Hana's misplaced, mistaken life. Watching her evoked a kind of gorgeous wonder that was so much greater than any other joy Hana had ever felt. It was the closest thing to religion she could imagine.

She thought again of the architect—this intense little Anton Reynolds—and the thought gave rise to a tangle of emotions. He reminded her of Andrew a little, with his gloomy brand of gallantry, and this, Hana sensed, was potentially dangerous. There were times when such men—Japanese and foreign alike—sparked a rash urge to fling her arms around them. To cram them, by trickery or seduction or sheer brute force, into that gaping hole that had become her life. She hadn't done it yet; she wasn't quite that far gone. Yet, somehow, she felt it coming . . .

She realized she was shaking a little. She stood up slowly, holding on to the sink for stability. When she'd managed to regain her balance she powdered her forehead, nose and chin, then meticulously reapplied her lipstick.

Then she stepped out into the hallway. Not in the direction of the doorway, but towards the living room. She wanted, she'd decided, to see the house.

"GRACIOUS," HIS WIFE exclaimed, "look at her run!"

Their dinner guests obediently turned to see Kenji's six-year-old daughter tumbling down the hillside. Watching them watch the child, Anton Reynolds found himself thinking about the odd authority Béryl had always had, even in an apron. Was it the crisp French accent? Her slightly mannish build and bearing? Whatever it was, she could probably have suggested they all run or even slide down the hill on their rear ends and most of them would have complied. The one possible exception being Kenji's wife, who was wearing highly impractical high heels.

Leaning back in his lounge chair, the architect sipped his Tom Collins and surreptitiously studied his builder's spouse. Before Béryl's command she'd been using her over-long cigarette holder (also, he couldn't help noting, rather impractical) to punctuate a point on modern English literature. "I know that all anyone really talks about is the sex," she'd been saying, a little too rapidly, as though she'd had several espresso shots before arriving. "But there is so much *more* to *Chatterley* than its self-evident carnal aspects. In my mind Lawrence is first and foremost an innovative modern writer. He deserves much more credit on that score."

"Indeed," George Yamashita had said, giving Anton a look that spoke volumes. Mary Yamashita—God bless her—actually blushed. They were both so clearly thinking what Anton had thought when he'd first seen Hana an hour earlier, striding towards him in a white sundress and towering pumps, looking less like a Japanese wife than a Mediterranean cruise-ship model: *Who the hell is this woman?*

Technically, of course, Anton knew who she was: the wife of his favorite building contractor, Kenji Kobayashi. Kenji sometimes referred to his *okusama* as a "modern woman" and "very Western," shaking his head as though repeating a fatal diagnosis. But Anton had imagined he meant modern by Japanese standards: a cold-wave permanent paired with a tasteful *kimono*, perhaps. Or a pair of vaguely Westernish shoes balanced out by a fan. So when this exotic apparition bounded up to him calling "Oh, so *this* is the fabled boss-man! De-*lighted!*" he'd had to tighten his jaw simply to keep it from dropping open in shock.

Nursing an ice cube now, Anton couldn't help wondering whether Kenji had anticipated and perhaps dreaded this reaction. Whether this was, in fact, the reason that neither Anton nor Béryl had met the woman until tonight. The strange thing was, he'd known Kenji for over a decade—ever since they'd worked together on Frank Wright's Imperial project. At first glance, the man had seemed to embody all that Frank had told Anton about Japan's legendary master carpenters: strong, honest and simple, with an almost spiritual connection to the wood he'd learned to work from his own father. "Real salt of the earth," Frank had said approvingly, and Anton had to agree. He had seen Kenji hold his lathe in his callused hands as gently as though it were an infant, and yet with enough force to pare off thick golden strips of curling scrap as effortlessly as he might brush sawdust off a workbench. He had seen him stroke a beam with his palms open and his eyes closed, and then perfect its angle without a bevel or a protractor. He was dedicated, too: when the earthquake struck in '23 he was back on-site quite practically before the last tremor had ended, like a general rallying his dazed troops. They all worshipped him. Even the drawn Korean laborers Kenji sometimes denigrated—to their faces—as "lazy as a race."

Nevertheless, Anton still had a hard time understanding how he'd ended up with such a cosmopolitan woman. In fact, as the evening unfolded in all its dusky perfection—splendid sunset, drinks on the still-warm slate of the patio, the gentle *plish* of the falling water weaving itself under and around and through the throaty heartbreak of the Negress singer Bessie Smith—that particular puzzle continued to nag at him, though the puzzle that was Hana Kobayashi herself began to make a little more sense.

"I was raised in London," she was saying, apparently in answer to someone's question, though she might as well have been answering Anton's own thoughts. "I went to a school there from the age of eight. Of course, this wasn't so unusual in the years when I was growing up. Lots of merchants like my father went overseas. What was unusual about my case was that when my parents came back to Tokyo—I believe that was the year that I turned ten—they left me behind."

"Mon dieu!" exclaimed Béryl. Anton saw her throw a glance at Billy, who was making his awkward way down the hill as well. "But *why* did they leave you alone? And for how long?"

Hana shrugged with a casualness that to Anton seemed, like her greeting, a bit too carefully choreographed. "To complete my Western education. I was there another nine years. Of course, I came back to Japan a few times, for holidays and such. But it was expensive, and in the twenties my father's business started to decline."

She reminded him of someone. But he couldn't put his finger on just who it was . . .

"What was the school like?" Mary Yamashita was asking, wide-eyed.

"Miss Pentworth's?" Hana fit a cigarette into her holder, then leaned back languidly to light it. "Have you ever read *Jane Eyre*?"

"It was that bad?"

Hana laughed. "Not quite. But I was effectively raised by British spinsters."

"So your parents didn't bring you back until you graduated?" Anton asked, intrigued despite himself.

She turned to look at him then, a warm, dark, knowing look that sparked a secret flush somewhere hidden within him. "Directly after."

"Did you *want* to come home?"

"Home," she said thoughtfully. "Well, I suppose not. You see, I'd wanted to go on to study English literature at university, or perhaps theater. I'd been told I might even get a scholarship. But by then my parents had decided that it was time for me to come back and become a proper Japanese wife." She paused, blew some smoke out in a graceful oval ring. "And so," she said, gazing at Kenji, "they found me a husband."

The contractor—who didn't speak English—nevertheless nodded congenially. *"Or-u-do Ja-pan,"* he said, pointing to himself with his beer glass. Old Japan. *"New Japan."* He indicated his wife.

"So desu nee," said Mary Yamashita in Japanese. "I wonder where that puts me and George."

"You? You're neither," said Kenji simply. He pointed to his round red cheek. "Japanese face only."

An uncomfortable pause followed. Anton cleared his throat. "Well," he asked, packing and lighting his pipe, "it seems to have turned out very well for the both of you. Will you send your daughter to English boarding school as well?"

Hana gave a wry smile and shook her head. "Kenji would rather send her to Manchuria. Particularly since the League of Nations came down on Japan for its—shall we say adventures?—there."

"And since Japan left the League of Nations?"

Hana rolled her eyes. "Foolish. Foolish, foolish men. I'm sure you agree with me, Mr. Reynolds, that the military is leading us all into disaster."

Once more sensing the gist of her conversation despite the language barrier, Kenji gave her a warning look. Even Anton raised his eyebrows. Not at the assertion, with which he wholeheartedly agreed, but at the uncharacteristic frankness with which it was made. These were dangerous days to speak out against the government. Just last month, two openly dissident writers had been shot to death by thugs the papers vaguely dubbed "criminals" but who were generally known to work for the military police. Anton himself had had two draftsmen detained last month, questioned about suspected Socialist ties at university.

And yet, this woman who inexplicably shared his contractor's name wasn't at all worried about offering up her two *yen* on the topic. In fact, she looked radiant. Also, a little defiant. *A real spark plug,* Anton found himself thinking. Then—and somewhat to his own surprise—he tried to picture her in bed. The image that came was faint and rather impressionistic—small white breasts, head thrown back, red lips wet and wide open—the standard hazy stuff of sexual fantasy. Still it was unsettling enough that for that moment he couldn't meet either set of dark Kobayashi eyes.

The Kobayashis' daughter arrived safely from her hillside descent and pounded across the patio on bare feet. "Mama!" she cried, as Hana opened her slender arms to her.

"Oh my gracious, Lady Yoshi!" she exclaimed in English. "Where is the fire?"

"No fire," chirped Yoshi back in the same language, and then stood on her toes to whisper something into her mother's delicate ear.

Hana lifted a penciled eyebrow. "Why can't you go yourself?" she asked, in French this time. "You're a big girl. I'm sure you can manage it." She pointed towards the open door. "Look. You just go straight through—wipe those feet first—and you'll see the water closet door around the corner."

Yoshi pondered this a moment, kicking her dirty feet. Off to their right, Anton saw Billy reach the patio and promptly lift his camera. The gesture triggered sour irritation; *enough* with the damn Brownie. Could the boy only live through the lens? He frowned and shook his head, though not before he saw Hana Kobayashi—doubtlessly sensing another opportunity to steal the spotlight—dart a glance towards his son, then himself.

"*Oui*," announced Yoshi, "*je peux*." And off she tottered towards the open back door.

"So impressive!" gushed Béryl, politely switching back to the one language shared by all.

Grinning, Kenji said something appropriately dismissive while Anton tried to imagine how this tiny East/West wonder had come to be. Of course, Hana had confirmed for them that the marriage was arranged. But why would it have been arranged with Kenji? The differences went well beyond "Old Japan" and "New Japan." She was an intellectual, he an Everyman. She was outspokenly progressive, he staunchly nationalist—and fully believed Hirohito was an *ikegami*, a living god. Where Hana was milk-pale and willow-thin, Kenji was dark and hard and round as a peasant. Anton could barely imagine them eating dinner together, much less sharing a bed . . . unprompted, her naked image popped into his mind again. *Spark plug.*

Annoyed, Anton rattled his glass. *Don't be an ass*, he told himself. He actually found her pretentious, teaching her daughter to perform like that, a little trilingual monkey. And of course, he was married—*happily* married. Béryl may not have been a film star, and she would never have worn those shoes. But she was something far better for him. She was a soul mate.

Returning his attention to the group conversation, he saw the Kobayashis exchanging tense glances. "Shouldn't *you?*" Hana was saying.

"It's the mother's job," Kenji said, tightly.

His wife sighed and stood up. "Let's hope it's not another false alarm," she said in English. As she smoothed her skirt down she caught Anton's eye, and he had the deeply uncomfortable sensation that she knew exactly what he'd been thinking—and approved of it. Then she turned, not towards the doorway, but towards his son.

"William-*san*," she asked, "had you wanted to take a picture?"

Oh Christ, thought Anton.

Billy was taken aback too. His face had deepened to almost the same red of his hair. "That's OK," he said, much to Anton's relief.

But then Béryl joined the fray, gushing over Hana as though she'd just offered their son a bag of pure gold. Explaining how Billy was "documenting" his life here with the camera "they'd" given him back, and Hana gaily pronouncing the idea "marvelous" because "all children need hobbies," and further noting that little Yoshi was training in English and French as well on a weekly basis, and was also taking piano. *Doubtless specializing in French and English composers,* Anton thought. Then she took out her compact and repowdered her nose, after which she meticulously reapplied her dark red lipstick.

"Oh, aren't you glamorous," sighed Mary Yamashita.

"Smile," said Billy, uncertainly.

Hana pursed her lips, which now shone moist and red. Then she set a hand on a hip and beamed like a starlet.

Pretentious, Anton thought, yet again. He was going to make some sort of sarcastic comment about getting her autograph when a worrisome *thud* sounded from the inside hallway, followed immediately by the thin wail of a startled six-year-old.

God. The house was strewn with expensive antiques and plateware he and Béryl gathered at weekend markets. Why on earth had the woman sent the child in alone?

And yet Hana didn't look worried in the least. Tossing off a blithe *"Quelle catastrophe!"* she hurried towards the house, her husband shaking his head in her wake.

"Quite the drama," Anton murmured sympathetically.

"It never stops," said Kenji, in a low voice. He looked into Anton's eyes. For a moment it seemed as though he were about to say something more, but he didn't.

"Children fall," Béryl was telling everyone reassuringly, and of course everyone was obediently reassured. Even Yoshi looked relieved as she raced out a moment later, making a jittery beeline towards her father's knee while crowing over how she had conquered the toilet.

Kenji Kobayashi swept his daughter off the ground, nearly crushing her in a muscular hug. At that moment his plain face softened: he looked almost handsome. It always touched Anton, the way men here could be the fiercest warriors on the planet and yet so unselfconsciously tender with their offspring. Little wonder that the War Ministry propagandists fell back on that father-child bond when writing about the Emperor and his people. For his part, Anton had never had a particularly tactile relationship with his own son. For one thing, the boy was bone and stringy sinew. It was like trying to cuddle a marionette.

But if Anton was truly honest with himself—and on this one thing it was quite difficult—it was also due to the aching memory of the other William. The first William. The one this William had never known about. That William—Willy, they'd called him—*had* looked very much like Anton, at least for the six short months he'd lived. Perhaps this was why Anton had become so disastrously enamored of him; had felt his normally cool and collected center liquefy with warm love each time he'd held the boy in his arms.

And why, when cholera took the child away from them after a mere half-year, it was as though one of his own pile drivers had driven its wedge straight through his heart.

Sighing, Anton took another sip from his glass before realizing that it was empty. "Who else wants another?" he asked, standing up.

Béryl threw him a look, her heather eyes questioning.

"Mary?" he asked, ignoring her. "George? Kenji, you're still drinking Kirin?"

"If it's not too much trouble."

"We'll be eating soon," Béryl said quietly, in French. "But why don't you make a pitcher. There's still some ice in the icebox. And my mother's crystal carafe is on the top shelf of the living room armoire."

Anton bowed slightly, butler-like. "Yes, madame."

He strode past the waterfall to the open doorway, pausing to leave his shoes in the *genkan* before ascending to the *tatami*-matted front hallway. In his rush he took the corner without looking and very nearly ran into Hana Kobayashi. The latter had clearly just reapplied her lipstick yet again.

For a moment they simply stared at each other, her eyes bright, his heart pounding.

"Oh dear!" she exclaimed finally, in her peculiarly clipped English. "Are you all right? I'm afraid I was in a bit of a dream. I really should watch where I'm going."

Anton heard himself laughing awkwardly. He was acutely aware of her perfume—something musky but with a hint of lavender. Again: not a scent he'd associate with a Japanese woman. She definitely reminded him of someone. But who? . . .

"I must confess," Hana went on lightly, leaning against the wall, "that I just snuck a peek at your home. It's every bit as marvelous as your lovely wife's garden. Did you really design the whole thing?"

"Soup to nuts," said Anton, though he had no idea why. He'd never even understood that expression.

"Well," she said, taking out a pack of Winstons and shaking one out before carefully inserting it into her holder, "I'd like to congratulate you on your inventiveness. And your—playful spirit."

"Thank you," Anton said, watching her slender fingers encircle the slim white cylinder. No one had ever described any of his buildings as playful. Nor did he consider himself, in any way, a playful man.

"I really mean it, you know." Hana propped the holder between her lips and blew smoke up towards the lazily spinning ceiling fan. "This is the sort of house I'd love to live in, if I had the choice. And not just because it has such a wonderfully modern washroom."

"Well, surely," Anton said, "Kenji could—"

"Kenji wouldn't," she interrupted. "It would never occur to my husband, Mr. Reynolds, to do anything that departed from the way his father, and his father's father, built houses. Why, I've had to practically beat him into providing our house with indoor plumbing. That's how conservative he is."

There was a strange shrillness creeping into her voice, and Anton found himself articulating a thought he'd begun to form with that first, a-tad-too-enthused handshake: *Something's off.* Something beyond the incongruous accent, the stridently erect posture. The sad little Dickensian story. He looked away, swallowing. When he looked back he saw that she had shut her eyes, as though she were in pain.

That she was tipsy was amply evident: both by the way she swayed slightly as she stood there and by the fact that her shoes were still on. Anton had never had a shod Japanese woman in his Japanese house before, and he wasn't sure what to do about it. Should he gently remind her? Offer to take the shoes back to the *genkan* for her? It seemed a strangely intimate suggestion, as well as one that left him pathetically breathless.

Then, however, she snapped her eyes open. "I'm sorry," she said crisply. "I really should get back."

She turned to resume her walk, and Anton inhaled for a sigh that was either relief or regret, he was really in no state to tell which. But then—

But then. A half-step away one of her high heels caught on something, perhaps a knot in the *tatami* weave, or a corner of the Turkish kilim Béryl had tossed atop the Japanese-style flooring, and Hana Kobayashi ended up falling *into* him. Purely out of instinct Anton caught her, his arm twining around a waist he couldn't help but note felt as different from Béryl's as bamboo stalk from a tree trunk. Just as reflexively, with his free hand he reached out to grasp her arm, just to steady her. But his fingers accidentally—so completely and purely by accident!—missed their target, instead landing quite squarely, palm-down upon Hana Kobayashi's left breast.

A moment of frozen panic. The Japanese woman looked down at his quivering fingers, and then back up into his mortified eyes. By that point Anton was already pulling away. But to his astonishment, Hana Kobayashi pulled him right back, pressing his fingertips more deeply into her flesh. She leaned into him with a helpless-sounding little gasp. When he still didn't recoil, she whirled them both about in a practiced and surprisingly forceful way, so that she was against the wall and he leaning into her. Then she was standing on tiptoe and pressing her lips against his own, even as Anton's own lips were shaping themselves into a bilingual apology: *Shitsurei, I am so sorry.*

If, at that moment, Anton Reynolds had been watching himself with his habitual cool command he'd have asked himself one question: *What the hell are you thinking.* But the answer was obvious: he wasn't thinking. Not at all. In fact, at that moment nothing in his head even qualified as a thought. There was simply feeling—an unarticulated sensation that Mrs. Kobayashi's kiss was a beacon of some sort. A soft, damp, intensely exciting beacon that, if he so chose, he could follow. A wordless notion that if he somehow could fully taste her mouth's moist meaning he could unlock a crucial secret, one that perhaps even he didn't know yet, other than that he'd been hiding from it his whole life.

And so: he kissed her back. He kissed her back and he kissed her back, tasting the smoke of her English tobacco and feeling the wax-like stick of her lipstick. He felt the firm point of her nipple pressing against his palm, and behind that the fast tattoo of her heart. He felt her tongue against his teeth and his own body quicken, his penis leaping almost painfully to life.

There, in the hallway of the dream house he and his wife had so meticulously built and decorated together, Anton Reynolds pressed Kenji Kobayashi's wife back into the wall. He dug his fingers into her tiny breast, hard enough that she gasped—in pain, yes, but also in encouragement, her own cool hand pressing his palm harder against her in case he somehow had missed the point. *Oh god*, he thought then. *Oh god I can't do this*. But then he felt her tongue flicker on his lips again and he stopped thinking. He simply opened his mouth to her in a way he'd never opened it with Béryl, who found "French kissing" *gauche* both as a term and as a practice. He felt the sweet discomfort of her jutting hip bone as it cut into his groin, and he pushed into her again, moaning slightly. She moved with him. Then she moved her hand off of his, and suddenly there was the warm shock of her unclothed thighs pressing against his belt buckle.

Dazedly dropping his own hand, Anton touched Hana below her tiny waist. Feeling the smooth expanse of her leg, the slightly harder crease of her groin, and realized—good *God*—that *she wasn't wearing underthings*, which somehow both repelled him while exciting him even further. He lingered briefly at the soft pelt of her pubic hair—at once more wiry and more sparse than Béryl's—before, very slowly, moving to the soft and warm split of her cunt. He half expected her to finally stop there, to push his hand away, but she murmured something in some language (Anton was too distracted by that point to distinguish which) that meant *"Oh yes"* or *"Oh please"* or *"Yes, right there."*

He felt her hand grasping him, and he found himself thinking his first coherent thought in what seemed like an eternity: *I am about to have an affair.* While this thought shocked him it did not stop him, or even slow him down, until two things happened to bring the encounter to its abrupt end. First, another woman behind them both shouted out: *"Kaji da! Abunai!"* (Fire! Watch out!). At the same time he detected through the musk and lavender and tobacco a whiff of genuine smoke. This instantly replaced his lust with fear: he'd worked with Japanese materials long enough to appreciate that what made them so desirable (lightness, flexibility, a certain dryness) also rendered them disastrously vulnerable to flame. Including, of course, his own "inventive, playful" house right here. In short, he knew how quickly he could lose everything.

And so he stopped kissing Kenji's wife and turned around to find not a woman, but his own son Billy, with his blasted Brownie still swinging from his neck. Billy, staring like a freckled apparition and pointing dumbly at the floor. Following that thin, pale finger Anton saw that his hallway had just been set on fire. It wasn't a big flame yet—just a cerise spark, started by Hana's fallen cigarette. As of yet, it was only in the glowing-and-growing stages. But it was enough to distract him—at least for the moment—from the disconcerting fact that his young son had just seen him fondle a stranger.

Acting reflexively, Anton spun and stamped upon the small flame, which (of course) burned straight through his sock. He cursed and hopped, still aroused and fully aware of just how foolish he must look. But those painful two seconds had done their work: both the flame and his erection petered out.

Panting, Anton looked back up to see that Hana Kobayashi had—with rather astonishing efficacy—dropped her skirt back into place. As her eyes met his she pressed her hands to her mouth.

"*Gomen nasai,*" she said, in that oddly bright, polite voice, as though she'd simply knocked over a glass of wine. "Oh dear. I'm sorry. I—"

"No—no. It's quite all right," Anton replied automatically. "No harm done."

"Papa?" Billy said, in a tiny thread of a voice.

"Billy," said Anton, turning back towards his son and running a finger—a finger that now smelled of Hana Kobayashi—over his mustache, "would you please show the lady outside and back to the party. Then bring me a dustpan and a damp cloth."

He managed to say this calmly. But when the boy simply stared at him Anton finally felt himself lose control. "Well?" he exploded. "What the hell are you waiting for? Go on!"

Billy rubbed his left eye, and for a panicked moment Anton thought he'd burst into tears, something his son still did with annoying frequency despite his age ("he's *sensitive,*" Béryl argued). Instead, he just said, "Yes, Father," still in that somewhat high and girlish voice. And, to Hana: "*Kotchira e kite, kudasaimashite.*"

Please come with me.

III. *U.S.S.* Hornet, *Pacific Ocean*

APRIL 1942

IT WAS TWO HOURS PAST DAWN WHEN HE REGISTERED THE THUMP of a heavy gun from one of the Cruisers.

Cam Richards sat up groggily as the 21-MC delivered its brassy message from the bridge: *"Now General Quarters. General Quarters. All hands man your battle stations. This is not a drill. General Quarters. General Quarters."*

His first thought was for the *Blonde Bombshell*, up there on the flight deck, her scrubbed hull vulnerable to whatever the sky might be sending down. His second was for his wife, who'd just appeared in his dream. In real life, of course, she had no idea where he was and wouldn't have been able to get to him even if she did. But in the dream she'd been here, standing on the *Hornet's* slippery flight deck in the pouring rain, wearing high-heeled red shoes and matching nail polish. She'd had one hand on her belly and the other on the *Bombshell's* nose, and she'd been frowning and trying to tell him something. But of course, with the engines firing and the wind roaring and the big ship's violent pitching and yawing, he'd had no idea what she'd been trying to say.

I wish, he thought now, *I'd replaced the storm door by the cellar before I left. I wish I'd had the record player fixed. I wish . . .* Then the carrier reverberated with another blast, and all these disparate, vague worries converged into two taut thoughts: *They've found us. They've found us, and I'm not ready.*

Exactly what he wasn't ready for was a little less clear. Flying, perhaps. Crashing, or damaging his plane. Killing his crew, or dying himself. Or perhaps—as was not at all unlikely for this mission— some grim combination of all four. He stumbled to his locker anyway, plunging his cold feet through the salt-stained legs of his pants. *I wish,* he thought, *I'd gotten more sleep.*

In fact, he had bunked down less than four hours earlier, having spent most of the prior night writing Lacy a letter.

> *Dear Lace, Well, I guess this is it—my last night aboard this floating hunk of metal. The mission starts tomorrow, and while I can't tell you anything about it in writing you can be sure I'm doing just that in my head, like I always do. It's kind of strange, but I've kind of started to feel as though nothing really happens until I do that. Run it all by you, I mean. Get your "OK." Though even if I could do that for real I probably wouldn't, because I don't want you to worry about me and well, this thing we're about to do tomorrow night would probably make you worry.*
>
> *For now, though, it's all peaceful. Another red sky tonight—"sailors' delight," as they say (remember when I taught you that?). It bodes well for a good flying day tomorrow, which is good because we are going to need all the help we can possibly get on this one. Everyone is pretty nervous. No one says as much, but you can see it in their faces and gestures, and in the way no one seems to want to be alone. The men are talking less than usual and swearing more if that's possible (and yes, I'm trying to rein it in a bit, for your sake, but it's pretty ~~damn~~ hard around here). Tonight we all must've spent four hours in the wardroom together, even after lights-out was announced. We knew that it might be our last opportunity for a long while to sleep in anything like a real bed. And of course*

we knew that we needed the rest. For some reason, though, no one felt much like breaking things up. So we shot the breeze and listened to Tokyo Rose on the radio until we got sick of hearing her downbeat songs and tunes. And we played cards. Would you believe it—I actually won! A whole set of Bob Eberly records. I'm hoping that's a sign that luck will be with us tomorrow . . .

Now, though, as he stood there numbly fumbling to zip up his fly, he had an awful feeling that it wasn't lucky at all, and he felt less inclined to follow orders than to go back and cower under his covers. As if in answer to this thought there came a sharp-knuckled *rap* on the cabin door. Cam gave his stuck zipper a last, futile yank, then snapped to attention as James Doolittle himself stuck his small head into the cabin.

"*Sir,*" said Cam, and saluted in shock: the commander had never paid him a personal visit before.

Doolittle waved away the formality. "Didn't see you topside or in the wardroom. Wanted to make sure you weren't oversleeping," he said. "We're going. Full flight gear."

Cam glanced at his watch. It was 0730. "We're going *now?*" he asked.

"We are. Right now."

The older pilot's face was grim. His nostrils flared beneath the nose that Cam always thought made him look like a hawk. He was already in full flight gear.

"We're *lifting off* now, sir?" Cam repeated, just to be sure.

Doolittle nodded. Cam felt his throat tighten further. *Calm,* he thought. *Breathe.* "What happened?"

"At 0600 we were spotted by a Japanese picket. The *Nashville's* opened fire to sink it—that's the racket you're hearing. But we have to assume the crew's sent word back. The sooner we lift off, the better." He clapped Cam on the shoulder. "Think you're ready?"

Cam forced himself to nod as he tried to work out just how much

this changed. For starters, they'd now be attacking Japan's capital
in broad daylight. And if the picket really had sent word back to
Tokyo, they'd have lost not just the cover of darkness but the ele-
ment of surprise. So there'd be ack-ack, and Jap fighters, and Cam
knew from training that those Zeros could hit 400 mph in a single
dive. There was no way the Mitchells—loaded down as they were
with extra gas and ordnance—could outrun them.

"How far out are we now, sir?"

"Roughly seven hundred miles."

Fuck. The original plan had called for a takeoff four hundred
miles from Japan's coast. Even at six hundred it was doubtful that
they'd have enough fuel to make their escape all the way back to
China, as the plan called for. "Can we carry the fuel to carry us two
hundred extra miles, sir?" he managed, though it felt as if someone
had tied a string around his windpipe.

Doolittle shrugged, as if to say *We'll see.* "We're each getting an
extra twenty-five gallons. Shouldn't change things too much. At
least, not on the bombing end."

He held Cam's gaze for a beat, meaningfully—or so it seemed to
the younger man. Then he let his hawk's eyes drop to Cam's still-
unzipped pants. Cam thought he detected a slight softening of the
pursed lips. "All clear on what you need to do, son?" the colonel
asked.

"Yes, sir," Cam said, zipping himself up hastily, thinking again:
I'm not ready.

"I'll see you topside, then."

Doolittle nodded and turned on his heel, all but sprinting in the
direction of the closest ladder topside. At first Cam just stared after
him. Last night, when he'd finally gone back below to his quarters,
the passageways had been as empty as a morgue, lit only by the
red no-smoking lamps, the bulkheads clouded by indistinct shadows. He'd seen one rat scurrying towards the stern with something

clamped between its teeth. One sailor headed below, probably to the engine spaces. Now the passageways were packed. Men raced grimly in both directions, through the watertight doors and hatches that would soon be dogged down to seal them shut. They jammed into any available head and fought their way back out again, buttoning up shirts and pants, jamming helmets over their heads. Cam heard shouts and whistles, orders and queries: *"What's the story?" "Are we hit?" "Where the fuck is Smitty?" "Which one?"* The stale air all but sparked with new energy.

Cam's hands shook a little too as he tucked in his belt end, unbunched his socks and slid his feet into his chukker boots. "It won't change things too much on the bombing end," Doolittle had said. *Sure,* thought Cam. *Just on the getaway end.* He gave his belt's brown tongue a yank so strong that the belt's leather bit indignantly into his hips. Grunting, he loosened it again. He shrugged into his flight jacket, strapped on his own chute and buckled his flight cap with shaking fingers. He double-checked the B-4 kit he'd repacked eight times since leaving land. It now contained what he'd finally decided were "essentials": caffeine tablets, shaving kit, the military-grade whiskey Doc White had passed around to them last week ("for medical purposes," he'd said, but with a wink). A little toilet paper—word had it the Chinese didn't use any, which was a fact Cam didn't care to explore further mentally. A few Mounds bars to hold him over, presuming he lived. All seemed in place. Still, as he made his way towards the topside ladder there lurked a low-slung sense of having left something important behind.

Pushing his way through the passageway, he rechecked his mental checklist: Lacy's ring was still tucked safely in his jacket's inner pocket, along with the Black Crackle Zippo with the silver USAAF wings on it that Doolittle had given to him, and every other lead pilot at their first wardroom meeting. His pistol was holstered in its appropriate place, his dog tags and Chinese phrase card were all where they should be. He'd packed his hunting knife, compass and flashlight in the *Blonde Bombshell*'s storage space. *Gas mask?* he thought. *Extra ammo?* But all that was on board too, he'd double-checked . . . He was already one deck up the aft ladder before he remembered: "All This and Heaven Too." Midge's records. He'd told everyone he'd bring them along with him so that they could play them at the victory party in Chungking.

For a moment, as panting sailors swarmed past him on both sides, Cam wondered why he was even thinking about a song when what he should really have in his mind was a prayer. But even before *that* thought was finished he was heading back down the ladder, chukker boot soles hitting the treads like a tin drum solo: *pap-pap-pap.* He imagined Bob Eberly's voice underscoring the rhythm, and the thought, while incongruous, still felt right. He decided right there that when he got back—if he got back—he'd tell Lacy how he'd turned around to get the records. He'd tell her about his strange dream, too: all that rain, those red shoes. The way she'd had one hand like that, newly manicured, flat and tight against her flat, tight belly. Did Lacy even *have* red shoes? He couldn't remember. But if she didn't (he told himself, hurling himself up the steel ladder and into the wet and overcast morning) he'd buy her some. Hell; he'd buy her a new phonograph player, too. He'd buy her everything.

THEIR DESTINATION HAD been announced on the same soft spring day Doolittle's crews and bombers were loaded onto the U.S.S. *Hornet*. Most of the AAFers were finding their sea legs and checking their planes at the time, and Cam and Midge had been among them. Unlike his brother Michael, Cam had never much liked the water. But the thought of his Billy swinging from a twenty-foot crane, then clunking gracelessly down on deck, had left him significantly more queasy than the bars they'd hit in the previous night. It had seemed to him that the big planes had looked queasy too, wedged as they were into spaces built for sleek two-man Dauntlesses.

Up until that point, their superiors had remained so tight-lipped about the mission that Cam had resigned himself to not knowing anything about it for at least a few days. Possibly not until the very day they flew off to whatever super-secret destination they were flying to. He certainly didn't expect a shipwide announcement as the Golden Gate Bridge faded from view. But that was exactly what happened: as he was leaning in to double-check the left Cyclone's RPM (he could have sworn he'd heard a slight stutter in it back on shore), the 21-MC PA system crackled on.

Cam signaled Midge to cut the engines, and the copilot opened the plane's side window and leaned out.

"God-*damn*," Midge said in annoyance. He'd been complaining of a hangover too. As his full nickname ("Midget") referred not just to his lanky six-foot frame but to his excessively short fuse, most of the guys had known enough to stay out of his path.

But as the feedback shrank into the reedy voice of the *Hornet*'s captain, Midge's face had assumed a new look, one of intent focus. He'd dropped his hands and sat up straighter, and looked back at Cam to make sure he, too, was listening.

"We thought you'd like to know," Mitschner's voice rasped on, "that this task force's target is Tokyo. The Army is going to bomb Japan, and we're going to get them as close to the enemy as we can. This is a chance for all of us to give the Japs a dose of their own medicine."

This short speech was met with stunned silence—a tiny pocket of wind, wave and seagull caw. Cam could all but hear what everyone was thinking: *Bomb the Japs? From the water?* It occurred to him that they'd all gone batshit crazy. But then he thought about all their training these past few weeks—learning to get a two-ton B-25 in the air at twice the speed and a third of the runway normally required—and it all started to make sense.

Apparently everyone else was thinking along the same lines, because the silence was followed by a deafening outcry. It seemed to Cam that every man on the vast ship roared his approval, though Midge was rendered uncharacteristically speechless. He stared down at the deck from his seat as though he'd been woken up from a nap there. Then he slapped his forehead with his flight cap.

"I'll be damned," he'd shouted down to Cam. "Tokyo. Well, we're in for it now."

His heavily stubbled face wore a grin, and Cam found his own (nearly hairless, as always) face doing the same. The plan's audacity shocked him, but it also sparked a giddy exhalation of relief, because finally, they were *doing something*. The treachery of Oahu would have an answer. The wasteland to which they'd all tuned in that first bright Sunday of last December would be avenged. And that was something that made it all worth it, because the most frightening thing about the Jap attack had been how powerless it had made him feel. It was a little bit like the stutter he'd struggled with for the first eighteen years of his life. Or being forced to fight in the dark. Or like having a gunnysack yanked over your head, and your arms and legs tied down, and having to just *sit* there, waiting for the next blow.

But they weren't sitting any longer. *Tokyo, watch the hell out*, Cam thought, on that sunny April 2nd. He'd tossed his pilot's cap into the bolt-blue sky, and even clapped arms with a nearby bellbottom, something he hadn't done since boarding since most of the Navy men seemed to see the AAFers as about as useful and appealing as drowned rats.

Now, though, the bell-bottom—a skinny guy with ears nearly as big as Dumbo's—clapped him right back, and shouted: "Thank you, boys." And then, to Cam's amazement, he tucked a pack of Winstons into Cam's palm. "For the trip," he said with a grin.

Later in the wardroom, after everything had settled down again, Doolittle confirmed their targets—Tokyo, Yokohama, Osaka, Kobe and Nagoya. He announced that each crew could choose its own strike. And when it turned out—not surprisingly—that everyone's first choice was the Imperial Palace he shut that road off right away. "I want to reiterate something our commanding general Hap Arnold stated last year. 'The use of incendiaries against cities is contrary to our national policy of attacking military objectives.' That means we bomb miltary plants and factories, and *nothing else*. Is that clear?"

There was a little head-scratching, but at first no one said a word. Then the *BustaGut*'s bombadier raised his hand. Mickey Franklin was from Iowa and had eyes like cows he'd milked there; sad, long-lashed and brown. His pale skin bubbled with acne. "Sir," he began, "I—I just want to make sure I understand this. You say our targets are military in nature. But there'll be civilians *working* at some of them. Isn't that right?"

Doolittle nodded. "As of now the plan is for an early evening lift-off, which would put us over Tokyo around midnight. Hopefully, the majority of factory workers will be at home by that point, and we'll make our point mainly with structural damage. But yes, it's almost certain that the workers are civilians. Some women, or even children. It can't be helped. This is war."

More silence. Then Bill Fitzhugh, Plane Two's copilot, raised his hand. "Isn't Hirohito a military target, sir?" he asked.

Doolittle shook his head. "He is not."

"But doesn't he command the Imperial Army?"

Doolittle's thick brows drew together. Though only five feet six inches—barely taller than Lacy, sans heels—he was easily the most intimidating officer Cam knew. This, in part, was due to his disconcerting way of focusing on the people he spoke to. Cam's first fear upon learning that this living aviation legend would be leading this "highly dangerous" but otherwise unspecified mission was not of injury to himself, or his crew, or even his plane. It was a very real fear that he'd let this stern little man down.

"Hirohito is a figurehead," Doolittle was saying. "All the experts I've met agree: if you hit him—if you even *hurt* him—you'll make the war three times harder. Nothing would unite Japan more than to have the Temple of Heaven attacked."

NOW, TWO WEEKS later, as he assembled all his pilots again, the commander looked visibly nervous. He held his left hand in his right, tightly, as though restraining it from doing damage. "More bad news, I'm afraid," he told them. "*Hornet*'s navigators say we'll face a twenty-four-knot headwind, pretty much all the way to Tokyo."

A collective groan: fuel would now be even more precious. "We've got a fucking Chinaman's chance of reaching China now," Midge muttered. It was less a complaint than an observation.

"But the plan's still the same?" asked Ted Dawson, the lead pilot of the *Ruptured Duck*.

"Drill's the same," Doolittle confirmed. "Get up quick. Hedge-hop as much as possible until you reach your targets. Drop your eggs. Follow your homing signals to the mainland, gas up fast. And then, get the hell out and over to Free China."

Doolittle's voice cracked slightly on *over*, and Cam felt a sudden lump in his own throat. He was thinking of the green ring in his jacket's breast pocket when the commander recovered and rubbed his palms together briskly.

"One more thing I want to add," he went on. "Given all these developments, the chances of any of you making it back at this point—well, they're pretty slim. So if you want out, now's the time to say so.

No shame or blame in the act. We've got six backup crews and a whole boatload of Dauntless pilots more than ready to take your places."

He looked around the group, his jaw clenched so tightly that Cam could almost make out his back teeth through his cheeks. He suppressed a shudder as his own eyes met with that dark and sharp gaze. But he didn't break it. None of them did. Behind them the wind roared and whistled, and they all swayed as the *Hornet* heaved upwards on the back of a massive swell. As it pitched back down again the chained planes clattered.

"Any takers?" asked Doolittle.

Cam's emotions were pitching as violently as the sea; for the first time in three weeks he felt almost seasick. Yet he knew he'd say nothing. Were the CO to look straight at him and say: *Cam Richards, you're newly married and your brother's joining up too, so in the end we really don't need you*—he'd still fight to fly with every last breath he had. So he returned Doolittle's salute and handshake, and returned, in kind, the commander's sober "Good luck." Then he turned to go see to his ship.

And ten minutes later there he was: strapped into his left-hand seat and diaper chute next to Midge, their breath pearlescent in the wet morning chill.

His palms were sweating despite the cold and the lack of coffee. Normally they'd have drunk a potful at breakfast—especially on this little sleep. But the call had come before breakfast and it was only after they were all strapped in that someone mentioned food and drink.

Reaching into his jacket pocket, he clenched and unclenched the lace-trimmed handkerchief in which he kept Lacy's ring. If he could have, he'd have taken it out. But he wasn't comfortable doing that; not now, with Midge right next to him and Miller, their navigator, a half-foot behind him at his table, worriedly studying his chart.

"I want you to wear this," she'd said, handing it to him on a dangling silver chain and blinking up at him in the moonlight. "Maybe it will bring us the same sort of luck it did my folks."

"I don't believe in luck," he'd told her. Which was true: what life had taught him was that you counted on yourself. Just yourself; to survive your scathing father and idiot bullies in high school; to master your own trembling tongue. Lacy, of course, knew all this and said as much:

"*I* know that," she said, in her *you-big-dolt-you* voice, "but I don't really give a damn what you believe. You just take it with you. You can hold it when you think about holding me. Which will be every single minute, am I right?"

Cam had laughed despite himself. "I don't know about that. But I'll hold it every night before I go to sleep, Lacy Lady."

She'd looked up at him for a moment, her green eyes damp but undaunted. Then she'd pulled his ear down to her lips.

"You'd better bring it back to me," she whispered. "Or don't bother coming back, you bastard."

And so for Lacy's sake, and also because he couldn't take her letters with him, or her picture, or anything that might identify who he was and where he'd come from in the event that they were discovered; and also because no matter what happened some small part of him would always be thinking about holding her, Cam took the ring. There was no way in hell he was wearing the thing around his neck, so he wrapped it instead in one of her lace-edged hand-kerchiefs, the same one she'd used to wipe her lipstick off his cheek. True to his word, every night before he slept he'd take the little white bundle out from his duffel bag. In a sort of somber ritual, he would press the red-streaked linen against his cheek and hold the hard small ring in his palm. It reminded him of his wife, yes. But it reminded him too of the tales his mother had read to him and his brother as children; stark, simple tales that started with "Once upon a time" and sometimes starred a stuttering idiot very much like himself who, in the end, and against everyone's expectations, took a deep breath, fought the dragon and won the princess. Though of course he'd already won his princess . . .

"You don't happen to have any food in there, do you?" asked Midge, breaking into his thoughts and looking pointedly at where Cam's hand disappeared into his jacket. And then: "Hey—Cam-man! You bored already? Are you *sleeping* or something?"

Cam turned to look at his second-in-command. As usual, Midge was trapped uncomfortably in his seat, his long legs wedged beneath the Billy's densely packed control panel. Cam had asked him once why he'd chosen this job when he so obviously wasn't the right shape for it. Midge had looked him in the eye and said—completely dead-pan: "Did you know that Yids don't believe in angels?"

Cam had shaken his head: he had not.

"Well," said Midge, "we don't. I learned that from the rabbi. And pretty soon after that I decided to be a pilot, since flying's about the closest I'm ever gonna get to heaven."

Now his friend tapped an unlit Lucky against his knee in a rapid-fire rhythm.

"You're not smoking that, are you?" Cam asked him.

"No," said Midge, "but Jesus God, what I wouldn't give . . . either for that, or a sniff of Doc White's brown booze."

"What's the matter, Friedman? Are you really *that* worried?"

He tried to keep his tone light, and to his credit Midge acted as though he'd succeeded. "Worried, Lieutenant? *Moi?*" he quipped, Groucho-style. "Why, what could *possibly* go wrong?"

Cam forced a smile, though they both knew all too well the endless answers to that one question.

"What *do* you have in there, anyway?" Midge asked, glancing at Cam's jacket pocket, and Cam looked down to see he still had his hand in there.

"Nothing," he said, quickly taking it out. "Good-luck charm."

"Thought you didn't believe in luck."

"Maybe I've changed my mind."

Midge gave him a strange look. "You brought those records along too, I hope?"

Cam pointed under his seat.

"Good," Midge said. "I hear Dawson brought his player for the get-down in Chungking."

Cam snorted. It still struck him as absurd that they'd brought their music along to a bombing. "If we make it to Chungking," he said.

"We'll make it," said Midge, as soberly as stone. Sticking the Lucky between his lips, still unlit, he slouched back moodily in his seat. A half-second later, though, his face lit up and he sat up again, his head nearly grazing the cockpit's steel roof. "Oh. Oh shit," he said. "There he goes. There goes the Old Man."

Heart thudding, Cam turned to follow his gaze. Doolittle's plane was indeed revving up. The propellers were spinning, and even from across the deck Cam could hear their near-ear splitting whine.

"Give 'em hell," shouted Midge. "You go get 'em, Number One!"

Then—to Cam—"Hey. Since you now believe in fortune and all, I'm wondering if we should've followed his example and just stuck to Number Six." Like many old-school fliers, Doolittle thought christening a ship invited bad luck. Most of the other pilots had figured out fairly early on that there was little enough luck in all this to begin with, and a full half of the Billys had been baptized back at Eglin. Cam had named his for Jean Harlow, both in memory of her untimely death and of that first movie he and Lacy had ever seen together. Also, he liked the play on *bombshell*.

"I guess we'll find out," he said now.

As the launch officer prepped his flags a seaman darted in front of him, jerking out the wheel blocks from beneath the nosewheel. Even with the ship's jolts and skips his focused moves had an extra, jittery spring to them—as though he were preparing to bounce down the aisle of his very own wedding. Cam peered above his crouched form and tried to see the commander, but all he saw was the sky and tower's reflection.

"Wonder if he's nervous," he said.

Midge snorted. "The Old Man? I doubt it. A man who survives the world's first outside loop ain't scared by much."

"He's still human," Cam said. "He eats and shits like the rest of us."

Doolittle was now standing on his brakes. Cam could just make out his silhouette through Plane One's Plexi windshield. His engines were at full power and his props had melted into translucent discs. The *Hornet* had swung into the wind now, to help the pilots lift off sooner. That was at least one good thing about this goddamn gale: wind that strong across the wings would both slow them on the trip but also lift them quickly enough to make it off the deck safely. And if they didn't . . . Cam suppressed another shudder.

Off the bow thirty-foot swells rolled towards them like so many snowcapped Mount Fujis. The troughs between them were canyons, dark and dimpled, sightlessly deep. As Doolittle's plane continued revving Cam tried not to imagine one of those monstrous waves swallowing the whole craft, crew and all. Then the red-haired kid jerked away Plane One's last block, the *Hornet*'s hull hit one particularly massive curl, and the flight deck lifted to what looked like at least forty-five degrees.

"Fuck *me*," said Midge, thrusting the unlit fag between his lips again and chewing on it. "Who came up with this crazy-assed idea again?"

Cam just shook his head, as he was fairly sure he couldn't speak. He pressed his lips together and watched the signal officer's stern face, his eyes on those advancing watery surges and his lips moving as he counted the seconds between them. He kept that flag arm lifted for what felt like so long that Cam had a crazed urge to go yank it down for him. At last, though, the waves complied, and Doolittle's engines hit the right notes, and the banner came down like a wet karate chop: *Go!*

As the officer sank to one knee to avoid the oncoming plane's wing, Doolittle released his brakes. Number One lumbered powerfully forward at what seemed like impossibly low speed, flaps in the full down position, and Cam felt like an invisible rubber band had looped itself around his chest. *They are never going to make it,* he thought, and felt his joints lock, as though they'd abruptly turned into ice. *They're going to go straight down. They're going to plow into the sea.*

Doolittle's nose did dip deeply as his wing wheels left the wooden deck. But to Cam's relief the lead pilot brought it right back up again, tipping his black nose towards the sky. Then he climbed, his double Cyclones straining valiantly against all that wet wind and all that gravity.

"Well, fuck *me*," Midge said again, but joyously this time.

Doolittle completed his three-sixty turn to fly down the *Hornet*'s length, checking his compass against the sign on the island that displayed the ship's gyro heading. Watching him, Cam felt the band around his chest snap off: he could breathe again. He dropped his gaze to the flight deck, where the carrier crew was cheering now. He couldn't hear much over the engines but he saw his own crew joining in, Midge drumming his big feet against the floor and clapping, Miller howling like a hound dog at a hunt. Despite himself Cam called out too, shouting *"Yeeeeeeeeaaaaaaaah"* into the rumbling air until his voice broke atop his smoke-roughened lungs.

In response, Doolittle banked right and dipped his wing in celebration. Then, not waiting for the next plane to takeoff, he sped into the fogbound west. Cam watched the glittering hulk of the ship for as long as he could, until its lines melted away against the surrounding steel-toned cumulus.

"I sure hope we see him again," Midge shouted. Cam nodded. For some reason he found himself laughing; dry, hard heaves that welled up from somewhere beneath his belt and that lasted a good ten seconds.

"You all right?" Midge asked, giving him a concerned look.

"Yeah." Cam wiped his eyes with his jacket cuff. When he looked up again, Plane Two was speeding towards the water.

"And here we go once more," sang Midge. "Like a clock. Bam-bam-bam."

Cam had never seen a clock that went *bam-bam-bam*, but it all pretty much went just like that. *Bam*: there went Plane One. Plane Two: *Bam*. Three, *Bam* again. Up until Plane Six they all managed their takeoffs without incident, though Plane Five—the *Whiskey Pete*—had them all fooled after a rogue wave threw the *Hornet*'s bow into an unexpected trough at the same split second the plane's wheels lifted from the deck. For one hair-raising moment, as the bow lurched itself skyward, it looked as though the plane had simply dropped off the edge and into the water. A moment later, though, the bow sank back and the bomber reappeared like the phoenix, its wheels scraping waves but its nose tilted towards the clouds. As she pulled herself up another roar swept the aircraft carrier. This time, Cam's crew didn't participate. They were all too busy prepping: they were next.

Cam felt the *Bombshell*'s nose bounce as the plane pushers edged the front wheel onto the white line; felt her hull vibrate as the bomb boys double-checked and latched the hatch. He threw a quick glance behind him, just in time to see Miller crossing himself, his round face as pale as the moon. And then the launch officer was looking right at him.

For one short moment it came back; that hopeless drone in his mind: *I am not ready.* But its dour hiss was quickly swallowed by the Cyclone's revved-up roar, and to his own surprise he was shouting over that into the interphone system: "Pilot to crew. Everybody ready?"

He was taken aback to hear how level—even commanding—his voice sounded, but apparently no one else was. A round of crackling *"Roger's,"* and then he barely had time to think *This is it; I can still get out* before the launch officer registered his trembling thumbs-up *are-you-ready* and returned it with a salute. Then, as smoothly as though performing a dance, he raised his checkered flag over his head. He sank down onto one knee, dropped his upstretched arm to shoulder level and pointed unmistakably down the flight deck: *Go.*

Almost by reflex Cam released the brakes and started to roll. And then they were racing down that slippery white line, his heart pounding with the rhythmic throbbing of the twin Cyclones. The dungaree blue of the sailors' uniforms and the dirty gray of the ship's island bled together as the *Blonde Bombshell* picked up speed. As they passed by the signal officer (now safely flattened against the deck), Cam pulled on the yoke so hard that he felt his elbows crack, and saw the sky lunge towards him like a wet concrete wall. They hit the ship's edge in the after-trough of another white-topped crest, and as his plane's nose plunged towards the water Cam's gut plunged right along with it. He was pulling up with all his might, and there was a brief moment where he had just the faintest sense of a tremor and thought he'd pulled them right into a stall. Clearly Midge—who shouted *"Shiiiit, Cam! Watch your airspeed! Watch the nose, for God's sake!"* thought so too.

But he leveled her out, feeling the strain now in his triceps and lower back. He crabbed a little into the headwind, pulled up a little more . . . and to his utter elation and terror they were aloft. The cream-flecked waves were below them, sinking away by the second.

It was only after he'd raised his flaps that Cam noticed the burn in his lungs and realized he'd held his breath for the take-off's entire duration. *Breathe,* he thought, and exhaled in one harsh *oooooof.* He banked right for his three-sixty to reset his compass, his knuckles white against the column. Fifty feet into the sky and the cloud cover was dense as sheep's wool. But his mind was now startlingly clear; filled not with the worries and anxieties of ten minutes earlier but the airy words of Lacy's favorite song, about sentimental breezes, and dreamy streams, and highways of adventure for him alone. He could hardly hear himself with all the noise, but he hummed it as they soared, his tone-deaf voice covered generously by the Cyclone's clamor.

FOR FIVE HOURS they flew northwest. After the first round of "good jobs" they had a brief conference about food and drink, and confirmed that the picture wasn't pretty. Apart from Giamatti, who always kept a couple of deviled-ham sandwiches on him ("I'm Italian, sir," he'd interphoned. "We don't do nothing unless we're fed"), there was, in fact, nothing at all to eat except for Cam's three Mounds bars, all smashed flat during takeoff. Things were as bad on the liquid side: Bergermann discovered a canteen of lukewarm water tucked behind his seat cushion, but that was all the five of them had to drink. Worried about blood sugar and dehydration levels, Cam ordered them to take it slow. But in the end they finished it all off in the space of that first hour; taking careful swigs from the canteen, divvying up the sandwiches into bite-sized squares. Midge ate his princess-style, his hairy pinkie lifted, as though he were taking tea at Buckingham Palace. "Well," he said when he was done, gazing out at the dew collecting in fat tears on the windshield, "better than nothing."

Cam nodded, though he himself found it slightly worse than nothing. The food tantalized his tongue and the water just wet his lips, and together the two set his stomach rumbling even more. And of course it was only now, with no food on the plane and the next meal nothing but a theory, that he realized he'd barely eaten these past few days—even when he'd had the chance. Like everyone else on the ship, he'd stood in line and filled his tray. But when it came right down to it, between an untimely bout of constipation and general agitation he'd chewed on little more than his own fingernails. He wondered if anyone else had overslept and skipped breakfast and was even close to this hungry right now, but he didn't ask. In fact, for the next couple of hours no one said anything beyond what was strictly necessary. They all knew that these might be their last few hours together, or alive. There weren't many words worth that weight in importance.

The one ray of light on the incoming trip was just that—a ray of light, breaking through cloud cover two hundred miles from landfall. That one shining shaft was soon joined by another, then two more. Then a dozen; until the clouds had all magically lifted. The low altitude and the heavy headwinds still made steering tedious work. But Midge took over for a bit when Cam went to use the honey bucket, and he got a chance to stretch and massage his aching arms. When he returned to his seat the sky was blue, and the water sparkled as though God himself had shaken gems all across its rippling surface. Midge looked up at Cam. For the first time since losing sight of the *Hornet*, he grinned.

"Thought I'd clean up some of that crappy weather for you while you were back there," he called.

Cam grinned back, though for some reason a lump also formed in his throat. As though his copilot really had done something of this magnitude. Just for him. "See?" he shouted back as he slid into his seat. "Hell with your rabbi. You *are* an angel."

"My rabbi also says there's no hell," returned Midge, and punched Cam in the shoulder.

"We're all going to hell if we don't find our goddamn landmarks," called Miller from the back. "Pardon my French." He'd been scanning the horizon through his binoculars for the past hour, looking worried, though when Cam asked if they were on course he'd nodded.

"We should be close now, shouldn't we?" Cam asked again now.

"As long as we've stayed on course. We'll probably hit the coast any minute now."

Cam's gut lurched, even though this was exactly what he should have been hoping to hear. To calm himself he thought back to "All This and Heaven Too," trying to remember all of the lyrics. He was puzzling over the last verse (was it *You give me love and your love is a melody* or *You give me love and your love is so sweet?*) when Miller and Midge started shouting *Land Ho!*

"Where?" he yelled back. "Where's the land?"

"About twenty degrees off the nose to the left," shouted Miller. "Right there. See that thing? It's the Inobusaki Lighthouse."

Midge retrieved his binoculars and gave the named coordinates a good hard stare. "Yup," he said at last, "you're right. Well, that's a sight. First damn land I've set eyes on in three weeks."

Cam felt his pulse pound. "Give me the binoculars," he shouted. "Take the yoke a second, will you?"

His fists were so cramped from clenching metal that it hurt to uncurl his fingers at first. But the shooting pains subsided as he pushed up his goggles and lifted the binoculars to his eyes.

At first all was blank; just two circles of white light intercut with the spiky silhouette of his thin, sparse eyelashes. He blinked a few times, shifted direction, and like a vision the enemy nation materialized, bathed in the light of the sun behind them.

FOR WEEKS HE'D been trying to picture it: *Nip-pon. Ni-hon.* He'd even copied the characters carefully into his notebook: 日 and 本. *Origin of the sun.* He'd learned this during a series of morning lectures offered in the *Hornet*'s wardroom. They were given by the Navy's last attaché to Tokyo before the war, a pale thin man named Lieutenant Commander Spencer Jackson. Some of the men called these talks "Skull Practice." Midge referred to them as *How to Make Friends and Influence Japs*, and he was usually late if he attended at all. Cam, though, was there at 0830 sharp every morning, front and center, with a focus he'd never given to Aeronautics 101. *A guy should learn something,* he'd written to Lacy, *about a place he's about to bomb.*

And in fact, he had learned something. Apart from how to write 日本, Cam had learned that the Japanese language system was not at all like China's, even though they used Chinese characters. They used Chinese characters because for thousands of years they—like most East Asian nations—had admired and emulated the Chinese, just as many Western nations emulated the French. Now, however, they were apparently past admiring them and just wanted their land—starting with Manchuria, which Hirohito's army had invaded in 1930 and had been tightening their grip on ever since. They'd even left the League of Nations in protest when the organization called for the withdrawal of Japanese troops from Chinese territory.

"Why the hell do they want it so much?" someone asked.

"They want it," LCDR Jackson replied, "in part because the astounding rate at which Japan has modernized has created desperate need for resources—lumber, steel, coal, farmland—that a nation of such size simply cannot supply. But the government also hopes to secure space for its population. They see Manchuria much as the American pioneers saw the West. They consider it their land of opportunity."

"Except," Midge noted, "that it's not their land."

"Of course it isn't," Jackson said. "And neither are Guam, Wake, the Philippine Islands or Borneo. That, Lieutenant, is precisely why we are bombing them."

"I thought we were bombing them because they bombed us in Oahu," said Giamatti.

"They bombed Oahu so we wouldn't try to *stop* them from taking over East Asia," Jackson snapped.

A small silence had followed, after which some joker in the back drawled: "Well, they sure as *sheee*-it got *that* wrong."

Based on these lectures, Cam had come to picture their Pacific enemy as a sort of mix between various Chinatowns he had seen, New York City (which he had not) and maybe Lilliput, based on the reportedly short stature of its people. From where he sat now, though, Japan looked like nothing so much as a bit of pale silk atop the waves. Its sandy coast was laced with fog, pocked by occasional white spots that from the distance twinkled like clean ice or marble. As he drew closer they turned out to be boats; trim fishing frigates and white patrollers like the one they'd sunk a few hours back. Cam was flying low enough to make out their crews, many of whom looked up as they passed. He steeled himself for alarm, ack-ack fire and/or pursuit, but to his vast astonishment the Japs didn't curse or shout. Instead—and at first he thought he was imagining it—they *waved*.

Cam dropped the eyepiece in order to rub his dry eyes. But when he looked down again there they were, lifting up their hands in cheerful greeting.

"Why the hell are they *waving*?" he asked, stupefied.

Midge took the binoculars back and squinted down. "Hell if I know. Maybe they think we've come to liberate them."

"I don't think that's it," called Miller from the navigator's seat.

Midge twisted in his seat. "Come again?"

"I think they *think* we're Japs," said Miller. "It's gotta be the insignia. It has that red circle on it, you know?"

"So?"

"So I guess from there, it must look like those red suns they paint on their Zeros."

"Those are suns?" Midge called back. "I thought those were just big red meatballs."

Cam shook his head in disbelief. Between Skull Practice and all that training he thought he had considered from every possible angle what might happen when they entered Jap airspace. He'd even imagined the *kamikaze*—the "divine wind" that the Japs for centuries had thought would protect them from any outside invaders—materializing out of nowhere and blowing them from the sky, just as it had blown Kublai Khan's invading fleet from the seas. That the skies would clear like magic and the enemy greet them with sunny smiles seemed nothing short of surreal.

"Well," shouted Midge, "whatever it means, they sure don't look like they knew we were coming. Maybe that patrol ship we sank didn't radio back after all."

It was as good a scenerio as any of them could have hoped for. Yet for some reason this unexpected gift of disguise left Cam feeling even more uneasy. As though they were hiding behind something too small to shield them from sight for very long. As though they were a big man crouching down behind a too-tiny boulder.

It didn't help his mood much that the gas gauge was now knocking well past the three-quarters peg—and this despite the fact that Bergermann had refilled the tank several times. Maybe, Cam thought, *this* would be the famed wind god's vengeance. Not a sixty-knot monsoon blowing them wetly down from the clouds, but a simple, sputtering lack of fuel.

Below them, the little white boats seemed to get bigger and to multiply, and their little captains continued waving encouragingly. After a while Midge waved back. It was a Queen Maryish sort of wave, with his palm stiff and his hairy fingers rotating together at the top of his knobby wrist. If anyone on the ground saw him they didn't get the joke.

"Stupid gooks," he snorted. "If we'd come in a wooden horse they'd have wheeled us right in."

"Yeah," returned Cam. "And we wouldn't have to worry about the fucking fuel."

Midge smiled tightly. But the exchange ended there. As they

approached their target it seemed increasingly to him that the mission itself was suddenly riding right there in the cockpit with them. Like a ten-ton gorilla, it did not leave much room for casual discourse.

When they finally hit shoreline they found themselves on the main beach, a gold-toned band surrounding greenery, lush and thick. Fishermen in boats became fishermen on land, their heaving nets filled with their writhing silver catch. There were sunbathers too, bunched beneath bright-colored beach umbrellas, the women in sunglasses and big floppy sun hats, the children in baseball caps and visors. They too waved up in lazy, sun-soaked greeting, but Midge was tired of his game now and ignored them. He was busy checking their readings and marking them down so they'd be able to report them back to HQ. Watching him, Cam noticed the thickening stubble that stretched across his friend's jawline. During their last Skull Practice class their instructor apparently noticed that some fliers—temporarily released here from the AAF's strict stipulations about facial hair—were experimenting with beards and mustaches. He'd advised them all to shave before takeoff. "Not to make you unduly nervous," he'd said, briskly, "but I'm told that one of the Japanese Army's favored torture techniques is the ripping-out of facial hair. Very slowly."

Of course Midge, like everyone else, had been clean-shaven at takeoff. But he was already starting to look like a damn grizzly. Cam—who like his brother could skip a day without much notice—had never seen hair grow so fast on anyone. If there'd been water on board he'd have been tempted to order the man to shave, right there. But there was no water, and as it turned out there wasn't really time either, because within moments they were crossing over the wavering white line marking where the shore became sand.

Then the line was behind them, the fine white grains sifting into what looked like an enormous checkerboard from some green-painted Wonderland. Farmhouses of silvered wood squatted atop rice fields.

People came and went carrying tools and bright cloth bundles and more children. As the *Bombshell* made its roaring way overhead, some of the farmers took off their straw hats and waved them back and forth slowly, as though pointing the way to Tokyo. Cam saw kids climbing peach trees—the girls with beribboned braids, the boys with little military-style buzz cuts, all of them waving, waving, waving. He wondered why they weren't in school. He wondered what they learned when they did go, whether it was just like what he'd learned, but in Japanese. He wondered whether Jap kids stuttered, and other Jap kids mocked them for it. *Kuh-kuh-kamikaze.*

He considered them, these peaceful-seeming and polite people who had sent Jap soldiers to China and Jap pilots to Hawaii, and who, in the process, had summoned him here. They didn't *look* like monsters, capable of plucking out a man's beard. They looked like ordinary humans, doing what their parents and grandparents had always done here and their grandparents' parents before them. For all Cam knew, they planned to continue in those same lives until they died, war or no war. Waking up, putting on hats and sandals and dull, loose clothes. Working through sun-filled Jap days. Eating dinner with their wives and children, and when dinner was through retreating into the dark to make more children.

"Pretty, huh," shouted Midge. His tone was disapproving; as though the Japs didn't deserve a pretty country.

Cam nodded. Then he looked up, gasped and pulled up again so quickly he didn't even have time to notify Miller.

"Hey," shouted Miller, looking up from his plethora of papers, "what's the idea?"

"Sorry," called back Cam, "but look at that, will you? The damn thing felt like it came out of nowhere."

They'd come to a lacquered temple with a huge, horned arch for a gate, the walls and beams painted a solid, gleaming red. The roof was covered with dove-gray tiles that looked as though they'd been made from clay, like the smooth scales of fish. As far as style went, the structure looked much like the tiny model Cam had seen once in a curio shop, carved into a small ivory horn in amazing detail. It was only as they drew closer that he registered how enormous this building was. The wooden door alone seemed almost the height of his ranch house at home. The massive gate was a hundred feet high, if not more. The red was a bright red, as bright as Lacy's nails after her weekly trip to the beauty shop.

"How do they get it so bright like that, do you suppose?" he called to Midge.

His copilot just shook his head.

The temple receded into a red blur and Cam rechecked his chart, scratching his head beneath his flight cap, and turned back to consult with Miller. "Where the hell *is* Tokyo anyway?" he shouted. "It's supposed to be right up ahead. But I don't see anything real different from what's below us now."

Miller squirmed a little at his table. He squinted down at his map, then down at the ground, then at the compass and back to his chart. "This thing's fucked," he shouted. "Not a damn thing on it corresponds to anything I'm seeing on the ground. I swear, they must've just kept it on from the last war with Japan. Whenever the hell that was."

He rubbed his forehead with one hand, then lifted his binoculars. He'd taken off his gloves in order to do some calculations, and Cam saw his wedding band gleam in the midday sun.

After another few minutes of scanning earth and paper, the navigator dropped his chart back onto his table and turned it around so Cam could take a look. "It's not where it's supposed to be," he said, "but I think that little notch there is where we're supposed to veer more towards the capital. I'd say about twenty degrees left. If we do that, and I'm right, we should make target within a half hour or so."

"You sure?" Cam asked.

"Fuck no," returned Miller. "Pardon my French. But I'm pretty sure that that's my best guess."

Shrugging, Cam adjusted his course accordingly. The gas gauge needle was now knocking at almost a quarter, though it might as well have been knocking against his heart. *A half hour,* he thought. *We'll be on fucking fumes by the time we make China.* That is, if they were still in the sky. It was said—and Cam believed it—that the worst crashes were the best ones to be in if you found yourself in a place where you had to choose. You died fast, at least: *Bam.* Slammed against concrete or asphalt. Pierced through by Plexiglas. Vaporized by a fuel-fed fireball. It was the less efficient deaths—the failed crash landings; the slow submerge in shark-filled waters—that were the worst. So instead of picturing his Billy flying dry he pictured a good, quick death for himself, and someone important—Jimmy Doolittle; George C. Marshall; even Roosevelt himself—calling Lacy to give her the news: *The one thing I can tell you, Mrs. Richards, is that your husband died instantaneously. He felt next to no pain.* He tried to picture Lacy's grief at this news, but all that came was her usual flippancy: *That big dolt,* he pictured her saying, smacking her forehead with one hand. *Oh boy. Am I gonna kill him.*

They crested another temple, this one stone-gray and earth-brown, and waved back at some cerise-draped, head-shorn monks ("Suckers," scoffed Midge). They flew over a small green hill. Then:

"Holy cow in New Delhi," said Midge. Because there was Tokyo Bay, spread out as smooth as blue ice below them. Mount Fuji loomed benignly, just like in *National Geographic,* all white and blue and purple mist. There were barrage balloons strung between Yokohama and Tokyo proper, and at first the sight of so much light and mist and water and bobbing white caused Cam's tension to lift a little. Then he remembered that the light only made them a clearer target to the anti-aircraft gunners.

"One good thing about coming in broad daylight," called Miller. "At least we can see the goddamn balloons now."

"Yeah," returned Cam. He'd planned on *Just like at the circus*, but all at once that didn't sound very funny. Instead he said: "We still on course, Miller?"

"Tight as Dick's hatband, sir."

Midge twisted in his seat. "Now what the hell does that even *mean*?"

Miller just shrugged, his eyes on his chart. His upper lip was beaded with sweat. Cam felt his own palms perspiring within his gloves as he checked his gas again (the peg below one-quarter now; *knock-knock-knock* went his heart). He brought the Billy up to 1,500, and throttled back until he'd reached bombing speed. "I think we're good," he shouted at Midge, less because he believed it than because the silence felt so goddamn oppressive.

It took them about five minutes to clear the bay, its myriad wharves and ceaseless dredging operations. They passed more boats—not just fishing skips but yachts and motorboats too. *Nice* boats. Even a few that (at least by Cam's utterly inexpert reckoning) folks like the Rockefellers or Vanderbilts might have envied. Then at last they were flying over Tokyo proper, over more light-looking houses with papered windows and gabled rooftops. Over streets packed with bustling housewives and shops draped with flags and banners, and a few stately, Western-styled banks with Ionic pillars and marble steps. There were broad brick structures that might have been schools, and at one of them the students swarmed out onto their flat red roof as the *Bombshell* flew over. It was hard to see from this height, but Cam had a vague and fleeting sense of boys in drab caps and uniforms and girls in braids and loose tops and flowing pants. The kids seemed to be jumping up and down excitedly, which gave him his first twinge of guilt. As though he had set out this morning to deliberately trick children. To foster their trust before bombing the shit out of their city.

"First target's coming right up on us," shouted Miller. "I'd give it five, maybe seven minutes, tops."

"Roger that," said Cam. "Let's get ready." He repeated the instructions into the interphone, getting another *Roger that* as he turned back to his own chart.

"Dead ahead?" he asked, prepping himself mentally for the hit.

"Maybe five degrees east, sir," said the navigator. "No more."

All three men were sitting straight up in their seats now, their eyes fixed on the sprawling city below. As they ticked off the steps to bombs away, Cam thought, *I can do this.* But the thought felt distant, and strangely unrelated to the actions his own hands were taking: steering their nose towards the target. Steadying her out. He felt the bomb bay doors scrape open, and then a raw and new silence wove between the hums and rumbles of the general cacophony. It felt as though every man on the plane—and even the *Blonde Bombshell* herself—were all holding their breath.

He felt dizzy. *Breathe,* he commanded himself, and exhaled strongly, his lips pursed. There was no margin for error now: even a slight deviation from their bombing coordinates could knock off Miller's readings, which could lead Bergermann to misread his bomb site and maybe miss the targets altogether.

They were over downtown now. Cam noticed a drab modernity to the buildings: for the most part they were square and gray, low and flat, jammed tightly against one another. At one point, though, they flew over one that looked surprisingly modern: a round building with arching doorways and wide, roof-to-ground windows that sparkled in the sun. As they passed over it he could see a large sign written in Chinese characters and English letters, and was even able to read part of it: *O-W-E-N E-L-E-V-A-T-O-R C-O . . .* Cam thought for a second. *Owen.* That was an American company. He knew its name from the letters stamped on the sliding escalator steps in Sattler's, back in Buffalo. It had never occurred to him that an American company would have an office in the city he was getting set to attack, though of course it made some sense that some would. Had Americans worked there before the war? They couldn't be there still, could they?

"We're approximately two minutes away, sir," Miller notified Cam.

"Roger that," Cam called back, and phoned the information back to Bergermann, who sent back another *"Roger that, sir."*

And without further fanfare (though what did he expect, a god-damn drumroll?) he felt the shudder of the first of the bombs releasing. The *Bombshell* gave a little bounce like a girl skipping in excitement, and *hey-presto*, they had laid their first egg.

And after that it was *bam-bam-bam*: a second red light blinking. Another grateful dip by the Billy. At the third light Cam knew their incendiaries were off—dozens of small experimental firebombs which would part ways like startled minnows once the wind hit, from there scattering to light dozens of small fires. At the fourth he heaved a relieved sigh and settled back into his seat, relishing how much lighter the hull felt now, and how newly receptive to his twists, turns and pulls on the yoke. They were empty.

"We done?" he called into the microphone, and got a static-filled chorus of *"Roger's"* back.

Of course, they weren't really done. They still had to get away, and stay airborne, and find someplace safe enough to land in. Still, Cam felt his toes unclench inside his sweaty chuckboots and his knuckles loosen just a bit on the pillar. Could it really be that easy? Had they actually *hit* anything? Just to be sure he dipped a wing and glanced back quickly—just in time to see Bergermann's five-hundred-pounder smash into the smelting factory.

What Cam saw next seemed surreal—he almost thought his tired eyes were making the scene up. But no: when he looked again the solid building really was blowing up. Not like an explosion, but like an enormous, brick-walled balloon. Its four walls were *expanding*, pulling away from one another as though the god of wind was blowing it full of hot breath.

He watched the heaving walls as they strained and shivered, strained and shivered, then seemed to freeze for an instant. Then, just like in the story his mother used to tell him, the factory blew apart, spewing ash and debris in all directions. Bits of matter were flung festively aloft. His last sight before losing visual was of paper—there must have been reams of it—exploding through the roof and the shattered windows and soaring up and up and up, into the clear blue spring air.

Then their little square of destruction was gone, and the streets once again contained intact buildings and little people. The people, Cam noticed, were now no longer waving at them. They were running, seeking cover and escape. The sight filled Cam with a sharp excitement that tightened his throat and jolted his belly and groin, and for a moment he badly wanted to give chase. He suddenly wanted to shoot them, the fleeing Japs in their dull and dusty city; less because they were Japs than because they *were*, finally, fleeing. He even thought briefly about interphoning Giamatti and dropping lower so the gunner could strafe. But then Midge called *"Watchit,"* and Cam looked up in time to see a bird of some sort—a big one, brown and white and black, its sharp beak split in a screech—streak across their windshield, inches from impact.

He blinked and the bird was gone, and along with it the trigger-lust. He shook his head, which felt suddenly light. *What the hell was that?* he wondered numbly.

Then he glanced down at his Hamilton and saw something even stranger: that the entire operation had taken roughly thirty seconds.

Thirty seconds.

"Holy cow," he muttered, and counted off again. The timing stood. Which seemed wrong somehow, that the biggest and probably most profound event of his life had taken less time than it took to brush his teeth. Midge must have been having more or less the same thought, since he leaned over and gave Cam a commending punch in the shoulder.

"That was quick," he shouted. "Thank God we can finally smoke."

"Just be careful with that thing."

"Aw hell, Commander," said Midge, sticking his now-well-furred lower lip out like a schoolboy, "there's no goddamn fuel *left* to ignite."

Technically this couldn't be true—at least, not as long as the engines roared. But Cam just sighed and gave his second the OK. He watched in silence as Midge retrieved his chewed-up Lucky, flipped open his Zippo and lit up. As the forbidden flame briefly illuminated his friend's long, hairy face, Cam felt a stinging wash of something almost like love.

ASTONISHINGLY, THEY MADE it out of Japan's airspace without a scratch, though they were briefly chased by six ungainly black biplanes. That first sight of them off the rear left made Cam's fists tremble, but almost before he'd felt the terror he heard a voice he only a moment later recognized as his own on the mike: *Evading! Lock target! Fire at will!* And though the tracer fire puffed and popped close enough to *ping* against the *Blonde Bombshell*'s steel sides, Giamatti let them have it, and before Cam dropped to shake them off he was rewarded with the sight of one black beast springing a leak of thick black smoke. They couldn't stick around long enough to see if it finally went down. But as they hedgehopped their way towards Kyushu, Cam heard the gunner shout like a kid who'd topped his old pinball record.

They shook the rest of the pursuits off by dropping down even lower, almost level with those shining telephone wires. But with her load gone, and more frighteningly almost all of her fuel, the *Blonde Bombshell* felt as maneuverable as a glider. Cam had no trouble steering her clear of the Jap fighters, which—true to Doolittle's predictions but to Cam's open astonishment—clearly bought that the black-painted broomsticks with which the engineers had replaced their stingers (like most of the alterations, to save weight for fuel) were actual guns, and so kept several yards off their tail. When Cam dropped even lower to hedgehop—barely missing the telephone wires but taking the tops off a few leafy ginkgos—they fell away, recognizing as they must have that diving that low from their altitude and at their heft would be little short of suicide.

In the end, the remaining planes gave a weak chase that seemed largely intended for show, and Cam lost them on the second half of an S curve he made by looping back towards Tokyo, then doubling back. Bergermann confirmed through the interphone that they were finally out of sight, and there was a brief round of cheers and shaky backslaps in the cockpit.

But as they turned to double back over the East China Sea the mere sight of the gas gauge made Cam's heart pound so hard it hurt. He kept his gaze strictly outside, on the lengthening shadows of late afternoon in southern Japan.

Below them, the buildings were starting to spread out again, the gray of asphalt replaced by dirt and grass and more rice fields dotted by waving workers and children who clearly hadn't yet heard the news. Then the view opened up again and the land was replaced by white-tipped waves and a darkening sky to the south.

The wind was picking up, and he wished he could veer off north a little to avoid the storm. But they had strict orders to steer clear of Russia, since as far as GHQ was concerned it was apparently better to land on Japs than on Communists.

And so Cam confirmed his course with Miller and adjusted his heading for Chungking. He rarely prayed these days, just like he rarely trusted fate. But as they edged out over the water and the needle edged into the red, he felt his lips forming a fervent plea:

Please. Please just let us get onto the ground safely. Please just let me live long enough to get back to her.

And for a while, at least, prayers and fumes seemed enough to keep them going. The clouds still loomed, but the headwind eased up a little bit and Miller announced that he'd finally found his bearings. At one point Midge slapped Cam's seat and shouted "Shit, *look*," and Cam looked down to see three massive Imperial carriers almost directly below them. But while the ships must have spotted them, and surely knew now about the raid, for some reason they ignored the *Bombshell* entirely. Within a few moments they, too, were out of sight.

The cockpit returned to rumbling silence. The horizon, when Cam squinted at it, was now as bloated with cloud cover as the sky had been at takeoff, the air above it darkly veiled with heavy rain. "That looks bad," observed Midge.

"Yep."

"Can we go over it?"

Cam shook his head. Under normal circumstances that'd be his choice too. But with the Cyclones running on dregs and Choochow Lishui god-knew-how-far-off, he didn't want to risk burning up the fuel. Better to save the gas and hope for a proper landing. He could only pray the storm was better inside than it looked on the outside.

On their current course, Miller figured they'd hit the monsoon in roughly twenty minutes or so. Cam decided to take a couple of minutes to stretch his legs and empty his bladder of whatever lick of liquid it might still contain; to take his flight cap off and scratch his hot, sweat-damp hair. His stomach—which had felt as tight and quiet as an untouched drum during the bombing—now felt full of tumbling, sharp-edged pebbles.

After he'd zipped back up Cam patted his pockets again, hoping to turn up something—an old lozenge; a lone stale M&M—that he might have missed earlier. The only thing he turned up was an already-chewed wad of Doublemint which defied his attempts to pry it free from its dirty foil and lint. He finally tossed it into the sloshing pot as well, resisting a bizarre urge to wish on it as it sank from sight.

As he made his way back the ship gave a full-fledged vertical jump, and Cam heard the bucket slosh ominously behind him.

"We're OK," called Midge, who was pulling the copilot yoke with both big hands. "Just hit a patch of turbulence. We're right on this thing's doorstep now."

Cam slid back into his seat. "We'll be all right," he said. "She can take it."

But as he strapped himself back down his heart was back in his mouth. Already, almost everything outside was as gray as cotton: he couldn't see an inch past the windshield. The rain was striking the bomber like a thousand tiny, punishing fists, and Cam could feel the Billy's wings shuddering as if in pain. Most worrying of all, he could've sworn the plane's left Cyclone was still stuttering. Though of course, this could also just be his frazzled imagination at work. Earlier, he'd thought he'd heard it humming and thrumming to "Deep in the Heart of Texas."

"That sound right to you?" he shouted, indicating the Plexi with his head. "I thought I heard a skip."

Midge inclined his hairy ear towards the east. "I don't hear it," he called. "But I'm still a little worried about this mess. You're sure you don't want to fly above it?"

Cam shook his head. "You all right back there?" he called back to Miller.

The navigator nodded, though his lips were tight and his face as white as talc. Cam remembered that for all the diminutive Texan's tall tales of bucking rodeo broncos, he out of all of them was the most prone to airsickness. He usually took something for it. But after ten hours in the air most powders and pills would probably have worn off.

"You need a bag or something?" Cam shouted at him, but Miller just waved him off and dropped once more behind his chart.

Just to be safe, Cam ran over the bailout procedure in his mind: *First warning: inform the crew of his decision. Second warning: order them all to jump. He, Midge, Miller and Bergermann would exit through the forward hatch; Giamatti through the rear. The commanding pilot is the last out of the plane.* This was all laid out in the Michael's flight operating instructions, which he and every other pilot had committed to memory. At least he knew the escape hatches worked: the ground crew had checked on them last night before putting all the Billys to bed.

But there were questions the FOI couldn't even begin to address. Like: How cold would the not-yellow Yellow Sea be, in April? And what about all those new phonograph records? Leaving them behind felt wrong somehow. Almost like a betrayal. But jumping into the unknown with a can of vinyl made no sense. *You did what?* he imagined Lacy saying. *Why, good Lord, Cam. You know I already know every word to that damn tune.*

The plane jolted again. *"JE-sus,"* shouted Midge.

"Oh God," added Miller. His voice sounded strangled, and when Cam looked back quickly the navigator's face looked gray and slick beneath his goggles. His eyes were closed, and he was holding his crucifix between his thumb and forefinger and shivering.

It took ten more minutes of shakes and dips and the sound and smell of Miller retching for Cam to finally realize that it wasn't working.

"OK. We need to leave this," he called to Midge and Miller. "It's too much strain. I'm afraid we'll break some—"

But before the words were even out the dank air filled with a sudden and startlingly loud *crrrr-ack!*—like a huge steel ruler slamming across the bomber's roof.

"What the fuck was *that?*" yelped Midge, hastily stubbing out his cigarette.

"L-lightning?" said Cam. He felt his fingers tremble, as much at the bolt as at the quaver licking at his voice. If the others noticed the stutter, though, they gave no sign. Miller was now holding on to his crucifix with one hand and his seat with the other. Midge was furiously checking their dashboard switches and readings. He flicked the autopilot switch on and off a couple of times; then the emergency power. When he turned to look at Cam again his furred face was almost bloodless.

"Fuck," he said. *"Look."*

He was pointing at the gas gauge, the goddamn dreaded gas gauge, and Cam could no longer avoid doing the same. When he did, it was as though his heart dropped straight out through the soles of his boots: over the past few seconds the needle had jumped from just into the red area to almost fully past it.

"Fuck!" he shouted, frantically yanking on the pillar in a reflexive effort to get enough altitude for a bailout. "How the hell did that happen?"

"One of the Jap fighters must've hit the gas tank," Midge said. Cam heard his deep voice crack.

As if on cue, the interphone crackled and Bergermann's reedy voice came on: "Bombadier to commanding pilot. Sir, I think we're dropping fuel."

Cam swallowed, tasting old chocolate and bitter bile. "You sure it's not oil?" he sent back, without much hope.

A long pause. Then: "No, sir. Pretty certain it's fuel."

Cam wrenched himself around in his seat. "Miller," he barked, "what are our coordinates? Are we high enough to jump? How far are we from Choochow?"

Miller seemed to rally. He consulted his charts and then shouted back: "Six thousand feet. We're just high enough to bail. Just barely. As for Choochow, hard to tell."

Cam glanced back through the Plexi. The clouds rolled out below them like thick, gray, boiling blankets. "Are we at least over land now?"

"Not sure. I think we're somewhere to the north."

The north, Cam thought. *Shit*. Did that put them in Manchuria? Manchuria was Jap-held—that much he remembered from Skull Class. He chewed his lip and pondered. Nobody spoke. Both Miller and Midge were watching him expectantly, and both looked fully at attention, the informality of the last few hours replaced with an unspoken affirmation of the crew's formal hierarchy. Cam was in command. It was his job to save them. *What do I do?* he thought. *What the hell do I do?*

He shut his eyes, and in his mind he touched Lacy's green ring. Then without even realizing it he had made his decision. He opened his eyes.

"We've got to bail," he ordered, and reached over to flick on the alarm bell and the interphone in quick succession, and after that to switch and set the autopilot. "Everyone: man stations. Midge—open the central hatch. Bergermann—check that everything's shut up—especially those bomb bay doors—and that your chute is on. Then get back here as fast as you can. Giamatti—"

"*Yes, sir.*"

"Release the hatch on the emergency exit in the aft turret. You're on your own there, so make sure all's in order. Everyone: check your chutes. If you want to bring anything with you, now is the time to get it. Make sure it all fits in your pockets. You'll need both your hands to pull the rip cord and steer down safely, and I want your arms free if you land on Japs."

A brief scrimmage followed. Bergermann emerged through the

crawl-through, his face the color of his shirt collar where it wasn't smudged black with engine grease and gunpowder. His jacket and pockets bulged with whatever it was he'd shoved in them in preparation for the jump. Out of the corner of his eye Cam saw Midge push his last three packs of Luckies into the zippered opening of his coat, and then Doc White's slim container of whiskey. Miller disappeared for a moment as he ducked beneath the navigator's table. When he reappeared, he held his Bible and two rolls of toilet paper, which he shoved down his flight jacket in rapid succession.

Cam considered the contents of his own flight bag. With the chocolate gone there wasn't much in there that seemed worth the effort. He couldn't jump with a straight blade, that would just be plain stupid. The whiskey might come in handy—but as it was in a glass bottle he was hesitant about that too. There was his compass and his hunting knife, but they were all the way forward, and he wasn't sure it was worth the time it'd take to retrieve them . . .

He finally decided to bail out as he was, just shifting Lacy's ring from his pocket to his own hand, to be safe. It was too small, of course. The delicate gold band was meant for a woman's slim digits and not Cam's callused and slightly swollen pinkie finger. But he managed to push it past the knuckle, a little more than halfway past the knuckle, where it throbbed with each bump of his pulse. Then he and Miller wrestled with the front escape hatch latch, until it released at last and the wet storm roared in on them.

The added sound and wind caused them all to jump back. Cam saw it flash across each man's face like mental lightning: the fact that they were about to hurl themselves from their familiar mechanical womb out into the torrential unknown. He held his breath, wondering if anyone would choke. But Bergermann—first in the proscribed bailout lineup (bombadier, navigator, copilot, lead pilot) made his way without hesitation to the hatch. He braced his feet on one side and his hands on the other. "All set, sir," he shouted, over the wind.

"Good," called Cam back. "Remember the drill. Face rear, and twist to the left against the slipstream as you drop so you don't hit your head. We're low, so pull the rip cord the minute you're clear. We'll try to convene on the ground—but everyone stay real low until we've figured out who we're dealing with down there."

The bombadier nodded and eased his feet through the hatch. Then—in a flash of lightning—he was gone.

Cam turned to Miller. "Ready, Lieutenant?" he asked, trying to keep his voice steady.

Miller's eyes were red-rimmed behind his flight goggles. Dried vomit clung to the corner of his lips, and he held his Bible through his flight jacket like an unborn child he was charged with protecting. Something in the gesture caught at Cam's memory slightly, the way a hangnail might catch on a smooth stretch of nylon. He pushed away the feeling and touched Miller's shoulder. The Texan saluted. "Ready, sir!"

After Miller's jump Cam continued staring at the escape hatch. He felt the wind's wet breath on his face, and for a moment last night's dream came back again: Lacy, on the *Hornet*. Calling to him in the rain. Her hand pressed tightly against her belly. Cam's own hand pulsed painfully through the restricted skin on his little finger, and he gripped the ring tightly, thinking, thinking. Then it hit him, and he felt his knees weaken beneath him.

"Hey." Midge had been tightening his parachute and taking one last defiant swig of Doc White's whiskey. Now he caught Cam's arm as he staggered slightly. "You all right, Commander? You want me to go after you?"

"No," Cam shouted, "I'm good. I just . . ."

Midge looked down at him, his dark eyes worried and alert. "What is it?" he shouted.

Cam shook his head. "It's just—" He paused. *He's going to think I'm a nut job.* But he found himself going on anyway. "I think—I think Lace may be pregnant," he shouted. And then he just stood there, frozen, as the words reverberated in the plane and against the storm and in his own rattling head.

Midge stared at him, his stubbly lips parting slightly in astonishment. Then he licked them and shouted—for all the world as if they were at mess together and not about to leap thousands of feet into unknown enemy territory: "No kidding. You sure?"

Cam nodded, though he had no idea how the hell he *was* sure. And yet he was. He was suddenly, unshakably sure that he was going to be a father. Just as he'd been sure that they had to ditch his plane.

"Hell," Midge said. "Well. Uh. Congratulations, sir." He searched Cam's face, openly concerned now. "You *sure* you don't want me to go last?"

But before Cam could answer the Billy gave another bounce—a hard one this time—and Cam found himself flung against Miller's table, with the papers flying everywhere. His temple connected with the desk's sharp steel corner, and there was a burst of light or maybe lightning. Then Midge shouted, *"Shit,* Cam, are you all right?"

Cam touched his hairline and felt something wet and warm. When he pulled his hand away it was dripping red. *Bandages,* Cam thought. *I should have packed the bandages.* But he felt fine—he felt OK. He turned to Midge to tell him this, but his shout was lost under the sound Cam had been fearing he'd hear since they first took off from the *Hornet's* flight deck: the Billy's left Cyclone stuttering and then coughing like a chain-smoker choking.

Then—just like that—it died.

Oh god, Cam thought as the plane banked left, sharply enough that both he and Midge were slammed together to the other wall of the cockpit, sandwiched against its trembling steel seam.

"Fuck," shouted Midge, straining to pull away. "We gotta go. She's already in a left-hand roll . . ." He started pulling his way past Miller's table, shakily, big hand by big hand. When he reached Cam he extended his free arm.

"Come *on*," he shouted. And when Cam didn't respond right away: "Come *on*, Cam. *Now.*"

It's pointless, Cam wanted to shout back. *You can't fight the goddamn god of the wind.* But he was too tired to argue, and so he just shook his head.

"Come *on*," Midge shouted again, his voice growing hoarse. "You've got to live through this, buddy. You're going to be a god-damn *daddy*, for Christ's sake!"

Cam stared at his friend. At first he didn't quite grasp what the copilot was saying. But then he did—and realized that it was true. So with what felt like a superhuman effort, amid all the rain and roaring and pain, he pulled his arm free from the wall and reached out. He felt Midge's strong hand clasp his own fingers, and winced as Lacy's ring crushed itself right into his palm. But the pain woke him a little more. He managed to pull himself forward.

"You go first," Midge shouted when Cam had finally reached the hatch. Cam tried to shake his head again—he was still the lead pilot, after all—but Midge just straightened his chute straps roughly, then pushed him towards the hatch. "You go first," he bellowed. "I'll jump right after."

It was too much to fight Midge and gravity and his own sput-tering, spinning plane. So Cam ducked his head down and tucked his knees up into the fetal position described in the handbook but never actually demonstrated. Grimacing, he pushed down and down until he was through. He was vaguely aware of Midge, jumping right behind him.

And then they were falling, falling into the rain-sliced night as the Billy screamed into the darkness, alone.

WHEN HE WOKE it was black and damp, the air close and stale and pungent and heavy with a fecal smell he both knew and did not know. He stirred slightly and pain shot through his bruised temple, and he thought again—groggily—*bandages.* Had he packed them in the end? He couldn't remember. In fact, he had no recollection of where he was and how he'd gotten here. His head was pounding hard enough that the air around it vibrated. He could actually hear it clanging: *clang, clang, clang.*

Experimentally, Cam moved his head a little and felt something soft and mud-like but far more foul beneath his cheek. *Shit,* he thought. Not out of rage or frustration but out of a sudden recognition that that was what he was lying in. He tried to pull himself up into a sitting position, but when he went to move his arms he found them both numb and unresponsive. His legs were equally unfeeling. They felt dead.

(*Clang, clang, clang . . .*) *Calm,* he thought. *You've got to try to stay calm.*

Breathing hurt his ribs, but Cam took a deep one anyway. *Breathe.* And with that breath, bits and pieces came to him: the *Bombshell* coughing. That awful cessation. The terrifying half-silence of a plane flying on one engine. He remembered hitting the bulkhead, and the blood, and fighting with Midge over jumping first. And then he remembered falling; blacking out briefly but then opening his eyes again to the plummeting darkness and knowing he was flying towards the earth, and though he knew it was impossible it seemed to him that there had been a tall black figure outlined in billowing white flying with him. *Holy moley,* he remembered thinking; *he really is an angel.* Then he remembered his chute opening and the fall slowing to a lazy drift, and then blacking out again.

And now here he was; blind, paralyzed. Lying on a pillow of feces.

Groaning, Cam tried again to lift his head. He blinked and discerned a difference between what he saw when his eyes were closed—which was nothing—and when they were open, which was a grainy smudge of light. The air didn't feel fresh, so at first he thought he was inside somewhere. But then he shook his head from side to side and felt the rough weave of something rank, rubbing against his cheek and forehead. Cloth of some sort. Sackcloth. *A sack,* he thought. *I've got a goddamn sack over my head.*

Claustrophobia washed over him, hot and nauseating and stifling. He tried to force it back, collect his thoughts. His heart was still pounding (*clang, clang, clang*) but as his mind cleared he realized that what he was hearing wasn't actually his heart. It was another sound; something far-off, a hammering of some sort. Metal on metal. Somewhere above that rose a muffled mumbling of men's voices, and the sound sparked a surge of excitement. *Maybe they found the Bombshell,* he thought. *Maybe they've even started fixing her . . .* and before he could think it through he was calling out for his crew: "Midge? Miller? You guys there?"

The words felt like blades cutting through his dry throat. The clanging stopped briefly. Then the shit beneath his cheek trembled and he felt rather than heard footsteps, followed by a rapid-fire exchange between voices not at all Midge- or Miller-like. These voices were deep and guttural, with rolls and dips Cam didn't recognize. What he did recognize was that they sounded angry.

Then hands were hauling him roughly to his feet, which Cam discovered he also couldn't move. The hands pulled him along by his armpits with his legs dragging behind in the muck. He registered that he'd lost one of his chukker boots. And maybe a sock. He felt a brief if pointless relief as the shit smell faded away, step by dragging step.

Amid more shouts and grunts he was forced to his knees, then kicked hard enough that he felt something crack. He doubled over from the pain, only to be jerked upright and kicked once more. Then without warning the sack was gone from his head, and he saw blue sky and white light and (though it was clearly day now) shooting stars. He shouted in surprise and squeezed his eyes shut.

"Wh—Where am I?" he croaked.

"*Nani!*" someone shouted; then something like *Hana-sana* and something hit his head, hard enough that he screamed and his eyes teared over. His ears were ringing now, but through the ringing he could still hear the voices, exchanging comments in that same harsh, unknown language. What had Spencer said was the difference between Chinese and Japanese? One was tonal. But was what he was hearing now tonal or not? And was it possible he'd somehow landed in Free China? He tightened his right hand into a fist, searching for the tight pain of Lacy's ring on his pinkie. But as far as his brain was concerned his hands may as well have been cut clean off. He somehow managed to muster the courage to try to pry his eyes open again, keeping them slitted at first. When there were no more blows forthcoming, he opened them all the way.

The first things he saw were the boots. Gleaming black riding boots that went up to the wearer's khaki-sheathed knees and that boasted a silver spur on each ankle. Cam lifted his eyes up further and made out khaki jodphers, a heavy black belt. Hanging from the belt was an elaborate curving scabbard, so long its silver tip nearly grazed the dirt. His gaze continued up to the man's smooth-shaven face and small, tight mustache; to a nose covered in ugly purplish-looking scars. The officer's black eyes were fixed flatly and unblinkingly on his own features, and for a moment Cam stared back in dull shock. Then the officer scowled and barked something, and one of the men standing behind him scurried forward. He hesitated in front of Cam, as though gathering his thoughts, until the sword-bearing man shouted again. The smaller man started and saluted him before turning back to Cam.

He cleared his throat. "Ah," he said, pointing at Cam's chest, "you—American."

It was less a question than a statement. Cam squinted at the man's insignia, trying to remember what uniforms Jap Army officers wore. He'd seen a picture in Skull Class, but try as he might he couldn't remember a single detail.

"You American!" the little man repeated angrily.

Cam nodded. To be on the safe side he gave his name, rank and serial number, which was what he'd been instructed to do in case of capture: "Cameron Richards. First Lieutenant, United States Army Air Force, serial number 400765."

The man looked confused at this, so Cam repeated it more slowly. On the second repeat the man nodded and turned back to the sword-bearer, speaking excitedly. The latter had never taken his eyes off Cam. His lips pursed as though he were viewing something with extreme distaste. Although, Cam thought, he might look the same way himself, staring down at a man rolled in shit.

Fingering his sword's handle, the officer walked in a circle around Cam, limping slightly with each step. He prodded him with a boot tip, then circled back and continued talking. The small man who'd apparently been designated translator nodded continually as the other officer finished both his harangue and his short trip and stepped back again slightly, still glowering.

The smaller officer stepped forward, wringing his hands. "Captain Yamazaki-*dono* say that you—*pi-rot*," he said, pointing again. "You—pi-rot. You . . . Tokyo."

Yamazaki. Cam felt his heart sink: it sure as hell sounded like a Japanese name.

The little man hooked his hands together and made a puttering engine sound. Then he clasped his hands together, dropped them towards the ground with an accompanying whistle, and finished by pulling them apart in a clumsy mime of an explosion.

Shit, Cam thought. His temple gave a piercing throb that almost knocked him over on its own, but he forced himself to sit up straight on his knees.

"I'm not a piro—pilot," he managed. "And I haven't been to Tokyo. I'm Cameron Richards. First Lieutenant, United States

Army Air Force, serial number 400765. I jumped out of my plane and hit my head."

His interpreter glared at him, then turned back to the other officer, speaking rapidly. The man with the sword growled something back. Then he turned to one of the men who'd clustered behind them, the only one who wasn't wearing a uniform. He was older than the others, and stockier, with thick black brows and small bright eyes—rather handsome, in a thickset, jovial way. Catching Cam's eye, he parted his lips in a wide, disorientingly friendly smile, revealing a large gold tooth just beneath his upper lip. He then bowed to Yamazaki and hurried off with one of the younger soldiers.

In their absence Cam chanced looking around furtively. They appeared to be on a farm of some sort, which made sense at least as far as the stench went. They'd learned in Skull Camp how Chinese farmers used human excrement to fertilize crops. But he didn't see anyone who really looked like a farmer, or for that matter any farm animals. He saw three tanks lining the wet rice fields, and a little further in the distance a crew of workmen who appeared to be building a barracks. *Clang, clang, clang.* It wasn't until he spotted a truck parked a few yards away that Cam found the final proof of who, exactly, had found him. The truck was a Ford, which struck him as surreal. But emblazoned on its side was a dull red circle.

Within a moment, the gold-toothed man and soldier were back. Between them they held a very thin Oriental, naked but for a blindfold and a pair of ragged trousers. The man was shaking and speaking rapidly, though no one appeared to be listening. At the sword-carrying man's command, he too was forced onto his knees.

The little translator stepped forward.

"*You,*" he began, more forcefully this time to Cam. "You. *Anoooo . . .*" Then, suddenly, his eyes lit up. "You *bomb* pi-rot," he cried with excitement, like a boy who'd just remembered an answer to a particularly difficult quiz question. "You *bomb* Tokyo. Kill many many. Childs."

Cam shook his head again. "Cameron Richards," he whispered. "First Lieutenant, United States Army Air Force, serial number 400765." *Oh god. Please let me live.*

Behind his back his fingers were now tingling painfully; the circulation was beginning to come back. Desperately, he felt for his right hand with his left. When he found it his heart seemed less to skip than just stop. The ring was gone. For some reason this was even more horrifying than the realization he'd been captured by Japs. *Oh god,* he thought again, and looked back at the gold-toothed man. The latter was now lighting a cigarette with a large, shiny lighter. Cam stared numbly at it before recognizing with a jolt that it was the Black Crackle Zippo Doolittle had given him and every other pilot on the mission.

Sensing his gaze, the civilian looked up again and gave another of his gold-glinting smiles. He slipped the Zippo into his breast pocket, and as it disappeared from sight there came a sudden rush of impotent rage. Cam wanted to say something. But what could he say? *Hey, that's mine, give it back?*

The officer with the sword was shouting again. "*Miro!* Ahhhh— *You!* You. You." He paused, grunted in frustration and spat something at the smaller man, who muttered back something that included the word *watchee.* The officer nodded and turned back to Cam again. "You," he commanded. "*Watch.*"

He barked another order, and a soldier stepped forward and grabbed Cam by the hair, forcing his face in the direction of the quaking Oriental. Cam found his breath coming quickly and shallowly, as though the air around him had thinned. He fumbled with his right hand to feel his left, hoping against hope that he'd simply switched the ring onto his other hand. For some reason, it felt like his last hope. But he felt nothing. Not the green ring, not his wedding ring. No metal at all. They'd even taken his watch.

The officer with the sword was now standing behind the kneeling man, touching his black hair almost gently. He looked at first like some crazed priest blessing a disciple, but then Cam realized—with another sickening jolt—that he was actually positioning the man's head. Pushing at the base of the neckline. Angling his pale, thin neck.

Smiling grimly, the officer stepped back and gauged his swing like a batter at bat. "You," he repeated to Cam. *"You. Watch."*

Obediently Cam watched, his thoughts and focus frozen to the trembling man's skinny neckline. To the skin that was not yellow but as smooth and white as ivory. Like old lace. *Lacy*, he thought, just as the officer pulled both of his arms back. Then he looked up at Cam, directly into his eyes. He *smiled*; just as the kids atop the Tokyo schoolhouse had smiled. Just as the man with the gold tooth had smiled.

Then, as Cam watched, the officer's expression shifted into one of horrific concentration. He bared his teeth and drew together his dark, heavy eyebrows. He let loose a shriek so high it might have come from a woman. *NO*, thought Cam; but already the blade was whistling down towards the kneeled prisoner, then hitting him with a wet-sounding *thwack*. And then the kneeling man's head rolled off.

Rolled. Right. Off.

The world tilted and blurred. Cam shut his eyes. He felt himself sway on his knees. But the soldiers—cheering now; as though their captain had hit a home run—propped him up again and jerked his head back and slapped his face on both cheeks.

"Watchee," someone hissed; and though he didn't want to see more Cam opened his eyes again. Yamazaki stood over the body. The latter had fallen forward. It was spurting blood from the sliced stump of the neck. The Japanese officer kicked the severed head and it

rolled a foot or so in front of Cam. Cam looked down at it, as he knew he was meant to do.

The Oriental's blindfold had slipped in the fall, and Cam saw that the man's dark eyes were open. They looked blankly into the clear sky, less alarmed somehow than concerned. The parched lips parted, as though forming some mildly worrisome thought. There was, Cam noted—with an odd, hermetic sort of distance—very little blood on this part of the body. Then the bile came back, and even though there was nothing in his stomach Cam felt it heave dryly, once, then twice, and then again.

When he'd managed to stop retching he looked slowly up at the officer, who was wiping his blade with a piece of fabric. The metal shone dazzlingly in the sunlight, but Cam barely saw it because his gaze was fixed on the rag. Only it was not a rag. It was an ivory handkerchief, delicately made, with handmade lace around the edges. When Yamazaki was done he threw it next to the head. And while the lipstick smears that Cam had caressed nightly on the *Hornet* were now obliterated by the Oriental's bright red blood, the black monogram in the kerchief's corner still showed clearly: *LSR.*

"You," the interpreter said, his voice oddly patient now, almost bored. "You. Pi-rot. Bombing. Tokyo. You . . . others. Where. How. How many. Tell Captain Yamazaki. Now."

He waited a moment, smiling faintly as Cam tried to gather his thoughts. Then the officer broke in, his voice bordering on hysterical.

"You *TALK!*" he screamed. "*HanaSE!* TALK!"

He strode over to Cam and brought the flat edge of the weapon down upon Cam's head, whistlingly fast. The world exploded into millions of sharp shards of light, and Cam felt his face hit the ground. Just as quickly, though, it was jerked up again. He gasped, tasting dirt on his tongue. Out of the corner of his eye he saw the gold-toothed man shaking his head in what looked like sympathy or disappointment.

Yamazaki screamed again: "TALK!"

Cam looked down at the Chinaman's head, and at Lacy's blood-stained handkerchief. He thought of Lacy in the rain, hand on her belly, calling him. He thought of Midge, that big Jew-angel, making Cam go out before him.

And suddenly, like an epiphany, it was all very clear. *Yes,* Cam thought. *Yes. I will talk.*

He took a ragged breath, darting another glance at the gold-toothed man, who nodded at him encouragingly. The gesture sparked a rush of hope so powerful that he swayed again on his knees. This time, though, he righted himself on his own. He *would* talk. He would tell them anything they wanted to know, and in return they would let him live. Trembling, he tried rehearsing it in his head. He stared at the gold-toothed man as he did; as though he were the one Jap there who might save him. *Help me,* he thought; and the man seemed to understand, for he beamed widely and said a few words to the crowd, and whatever he said shut them up.

Then all eyes were on him. Cam licked his lips. But when he opened his mouth, the words failed him. He tried again, starting with the name of the project. Again, the words dissolved like cold ice on his tongue: *"Puh—puh—puh . . ."*

He shut his eyes again, the tears sheeting down his shit-smeared cheeks. *Please,* he thought, shaking his head. When he opened his eyes the sword-bearing officer had taken a step towards him, his face white and drawn in fury.

"Nazeda," he screamed. *"Bakani SuruNA . . ."*

He lifted the sword again, and brought it down; this time just inches from Cam's face. *Please,* Cam tried to say. *Please, don't . . .*

But now nothing came out at all. The needle knocked against the peg. He was empty.

The officer spat on the ground by his knees. Then, very slowly, he walked around so he was behind Cam, slightly to his left. There was a moment of ringing silence before Cam felt the officer's hand on his own head. Gently, almost. Positioning it. Pulling down his collar. *Please,* he thought again; and felt a warm wetness spreading between his legs. He could see the small audience of soldiers watching, entranced. He could tell from those shining eyes what was happening; that the officer's sword was going up; that it was quivering in the air. He saw the men hold their breath, awaiting the blade's whistling descent, and thought—idiotically, automatically: *breathe.* He shut his eyes in silent prayer, his tingling fingers clenching spasmodically, as though the green ring might still bring him home safely. *Please,* he thought. *I'm not ready . . . I'm not . . .*

But it didn't work. It didn't do anything at all. He heard their raw shouts, and the whistle of the blade, and his own voice rising up sharply as though to block the blow, only of course it didn't.

The last thing he heard was the scream.

IV. *Shin Nagano, Manchuria*

APRIL 1942

"I STILL DON'T UNDERSTAND," YOSHI SAID.

"Don't understand what?"

"Why you can't come home."

Kenji finished off his rice with a deft scoop of his chopsticks, picking up the last two grains in his *bento* box and shoving them neatly into his mouth. He chewed briefly, swallowed. Then he sighed. "Yoshi-*chan*," he said. "Do you remember what I told you when I began the Emperor's work here? About the fox and the treasure box?"

It was her second day in Shin Nagano, and they were eating lunch on a grassy knoll overlooking her father's building site, to the *clang-clang-clang* of hammers on steel. In their laps were "Rising Sun" lunch sets—lacquered boxes containing red *umeboshi* pickles nestled into neat white squares of rice. Yoshi's tasted good enough, though she couldn't help noting its simplicity—particularly compared to the extravagant dinner Kenji had bought her when she'd arrived in Harbin two nights earlier. Though granted he had warned her—over filet mignon, caviar, candlelight and the delicate strains of Chopin as played by a Russian lady on a white piano—that most of the trip wouldn't be like that.

"Yee—ess," she affirmed now, slowly. "You said Manchukuo is Japan's treasure box. It contains her riches, her future. And the *hizoku*—bandits—are like foxes. If we don't defend our treasure box, then the bandits will steal it all away."

"*So da,*" he said now. "That's exactly right. Manchukuo is our nation's treasure and our future. And as such, my job is not just to build it, but to defend it."

"But all the time? You really need to live here all year long?"

Her father gave her a look that seemed at once fond and exasperated—the sort he'd given her when she'd still been prone to asking for ponies. "Yes," he said. "It's a full-time job."

"But aren't *they* doing the job?" She pointed down at the coolies with her chopsticks. One stood on the metal rafters a good fifteen feet off the ground, his bony feet planted on bamboo scaffolding. As Yoshi watched he shouted something down to the Japanese officer overseeing them, a thin man with a limp, shiny boots and an enormous sword dangling from his hip. The officer shrugged and looked at his watch. Then he barked at the tall Japanese boy Yoshi had noticed earlier who was sitting near the site on the other side, whittling the tip of a wooden stick into a sharp point. The boy nodded, set the stick down and clambered to his feet to fetch a plank from a pile of them slightly off to the right.

Following her gaze, Kenji leaned back on his elbows. "They're not builders, Yoshi-*chan.* In fact, most of the Chinks down there are prisoners. Take your eyes off them for a minute and they'll knock the whole damn thing to pieces. And Yamazaki-*san* was an accountant back in civilian life."

Pulling his cigarettes from his breast pocket, he frowned for a moment before producing a lighter Yoshi had never seen (huge, black, with silver wings on it). He looked older, she noticed. Over the past six months his short hair had gone almost completely gray, though his skin, bronzed by long hours on the North China plains, had darkened in equal measure.

Studying her father, Yoshi was suddenly swept by a wave of the same longing she'd often felt watching him leave their Tokyo house: a sense that when he left her, her own world somehow thinned a little, like air at the top of a steep summit. A fear that that final glimpse of him, lunch and toolbox in hand as he turned the corner at the end of their street, might actually *be* her last glimpse; that he'd disappear for good. "But couldn't you could spend at least a week or so each month back in Tokyo?" she pressed. "I miss you." She hesitated a moment before adding: "Mama does too."

Kenji offered a wry smile. "She told you that?"

Yoshi poked a pickle. In truth, Hana hadn't actually said this, any more than she'd shown interest in coming on this trip to the continent, though Yoshi had begged her for weeks. She'd hoped the brisk continental air would help cure whatever illness was steadily seeping into her mother's limbs and breath and gaze. She had imagined falling asleep in adjoining first-class sleepers on the South Manchurian Railroad and reading together over tea and toast in the dining car. She'd even imagined Kenji meeting them at the Harbin Central Terminal, the three of them magically becoming a "normal" family again.

Once Hana had made up her mind, though, she refused to allow it to be changed. "What on earth would I do in *Manchuria*? Ride a camel? Herd sheep?"

"You could buy new furs," Yoshi suggested. "Papa says there are lots of places to buy furs there, very cheaply."

"*Cheaply*," Hana corrected (they were speaking in English). "Two syllables. *Cheap-ly.*"

"Cheap-ly," Yoshi repeated.

"I'd assumed furs were cheap—or *inexpensive*—there, yes," her mother added. "Why else would your father have brought me three already? It's not as though he takes me places where I could wear them . . ."

"Is she behaving herself properly?" Kenji asked now.

"Who?" Yoshi turned to look at him.

"Who do you think?" he asked, laughing at her. "Your mother, of course. Any more visits from the *kempeitei?*"

Yoshi shook her head. Last spring, two men wearing khaki trenchcoats and silver badges had shown up in the *genkan*. When Hana dismissed their papers they took her away anyway, helping her into a pair of house slippers that didn't match her dress at all and walking her stiffly between them to their car at the curb. In the hours that followed Yoshi did her homework, read for an hour and then—at six o'clock—laid out two places on the *kotatsu* for dinner.

But her mother didn't return that night, nor the night after that. On the third day, numb with worry and groggy from lack of sleep, Yoshi finally told her best friend and neighbor Satako what had happened. Sa-*chan's* mother telegrammed Kenji, and the next day Hana reappeared, gaunt and unwashed, with ladders running up and down her stockings. She'd kissed Yoshi on the head without looking in her eyes and retired to her bedroom upstairs. In the year since she'd emerged from it only to go so far as the green *chaise* in the downstairs parlor.

"Good." Kenji nodded. He was still toying with the big black lighter. Curious, Yoshi held out her hand for it. "Is that new?"

"What, this?" He handed it over. Yoshi turned the device over in her hands, touching each small silver wing and brushing over the English inscription. *To Lieutenant Cameron Richards*, it read. *With Deep Gratitude and Great Admiration from the United States Army Air Corps.*

"It's American?" she asked, surprised.

Kenji nodded. "From that downed pilot I wrote you about."

"Oh, right." Yoshi smoothed her hair with her palms, trying to recall what he'd written. Something about an American crashing not too far from New Nagano. Kenji himself had found him—

unconscious—on a scouting excursion for locations for a new set of Army barracks. *We're bound to win the war,* he'd written, *if those stupid Americans can't even fly their own* planes . . .

"Aren't they allowed to smoke?" she asked now.

He shook his head. "Can't have prisoners lighting fires. Besides, he doesn't need it where he's gone."

Yoshi blinked. "He died?"

"*Nn.*"

"Of his injuries?"

"You could say that." Kenji stubbed out his cigarette in the grass. He nodded. "*So ieba*—that reminds me." He patted his breast pocket again, then pulled out a tiny bundle. "This is for your mother."

Handing the lighter back, Yoshi took the little package in her hands. It was a drawstring bag made of bright Chinese silk, embroidered with some lighter-colored thread in a floral pattern. Shaking the bag's contents onto her palm, Yoshi saw a ring. It was made of tarnished silver, intricately wrought. The setting was crafted of finely forged loops and ribbons, unfurling around a glistening, dark green stone. It was easily the most beautiful thing Yoshi had seen in the day and a half since leaving the Yamato.

"When I saw it I immediately thought of *Okaa*-san," Kenji was saying. "She likes Western things, *nee*? And she certainly doesn't need another fur."

"Where did you get it?"

"Oh, I just picked it up somewhere . . ."

Yoshi toyed with the ring, trying to picture it on Hana's slim white finger. The image brought on an unexpected wave of homesickness. What, Yoshi wondered, was Hana doing at this very moment? Was she remembering to take all of her pills and powders? Was she changing out of her nightclothes when she woke up? Or was she sitting on her bed or the green *chaise* writing letters she would never send to people she never spoke about (an Andrew, an Anton)?

"Put that someplace safe, *nee*," her father was saying. "I want her to know I'm thinking of her."

If you were thinking about her you'd come home, Yoshi thought, but then decided that was probably unfair. Her father was a kind man; everyone she knew said so. He was simply working to make a life, both for himself and his country. After all, back in Tokyo he was little more than a carpenter, even if he'd married a samurai's granddaughter. But here—she looked at him sidelong as he surveyed his building site and his soybean fields and, beyond that, the village he'd built from nothing—here, he was a kind of king. A king who had made food and villages spring from barren Chinese steppes; a king who was helping Japan find her dignity, free of Western imperialism and hypocrisy. (*King Kenji,* she thought experimentally, in English.) And at least the ring showed he hadn't forgotten Hana completely. After the war was over he'd come home again. After the war was *won.*

Feeling slightly better, Yoshi stretched her fingers out towards the barracks, imagining she was a heroine in some Hollywood movie— Scarlett O'Hara or perhaps Dale Tremont from *Top Hat.* She pictured Fred Astaire or Clark Gable bending over her elegant hand. Pressing it to their lips; murmuring something dashing. *Madame, I'm enchanted . . .*

"Don't you lose that, now," Kenji cautioned. "Remember, it's for your mother. We got you that fur cape in the Russian district."

Yoshi nodded, slipping the ring off again as Kenji stretched his burly arms towards the sun and heaved himself to his feet.

"We should start heading back soon," he said, pulling another cigarette from his pack. "I wanted to introduce you to Miss Oguchi, our schoolteacher. I thought you could help her in the new schoolroom a little—heaven knows she could use some assistance. But I want to have a quick word with Captain Yamazaki first."

"All right." Yoshi slid the ring back into its pouch. "Oh, Papa?"

"*Nn.*"

"You said the Chinese men down there are prisoners. Why?"

He frowned. "What do you mean, why?"

"Why are they being—imprisoned?"

"Why, they're *hizoku*, of course."

"What did they try to steal?"

He tucked in a loose shirttail. "Our land, Yoshi-*chan*. They tried to steal our land."

Yoshi nodded, though inwardly she couldn't help wondering: How does someone steal *land*? It wasn't like stealing jewels, or money. Or even a car—though this was something her father also seemed worried about. When he'd driven her from Harbin station she'd noticed that he'd painted his old Ford (which he'd brought with him from Tokyo) the same mossy green as the Japanese Army trucks one saw everywhere here. He'd also painted a round *hinomaru* sun on each door, like round red cheeks on a Russian doll.

As her father jogged down the gentle slope Yoshi carefully reknotted the little bag's silk strings, then slid it into the outer pocket of her school satchel, where it would be safe. She was just setting about retying the *bento* boxes into their bright red *furoshiki* when she heard an unfamiliar voice directly in front of her: "Hey there! Are you Yoshi-*chan*?"

Startled, she looked up to see the boy she'd seen whittling earlier standing just a few feet in front of her.

"Yes," she said, warily.

"Good afternoon." He bowed, the words slightly mocking. "I'm Masahiro Shinagawa." He assessed her for a moment, his expression musing. Then he pointed at the two neat bundles she'd just finished tying. "Your dad sent me up here to fetch those. I'm to bring them back to my mother to wash."

"These?" Yoshi looked back at the *furoshiki*-bound boxes, confused. Kenji hadn't mentioned where he'd gotten them from, but she'd assumed it would be her job to wash them. "All right." She held them out stiffly. "Here you are."

As the boy took them, she smoothed her hair and studied him beneath her eyelashes. She wasn't used to talking to boys; at least not one-on-one. Back in Tokyo girls and boys went to separate junior highs after primary school, and were carefully chaperoned whenever they were together.

"Your father has talked a lot about your visit," he was saying. "I hope you had a comfortable trip."

"I did, thank you."

He squatted to knot the two boxes together onto his pole, peering up at her in the sunlight. "He was right."

"About what?"

"You're very pretty."

"He *said* that?" Yoshi felt her cheeks heat, in part because of the forwardness of his comment. She couldn't imagine some boy in Tokyo saying such a thing out of the blue. But it was also because Kenji had never told *her* she was pretty. Hana had on occasion, but always in a way that seemed to include or imply a *but*: "Oh, Yoshi-*chan*," she'd say, when Yoshi came down with her blouse buttoned crookedly, or a run in her tights, or an ink stain on her hands or her cheek. "You are so pretty, *but . . .*"

"Sure he did," the boy was saying. "And you are. You're like the girl in the Kanebo soap advertisement."

"*Uso,*" she said, flustered. "You're lying." She wanted to pinch herself: was she really standing here on the Manchurian plain, being flattered by an almost grown-up farm boy? An image came: she was Grusinskaya, the mournful aging ballerina from *Grand Hotel*. And this boy, this Masahiro Shinagawa, he could be Felix von Geigurn, the dashing baron-*cum*-jewel thief who sets out to steal Grusinskaya's pearls but instead ends up with her heart.

"How old are you, anyway?" he was asking.

"Thirteen. And a half." Technically the "half" wasn't true yet—she wouldn't even be thirteen for two weeks. But somehow just saying "thirteen" sounded too young.

"*So ka.* I'm seventeen."

"Oh," she replied. "That's—that's old."

He burst out laughing, and Yoshi felt herself turn even redder. *Baka,* she thought. *What a miserable actress you would make.* She stared at the ground, digging the black tip of her shoe into the brown earth until his chuckles subsided. "I'm sorry. I didn't mean it like that."

"I know." Still squatting, he pulled a toothpick from his *monpei* pocket and stuck it between his teeth. He had, she noted, very white teeth. She wondered if he had some special pioneer-style way of cleaning them. "How do you like *Manshu* so far?"

"It's . . ." Yoshi hesitated, not wanting to sound foolish again. Manchuria was nothing like the government posters and pamphlets she'd seen, with their bucolic scenes of lush fields and flush-cheeked Japanese workers. Instead, the village that had greeted her yesterday had seemed the dirt-brushed skeleton of some utterly alien community. Though well-constructed (Kenji had seen to that) Shin Nagano's round, rough town buildings had struck Yoshi as strangely clunky against the smooth Mongolian plains. Beyond them in the yellowing fields, skinny cows and swaybacked horses mingled, looking equally out-of-place amid disgusted-looking camels. It was about as different from bustling, international Harbin as one place could be from another.

"It's very . . . simple," she said finally.

He lifted a brow. "Simple?"

"In a good way, of course," she added quickly. "Harbin was just so busy."

He nodded sagely. "Great city, though, isn't it? Did you get to go to the zoo?"

She shook her head. "We just spent the night and then came straight here. My father said he had work to do."

"He's always working, your dad," the boy said admiringly. "He's the whole reason this village exists, you know."

"I know." Yoshi felt another flush, this time one of pride. "He's always been like that."

The boy nodded, as though this came as no surprise. "He's a real inspiration. The Emperor should give him a medal."

Standing, he rehoisted the pole onto a shoulder. Yoshi set about brushing lunch crumbs off her blue jumper, expecting him to turn and go. But when she looked up he was still there. Just . . . *looking* at her.

"Why are you staring?" she asked, finally.

"Because," he said, very seriously, "you are interesting."

"Me?" She laughed, the sound shrill and silly in her ears. "*Ie.* You're much more interesting than me."

He quirked a brow. "How so?"

"A Japanese boy living in China? *That's* interesting. Much more interesting than a Japanese girl from Tokyo."

He shrugged. "I'm Manchurian more than Japanese. I barely even remember Nagano-*ken.* My sisters have never even been there." He looked out over the barracks, where the Chinese coolie was now leaning precariously over to retrieve another board from a coworker on a ladder. "Besides, pretty soon there will be as many of us here as on the mainland. If not more. After all, Manchuria is Japan's lifeline."

Yoshi nodded: it was something Kenji said often.

"Anyway," she said, "I should probably go down and join my father." She waved vaguely towards the construction site, where Kenji was deep in conversation with the *Kantogun* officer with the big sword.

Masahiro Shinagawa nodded. "I need to get these home before the Pioneer Youth Defense Corps meeting tonight."

She heaved a silent sigh, half disappointment and half relief. "Well, it was nice to meet you." She bowed formally. "Perhaps we'll meet again before I go back to Tokyo."

He gave her a strange look. "You'll be with your father this week?"

"This week and half of next."

He bowed back. "Then I'm sure we'll be meeting again. *Jya, nee.*"

And with that he turned, and on his bare and dirty feet began the short climb over the hill. The kerchief-covered lunch boxes swung with each stride. Yoshi watched him go, a little unsure of what had just happened, feeling her pulse beating in her throat.

"Yoshi-*chan!*"

Her father was waving at her to come meet him. Yoshi shouldered her satchel and made her way carefully down the hill, the site's *clang-clang-clang* growing louder with each step. When she reached them she paused for a moment, slightly intimidated by the officer's scarred, pockmarked face. Noting her hesitance, he grinned and beckoned her closer. Shyly, she sidled next to her father.

"This your own little soldier?" the officer asked Kenji.

"It is indeed," Kenji said. He patted Yoshi's shoulder. "Captain Yamazaki and I were just talking about how well everything's going," he told her. "Between Burma and the Solomons I'd say we have this whole thing wrapped up within a year. Japan will lead the East, Germany will lead the West."

"*So da,*" nodded the captain. "You young folk have a glorious future ahead of you." He winked at Yoshi. "Perhaps you'd like to join us tomorrow for the Greater Japan Women's League of Defense exercises? I supervise the village girls here every morning at six."

"Of course she will," boomed Kenji immediately, to Yoshi's dismay.

"Good. I'll look forward to it," Yamazaki said, and gave Yoshi a miniature salute. Yoshi hesitated for a moment, trying to decide whether to salute back or to bow as she would have in Tokyo. She finally opted for the former, which the captain seemed to find highly amusing.

"*Papa,*" Yoshi intoned, as the captain strode off, "why did you tell him I'd join the exercises?"

"What?" he asked, feigning innocence. "Don't you practice National Defense at your fancy city school?"

Yoshi nodded, though what her class did after assembly each morning looked more like ballet practice than battle preparation. They didn't even have enough spears to go around; half the class used beribboned batons instead. They certainly didn't have a *Kantogun* officer putting them through their moves. "I think I'll be tired tomorrow morning," she said cautiously. "Six is awfully early, isn't it? And I've been doing a lot of traveling. I should probably sleep."

He shook his head. "Not possible. I let you sleep this morning. But everyone here gets up at five to sing the anthem and bow to the Emperor's palace."

Five? She groaned inwardly. "To Pu Yi?"

"No, silly girl. The real emperor. The *Tenno-heika.*"

"Oh." She frowned, trying to come up with another excuse. But her thoughts were suddenly interrupted by a shout and a loud crash behind them. Startled, she turned to see that the man who'd been working on the barracks roof was now lying on the ground on his back. As she watched, the other coolies dropped their planks and tools and hurried to cluster around him.

"*Nan de cuso!*" cursed Kenji, striding towards the scene.

Yoshi hesitated, then trailed after him. When she reached the workers the one who'd fallen was groaning and clutching his shin while his colleagues tried to lift him to his feet. Though no one else appeared injured, they all looked almost as stricken as he did.

"What happened?" she asked Kenji.

"Goddamn Chinks weren't paying attention." Her father was

kneeling to feel the man's leg, his thick fingers pressing and probing and his eyebrows knitting while the man yelped in obvious agony. Kenji stood, brushing the dirt from his knees and surveying the frightened group grimly.

"Second time this week that's happened," added the captain, who'd come to stand behind them. "They don't give a damn that it's for His Majesty's soldiers. They might as well have been building a doghouse for all they care."

He spat in disgust, then tilted his head irritably as one of the laborers addressed him in a low voice.

"What's he saying?" Yoshi whispered to Kenji, who followed the exchange with narrowed eyes.

"They keep saying the site's not safe; that they need more manpower and more scaffolding to finish on schedule. And they want to take this idiot to a doctor."

"His leg does look bad," Yoshi noted sympathetically, glancing again at the worker's stricken face. "You have a doctor in Shin Nagano, right?"

Kenji snorted. "Not for the likes of him. He's set us back at least a day with this nonsense. And Dr. Ohta has better things to do."

"Really?" Taken aback, Yoshi looked again at the wounded man. The latter's face was as pale as paper; his eyes had glassed over in pain. She looked uncertainly back at her father, who was muttering again with Captain Yamazaki.

"Papa . . ."

He waved her away distractedly. "Why don't you head back towards the car, Yoshi-*chan*. I need to talk with Captain Yamazaki again quickly—figure out how to solve this mess."

She hesitated, then tried again. "I—I might be able to help him. We've been studying first aid in school in case the war comes to Tokyo. If we can find a splint, I can maybe set the break . . ."

It seemed a good plan: she could practice her new skills, and the coolie could get better without bothering the doctor. But Kenji just glared at her. "Didn't you hear me? I said *go*."

His voice was thick with barely contained rage. Stunned, Yoshi blinked, afraid she'd burst into tears.

Papa, she thought, and gazed pleadingly at him. But Kenji had already turned back to the officer.

Swallowing hard, Yoshi turned away as well. She began blindly walking towards the dirt road to the village, past the stack of planks and the dropped tools and the place where Masahiro Shinagawa had been sitting cross-legged. When she got to the Ford she slumped against the sun-warmed steel. She felt herself shaking, because of the accident as well as her father's response to it.

It's all right, she tried telling herself. *He's just under a lot of stress. He wants everything to be perfect for the Emperor . . .*

Yet even as she thought it a part of her realized that it wasn't just her father's anger that had frightened her. It was something in the coolie's expression, and in the way his coworkers had huddled around him like that, helpless and terrified.

Still shivering, she pulled open the Ford's passenger-side door and slid into the front left seat. *Copilot's seat*, Kenji had always called it. The backseat was *tailgunner. Well, City Princess?* he'd asked this morning. *Copilot or tailgunner today?* Pulling her satchel into her lap, she began unbuckling the front flap, intending to take the ring out again to distract herself. As she fumbled numbly with the silk strings, though, she was startled by another loud sound from the site.

Not a shout or a thud, but the echoing *crackkkk!* of a gunshot.

Pulse pounding, Yoshi twisted and half stood in her seat, squinting back at the now-silent building site. She saw six of the workers sitting quietly off to one side. The seventh—and her father and Captain Yamazaki—were nowhere to be seen.

Kenji arrived ten minutes later, sliding into the driver's side, and started the engine. "Fucking Chinks," he muttered, throwing the

Ford into reverse. "The 186 is arriving in just ten days. How the hell am I supposed to have a damn roof over their head in time *now*?"

They drove for several miles on the rough, rock-strewn road in silence.

"Papa," Yoshi finally said, in a small voice.

"Yes?"

"Do you work in the Army now?"

It was a question she'd asked often when she was younger, when he stopped bringing home Westerners for dinner and began showing up instead with Japanese officers in their moss-green uniforms and shiny pins. But he'd always shaken his head and explained that merely working for the Imperial Army didn't make him a soldier— any more than working for Owen Elevators or the Ford Motor Company had made him a *gaijin*.

Now, though, he merely ran a hand through his short hair. "It's a war we're fighting, Yoshi-*chan*," he told her. "We're all in the Army now."

YOSHI SPENT THE next week learning about life in Kenji's "New Paradise." Most people referred to *Manshu* as "地上の楽園" (Paradise on Earth) or "新天地" (the New World). At school they called it "王道楽土" (The Royal Way for Paradise). For some reason, though, none of these titles suited her father. Ever the builder, he'd created his own, which he'd used in his letters home to Hana and Yoshi: *The New Paradise is a bit like Hokkaido, only without all of the snow and with longer days.* Or: *There is almost no need for fertilizers here in the New Paradise; crops grow in an extraordinarily short period of time.* Or: *The cities of the New Paradise have all the grandeur of a Berlin or a Paris, but with a uniquely Asian essence.*

To Yoshi, however, if Shin Nagano felt *new*, it felt very little like a paradise. She slept in a small, rough room in Kenji's tiny, sturdy house in the village center. She ate meals comprised mostly of Shin Nagano produce: rice and soybeans, turnips and carrots. She helped plump, sunburned women weave cloth and pound *mochi*, catching her fingers in the shuttle and pulling the muscles in her forearms.

Kenji quizzed her daily on what schedule corn and soybeans were grown; on how to read a rain cloud, on how to test soil for acidity. He brought her back to the building site several times as the barracks gained three walls and a roof, and discussed the building schedule with her, and the planned arrival of the new troops in early June. They never talked about the coolie who had fallen from the scaffold, and Yoshi never saw him again. Two days later, however, four new coolie prisoners had appeared on the site and the project was back on schedule.

On most mornings they rose together at the first crow of the cock to join the other frontierspeople in the village center, bowing thanks to the Emperor who'd made this new life possible. Afterwards, Yoshi helped Oguchi-*sensei*, the schoolmistress, as she tried to keep her raucous, barefoot children in order. The schoolhouse Kenji had built them still lacked desks or chairs or even a map of the growing empire, so they sat in a sun-shaped circle on the floor unless they were exercising or bowing to the *Tenno*'s portrait.

The portrait itself—huge and hung front and center—was the only thing that looked anything like Yoshi's school back in Tokyo. In fact, it was the very same portrait; the one she'd bowed to in assembly every day now for over a decade, and the one her teachers had raced back and risked their lives to save when an enormous fire almost burned the school down last year. It felt surreal to her that squeaky-clean schoolgirls in the capital and farm children with dirty toenails all bowed to the same *Tenno-heika* and his family, and she wondered if they had the same thoughts about them. Whether any of the smaller children thought—as Yoshi had, when she was little—that these far-away-seeming people lived their whole lives in just those poses: outside the palace, stiff and starched, as motionless as Kanon statues at a temple. She'd pictured servants blanketing the family against the cooler nights, and holding royal umbrellas over their sacred heads whenever it rained or snowed.

"When do they go to the bathroom?" she'd finally whispered to Satako one day, in the midst of morning assembly.

"*Shhhhhh!*" Sa-*chan* warned her. But not before the teacher's ruler came down, *thwap*, on Yoshi's shoulder for her disrespect.

Her main job was helping the children master their Imperial Ancestry lessons, so she quizzed them on it day after day after day. Hirohito (she recited with them) was a direct descendant of the very first emperor Jimmu, the son of Hikonagisa Takeugaya Fukiaezu no Mikoto, the son of Toyotama, the daughter of the sea god Owatat-sumi, and Hikohohodemi no Mikoto, who in turn was the son of Princess Konohana-Sakuya and Ninigi-no-Mikoto, who was the son of Ame no Oshihomimi no Mikoto, who was the son of none other than the great goddess of the sun Amatarasu herself. "And so you see," she would conclude, as her own teachers had all concluded for her, "since we are the Emperor's children, we all have a tiny bit of the sun in each of us."

Usually the children would nod and smile. But one day one of the girls raised a hand and asked: "Do the *Tonin* have sun in them too?"

It was the first question Yoshi had heard that she couldn't answer immediately: she opened her mouth, then hesitated, unsure of what to say as a small boy in the back row leapt in to fill the gap.

"The Chinks don't have sun in them. They've got something else."

"And what's that, Jiro?" asked Oguchi-*sensei.*

"*Doo-doo.* It's why they all smell so bad."

As the other children erupted in laughter he beamed back at them proudly, a smile he maintained even as Oguchi-*sensei* hurried him outside to be punished.

AFTER CLASS SHE'D spend an hour or two working on the project her history teacher had assigned her for this trip, a five-page report on life and culture in a pioneer village. The rest of the days she spent with Kenji, following him on his errands, waiting for him while he talked with Captain Yamazaki or made phone calls in his office. Sometimes she'd spend the time trying to sketch what she was seeing in her diary so that she could show Hana later on: the town's arched wooden gateway, with its engraved slogan *Goodwill Between Japan and Manchuria.* The Town Hall, with the American pilot's grave (a sad brown mound, unmarked) behind it. The archery field and the silos. The village store, which to Yoshi looked more like a tiny, falling-down shed with *Kumamoto's Dry Goods* scrawled in paint on the door.

And of course, the fields: *Manshu's* famed, fertile, windswept fields, with Japanese farmers working them side by side with Chinese. Digging and sowing, prodding lumbering black oxen who pulled the plows that dug the rows for the new crops that fed them all. Before the Japanese came, Kenji told her, the Chinese had relied on ancient, unsophisticated methods of farming. As a result, the fields that grew so fertilely for the Emperor's pioneers had produced less than half of their potential. "They were like cavemen," he told her once, in a tone that seemed both fond and faintly disgusted. "They didn't even use oxen or horses to plow. It's part of why we have to be here—to teach them the ways of modern agriculture."

"They must be very grateful," Yoshi said, slightly dubiously. None of the Chinese she saw seemed particularly grateful. A few, like the young woman who cleaned Kenji's house and cooked his meals, were polite and even at times cheerful. The housekeeper gave Yoshi sugared orange and lemon slices and seemed genuinely pleased when Yoshi called them *"haochi,"* delicious. But most of the other Manchurians she saw struck her as both sullen and frightened; not at all like the beaming peasants who stood arm in arm with Japanese officers in the posters around Tokyo proclaiming *Two Nations, One Dream.*

"They're not nearly grateful enough," Kenji said.

SHE SAW MASAHIRO SHINAGAWA almost daily, exchanging glances with him during the morning bow to Tokyo and then passing him in the village or in the fields. It was usually just long enough for a brief exchange of greetings, but each time Masahiro gave her that brilliant, white-toothed smile that left her breathless. Casually, Yoshi tried to ask her father about the farm boy—where in Nagano-*ken* he'd been born. What his family was like. Kenji, however, remained curiously tight-lipped about him.

"He's a good, patriotic lad," he offered shortly one day. And then: "It's a shame about his father."

"What happened to his father?"

"He passed away. Influenza. We had a bad outbreak of it here last year."

"Oh, poor Masahiro!"

Kenji just shrugged. "Masa's a strong boy. I feel worse for his sisters. Little Aki and Maki . . . it's hard to grow up without a father."

I know, Yoshi thought; but she didn't say it.

Then one brisk spring afternoon two days before her return to Tokyo, Kenji announced that they'd be going to "the Widow Shinagawa's place" to check on her barn roof. He said it casually, but Yoshi felt his eyes on her, assessing her reaction. "That sounds good," she told him, as calmly as she could, but she felt her scalp prickle in anticipation.

At first glance, the little house struck her as modest, neat and safe. It had well-swept wooden floors, a new-looking *tatami* room in the back and spotless glass windows. There was a crackling fire in the fireplace, which was where Yoshi found Masahiro, shucking peanuts into a woven basket. Her pulse skipped at the sight of him, and though she'd been looking forward to visiting him for almost a week now she was suddenly overwhelmed by self-consciousness. She wished she'd worn her blue dress instead of the yellow one. Or at least put her hair up to make herself look older.

The widow was a sturdy, round-faced girl-woman who seemed barely older than Yoshi, though given her son's age she had to be. She had her gurgling baby girl on her back and her toddler on her hip, but she still offered to make lunch for Yoshi and Kenji. She bustled straight to the tiny kitchen area and emerged again with two *hinomaru* lunches in the same boxes from which Yoshi and Kenji had eaten the day the coolie fell. In a high, quiet voice she offered father and daughter well water or "special" white tea from Harbin.

While Yoshi and Kenji ate, two-year-old Maki-*chan* played on the floor with an impressive menagerie of carved wooden animals. The child had her mother's face and fresh red cheeks, and while the adults chatted she blinked up at Yoshi, her eyes wide with guileless interest. After a few moments she pulled herself up and toddled over on pudgy, drunk-moving legs. Reaching Yoshi's chair, she deposited one of her saliva-streaked toys on Yoshi's lap. "Horsie," she chirped. "*Anno nee?* Here's Mr. Horse."

"Thank you," Yoshi said, gingerly turning the tiny creature over in her hands. Apart from the drool it was quite lovely; roughly yet cunningly carved. The wood looked and smelled familiar to her, though she couldn't name it right away. At a pause in the discussion she handed it to her father.

"Papa," she asked, "what kind of wood is this?"

He reached across the table for the trinket. "Mongolian spruce," he pronounced. "Dense stuff. Very hard to carve." Holding the animal up, he addressed the widow. "*Ne,* Shinagawa-*san,* was this one of Masa-*kun*'s?"

The farm woman ducked her head. "Oh, it's nothing. As you know, he likes to tinker."

"The Shinagawas had a toy shop when they lived back in Nagano," Kenji told Yoshi.

The widow laughed. "Though by the time we left—that was after the price of rice dropped so sharply that everyone was practically penniless—no one had money to buy any toys. Such a shame."

Yoshi darted a glance at Masahiro, who at the mention of his nickname had looked up again from his work. Not at Kenji, nor his mother, but directly at Yoshi; as though she were the one who had spoken. When he caught her looking back he smiled at her, so subtly it might have been a trick of sunlight.

Her father was still holding the little wooden horse to the light. "Eh," he said appreciatively, "you're getting better and better, my boy. It's a very nice toy."

"Toy!" shouted Makiko, and tossed a mountain monkey towards the fire.

The widow sidestepped, deftly blocking the flying simian and stopping its skid with her foot. "Thanks to you, he's also become quite adept at carving bamboo bayonets."

"It's a good skill to have," Kenji said, nodding. "It will serve him well in the future."

Something about their tone was making Yoshi feel odd. "I like carving," she said, though she didn't really know if she did. It had never before occurred to her to try. But Kenji had already turned back to the widow.

"You know," he said thoughtfully, "it might be time for me to teach Masa-*kun* a little bit more about the building business. Perhaps after Yoshi goes home we can set up a schedule. Have him come by a few more afternoons weekly to help Yamazaki-*san* manage things."

"*Yoshi go home!*" squealed Maki, clapping her fat hands.

"*Hush,*" the widow told her. "Don't be rude, Maki-*chan*. We *like* having Yoshi-*chan* here to play with us, don't we?" And then: "And that's too kind of you, Kobayashi-*shachyo*. I'm sure it's too much trouble."

"No, no," said Kenji expansively. "It's my pleasure. When does school end again?"

"He'll be finished for good in May."

"And from there go on to one of the military academies."

"*Saaa,*" sighed Shinagawa-*san*, her large eyes on the ground. "That has always been the plan. Though heaven knows where we will find the money."

"Don't worry about the money," said Kenji shortly. "I've told you. We'll find you the money. Families like yours, who have done so much for the nation—you deserve to be rewarded."

He stood up and stretched, then made his way over to Masahiro at the fireplace. "Eh, Masa-*kun*," he said, and gave the boy a slap on the shoulder. "You'll make the *Tenno-sama* a damned good officer, I'm sure."

"Yes, sir." Masahiro's eyes darted towards Yoshi, then away again just as quickly.

"What do you want to be?" continued Kenji. "A naval officer who shoots down Yankee carriers? Or maybe a soldier of the sky? Are you going to fly off and bomb America, like those brave boys of December? Or do you still want to stay here and protect our land?"

"I'm still thinking that after graduating I'd like to join the *Kantogun*, if they'll have me. "

"An honorable choice," Kenji said. "It's a dangerous job, anyway, flying those damn planes. Though I hear the pilots get the better food." He chuckled. "Your mama here will really have to fatten you up before you go off, that's for sure. It's a good thing her cooking is so good."

"Oh no!" the widow protested, covering her mouth in embarrassment. "Really! You know I'm terrible. Takehiro always told me so."

She shifted her baby to her other hip. At the motion the infant burst into a loud and surprisingly husky wail, and then refused to be bounced back into good temper. "Oh dear, she's hungry again. If you'll excuse me . . ." The widow bowed and retreated to a nearby rocking chair, unbuttoning her blouse and exposing one plump and almost startlingly white breast. Both the movement and nursing were performed with an openness that Yoshi found slightly shocking, though she also found she couldn't help but keep on looking. Makiko looked too. In fact, as her sister latched on she wove her unsteady way over and leaned casually against her mother's hip, like an American cowboy leaning against a bar. She even reached out one pudgy little hand and laid it casually on the widow's other breast.

"Mine?" she asked.

"No," the widow said pleasantly. "That's your sister's breast, Maki-*chan.*"

Breast, Yoshi thought. *Mune. Sein.* She wondered what the word was in Chinese, and whether Masahiro knew it. It was an odd thought, and uncomfortably intimate, and yet it left her feeling both ashamed and sheepishly excited.

After the baby had finished, Kenji—who apparently saw nothing untoward in this open suckling; who, indeed, was nodding with a peaceful sort of approval—opened a fresh pack of Golden Hawks for himself and got to his feet. *"So ieba,"* he asked, "you said the patched roof that was leaking?"

"What?" asked the widow, looking confused. She glanced at Yoshi, then nodded. "Oh yes. I fear the first stall might have been damaged in the last thunderstorm."

"Hmm. And why do you think so?"

The widow glanced at Yoshi again through long and faintly bovine eyelashes. "The straw in it was damp," she said softly. "I can't understand how that would happen if there wasn't a gap or hole in the roof above it."

"Well," said Kenji, "why don't we go take a look at it together."

The widow waved her plump hands. "Oh no. I couldn't trouble you. You've done so much already."

"Nonsense. I'm the village builder. It's my duty."

Brushing crumbs off his pants, he stood, and out of habit so did Yoshi, even though the thought of seeing yet another barn in this barn-full town made her stifle a groan. But to her surprise her father shook his head. "You stay here, Yoshi-*chan*," he told her. "Watch the little one for us with Masa-*kun* here."

"All right," she said, uncertainly.

Her father smiled at her. "That's a good girl. *Ii ko da.*"

My good girl. The words sparked a rush of pleasure, and Yoshi had to think back hard to the last time she'd heard them. It had been back in Tokyo, of course—one of those rare nights when her father came home before her bedtime. He'd asked her about her day, and then given her a gentle chuck beneath her chin, and let her touch his gold tooth for good luck. *Ii ko da,* he'd said.

Now, shuffling his big feet back into his shoes, he gave her his broad, twinkling smile. "Don't get into trouble, now," he said, and offered a wink before hurrying out after the widow.

WHEN THE DOOR had creaked shut Yoshi glanced over towards the fireplace. She and Masa were completely alone this time. The thought set the fine hairs on the back of her neck prickling at attention. She felt her blood beating its warm rhythm in her temples; felt her breath come fast and short, as though the room were losing air.

Calm down, she told herself. *He's just a boy. Who cares if you're alone together or not?*

She sensed Masa's eyes on her, as though he were thinking the exact same thing.

Swallowing, Yoshi glanced down towards her own neatly aligned, white-socked feet. Of course, she reminded herself, they weren't *completely* alone. There was Maki, after all, who was the whole reason they were here in the first place. She looked over at the toddler, who was now lying sleepily at her brother's feet, a carved wooden cow clenched in one fat fist.

"Does she nap?"

Masa shrugged, still shucking. "Sometimes, I guess. I'm not here during the day much, so I don't know her schedule."

"You don't work Saturdays too?"

"Most Saturdays." He shrugged again. "I only stayed home today because I heard you were coming."

Yoshi felt her cheeks heat. "Why?"

"Because," he said simply, "I wanted to see you."

For a moment she felt as though every muscle in her body had frozen. To test herself, as he went back to his peanuts she tried tapping the opening of Satie's *Gymnopédie* No. 1 against her knee; the right hand seemed to work well enough. After a few bars she added the left hand, pressing a fluttering triad against the side of her leg.

"What in the world are you doing?" Masahiro was staring across the room at her hands.

"Anooo . . . nani mo," she said quickly, blushing and shoving her hands under her thighs. "I—I just was thinking."

"About what?"

"About Erik Satie."

He lifted a brow. "What's that?"

"The composer? From France?"

"Never heard of him."

"Jodan desuyo!" she laughed.

He shook his head, looking slightly irritated. "Did he write marching music?"

"No, classical. I play it on my piano sometimes, back in Tokyo."

"You have a piano? In your *house?*"

"It is my mother's," she said, feeling strangely apologetic. "I've taken lessons since I was three years old."

"Your mother taught you piano too?"

"No, a German Jewish lady did."

"Jews can't be German."

Yoshi considered this. "Well, she still *speaks* German. She and her family live in Yokohama. She comes into the city twice a week."

He nodded slowly. "You see, you *are* interesting. No one plays piano up here."

"They do in Harbin. At the Yamato Hotel. A Russian lady in evening dress plays it."

"You stayed at the Yamato when you were in Harbin?" he asked, sounding skeptical.

"Just for one night. The night I got here."

"Very luxurious." He dropped his gaze to the nut he was holding. "Rotten," he added, and tossed it into the fire.

Yoshi stared at him in confusion. Was he angry at her now? Had she made a mistake in bringing up a fancy hotel? *He doesn't think I'm interesting,* she thought miserably. *He thinks I'm strange . . . unpatriotic.* It was a feeling she knew all too well; standing in line at the fishmonger's, the neighborhood housewives behind her whispering just loudly enough for her to hear the words *English* and *kempei* and *spy.* In school, the teacher lecturing the class on anti-patriotic behavior and telling the class to "be sure to report any strange, *foreign* happenings on your street." He hadn't looked at Yoshi directly, but several other girls had; she'd felt their eyes like sharp needles on her face.

Suddenly, the little room seemed less cozy than stifling. Feeling dizzy, Yoshi stood up abruptly.

"Where are you going?" asked Masahiro, as she made her way towards the door.

"I've—I've got to ask my father something."

"What?" he asked; but she just kept going. Crossing the room in three strides; stepping into the *genkan*. Scanning the piled footwear there for her shoes. As she found them and hurriedly shoved her feet into them she heard him stand up and follow her to the doorway.

"Can't it wait until he comes back?" he asked, frowning. "Don't leave yet. Why do you have to ask now?"

"Because," she lied, her face burning as she knelt to buckle the straps, "I'm afraid I'll forget."

"Forget what?"

"When—when my train is leaving Monday," she mumbled. "I need to start packing."

"I'll come with you," he said, and began stepping into the *genkan* as well.

"No," she said, breathlessly. "I'll be right back." She glanced around wildly for her coat. It was nowhere to be seen; the widow must have hung it up elsewhere. Yoshi paused, then turned towards the door and pulled it open.

"I'll be right back," she repeated, and practically leapt out into the brisk Manchurian air. As she hurried across the dirt and grass she took one last glance over her shoulder. Masahiro was watching her through the window. She couldn't read his expression, but it certainly didn't look happy.

He thinks I'm strange, she thought again. Why had she ever thought that he would see her as anything else? *Manshu* was miles from Tokyo, but it was still Japan.

She picked up her pace, sprinting across the grassy yard with the same mixture of desperation and childish hope she'd felt years ago running into Kenji's arms. Reaching the barn door in a rush of relief, she paused to run her hand through her hair. Then she reached out and laid her hand on the rough steel handle . . .

And froze.

The sounds coming from behind the door were both unfath-omable and unmistakable—animal-like grunts and moans that no animal other than humans could produce. The widow's voice had lost its earlier, soft edge of shyness and was now breathy and excited. As the rustles and thuds escalated it almost began to sound like she was screaming. If she'd dared, Yoshi would have screamed right along with her.

As for her father's voice—well. It *was* her father's voice. This much she knew. She was afraid to think it through any further—what, exactly, the two adults were doing to each other in there. What it meant. She'd heard whispers during school, and even seen an old woodblock print that had been passed below the desks in her class-room. *Doing it*, they called it. But what was the *it* in *doing it?*

Mama, she thought, and the word felt like an iron weight, bruising her brain. For an instant, she imagined giving in, simply lying down. Perhaps she'd freeze to death, right here on the hard ground and scrabbly grass. Perhaps her father would find her, and be sorry. Ten-tatively, she sank down on her haunches. But then the sounds came again: a low moan. A quiet bellow. A gasp. Her stomach tightened abruptly; the clean white rice and red pickles churning together in a noxious, nauseating slop.

Swallowing back bile, Yoshi pulled herself up to stand again, careful not to make any noise. She looked over at the Ford, parked by the dirt road. Then she looked back at the Shinagawa house win-dow. Masahiro was no longer standing there; she pictured him back at the fire. Shucking his peanuts. Maki sleeping at his feet.

Yoshi hesitated a moment. Then, arms crossed over her stomach, she began slowly walking back towards the house. As she approached the neatly sanded little door, her father's last words to her seemed to circle not only in her head but in her gut as well, stirring up a noxious cloud of self-loathing that threatened to uproot the lunch that had only just settled. *Ii ko*, she thought dully. A "good girl" who sat inside, making idle chatter with a boy while her father did unspeakable things with the boy's mother. A "good girl" who left her sick mother alone for two weeks to spend time with the man who'd betrayed them both.

She kept walking, though she had no idea what she was going to do when she got back inside. In fact, she had no desire to get there at all. She wished she were back in Tokyo, or on the super-high-speed *Asia*, or even back on the stomach-churning boat ride from Japan to its Korean colony. Anywhere but this pristine and poisonous place, this "New Paradise;" this "lifeline" land to Japan that, at this moment at least, suddenly felt more like a life sentence to her.

She tried to think of a Western movie; something to escape to, if only in her mind. But what came was not the usual celluloid confection filled with dancing blondes and dashing Confederates. This was a different movie, plain and pain-filled, without a trace of color or spotlight. Grainy and dull, it starred a drawn, lonely girl who was losing her mother and now her father. A girl always on the outside, wherever she was; always saying the wrong thing and looking the wrong way. A girl who would never be seen by anyone as "normal."

Yoshi watched without expression as the girl-star of this bleak feature walked woodenly up to a wooden door. She knocked on it softly, the echo hollow and blank. Then, hearing no response, she pulled it open and entered, shutting it silently behind her.

INSIDE, THE LITTLE home looked as it had before: neat and swept. Smelling of old tea and cooked rice. But it no longer felt safe to her. Nothing did. Not the crackling fire that still flared in the brick fireplace, nor the long-limbed boy who was once more sitting beside it.

At the sound of Yoshi's soft footsteps Masa Shinagawa looked up. Their eyes locked, and she was left with a sharp impression: a brief and shining burst of near-blackness.

"Did you find them?" he asked.

"*Hai.*"

"Did you ask your father your question?"

"No." Knees trembling, Yoshi sank onto a nearby floor cushion. She didn't bother folding her legs beneath her but instead crossed them before her as a man would—something her father, were he here, would have chastised her for. *But he's not here, is he?*

A little ways away, Maki-*chan* was awake again, playing with another carved animal. Seeing Yoshi, she held out her shiny, pudgy fist. "Mousie," she chirped. "*Anno nee?* Here's Mr. Mouse."

"Thank you," Yoshi said mechanically, taking the thing with unfeeling fingers and suppressing the urge to kick the child and throw the *motchya* into the fire. Instead she turned it over in her hands, at first just pressing its sharp edges and angles into her palm hard enough to cause pain. Slowly, though, something in its design caught her attention. As Maki had said, it was a mouse. But it wasn't the four-legged, rodent-like variety of mouse. It was, rather, a spindle-legged cartoon one with big round ears and gloved hands.

For a moment, it seemed like another bad joke. A garish prop from the nightmare she'd stumbled into. "Is this—Mickey-*san?*" she asked, to no one in particular.

"Mouse," repeated the toddler, now crawling away.

Yoshi held the creature up to the firelight, suppressing a hysterical giggle. Before the war, her father had loved Mickey and Minnie, Donald and Pluto. He'd even brought Yoshi windup versions of them all, made at a toy factory he'd built in Kurashiki. These days, however, it was universally understood that such images were unpatriotic. What few toys were left on the shelves of Tokyo's toy stores were mainly toy soldiers, tanks and guns, the heroes of some as-yet-unfought tiny war.

"Do you like it?" Masa asked. He was looking at her again, his eyes both kind and (was she imagining it?) sympathetic. "I can make one for you."

"Is it really Mickey Mouse?"

"*Saaa,*" he said slyly. "I won't tell."

Less than an hour ago, his flirtation would have left her breath-less. Now, though, it only made her angry. "I'm not joking," she said sharply. "Is it really Mickey Mouse? Like the American cartoon?"

Masa shrugged, looking wounded. "I made it, didn't I? Doesn't that make it Japanese?"

Yoshi looked down at the floor. The room was soundless but for Maki's slightly congested breathing and the quiet crackle of the fire. Then, from the corner of her eye, Yoshi saw Masahiro push his stool back and stand. She gave no signal that she noticed, even as he moved quietly across the room and sank down directly in front of her, cross-legged. Close enough that their knees almost touched.

"I could make one for you," he said quietly. "A special Yoshi-carving. A deer, maybe. Then again, I think maybe that's not quite right. Too quiet. Too . . . I don't know. Too weak."

He eyed her thoughtfully with his black, shiny eyes. "How about a hawk?"

"A *hawk?*" She laughed, the sound as harsh as a cough against the forced quiet. "Is that how you see me? With claws and a big sharp nose?"

"I love hawks. They are strong. And beautiful."

I'm not strong. Or beautiful. She looked away. And yet she wanted him to give her something—some token she could take on the *Asia* with her and grip tightly for the whole trip back to Tokyo. Something that had nothing at all to do with her father, or Manchuria, or the war . . .

"I carve good hawks," he told her, his tone almost wheedling now, his right eyebrow lifting suggestively. He looked so much like a sly salesman that Yoshi found herself smiling.

"All right," she said, despite herself. "A hawk, then. But a *girl* hawk."

He nodded. "It will be a girl hawk. A beautiful, delicate, strong hawk." He darted the carving towards her teasingly, and more out of reflex than anything else Yoshi batted his hand away. As a gesture it wasn't anything, really. But when their fingers touched in midair she felt it in her hips, her knees, her foot's low arch.

I am touching a boy, she thought, awed; and for that moment it burned every thought of the barn from her head.

And then before she knew it the boy had shifted his fingers, just as deftly as he'd sifted pearl-brown peanuts from their shells. The mouse was on the floor, and his hands were not just touching hers but *clasping* them, tightly but gently, like protective shells. Yoshi stared down at their fingers. Was this adding to Hana's betrayal? Holding hands with the boy whose mother was doing far more than holding hands with Kenji now in the barn?

Unnerved, she pulled away. But he pulled her back again, almost abruptly. As he leaned over towards her face she turned her cheek, slightly frightened. He just whispered in her ear: *"Don't worry."*

The words tickled like tiny feathers. Yoshi felt her scalp prickle; something in her knees seemed to liquefy. "About what?"

"About anything. It will all be all right. I promise. You can trust me."

She hesitated, feeling the tears prickle at her eyelids. It was wrong—immoral and delinquent, really—to hold hands with him like this. In a room, by themselves, with their parents outside doing *it.* And yet sitting there, she had the unexpected sensation that these illicit hands were *her* lifeline. That they might be the only thing keeping her upright at this moment.

And so she stayed that way with him, holding hands and locking eyes, for what seemed a very long time: while the barn door outside creaked open, and footsteps followed, and Maki raced to the *genkan* squealing "Oka-*chan!* Otoo-*san!* Okaeri!" Even while the front door slammed open and shut again, and they heard the widow's voice calling: "Makiko! What are you doing here in the *genkan?* All those shoes! Dirty! Dirty!"

"Oh, let her," boomed Kenji. "Nothing wrong with clean, honest New Paradise dirt. It'll help her grow up strong and sound. Like her mother."

It was only when Kenji's feet began to creak against the floorboards that Yoshi and Masa dropped each other's hands. Even after they were gone she felt the ghosts of his fingertips, pressing gently against the outer edge of her palms.

"Maki called him 'Father,' " she said in a low voice. Masa just smiled, a little sadly; and it was at that moment that she somehow knew: the child called Kenji "Father" because he *was* her father. The baby was Kenji's baby as well.

Feeling that she might be sick, Yoshi turned towards the door again. But once more Masa stopped her, putting his hand on her shoulder. She turned back, hoping for an explanation of some sort. An assurance that everything she'd heard and seen this past half-hour meant nothing: the quiet intimacy in her father's voice when he spoke with the widow and her children. The impossible sounds in the barn.

But what Masa said was: "A hawk." He winked. "I'll have her for you tomorrow. You can take her back to Tokyo with you when you go. And when I see you there, I'll bring a boy hawk to keep her company."

She rubbed her eyes with her sleeve. "I'll see you in Tokyo?"

He smiled his white smile, as though she'd asked something so obvious and innocent that it actually charmed him.

"Like I said when I first met you," he told her, "I'm sure we'll be meeting again."

V. *Dugway Proving Grounds, Utah*

APRIL 1943

THE STRUCTURES ROSE AGAINST THE BONE-BLEACHED UTAH SAND, starkly different but equally out of place. German Village (or "Kraut House," as it was affectionately called) was farthest from them. Like its Japanese counterpart, it wasn't really a village; just a sensible structure modeled after a Berlin tenement house. Its walls were brick, its roof gabled and reinforced with wood and steel and tin.

Japanese Village—the house Anton Reynolds had built—was some yards closer to the concrete bunker in which he now stood. Seen through Army-issued binoculars, it seemed a flimsy doppelgänger of its Teutonic neighbor. Its walls were wood and paper, its roof mud-fortified plaster, topped by porcelain tiles that unfurled gracefully like gray waves in the winter sunlight. Studying the tiles now, Anton, who had hand-fired them himself, had a fleeting image: his wife's eighteenth-century Ibaraki serving plate, set squarely in the path of stampeding cattle.

It was an odd thought. Also an embarrassingly transparent one. Like those dreams he kept having of their country house in Nagano turning to ash before his eyes. Béryl, who was usually the one to wake him from nightmares, had been against Anton's taking this commission from the start. "I still don't understand why you went out there," she'd complained last night when he'd called her from the Camp Dugway Officers' Compound. "Isn't it enough just to have built the wretched thing for them?"

Anton himself had thought it enough too; or at least he had thought so at first. After completing the tenement in New Jersey (the site was closer to his New Hope office, and the village, like many of his Japan-inspired buildings, was designed to be easy to both break down and reassemble), he'd signed the documents the Army asked for to authorize its delivery and shipped it all out to the Army base here.

That night he'd wrapped every letter, release, waiver, form and blueprint related to "Operation Meetinghouse" in a thick swaddling of newspaper and butcher's twine, and put them all into storage in his office. Not in the usual place (the steel cabinet beneath the print of the bobbed, flapperish Japanese woman that hung on the office's eastern window), but in a cobweb-covered steamer trunk that had been abandoned to the musty damp of the garden shed. He tossed the parcel in, shut the steamer's heavy lid with a *thud* and locked it. He dropped the key into the Delaware River. As a gesture this act was largely symbolic; the lock had been broken for years, which of course was why the trunk was in the shed to begin with, instead of in the attic with all the other travel gear. But for some reason it made Anton feel a little better. As though the whole unpleasant business were finally finished.

"*Owarida*," he'd thought, watching the tarnished silver trinket sink and sway from sight, to some unknown resting place in the murk and mud at the river's bottom. "It is over."

And in the weeks that followed he'd acted as if he actually believed it *was* over: throwing himself into his other work with a forced sort of focus. Staying up two nights running to complete the floor plans for the modernization of an artist's ranch house in Lambertville. Locking himself in his office on weekends to work on an addition to a stone farmhouse outside Philly. He'd spent three weeks in Montauk, slugging bad wine from fish-shaped bottles and shaping a sprawling beach house for a fey fashion designer.

After Japanese Village, though, all that seemed flat—even trite. Truth be told (though officially it couldn't be; the Defense Research Committee had been quite clear on this point), the Dugway project had been Anton's most engrossing since his return from Tokyo. For one thing, it was the first exclusively Japanese structure he'd attempted, including the seventeen years he'd actually *lived* in Japan. No intellectual melding of West and East here; no Cubist windows or Internationalist-styled galleries or subtle Moorish touches to window arches or doorframes. From foundation to chimney, the whole thing was to be built just as traditional Japanese builders would have built it. The government would contribute whatever was needed.

"Except Japanese builders," Anton had noted to the DRC official who came up from Virginia to propose the project to him, and to show him maps and aerials of how ineffective prior bombing attempts like the Doolittle Raid had been, and how they clearly needed both target practice and more sophisticated weaponry.

"Well, right," said the official, a Colonel Neal Jamison. "We're not saying it's going to be easy to build it there, but we can give you inmate labor. Not from the Jap camps, mind you—that's been deemed too risky. But good American labor. The Utah State Correctional Facility will be right next door."

If he read the distaste on Anton's face he didn't let on, though since Anton was sure they'd done a full background check on him Jamison had to know his top draftsman was a Nissei Japanese from San Francisco. George Yamashita and his family had been interned at Butte Lake up until just a few months earlier, and it was only thanks to a good Jewish lawyer and Anton's significant fiscal sponsorship that they were finally free. All three were now working on the New Hope farm. Technically, George was an "agricultural consultant," though unofficially he was still Anton's right-hand man. This, however, was their secret. If the DRC knew a real "Jap" (at least by their definition of "real") had had a hand in Jap Village, they would have locked them both up for good.

In the end, though, it hadn't been the building process that had proven the biggest challenge, or even locating builders who *could* build the thing. It was the materials. With the war embargo in place, elements as basic as the right types of wood and plaster became all but impossible to find. Guided by George's detective skills (though Berkeley-born, he had a sixth sense for sniffing out Japan-compatible goods), fueled on twice-brewed coffee and Béryl's pimento cheese sandwiches, the team had brainstormed for suitable substitutes: rattan for bamboo. Rocky Mountain Douglas for Japanese spruce. Hawaiian lava instead of Hakone mud plaster. *Kawara* roof tile had also vanished, and after some experimentation Anton settled on a blend of mission clay and red river, glazed over with fine white sand. These he and Béryl had shaped and fired in a kiln Béryl had bought from a sculptor friend when she decided—briefly—to try her hand at pottery.

Even trickier to proxy was the rice paper necessary for the inner walls and sliding *shoji* doors. They spent six weeks sampling alternative American weights and varieties—onion, common bond, medium pulp. Stretching them against plywood frames. Holding them to the sun to see if they had the right look and feel. They'd finally agreed on vellum. It didn't distribute light in the same way (and what had Tanizaki said of *shoji*—that it should "filter sunlight onto a room's wall, as water filters the ink's darkness onto the artist's blank page"?). But it felt right in the hand. Sliding each new door experimentally back and forth, back and forth, Anton had to admit to a swell of pride in his creations, even as he tried not to envision them on fire.

The finishing touch was the floorwork. *Tatami*-rush imports had been banned for a year, but a string of phone calls led to San Francisco, then to Chinatown, and from there to Gump's Department Store on Post Street, where Anton found precisely four mats. Four. They needed forty.

Bowing to the inevitable, he'd telegraphed this to USDRC and suggested that the project simply go with straw, which they could dampen first. It would burn faster than *tatami*, but was as close as they could come here. To his surprise, however, less than a week later he'd found five dozen more mats waiting for him at the Hoboken building site, stacked neatly on the back of an idling Army pickup truck. When Anton asked the driver where they'd come from he was told that they'd been "borrowed."

Anton had tried not to think about the mats' "lenders" as he inspected each of the units individually. Like the ghosts of his flaming *shoji*, though, they came to him anyway, their former lives whispered from the scars and nicks etched into the rough weave: dents from a low table, laden with food or books. Nail varnish from a careless pedicure. A sickle-moon scuff mark, the approximate shape of a toddler's sandaled heel. They haunted him, these small marks left by lives upended. But as Anton repeatedly reminded himself, he had taken the job. He had to agree to the rules.

For the construction work he'd ended up with Maroni Brothers and Company, a New Jersey-based outfit of foulmouthed but dependable Italians. None, so far as Anton knew, had been locked up as enemy aliens after Italy joined the Axis, though he strongly suspected some had done time for more palpable crimes. On visiting their Hoboken headquarters, with its smoky air and yellowed walls decorated with pinup posters and Virgin Marys, side by side, he had to smile at the absurdity of it all: with their big hands and hairy chests, their clinking crucifixes and hair pomade, the Maronis couldn't have differed more from the neatly trimmed and usually near-nude laborers with whom he was used to working in the East. But as the village went up—post by post, beam by beam—he was satisfied enough by the men's capability. And even here in New Jersey, constructed under those hirsute Occidental hands, the simple beauty of the structure all but awed him.

Because for all its gloomy end-purpose, Japanese Village embodied everything Anton loved about Japan's architectural traditions. It possessed an almost ethereal utilitarianism, was uncompromisingly solid yet as effortless in design as the air. It was sound enough to weather monsoons and the carpet-like mold that grew everywhere in the moist Kanto summer. But inside the feel was of a delicate, almost chapel-like calm. In fact, wandering through the clean-smelling halls after the building's completion, Anton—whose unease over the project seemed to grow with the house's skeletal infrastructure—found himself unexpectedly soothed. He was filled, in fact, with the kind of reverence for his profession that up until that point he had felt only in the Orient. It was almost like a small homecoming, though he had to remind himself it was not. For wasn't that the whole point of this grim exercise in the first place? Putting his "suspect" admiration of Japanese style to good use? Showing the damn Americans his damn Americanism? And, of course, putting an end to all these militarist shenanigans so that the war would finally end, and the people of both nations could get back to their lives?

"That may be *your* point, now," Béryl had said, when he voiced his concerns. "But there is a difference, *chéri*, between taking your country's side and killing civilians."

"Who says they're civilians?" he asked her defensively.

"Anton," she chided, "it's a tenement. Not a barracks. The American Army is clearly planning to bomb non-military areas."

"You think that makes it murder?"

She shrugged, a very French-looking shrug.

"It's not murder," he told her. "It's war."

She shrugged again, as if to say *What's the difference?*

His son Billy, home on break from Princeton, was more temperate when Anton told him about the project. Initially he stared down at his shoes, blinking several times as though he might cry. As a rule, Billy's mood swings annoyed Anton, but this one he found slightly unnerving.

"You think I'm wrong?" he asked. "Your mother seems to think it's murder."

The boy—now a freshman—shook his head. "No. No, I don't think that. I just . . . our friends there. How do you know you won't be killing them?"

Something inside Anton sagged a little at the question. "Why do you say *them*? We're Americans. We're all on the same side."

"I know," his son replied impatiently. "I was as upset by Pearl Harbor as anyone else. It was cowardly, atrocious. Indefensible. But—and this may seem petty, or naïve or whatever—but I just can't get around the idea that in order to win the war we have to kill people who had nothing to do with starting it."

"They didn't try to stop it, either," Anton pointed out.

Billy looked at him, and Anton cleared his throat. Some *had* tried to stop it; he knew that. One by one, though, those few brave souls had been silenced by the military, if not through imprisonment, then something more sinister.

"Anyway," he went on, studying the polished wingtip of his oxford, "I'd imagine that anyone we knew there likely managed to leave the country. Or else, at least to leave the big cities. But if they haven't—" He shrugged, hoping it looked more casual than it felt. "It's war. People die in war. And the sooner they do it, the sooner the war ends."

Billy lifted a red eyebrow. "You really think it's that simple."

"Unfortunately, I do."

And he did. Still, hearing himself say it that way bothered him more than he would have admitted. It reminded him of something repulsive he'd read somewhere; a comment made by the Army general who'd led the air raids in Europe: "If you kill enough of 'em," he'd said, "they stop fighting."

ONCE THE COMPOUND was up the last task was to furnish it. All the Japanese goods stores from the West Coast to Honolulu were now closed, but Anton's team had found rough equivalents to the standard items he'd known in Tokyo: wooden tables and storage chests from Chinatown. Some odds and ends (folding screens, a big iron kettle) from an RKO prop room in L.A. There were also more "borrowings" donated by the government: a wooden bath bucket. Seating cushions. A wooden drying rack. One truck even showed up with a dollhouse—a two-story, intricately designed and furnished villa, complete with sliding *fusuma, futons,* lanterns. Even a tiny ceramic tea set. The little house was as unpeopled as Japanese Village itself, probably because its minute residents were installed on some homesick child's camp cot. But the fingernail-sized cups and plates—blue-and-yellow-glazed *koto-yaki*—bore the residue of some final, diminutive feast. The little bowls were still sticky.

With the dollhouse installed in the southeast corner of a downstairs sitting room (though Anton had no idea what a geomancer would say about that), the project was officially complete. The team toasted itself with the last of Anton's Tengumai *sake.* He christened the house with the emptied bottle as though it were a ship embarking on a maiden voyage. Which in some ways, it was.

"*Kampai,*" he said, lifting his *sake* cup. "To the most Japanese project of our careers."

"And," George added—to his credit, without an ounce of discernible irony—"to good American labor."

Japanese Village stood in its Jersey lot for six days, resisting

November winds, vocal slights and stones flung by local youths. On the seventh day, a Friday, the Army flatbeds pulled up again and the Maronis launched the painstaking process of breaking the house down. George and Anton watched from deck chairs, Budweisers in hand and ears tuned to what felt like a verbal barrage at each hammer stroke: *Motherfuckin' Nips. Yellow rat bastards. Hitler's dick-sucking Chinks.* (Like most Americans, the crew saw little reason to differentiate between the Middle Kingdom and Edo.)

When the building lay in pieces the Italians crowded around it once more, like a mob swarming the prone form of a hapless victim. *"Sayonara,* Jap Village," said Gio, the eldest brother. Looking directly into George Yamashita's eyes, he kicked one of the crossbeams lying on the ground. Not with enough force to break it, for of course it was too soon for that. But hard enough to make his point. "Fuckin' Nips," he repeated. "We're gonna give you just what you goddamn deserve."

Astoundingly, George smiled. "Damn straight," he agreed.

"How do you stand it?" Anton asked him later, when the village was gone and they stood alone on the butt-littered lot. "How do you let them speak like that to you?"

"Aren't you the one who's always saying what doesn't kill you makes you stronger?"

"I suppose so," Anton admitted. "But that sort of thing might just kill me. It's worse than the way the Germans treated me at university."

George shrugged. "It'd be just as bad back in Tokyo," he said. Which was true: by the time the Yamashitas left Japan they'd been repeatedly harassed by the *Kampetei,* the Imperial Army's not-so-secret secret police. George had been detained twice as a suspected "spy" for questioning, and so had his Hawaiian-born wife. The police rifled regularly through the couple's neo-Edo-style home in Ebisu. They even tailed George's nine-year-old daughter home from the American School one day. Ridiculously—or frighteningly, really—they asked her to "watch" her parents for them. *The walls have ears,* they'd reportedly told her. *The cabinets have eyes.*

"It's the price of being American," George said now. "We all pay it." He sighed and scratched his head. "Some of us just have to pay a little bit more at the moment. I just hope the damn war ends soon." He cast a glance at the lot. "And I hope this helps it happen."

Over, thought Anton. *Owarida.* He was through.

And yet once more he was not. For when Colonel Jamison called a month later to inform him of the test date, Anton found his resolve to stay away weakening. It frayed further upon learning that German Village architect Erich Mendelsohn would most definitely be present, as would Curtis LeMay, the Air Corps major largely behind Operation Meetinghouse, and a man so enthused about his incendiaries that he was known to his men as "Bombs Away LeMay."

Though curious to meet this self-declared paragon of air power, Anton did not want to go. With his entire travel-worn, war-torn being he simply wanted to put Dugway behind him. But as Jamison had talked on, spewing phrases like *"the optimal end-result"* and *"your demonstrated expertise"* and *"expected missile velocities versus windspeed and likely impact,"* the Village rose before him, a doomed apparition in his mind's eye. Its walls were smooth, its light soft. Its fish-tiled roof sloped gently. He couldn't avoid the fact that it was *his* roof. His creation. By the time Jamison had gotten around to discussing a possible bonus for attending the exercise, Anton already knew he couldn't leave the building to its unhappy fate, unwitnessed by the man who had helped to bring it into existence. The man who, essentially, was its father.

"Well, Mr. Reynolds?" asked Jamison. "What do you say, sir?"

"I must check my schedule," Anton said, though he knew perfectly well that it was clear.

After ringing off he'd sat down again at his drafting table, gazing down at a pile of Montauk land-use permits without reading them. He solved his *himitsu-bako*, the puzzle box Kenji Kobayashi had given him after they first worked together on the Imperial. Anton always kept it within reach; perhaps perversely, it soothed him. Now he unsolved it, then solved it again. At some point it was midnight and he fell into bed, more tired than he could remember being in months, yet it still took over an hour to fall asleep. And when he did, it was only to have the dream again:

He was outside of the Karuizawa country house, snugly enfolded in the throaty chorus of crickets and tree frogs. The night was balmy, the air heavy and sweet in the way only Nagano midsummer air can ever be. Anton was packing his favorite cherrywood pipe, planning to enjoy it as a post-dinner *digestif*. He struck a match to flint. Then, quite suddenly, all of the sounds around him stopped. They just *stopped*; as though the summer was holding its own, loam-sweet breath.

He heard just one thing more: a single word. *Anata*: "darling." It was a woman's voice, raspy and yet throat-catchingly gentle. A smoker's voice, with a crisp British edge. Anton knew it, too. He knew those three deep, singsong notes. *A-na-ta.* But in the dream he couldn't match them with a face.

Then the ground was rocking, thrashing below him with the same surreal violence he'd felt during the Kanto quake in '23. *Béryl*, he thought. They were still in the house: his wife and his child. His child—the one that had lived.

Throwing down his pipe, he sprinted towards the front door, his legs straining with the waterlogged awkwardness of dream-flight. Then he was on his belly, his teeth jammed together by the fall's force and the house suddenly collapsing before him. Not splitting into glass shards and split beams as an earthquake-ravaged house should, but blackening and drying up and *crumbling*. Like a child's dried sand castle in the wind.

HE WOKE AT 3 a.m. weeping in wet silence, and lay still until the darkness stopped wheeling at last and he could make out the shapes of his room: the screen in the corner, hand-painted with an abstract willow tree during Béryl's screen-painting phase. The Ibaraki plates she'd collected from weekend markets and antique stalls, displayed atop the antique Chinese armoire. The framed citations from the Japanese Architectural Association and Tokyo Christian Women's University. His own diploma from the University of Prague. And nearer to him, right beside him, Béryl. Sleeping on.

Anton gazed at her a moment, his wife. Her strong eyebrows, her sharp little chin. Her lines and angles that had softened slightly in middle age: her spreading waistline, the once-slim arch of her neck. She'd never been petite and time had only expanded her, blown her fuller with life and flesh while at the same time whittling and sharpening Anton's own shape down to the bare minimum ("Jack Sprat," she sometimes called him). But she was still Béryl. Still every bit the appealing, square-jawed girl he'd met aboard the last steamship to leave Portofino before the Great War hit Italy.

For a moment Anton was tempted to shake her awake. Just to hear her voice. He wanted her to talk; to laugh at him. To disperse the thick unease in which the dream and that other voice had wrapped him. But he didn't. Instead, he slipped on his *yukata* and his slippers and padded downstairs into the studio.

ONCE IN HIS office he sat again at his drafting desk, staring at the print that hung across from his desk. It was a woodblock entitled *Mo-dahn Garu*—another of Béryl's finds. She'd picked it up in some art store in the back alleys of Shibuya, and hung it in the Karuizawa hallway barely two weeks after the Kobayashis' visit. When Anton first saw it he'd stopped dead in his tracks, his heart pounding as though he'd walked into a trap. The woman pictured had bobbed hair, fresh-painted red lips, and a long cigarette between her long fingers. She wore a flapper-style dress and an expression of dry amusement. And she looked disconcertingy like Hana Kobayashi.

In that first moment, he'd had the insane idea of removing the thing. Of hiding it somewhere, like incriminating evidence. Instead he mentioned it casually to his wife that night as they sat side by side in their reading chairs.

"That's a nice print you've found," he said, "the new one in the hallway."

"Isn't it?" She didn't look up from her *Arts and Crafts International Monthly*. "I thought it would pick up the blues and reds of the carpet well. He's very interesting, this Kotani fellow. I'd like to see one of his exhibits."

"Hmm," said Anton. And that was that—the sum total of their exchange on the topic. No subtle accusation in her tone or her eyes. No sidelong gaze to see how he reacted. Somewhere, Anton thought, the gods were laughing at him.

Now he studied the woman, still fresh and bright and unfaded. She looked back; a little to the left, over his shoulder. She still appeared wry and amused to him. But it seemed to him that there was an added note to her mood. Was it sorrow? Recrimination?

Sighing, he dropped his head into his hands, digging his fingertips into his scalp as though by doing so he might somehow dig out the memories trapped there.

But of course, it was no use. And so he sat up and closed his eyes, and miserably let them enfold him.

———

THE WORST PART about their affair was that it might so easily have ended just as it had started: as a mere bumping of bodies in a hall-way. A momentary lapse of judgment and fidelity. Anton had had every intention that it *would* end that way, and had made sure to behave accordingly: avoiding Hana Kobayashi's eyes over dinner that night. Answering her questions in monosyllables. Shifting his foot away from hers quickly when, purely by accident (or was it?), their toes brushed beneath the table. At the Kobayashis' departure he dodged Hana's Euro-style double kisses, offering instead a hearty American handshake.

Even when the package arrived at his office downtown the next day—a bottle of Glenfiddich which must have cost a small fortune in Tokyo and a copy of D. H. Lawrence's *Collected Works*, his plan, at least initially, was to send them back. Then he read the note, written in schoolgirl-perfect cursive: *I'm so very sorry for all the trouble I've caused you. Please let me take you to lunch to make amends.*

He ripped it up of course, putting the torn bits in his pocket to distribute among different garbage baskets in Aoyama. He repack-aged the gifts, though he did flip through the book a bit first. He found it lyrical and even beautiful in parts, if also self-indulgent, childish and slightly manic. Not unlike the woman who'd given it to him.

After closing the cover, though, he reconsidered his initial inten-tion to simply return everything. It had nothing to do with the book's—what had she called them?—*self-evident carnal aspects.* He just didn't want to be rude, particularly not to his best builder's wife. And she had seemed so confused that day. So desperate. The right thing to do, the *mature* thing, was to meet in a safely neutral and public arena, gently explain that he was married, and somehow communicate, tactfully of course, that she might need professional help. Particularly if (as Anton partially suspected) she was suffering from some sort of nymphomania.

And so he had his secretary write her back on office letterhead, informing her of his availability. In as casual a voice as possible he told Béryl that he'd been invited to a lunch intended to make amends for the fact that Hana Kobayashi had almost burned their house down.

"Oh, that's nice," said Béryl. "Do you know where they're taking you?"

"Not yet," said Anton, not correcting her misinterpretation.

The next day Hana responded with a lavender-scented notecard stipulating Tuesday, noon, at the Imperial. Anton went (and he would have sworn this on his dead brothers' graves) with the very cleanest and most honorable of intentions.

He found her at a windowside table, in a slim-fitting white suit and broad-brimmed hat, her lips and nails a striking but tasteful maroon. When she saw him she smiled and raised her cigarette holder like a tour guide raising an umbrella. Anton had to admit that he saw not a trace of desperation or confusion in her face.

When he reached the table he extended his hand, slightly awkwardly. But to his surprise she stood up and bowed deeply. "What I did was unforgivable," she said, in highly formal Japanese. "I nevertheless have the arrogance to ask you to extend to me your forgiveness."

Though he wasn't sure for which act the apology was meant (nearly setting his house afire? Risking breaking up his marriage? Both?), Anton forgave her nonetheless. He was urging her to sit back down when the waiter arrived with their menus and two champagne flutes held aloft on a tray.

"I took the liberty of telling him our various roles in this building," Hana said, in response to Anton's inquiring look.

"Our roles?"

"Well, my husband was the chief builder here, after all. And didn't you help Frank Lloyd Wright with the plans for the building's erection?"

Anton nodded, wishing both that she hadn't mentioned Frank Wright, and that she'd used any word other than *erection.* "I did. I came over with him, as a matter of fact."

She leaned over the table towards him. "I'm sure everyone asks you this," she said conspiratorially, "but what was he *like?* To work with?"

Anton hesitated. He'd come prepared to face every possibility with her that he could think of: mournful apology, furious tirade. Heartfelt declaration of love. He'd even thought up responses to any further advances she might attempt. He was unprepared, however, for another interrogation about his dealings with a far more famous architect than himself. He suppressed a sigh.

"In the beginning it was quite wonderful. I was only twenty-three, after all. Being offered the chance to work in a place like Tokyo, with someone of Frank's stature . . . I'm sure you can imagine."

She nodded, her lips slightly parted, the pink pearl of her tongue tucked in one corner. He had a brief, searing flashback to the way that tongue had felt and tasted—soft and tart, faintly salty and slick. He shook it firmly from his mind.

"I'll never forget that first ride through Yokohama. It was on New Year's. Everyone out in their most glorious colors and patterns, waving those little *hinomaru* flags. The air smelling of incense and hot chestnuts and toasting *mochi* . . ."

He paused a moment, seeing it: the controlled gaiety of the street. The beaming bows of congratulations between neighbors. The almost spiritual moment when he saw his first ancient temple, as austere and pure as though it had grown from the ground. Frank and Miriam rode in one rickshaw from the wharf to their hotel, and Anton and Béryl in another. As the Wrights pulled ahead Frank called back at them: "Losers get to carry winners up Fuji! Ha-*ha!*" Miriam (good God, Miriam! With her satin turbans and silver morphine needles stowed away in her French garters) was screeching at him over one thing or another, as usual. They'd only just gotten married (finally) but it was clearly almost over between them.

"It must have all seemed so strange to you," Hana was saying, taking a sip of champagne.

He tore his eyes from the red kiss left on her flute and shrugged. "I'd traveled quite a bit by that point already."

"Still. I sometimes think that the Orient is more than a foreign place for a Westerner. It's more . . . I don't know." She tilted her head thoughtfully. "Almost alien."

"Alien in what way? Like Mars?"

She laughed, lighting another Winston. "A little. When I moved to London as a child, I remember having the strange idea that Japan must have grown from an entirely different sort of soil than England. From different elements, even. Even the most basic standards—the color of tea. The way music sounded. Even the way a door should work. They were nothing like those things in the West. There's just no relation."

"It's true," said Anton, realizing with some surprise that he'd had ideas not unlike this himself.

She offered him a cigarette, which he refused, taking another gulp of champagne and opening his menu. As he perused the appetizers he finally realized who it was she reminded him of. It was Miriam Noel Wright.

"The salmon with hollandaise asparagus is quite good," she noted, as though he'd never eaten here before.

He raised a brow. "Thank you. I've had it."

When the waiter appeared he ordered the beef bourguignon and a side of iceburg lettuce with blue cheese. He watched his glass get a refill with slight consternation: he didn't realize he'd emptied it so quickly. Hana ordered more champagne too, and took a roll from the basket. She handed the menu back with a small head-shake.

"You're not eating?"

"I can't eat when I'm nervous."

"Nervous?"

She exhaled a lazy plume of smoke, studying him as though try-ing to decide something. Finally, she said: "Certain people—certain *men*—have that effect on me."

At first Anton wasn't sure he'd heard correctly: she'd said it in the same way she might casually bring up a food allergy. When he did register her meaning there was a moment of disorientation. *She's not well*, he thought, as he had two weeks earlier. It occurred to him that it might be a good time to reemphasize the fact of his marriage.

But by that point she was already back to Frank. "So," she said, brightly, "in the beginning it was wonderful, working with the great man. And then?"

She was still watching him, her eyes narrowed and intent and somehow faintly amused. He had the uncomfortable sensation of having lost control of something, though he wasn't quite sure what it was. He took a sip of his champagne. "Ah—and then," he said, slowly, "then the project began. And—well, let's say it wasn't what I'd expected."

"As in more difficult?"

"As in god-awful."

She let loose a deep and uninhibited laugh, not bothering to cover her mouth as most Japanese women did, and Anton felt absurdly proud of himself for having put the smile on her face.

"Kenji said he could be tempermental," she said.

Anton grimaced. "That's one way of putting it. When I appren-ticed with him in Wisconsin I was his star student. Here, nothing I did was good enough. Every draft, every design disgusted him. He called me names that wouldn't be proper to repeat. I took more abuse that first month than I'd taken in my entire life up to that point."

His lunch arrived, swaddled in silver, and was placed before him on the pristine linen tablecloth. The waiter lifted the cover with a theatrical flourish. *"Beef bourguinon,"* he said, as though announcing a royal visitor.

As the man bent to brush a scattering of bread crumbs off the table, Hana whispered something in his ear. He nodded expressionlessly, folding the crumbs into a starched napkin which he deftly tucked into his apron. He then took Anton's unused soup spoon and butter knife, placed them neatly on his tray, and departed.

"So what did you do?" Hana asked, sitting back with her arms crossed, the half-full champagne flute tilted in one hand. "Endure the abuse for the experience?"

As light as the champagne was, Anton could feel it weighing down both his thoughts and his movements. If the alcohol affected Hana she gave no sign: she looked as fresh and self-possessed as she had when he first saw her, though her cheeks had taken on a faint glow. *Such lovely cheekbones,* he thought, and before he could stop he imagined tracing them with his fingers.

Clearing his throat, he shifted his focus to sawing off a small piece of meat with his steak knife. As he lifted it from his plate her dark eyes followed the movement, lingering on his lips briefly after he'd pushed the morsel into his mouth. He shifted, uncomfortably aware of an erection stirring.

It took a moment to remember where he'd been: "After three months I realized it was pointless. For whatever reason the man had decided to see me as a problem. Nothing I did was going to change that."

She nodded, chewing lightly on the ivory mouthpiece of her holder in a way that sent shivers down his spine. "So for you, it was better to simply leave."

"Leave Wright. Not Japan."

Dropping his gaze to his second champagne glass, Anton hesitated. He hardly ever drank anything at lunch. *What the hell,* he thought, and finished it off.

"I was in love by then, you see," he went on. "With the people, the tradition. The building aesthetic. So I joined forces with another architect who had just landed here. We set up a new firm together in Aoyama."

The waiter returned, bending to whisper in her ear again. Hana listened expressionlessly, then nodded. The man pulled something from his pocket and slipped it into her hand, then bowed again and departed.

"What was that?" Anton asked, as she clasped her hands in her lap.

She shrugged. "Just something I'd left here the last time I came. So how did Mr. Wright take your resignation? With *élan*?"

The word made him smile for some reason. "Not in the least. He stood there a minute, glaring at me. Then he stalked from the room. The next day I got a letter from him—I still have it somewhere. He called me a coward and a traitor."

Her dark eyes widened. "A *traitor*?" she repeated. "That's the word he used?"

Anton nodded. "In the military, he wrote, I'd be lined up and shot for treason."

He chuckled, carefully trimming off more beef and noting fuzzily that his champagne had been refilled. Also, he'd dropped his napkin. When he ducked down to retrieve it he found himself, face to leg, with a smooth, curved calf, a strappy platform sandal. He'd never thought much about toes. But Hana Kobayashi's were perfect: graceful and pale, tapered elegantly in length. They were meticulously colored the same deep red as her fingernails, and for some reason he imagined her painting them while naked.

This has gone far enough, he told himself.

He sat up again woozily, planning to look at his watch and make some noise about having to leave early. What he saw on the table, though, stopped him in his tracks. Next to his plate was a hotel room key: Number 27.

He looked up to see Hana Kobayashi across the table, watching him with that same intent, faintly amused expression.

"What—what is this?" he asked, waving at the key.

"A room key," she said, her tone almost gentle. She stubbed out her cigarette and pulled out a compact and a silver lipstick case.

"No," Anton stammered, as she began calmly reapplying her lipstick. "I mean, I *know* it's a room key. What is it doing next to my plate?"

His heart was hammering so loudly he could scarcely hear himself speak. Hana, however, seemed unruffled. She resheathed her lipstick, dropped it and the compact back into her expensive Italian purse. Then she stood up, smoothing her white jacket over her hips in a way that outlined her figure in the window glass.

"It's waiting for you," she said. "Like I will be. Upstairs. In room 27." She glanced down at his half-finished beef. "But don't rush. Enjoy your meal."

Stunned, Anton watched her walk smoothly towards the exit, pausing briefly to murmur something to the maître d', who nodded and bowed. Then—like magic—she was gone. She hadn't looked back at him once.

For a moment he just stared at the neo-modern doorframe (his design) through which she had made her exit. Then he finally looked at his watch. They'd been sitting at the table for barely more than forty minutes; he hadn't even started his salad.

The glittering room seemed to swim a little. He removed his glasses, cleaned them absently in his lap. As he perched them back there was a fleeting image of himself, perched on the edge of a precipice. It was such an obvious metaphor that he was almost embarrassed by it, yet his embarrassment didn't make it go away. It hovered before his mind's eye, forcing him to look at it. To ask the obvious question: *What was he going to do next?* Jump into the abyss? Scuttle away from the edge?

He thought of Béryl; of her cool, habitual cheek-peck this morning. He thought of Hana in the hallway, pressing his palm into her breast. He looked at his own champagne glass, dry and empty and erect, and Hana's, half filled with golden liquid, the rim sparkling beneath that bow-shaped red imprint.

What I am about to do will change my life forever, he thought.

He pocketed the key and stood up.

HE FOUND HER sitting at the vanity, staring at herself. She had taken off her shoes and her hat, but the rest of her suit still looked pressed and pristine. When she caught his gaze in the glass her expression didn't change, though he thought he saw her swallow.

Hesitantly, he moved towards her, his pulse throbbing in his temples. Despite everything he still half expected, and even half hoped, that she'd stop him before he reached her. Say he'd misunderstood her; that they were both married. That he was a pervert, and how *dare* he follow her up here.

But of course she did none of these things. She watched his approach, her expression opaque, her back as straight as a dancer's. When he reached her and stopped just behind her in confusion, she stood up and turned to face him. Her expression was pleading, and slightly haunted.

"You must think I'm a horrid person," she said.

"No," he said. "I don't think that. I don't think that at all."

He reached out and, very slowly, brushed her cheekbone with this thumb, as if brushing away a single tear. She smiled a hopeless smile, and touched his thumb with her own. And then suddenly it had started, as inevitably as it had started in the hallway, as he'd inevitably always known it would.

This time there was no Billy. No fallen cigarette. There was only him and her. A bed and a bolted door. Without letting himself think (*don'thinkdon'thinkdon'think*) he drew her towards him, holding her so tightly her stockinged feet left the ground. For a fleet second they stayed that way: his face buried in her neck, her white hands clasping his so tightly it almost hurt him.

Then they were on the bed, the white jacket and the blouse unbuttoned roughly, the white skirt hiked up to her waistline. Her torso arched into his as he bore down on her thin frame, and he stared into her face. She was grimacing in something that might have been either pain or desire, but either way made him desperate to plunge into her, *right now.* He was too agitated to even take his pants off, and they bagged around his knees like a clown's as he found her smooth thighs and guided himself between them. She felt different from Béryl—small and tight. And *wet*—so wet that he briefly thought of a sea: a tight, wet, warm red sea through which he was thrashing and gasping. He heard a strange voice above his heartbeat, strangled and furious. It took a moment to recognize it as his own; to realize that not only was he rutting and bellowing like an animal but that she was screaming and panting right along with him.

There was an instant when he was almost frightened—by the ferocity of it; by the desperation. He looked down again and saw her mouth stretched open so tautly he could see the clean pink recess of her throat; the uvula dangling like a glittering garnet in the back. Her eyes were clenched shut, the lashes dampened by trickling tears—something that with his wife would have caused Anton to pause and ask whether she was all right. But with Hana Kobayashi it had precisely the opposite effect. It made him want to push harder and faster, to *hurt* her even—a feeling he'd never had towards a woman in his life. But the friction building against his cock was also something he'd never felt, mounting like some tantalizing form of utter ecstatic release that was always one push, just one more push away. The force and weight behind his thrusts made her bounce and jerk against the bedspread like a rag doll, and this excited him too, though later on he would feel deeply humiliated by it.

When he came it felt as though his entire body was on fire, with heat almost exploding from every pore. He spasmed uncontrollably, collapsing on top of her as his skin trembled with exquisite sensitivity. But to his confusion she pushed him away.

"No, *no, not yet*," she moaned, and then said something in French. Then she'd somehow rolled him over and was astride him, her palms flat against his chest. There she rocked herself back and forth, gritting her teeth and grinding against him until he felt something inside her quiver and soften. She threw her head back, and the sound that came from her lips sounded like a cry of utter desolation.

Afterwards, they lay side by side on the damp bedspread, half-dressed and rumpled and almost motionless. Anton's head was reeling. His mouth and throat were as dry as though he'd just run through a sandstorm. He turned his face towards hers and found her staring at the ceiling that he and Frank Wright had designed together. She stared up at it so fixedly that he shivered, thinking *That's what she'll look like when she's dead.* Then, appalled at his own callousness, he reached out and touched her cheek again.

When she turned and met his gaze she was no longer crying, but her eyes were still swollen and damp. Her apparent misery made him feel as though he should say something, and he opened his mouth to do so—only to find he had nothing to say.

It was she who spoke first. "Thank you."

"For what?" Anton asked, incredulous that someone he'd apparently made so despondent would then express gratitude for it.

But she just shook her head, as though the enormity of the answer made even trying to voice it pointless.

THEY MET OFTEN, once or twice a week. Sometimes at the Imperial, sometimes at other hotels. Sometimes at a Shinjuku tearoom his Japanese friends used to meet discreetly with their mistresses, though

Anton himself never used that term—*mistress*—when he thought about her, which was nearly continually. In his mind a mistress was someone almost akin to a wife; a woman you loved and yearned for and perhaps even had children with, but were forced to keep on the side for the sake of propriety, politics or marital peace. What he had with Hana felt like something entirely different: a battle he kept fighting and losing. A chasm he kept falling into. A mistake he couldn't seem to stop making. Their affair was so *wrong*—and wrong on so many levels beyond the mundane framework of infidelity. It was wrong because he was betraying not just his wife but his best friend, the human being he most respected and loved in the world. It was wrong, too, because Hana, as he increasingly came to learn, was far more damaged than he'd ever imagined.

Sometimes when he was late he'd unlock the door to find her weeping on the bed. "I thought you'd left," she would sob. "I thought you'd left me too, like everyone leaves me."

Who? he'd wanted to ask her. *Who leaves you? When?* But she never gave him the chance, for the moment he approached her she'd strip off her clothes and his and force him onto the bed or floor or desk. Then they would do what he could only describe as *fuck*—make love to him so furiously and harshly it sometimes left a rash.

But even at her most passionate, there was always a sense for Anton that something was missing; something that had either been stripped from her or plucked out by her own will, or maybe never had the chance to form in her at all. She was beautiful, and startlingly intelligent, with a caustic sense of humor that could make him laugh until his gut hurt. She was the most uninhibited woman he'd ever slept with, which granted wasn't saying much, since an aged Viennese prostitute and his wife were the only others on that list. But there was something in her extremism that felt almost nihilistic; as though sex for her were a way of punishing herself. And she could say things that sent chills down his spine.

"Do you ever wonder," she said one afternoon (after an explosive, bruising tryst that had begun in a taxi and ended on a hotel's back stairwell), "what it would be like to jump off a roof? To end it all?"

"No," said Anton, startled. "Do you?"

"Sometimes."

She lay back on the bed they'd just collapsed on, her index finger casually tracing the nipple that still bore traces of his teeth marks on it.

"Why?" he asked, troubled. "Are you depressed?"

She gave him a look that was half-scornful, half-pitying. "Sometimes," she said again. Then she sighed and reached for his cock.

Another time she asked him to describe exactly what he'd felt when he first laid eyes on his wife-to-be. It felt like a transgression, but he couldn't help telling her—just as he hadn't been able to help climbing onto her a moment earlier, or the week before, or the first day he'd met her at the Imperial. He described how he and Béryl had both been coming back from Portofino, part of a panicked crowd racing for the last steamship out before war hit. Béryl had been a strong, stout girl, holding in her hands a green-glazed urn Anton later learned she planned to use as a washbasin. He held nothing but a valise and his third-class ticket, and as he rushed to claim his bunk he'd almost collided with her.

"I heard her gasp," he told Hana. "It was a soft, deep, breathy sound that for some reason I knew I'd always remember. And then she dropped the urn, and I somehow managed to drop my valise in time to catch it." He shook his head, wondering—as he often wondered—what would have happened if he hadn't.

"Then what happened?" asked Hana, her eyes glittering in the candlelight.

"I said the only thing I could think of."

"What was that?"

" 'That's a very nice urn, miss.' " Hana gave a short, throaty laugh.

"She told me it had cost next to nothing in an alley outside Naples, and that it reminded her of a work by the Polyphemos Painter. And then she laughed at my expression."

"Why?"

Anton smiled ruefully. "She said I looked as though she'd just spoken Swahili. Which was true. Between the Greek name and her French accent and my own English, which wasn't very good then, I had no idea what in hell I'd just heard."

He'd understood other things, though. Looking into those astonishing hazel eyes, he had sensed so much: a bounty of fantastical ideas, a wealth of intuitive, astute observations. A propensity for righteous tantrums and sweetly foolish gestures. He hadn't fallen in love then—not quite yet, and when he finally did it was less a tumble than a carefully choreographed step. But he'd known that this was a girl he wanted to talk to throughout dinner, and into the sea-scented night, and possibly for the rest of his life . . .

Of course, he didn't say any of this to Hana Kobayashi. He just stretched, and asked the ceiling, "What about you? What was it like when you first met Kenji?"

She didn't answer for a long time. And when she did, she said something else that made him wince: "It was like death," she said. "Or maybe, the beginning of dying."

He turned to face her. "What do you mean?"

She bit her lip. "Until I met him, I'd been able to hold on to the idea of myself that I understood. That I was essentially a Westerner, and that my stay here was temporary. I'd always thought that one day I'd be able to go back to England and pick up the life that I'd left there."

"So why didn't you? Why didn't you tell your parents that you didn't want to get married?"

She shook her head. "You don't understand. I had no *choice*. It was either marry him or live the rest of my life in their house, playing the aging spinster daughter. There would have been no chance of ever going anywhere again. They were so disappointed in me."

"Disappointed? Though you'd gone to England on their account, and learned to speak English and French so fluently?"

She sat up halfway, reaching for her Winstons and lighting one, her dark lashes seeming even longer than usual in the flickering flame of the lighter. "You see, they didn't want me to come back English *myself.* They wanted me to come back a perfect Japanese girl, with her Japanese habits and mannerisms and aspirations for her life intact. And impeccable conversation skills in three languages."

"And that's not what they got?"

She gave him a bemused glance. "You know me better than that by now, surely."

Anton cleared his throat. "So they found Kenji for you," he said, reaching for his pipe and his glasses, which—after crushing one pair against a headboard—he now took off before making love.

"They spent two years to find someone else, before realizing that no one else wanted me."

"So why did you go along with it?"

"Why not?" She shrugged. "It was a way to get out. And at least Kenji had money and foreign connections."

Anton nodded slowly, trying to put it together. "So how is that like dying?"

She sighed wearily. "Because I was fooling myself. Deep down inside I knew that marrying him would seal my fate." She exhaled a smoke stream. "I just didn't know how completely it would shut everything else off."

As was so often the case, he had no real idea what she was saying, nor how he was supposed to respond. He knew only that she was lonely; quite possibly the loneliest person he'd met in his life. And that nothing he did—not holding her in the dark, not burrowing down between her legs, not even suggesting (in one rash and entirely libido-driven moment) that they run away together—would ever change that. The only thing that seemed to give her even the slightest bit of real joy was talking about her daughter. Yoshi-*chan*, the trilingual wonder.

"Why are you so focused on teaching her foreign languages?" Anton asked once, after Hana related Yoshi's latest literary conquest: finishing all of *Grimms' Fairy Tales*, in English, on her own. "Especially since they didn't help you?"

"Because they will help her. They'll be a door for her, later on."

"A door?"

She nodded, running her fingertip from his collarbone to his navel in one electrifying line. "Things will be different here by the time she's an adult. They will give her tools to do what I wasn't able to do, in my lifetime. A way to get out."

"Why do you think she'd want to get out?" he asked, tensing as her hand delved lower and hovered teasingly over his groin.

"Because," she said, smiling slightly, "there is nothing in this country for women who don't want what men want for them. She's already smart enough to understand that, too. She's got it in her head now that she wants to move to Manchuria one day."

"Manchuria?" asked Anton, both dismayed and guiltily hopeful at the idea of putting so much distance between them.

She shrugged. "It's only because Kenji's been spending so much time there. By the time she's eighteen she'll be ready for real travel."

And then her hand was on him, and they stopped talking.

More than once upon leaving her (his skin rubbed raw, his limbs sore, his conscience clamoring like a five-alarm fire bell) Anton would tell himself again that this was it. That tomorrow he would write that note that he kept putting off; the one that would end things, kindly but firmly. The note that did finally end it, though, was not from his hand but the ambassador's. It arrived on Anton's desk one day in late November of '37, notifying him that in the face of Japan's continued hostilities towards China, the president's endorsement of the Neutrality Act and the growing likelihood of an American embargo on Japanese goods, the embassy was urging American citizens with business concerns here to put them on hold and prepare to leave the country.

By the end of the month Béryl was researching American East Coast private schools, and Anton had contracted to build a neo-modern Ashram in Bombay. By year end he'd made arrangements to hand the firm off to Japanese associates, and to have both houses looked after by neighbors. What he hadn't done was tell Hana.

It wasn't that he didn't mean to. He was sure she'd hear about it eventually from Kenji anyway. But every time he tried to put it into words they would pull their old disappearing act. Then it was two months before their steamer left, and then one, and then two weeks. Then two days, which was the last time he met her at their tea house. They had their usual exertive and inventive coupling, and after she'd untied him Hana drifted off on the *futon.* This happened often lately, as she was having trouble sleeping at night. Usually Anton would wake her before going out. This time, however, he just stood over her, looking down. Taking in the long lashes, the bow-shaped mouth. Those perfect, perfect cheekbones. Though he was standing upright he felt a weight on his chest, as though his rib cage might collapse or explode. But of course, it did neither. And then it was time to meet Béryl to go over their packing and emergency contact lists and figure out some solution for the dog. And so Anton reached down and stroked Hana Kobayashi's sleeping cheek.

And then he left.

Now he stared at the woodblock print, his fingers resting on Kenji's puzzle box. *Its not murder, it's war,* he thought. And then: *It wasn't my job to save her.* But the words felt empty, a rote prayer to a god or goddess he no longer really believed in.

He packed and lit his pipe, and the dream came back to him in all its chimerical grief: the match striking flint. The breathless pause of tree frogs. The voice—Hana's voice. *Anata.* Anton squeezed his eyes shut against it all. When he opened them again he found himself poised for a fight, with his left arm drawn back tautly by his ear. His fist trembling. His bleary eyes glued to the Kotani.

Later on, he would have no recollection of hurling the *himitsu bako.* There was just the sharp *crack* of varnished wood against plate, a tinkling shower of shards, falling to the floor. A brief, stunned silence as he registered what he'd just done. After that, the *swish* of the broom as he numbly swept the splintered wood and glittering glass bits into a dustpan.

Anton carefully ladled the mess into the bin Béryl had crafted during one of her basket-weaving phases. An hour later—at 0600 hours Washington time—he picked up his phone and dictated a telegram to Colonel Jamison. Four words, with neither salutation nor sign-off:

I'LL BE THERE. STOP

ANTON ADJUSTED HIS field glasses and shifted his scrutiny back down to Japanese Village's front-facing wall. As odd as it was to see it set in front of a German apartment complex and behind that Utah's Wasatch mountain range, it maintained all the grace and purpose he remembered: even here, it truly *looked* Japanese. His imagination had no trouble at all filling the airy structure with the daily life he still recalled with such vividness: housewives brusquely chasing dirt and dust from the *tatami* with brooms and rags. Heaving out the bedding for a good beating. Small girls jumping rope, their black braids bouncing in time with singsong rhymes: *Don guri korokoro Don buri ko . . .* Boys playing *onigokko*, or finger-wrestling, or simply running around and shouting, which was what Tokyo's small boys seemed to do primarily (Billy being one exception). He saw dogs sleeping in the structure's doorways, the nightsoil collector's cart plodding past . . .

"They're late," said Erich Mendelsohn, the German Jew who'd given the Berlin skyline much of its Expressionist mood before fleeing the city in 1937. Heavyset and heavy-breathing (Anton had never seen him hurry at anything, but he always breathed as though he'd been running at full tilt), Mendelsohn had built his squat, stolid village right here on the proving grounds. Unlike those of Japanese Village, its materials—brick, mortar, steel and cement—were too bulky to transport by flatbed.

"Late," he reiterated, frowning. He was looking at his wristwatch.

"Yes, well," said Anton blandly, though his stomach tightened, "it is an exercise."

"It's no way to win a war. The Reich pisses on a goddamn schedule."

As if in response a rumble of male laughter floated back from the group standing closer to the shelter's front. It was composed of three men. Two were suits, probably from Standard Oil and Boeing. They were fawning over a third man, a fleshy block of an officer, whom Anton recognized from the breakfast this morning.

Curtis LeMay had a cartoonishly square chin, a bulbous nose and the droopy, pouched eyes of a bulldog. His unnerving appearance was made no less so by the fact that half of his face appeared fully paralyzed. Anton had met him formally the previous morning, at a breakfast organized by the NDRC at the Dugway Officers' Compound. After Jamison introduced them ("Major, this is Anton Reynolds, one of our doctors of architecture") he'd been aware of LeMay giving him an appraising look over his coffee.

"So, Doc," LeMay drawled, "they tell me you've lived in Japan." He pronounced *Japan* with pointed emphasis on the *Jap*.

"I did," Anton said. "I had a practice in Tokyo."

"Mr. Reynolds," Jamison cut in, "helped design the Imperial Hotel in Tokyo. With Frank Lloyd Wright."

Anton nodded, suppressing a reflexive eye-roll.

"That's the one that survived the big earthquake?" asked LeMay.

Anton nodded. "There was some sinkage. But the floating foundations we'd created seemed to absorb most of the tremor."

"But it was the fires after the quake, from people's cooking stoves and whatnot, that took out most of the city in the end." The major's voice was slow but emphatic. As though each word carried irreparable meaning.

"Over sixty percent of it. Yes."

"And in your view, Doc, a major fire in Tokyo today could still cause equivalent damage?"

Images rushed back like a gruesome slide presentation: Ueno Train Station, reduced to smoldering and blackened bone and ash. Yoshiwara pleasure district, stripped of storefronts and flutter-sleeved courtesans. Its canals choked with swollen corpses. And then, for some reason, Hana Kobayashi on her back, naked. Her mouth opened so tautly it almost hurt to look at it . . .

"It would depend on the conditions," he said, running a finger beneath his collar. "Humidity. Wind. But yes. At least in theory, it could."

LeMay's thick lips tightened around the Cuban cigar he'd replaced there. As he spoke it wagged, a stumpy little tail. "Good. All very good." He fingered the stub meditatively. "Can I ask you one more thing, Doc?"

"Of course," said Anton, wishing Jamison hadn't introduced him as a "doctor of architecture."

"Why did you stay there, with the *Japs*, for all those years?"

It was a question Anton had fielded often, and with some care—particularly when asked by people like LeMay. He usually answered it with something like "My wife liked it there," or "They needed American guidance in their building," or simply "We just woke up there one day, twenty years older." Like some drowsy, transpacific Rip Van Winkle.

Confronting LeMay's granite-gray stare now, though, Anton heard himself forming a completely different and somewhat defiant response. "I am an architect, Major," he said. "I suppose I stayed because I admire their buildings."

LeMay smiled again. Once more, it was less a softening of lips than a tightening.

"Well, then," he'd said, "I sure hope you're not too attached to them."

ANTON SWUNG HIS gaze up. He scanned the sky. Nothing appeared there but a lone prairie falcon, looking powerful and golden in the early morning sun, looking, it struck Anton, eternal. It screeched, its call plaintive and familiar. When an engine sputtered to life outside, all helmet-covered heads turned towards it. To everyone else's obvious disappointment it turned out to be the same Army truck that had brought them here, protesting being put into reverse. The men in the bunker watched wordlessly as it backed up, its wheels whining against the sand.

"Hmph," breathed Mendelsohn. "False alarm." He mopped his brow.

Anton returned his attention to the hawk, still circling in the sky. What did it see from all the way up there? Clearly, much more than he could. Apropos of nothing the bird fell into a sharp nosedive. *Noh aru taka wa tsume wo kakusu. The wise hawk hides its talons from its prey.* It was something Hana had once told him when he asked her why she didn't do more with her skills: work as a translator, for example. Or teach.

But this *taka* wasn't hiding. It was almost showing off. Diving, hurtling with streaking speed towards the sand, then climbing effortlessly back up into view. Entranced, Anton dialed up his lens power to its fullest capacity.

"Did you wager?" Mendelsohn was asking.

"What?"

"LeMay has a pool going. About how each village will stand up."

"Does he." Anton lowered the glasses again. "Did you put in?" The suits were now nodding as the major spoke in a low voice, gesturing at one of the pamphlets he'd brought with him. Anton had one in his briefcase: *Air Power: Why It's Essential to America's Future.*

"I did," the German said glumly. "Ten dollars on German Village. At least forty percent damage. Though I must say I hope for more."

"And mine?"

"A safer bet. Sixty-five percent."

Anton felt a surge of defensiveness, as though he and not two thousand years of Japanese tradition were responsible for the design's vulnerability. "Really? As high as that?"

Mendelsohn shook his heavy head. "Probably higher. Your walls, my friend, are made of paper."

Which, of course, Anton couldn't dispute. "I don't think I'll put in," he said, with false ease. "I wouldn't want to hurt your chances of winning." He looked back at the two houses, standing quietly against the teal-green salt scrub. "Doesn't it bother you at all?" he asked in a lower voice. "All that work—just destroyed?"

"No," the German said flatly. It was, Anton reflected, perhaps an unwise discussion in the circumstances. But he sensed that that wasn't behind the German's frown.

"What about your old home?" he pressed, unable to stop himself. "Your old friends and neighbors, your work associates? You don't feel at all conflicted?"

Mendelsohn turned to look fully out at the bunker's wide-open entranceway. For a moment he didn't speak. "I built Berlin its most modern museum," he said, finally, his voice still low. "And three of its schools. I even built one of its goddamn *churches.*" He mopped his brow again. "Then, six years ago, they tell me I'm a foreigner in my own country and strip me of my license. They took my awards back. I write to my mother and sister every week. Do you know, no one returns my letters anymore."

He broke off, cleared his throat. When he turned his eyes were red, and Anton felt a rush of sympathy. But when he started to speak the German shook his shaggy head. "Do you have a religion, Mr. Reynolds?" It was a question, but it sounded like an accusation.

"Somewhere back there," Anton said, carefully. "Lutheran, Roman Catholic. To be truthful, though, I'd say I'm more of a Buddhist at this point."

"Like the Japs."

"Like some of them, yes." He attempted a smile.

The German remained sober-faced. "Where is your mother, Mr. Reynolds?"

"Prague."

"And you're not worried? The Nazis treat other nationalities almost as badly as they treat my people." He said *my people* with distinct irony. It reminded Anton of the way LeMay had pronounced *Japan.*

"I hear from her frequently," Anton said, dodging the question, though of course he thought immediately of his two brothers, executed by the Nazis for their roles in the underground resistance. He thought of his mother's repeated responses each time he asked her to consider coming back to America: *I see no need to leave, darling,* she'd written. *If one keeps a low profile, nothing has really changed here.* The hard coil in his gut tightened further.

"Nothing's really changed there," he said.

Mendelsohn shot him a meaningful look, then turned back to

the buildings. "Sixty-five percent," he reiterated. "But in truth, I hope—I hope to *Gott*—that they both burn straight to the ground."

As though to underscore his words a low rumble filled the room, deeper and more resonant than the big truck's engine. In the beginning it was all vibration, but as it drew closer the noise thickened into the distinct whine of a multiengine plane, flying low. A moment later the bomber appeared. Two silver lines, crossed: a gleaming crucifix in the sky.

The hawk dove once more, dropping from sight.

"There she is," LeMay called to them over the din, "the *Blonde Bombshell II*—a B-29. The Army Air Corps' latest Boeing design. Feast your eyes, gentlemen. What you are seeing is the future of the U.S. Army—and of modern warfare."

Twenty-three sets of Army-issued binoculars swung obediently towards the sun.

"Clever name," observed Mendelsohn, in that same flat voice. Anton couldn't tell if he was joking.

The plane was enormous, perhaps a hundred and fifty feet across and a hundred more in length. Jean Harlow was splayed across the bow in bright paint, her breasts outlined in such detail that the artist might as well have depicted her naked.

"Take a good look, Mr. Reynolds," LeMay called over, looking straight at the architect. "That's the she-wolf that's going to blow your house down today."

"That is, if she can stay in the air," Mendelsohn murmured. Anton nodded: a similar prototype had crashed to earth just last week, killing Boeing's Research Division chief and half its design team. Jamison had soberly assured this group that they'd identified the problem, and that a similar "incident" was in no way likely today. Still, Anton couldn't help but imagine it: the *Blonde Bombshell* screaming towards them. The hushed shock, and then the shouting panic. The bunker shattering as completely as had his *himitsu-bako*.

What did the Army say, when they bombed American civilians in the Utah desert? Would they tell Béryl he'd died in the line of duty? Would it earn him a posthumous Purple Heart?

Yet the *Bombshell* showed no sign of faltering. Almost lazily, it circled the proving ground in the opposite direction from which the hawk had. Once. Twice.

"That's Captain Frank Marshall in the pilot's seat," Colonel Jamison shouted. "One of Curtis' disciples. Flown three missions over Germany."

"That's right," LeMay confirmed. "Though he agreed to do this for me only if he could get reassigned to do the real deal in Tokyo. I told him, if you hit the mark, you can have Yokohama and Osaka too." He smiled. "Hell. I'll even throw in Hiroshima."

Another round of cocktail chuckles, more seen than heard at this point. Anton shifted his gaze to the bomber's eight small squares of front window, but failed to make out the pilot's head. Instead, he saw Hana's back and gently bumping spine, arching like a slim white bridge beneath him. He tried to imagine his village as LeMay's Jap-hating pilot was seeing it. But all that came was Hana, lying as she'd lain when he left her in the teahouse, her hair fanned out like a black halo. Then there came a slight but discernible shift in the plane's drone—a kind of distant, metallic grinding.

"Here it comes," Mendelsohn shouted.

On cue, the *Bombshell's* bays opened up in a huge, robotic yawn, releasing a small hail of incendiaries that looked almost harmless, even pretty. As they tumbled towards the earth Anton felt his bile rise. He'd somehow thought there would be more warning before the airstrike. More commentary, or a countdown. But looking around he saw surprise on no other faces. The men were rapt and intent, the room emptied of all sound but the whistle of the tumbling incen-diaries, the thunderous scream of the plane's engines. Every set of tin-rimmed eyes followed those shining spheres as they made their trip to the target. *You are American,* he reminded himself. *This is why you built it. Every step, every plank was for this.*

And then: *It wasn't your job to save her.*

He watched in vague wonder as the first bomb hit the village, hit the rippling roof, chipped a few smoke-toned tiles. Flared briefly. It looked for a moment as if it merely went out after that, and, perhaps treasonously, his heart lightened a little. But then the others hit, one small gleaming slash after the other. A hailstorm of steel and fire and jellied petroleum against a roof made, at worst, for a light snow. There was a breathless second where the cold air seemed to hold its breath. Then the entire rooftop was a-dance with flames.

"There she goes," shouted LeMay. "Happy New Year's, fellows!"

Scattered clappings, some catcalls. Another handful of dancing orbs. A few more flashes, a groan. The whole village was alight now, a massive wall of flames. The heat from it hit even two hundred yards away: Anton felt his helmet warm against his brow. His eyebrows stung and his ears rang with a huge *whoosh* and an earsplitting boom, as if the air itself inside the house had caught fire. He closed his eyes again and saw the trunk, the bathstool. The tiny, dolless dollhouse with its sticky little bowls. He saw his *shoji* explode like so many distress beacons, the flames starting at floor level and running neatly upwards, until they reached the seething sheet of swirling gasses and sparks that by now must surely have engulfed the room's ceiling.

He shut his eyes and saw another image: a woman's dark silhouette, slim and unclothed. Leaping into a flickering red plain.

When he looked again the building's outside structural beams had caught, and the walls. The house groaned a creaking, sighing death call. It leaned slightly to the right. Then a bit more, as though teasing them.

"Go on then," shouted someone; and obediently, it collapsed to the ground in an inverted rainfall of orange and red sparks. More applause.

"Damn," shouted LeMay, above the din. "He hit it. He hit the fucking thing, right on the mark."

Mendelsohn turned back to Anton, his whole face red but elated. He took his helmet off and his brow streamed with sweat. *"Amazing,"* he shouted, as the sound of the engines dimmed and the crackle of the fire outside softened, bit by bit. "I believe, Mr. Reynolds, that I have won my wager. Just look at that damn thing *burn*."

Anton looked, his eyes tearing—it was the heat.

"Congratulations, Docs!" LeMay shouted over at the two architects. "Here's hoping we do as well on German Village!"

"Hear, hear," cheered Mendesohn. He grinned at Anton expectantly.

But Anton had lost his voice. His throat was dry, his head ached. The room reeked of acrid-smelling smoke. He rubbed his eyes to clear them, then looked at his wristwatch. *Holy Christ.* It seemed impossible, but it had taken just fourteen minutes. Fourteen minutes, and the entire village had been reduced to a burning heap of ash. And it wasn't done yet. The flames were lower now but still flickering, hungrily licking the blackened sand.

There would be nothing left. Nothing left at all.

VI. *Tokyo, Japan*

MASAHIRO WAS ON THE BACK OF A TRAIN, REACHING FOR HER, calling, and Yoshi was trying to catch up to him—arms outstretched, fingers aching to connect. *"Wait,"* she kept calling. *"Waaaaait!"* But her voice was drowned out by the train's whistle, a bilious blast that seemed to fill the entire universe. The neat steel wheels began turning. The gleaming smokestack chuffed smoke. She watched in desolation as it picked up speed and force, carrying Masa away on shining tracks and neat brown slats, shrinking into a glimmering dot on the horizon. Oddly, though, as the train shrank into the smoky distance its whistle didn't shrink along with it. Instead it swelled to a bellow, and from there into a slow and mournful wail . . .

And then she shook her head against her pillow and pinched her own arm, hard, and realized that she wasn't abandoned, but simply asleep.

Reaching beneath the *futon* she pulled out the little Seiko she kept buried there so she wouldn't accidentally wake Hana when she woke at six to go to school. For a few groggy moments she fumbled and squinted, still fighting the panic. The clock stared back at her in baleful silence (2:02) and she realized that the noise that had woken her was neither the clock nor her dream-train, but a high-pitched wail coming from outside: an air raid drill. The second one tonight.

"*Mo—iya da!*" She groaned into her still sleep-warm arm. She'd worked two straight shifts at the balloon factory yesterday to which she'd been assigned, cutting and pinning silk scraps that would later be inflated into white spheres, attached to bombs and sent sailing across the Pacific. Then she'd met with the Patriotic Girls Fire Team for their biweekly bucket drill. Then she stood in line for an hour at a tiny fish store across town, awaiting a rumored mackerel ration that turned out to be just that—a rumor. For a moment she was tempted to pull her pillow over her head and try to go back to sleep.

But then her hand clasped around something small and sharp-edged she'd tucked beneath her pillow with the clock. Her hawk; the cunning, graceful carving Masa had given her the day she'd left Shin Nagano. She thought of Masa, who would be steaming into Tokyo Station in just a few hours. *I know no one in the capital thinks the bombing will get serious,* he'd last written, from a censored battlefront somewhere in northern China. *But Yoshi-chan, I've seen here what bombs can do. Please protect yourself—if only for me. I want you in one piece when I see you.*

Yoshi forced herself to sit up and throw her quilt back. "Mama? Mama. You've got to wake up. They've sounded the siren again."

At first: no response. Then a moan: "*Nn.*"

"Wake up, Mama. We have to go back to the shelter."

Outside, the siren paused just long enough for Yoshi to detect a slight rustle coming from the direction of Hana's *chaise.* They slept in the ground-floor parlor now, in part because it was closer to the bomb shelter outside but also because it was where Hana spent most of her time anyways, swathed in cigarette smoke and blankets, propped up on her green loveseat, writing her letters that were never sent or read.

Yawning, Yoshi reached into the black space beneath the Yamaha baby grand, fumbling until she found the emergency bundle they took with them on every air raid. She also retrieved the padded bomb hoods she kept with it. *"Oka-san,"* she repeated, lifting her voice and standing, "I'm coming over now. Please sit up."

"Nan de," grumbled Hana.

"What do you mean, 'Why?'"

"They're just doing this to torture us. There probably aren't even any planes. There weren't before . . ."

Yoshi sighed. "Still. The neighbors will notice if we don't show up again. We'll get reported."

Which was not entirely true: of their two neighboring families only the prim and prurient Hanedas regularly reported people to the Neighborhood Association head. The Fujiwaras—with their seven daughters and one son (now at military boarding school in Aomori)—were both too busy and too kind. Moreover, Yoshi and Satako Fujiwara had been friends since early childhood, jumping rope and riding bicycles. Whispering girlish secrets via string and tin cans. Still, the threat of a bad report seemed as good a stick as any to use to get her mother in motion, though it didn't prove good enough. Hana grumbled a little, in French and English: *Merde,* Yoshi heard. And then: *Bloody Yanks.* But she did not hear Hana's thin feet hitting the floor.

Sighing again, she pulled her own bomb hood over her head and groped her way over to the couch. The darkness felt visceral, as thick as pitch. Like every other home in the city, their windows were covered according to regulation, curtained by a dense black fabric that, paired with the lampshade's black shroud, made the days dark and the nights opaque. But as she shuffled forward, her arms waving before her like antennae and her head still fuzzy with sleep, Yoshi's eyes adjusted and she made out her mother's form on the settee.

"Mama," she said again. She took hold of one of the limp, bird-boned wrists. *"Okinasai.* You have to get up."

Hana twitched her hand free. *"Nan de,"* she grumbled again, without opening her eyes. *"Mo.* Leave me alone."

She's sick, Yoshi reminded herself, and then made herself remember what had happened just last week. She'd come home late from school after a long day spent working on care packages for Imperial Army soldiers fighting in the Phillipines. Usually Hana was awake in the early evening, and would greet her daughter's return with either a *Welcome home* or a complaint, depending on her mood. On this night, though, when Yoshi stopped by the parlor Hana wasn't in her usual spot upon the couch. In fact, she wasn't in the room at all—a fact that sparked a wave of panic. Had the police come back for her at last? Then she heard it: something crashing, something dropping upstairs.

Yoshi raced up to the second floor. Without bothering to knock, she flung open the door to Hana's bedroom. She was immediately hit by a wall of scent so strong that it made her blink: dank smoke, French perfume. The ever-present English lavender, underscored by a sour hint of old sweat she'd come to associate with her mother's "sick" days. She saw Hana's slim back, erect and straight by her vanity, sheathed in an off-the-shoulder gown of vivid emerald silk Yoshi hadn't seen for at least eight or nine years. The floor was scattered with cigarette butts and ash, glitteringly intermixed with glass shards from a shattered perfume bottle.

"Mama," Yoshi had said. Then Hana turned to face her, and she gasped.

In one hand, her mother held a gleaming tube of lipstick she had just finished applying. Her hair was as lank and uncombed as it had been that morning when Yoshi left, but her face looked perfect. Polished. As white and finely painted as one of the porcelain dolls in Yoshi's old collection.

"He said he'd marry me, you know," she'd said matter-of-factly, as though this one point explained everything. "And then he just left. Just like everyone else."

"What?" Yoshi had asked, bewildered. "Who?"

But Hana just turned back to the mirror, humming "Blue Skies" beneath her breath.

She's sick, Yoshi reminded herself now. *Be patient.* She tried again: "It's not just tonight. The B-*sans* have been flying over a lot these past few weeks. Papa said in his last letter that they might be building up to something."

"Let them build," her mother responded querulously. "If I'm going to die I might as well die in my own home."

Yoshi bit her cheek. Her stomach was aching with that taut, acidic ache that was so constant she couldn't recall what it felt like *not* to have it. Crossing her arms, she pressed her elbows against her abdomen, which helped to ease or at least obscure the discomfort. It did nothing, however, to curb her ballooning impatience.

"Mama," she said, shouting to be heard over the sirens, "you know I won't go out without you."

Hana mumbled something Yoshi couldn't make out at first. *"Nani?"*

"Au moins," said Hana (as the sirens quieted again), *" je n'auri pas à mourir seule."*

"What?"

"At least," Hana repeated, in English, very slowly, "I won't have to die alone."

Yoshi stared at her, automatically translating the phrases: from French to Japanese. From Japanese to English. From English back to French again. After there was just blankness, coupled with the surreal sensation that if she opened her mouth even the tiniest bit, what would emerge would be that same dead, bleached screech of the sirens.

Byoki da, she tried to tell herself, as she always did. Her Hana-mantra: *Byoki da. She is sick.* But what came this time instead was one word—three, in English—that Yoshi had *never* let herself think these past months. One word that explained nothing, and destroyed everything, and was not true at all. And yet she felt it spring up from her gut, felt it spit its way up her esophagus to then wait biliously on her tongue:

Kirai.

I hate you.

And for that moment, she did. She hated her mother for the unnamed illness that played out in their home life, a small-scale madness mimicking the large-scale madness of the outside world. For doing nothing to win her husband and Yoshi's father back home from his other life and family on the continent. For not even *knowing* about Kenji's double life; or, for that matter, about anything that had happened over the past three awful years. Yoshi hated her mother for lying in her listless cocoon of sheets, shawls and blankets, day by day, while Yoshi did the things mothers were supposed to do: stood in line for rations that often as not ran out before her turn. Packed *bento* boxes that seemed to mock the whole concept of lunch (a single spoonful of unhulled rice, small pickled plum, three sheer shavings of turnip). While Yoshi sowed and reaped the little garden she and Satako had planted in the backyard so they'd at least have carrots and cabbage and potatoes sometimes. While she scoured the house for the last small bits of metal, jewelry and change to drop into the Patriotic Housewives donation basket. She even attended Neighborhood Association meetings to report how much extra food they had, so as to more effectively distribute and share it with those in need. All this was in addition to her own overwhelming work, which now included breaking down buildings for firewalls, digging slit trenches beside the roadways and practicing bucket relays until she couldn't feel her arms. *After* which came her schoolwork . . .

Kirai.

As the next round of sirens started she grasped Hana's sharp shoulder hard, as if to brace for a collision. She felt slack skin and brittle bone, the weak beat of her mother's blood. She felt the thought pulsing through her own blood like a heartbeat: *Kirai. Kirai. Kirai.* And then: *I'm going to tell her. I'm going to say it to her face.*

She licked her lips. "I . . . ," she began, hoarsely.

But before she could finish the sentence Hana brushed her hand off. She blinked several times, as if she'd just woken from a nap. As the sirens swelled to their crescendo she stretched her skeletal arms towards the parlor ceiling, conducting an orchestra of doom. Then she turned to Yoshi, frowning.

"You really think this is necessary?" she asked.

Yoshi felt the sting of tears against her lashes, though whether in relief or frustration she didn't know. "Mama," she said helplessly, as the sirens moaned their way back into silence. *Kirai*, she thought again; but already the thought was shuttling off like Masa's dream-train.

"Here," she said instead, holding out Hana's bomb hood, "put this on for me."

Hana rolled her eyes but complied, pulling the fluffy bonnet over her hair and ears and tying the white strings beneath her chin. Yoshi had made the hoods herself during Student Defense Training three years ago: two layers of quilted cotton stuffed densely with padding. They were supposed to protect them from flying debris and sparks.

"Bring my Goldens," Hana instructed.

"They're already in the bundle."

"Then there's my book on my nightstand. Can you get it for me?"

It's a coffee table, Yoshi thought, *not a nightstand.* "I don't know why you keep bringing it. You know there's not enough light to read by in the shelter." Not that she'd ever seen her mother actually read the book anyway. She'd never even seen her lift its dusty blue cover. Not once; though Yoshi had flipped through it a few times when Hana slept or left the room. Her English literacy was good enough that she'd read *Little Lord Fauntleroy* in three days, barely needing to refer to her dictionary. But Hana's book had almost seemed written in another language altogether. It was filled with phrases like: *"tha mun come to the cottage one time*" and "*she was gone, she was not, and she was born: a woman*"; phrases Yoshi absorbed with equal parts awe and sheer confusion.

"I like it with me," said Hana now stubbornly. "Besides, when the house burns down I'll need something to keep me occupied."

It wasn't worth arguing over. Tightening her jaw, Yoshi pushed her way back past the piano. As she fumbled for the novel her fingers brushed first against Hana's tepid glass of dust-topped water, then against the chipped ashtray which, when empty, read *Hôtel du Louvre* but was almost always overflowing with stale ash and slender stubs. They finally felt the novel's soft broadcloth cover. Brushing dust and cigarette ash from it first, she stuffed it into her satchel. She took one last survey of the room. "Have you seen Bella?"

"She's probably back in the piano."

Yoshi glanced past the Yamaha's heavy lid. The one-eyed little cat who had followed Yoshi home one day liked to sleep on the strings sometimes, though it couldn't be all that comfortable a bed. Yoshi didn't see her there now, though.

She'll be fine, she told herself, pulling her own bomb hood on. *She still has all of her nine lives.*

Linking her arm through Hana's, she walked her mother to the *genkan,* where she navigated Hana's blue-veined feet into their rubber gardening boots and shuffled into her own old *geta.* She shrugged on her wool coat and wrapped Hana in her balding camel-hair trench-coat. Then, reshouldering her satchel and the emergency bundle, she put her shoulder to the door, pushing it past its usual sticking-place in the doorjamb.

THE KOBAYASHI FAMILY shelter was—as Kenji had proclaimed vic-toriously upon completing it—"the Bentley of underground bomb shelters." Unlike the shallow dugouts pocking other neighboring gardens and lining Honjo-*ku*'s main streets (none of which went below five feet, since after that they hit water), Yoshi and Hana descended nightly into a solid, walled room that was ten full feet underground, and reinforced by layers of metal, cement, wood. It had enough space for a little shelf and a small, slab-style wooden bench, atop which Hana grumblingly settled now.

Peering down from ground level, Yoshi dropped their emergency bundle gently onto the shelter floor, then climbed halfway down herself, pausing on the ladder to pull the three layers of tin and plywood sheeting back across the entrance hole. Seating herself next to Hana, she lit the ceramic lantern (they'd had to donate the tin one for the front). Then she leaned back, breathing in the familiar yet still-unsettling odors: dirt and metal, sulfur and pine.

As though satisfied that the two women had finally fulfilled their requirements, the sirens outside screeched to an abrupt halt. Yoshi tilted her head, listening for bomber engines. She heard nothing beyond some lone dog's howl in the distance.

"You see? No B-*sans*," Hana observed. She sounded affronted, as though the Americans were guests arriving late to a party. "I don't even hear *our* planes. Really, I don't understand why they keep insisting all this is necessary."

Yoshi tightened her lips, though she couldn't really argue. Everyone knew that the air raid laws were little more than precautionary measures. Still, it seemed unwise to take chances.

"Speaking of planes," Hana was yawning, "are you still involved in that airplane club?"

"*Hai.*" Yoshi fidgeted a little, wondering when they'd be allowed to go back to bed. "We are performing a reenactment on Saturday. At the Great Air Victory Celebration. Actually, Satako and I have to stay overnight at school tonight to finish up all the model Zeros. I told you about that already, didn't I?"

Hana shook her head in a gesture that could have meant *yes, no* or *who cares.* "Which victory are you performing?"

"The Midway. The girls wearing the American B-*sans* are going to carry black and red streamers. When we shoot them down, they'll unfurl them like fire and smoke."

"That's clever."

"It was my idea," Yoshi said, a little proudly.

"Of course it was," Hana snapped. "You've always been the smartest of the bunch, you know."

Yoshi nodded, though in fact she didn't know this, and found it hard to believe. If she were the smartest in the bunch, how was it that they were still here—that she hadn't talked Hana into fleeing to the country? And how was it that Hana herself was still so sad and so sick? Wouldn't a smart girl be able to make her better?

"Your father says brains aren't important in a girl," Hana went on, "but I know they will stand you in good stead. I believe you'll do great things for yourself one day, Yoshi-*chan*."

It was another compliment—the second in as many minutes. During the drill two hours earlier Hana had simply dozed in silence, but she was being unusually talkative during this one. Yoshi knew she should have been grateful; between her workload and her mother's erratic sleep patterns they rarely had a real conversation. At the moment, though, it only added to Yoshi's creeping sense of unease. After the past weeks of wordless descents into the cellar together, having her mother seem almost normal felt slightly jarring. The way the sight of her in full makeup had last week.

A tiny, tingling shiver announced itself on Yoshi's neck. *Baka*, she told herself. *Don't be an idiot.*

She reached down beneath the wooden bench and picked up her school satchel. It was too dark to see much, but she could make out enough to open the top flap and extract the thousand-stitch belt she'd been working on. As she unrolled the wide white strip of cloth on her lap she felt Hana's eyes upon her.

"Did you finish it?" her mother asked.

"Almost. There are five stitches left to do."

She'd been carrying the sash with her for nearly three weeks now, and collected stitches from mothers and grandmothers and young girls who barely knew how to sew, from Sa-*chan* and her five sisters and her harried, heavily pregnant mother. From old Mrs. Maeda and the members of her batik-dying club later. Her female teachers at school had each added a stitch as well, as had the various heads of the different work groups at the balloon factory. For the rest of the stitches she had taken to the streets, holding it out to women who passed by, along with her red-threaded embroidery needle. "Please," she'd asked, "a stitch for a brave soldier at the front in China. Do you have a moment?"

And with the one exception of the woman who spat something at Yoshi in Korean, and one more who apologetically explained that she was blind, they did. Smiling shyly or nodding soberly, setting down bags and small children, sometimes even missing the charcoal-burning tram or bus for which they'd been waiting, the women of Tokyo bent their dark heads over the white cloth. Contemplating it. Choosing where to put their round red knot of protection. "Where is he?" they would ask. "Does he have enough to eat? Does he write often? Has he lost many friends?"

Such questions sometimes brought Yoshi to the point of tears. Not because of the answers they required (*no, no* and *yes*) or because she doubted the belt's mystical powers of protection, but because the process had given her a feeling she was completely unused to. A feeling of *you are one of us.* It was this feeling, in turn, that lay behind Yoshi's reluctance to show the *seninbari* to Hana until now. Not just because Hana quite literally *pooh-pooh*ed popular notions about the sacred Yamato spirit. But because if Yoshi was truly honest with herself, she wasn't at all certain that a stitch from her mother would protect Masa so much as harm him—just as everything Hana touched seemed to somehow end up harming Yoshi.

Now, though, her mother's thin hand reached out into the darkness between them. *"Misete,"* Hana commanded. "Let me see it."

Yoshi handed it over, watching with slight anxiety as Hana ran the white length through her hands, examining each red dot, each indicated line and limb.

"It's a tiger?"

"Nn."

"My uncle had a tiger *seninbari,*" Hana noted. "From when he fought the Russians in Port Arthur. *Obaa-chan* collected the thousand stitches for it. After the war was over she had it framed and hung near the *okuma.* I'd forgotten entirely about it until now."

"Did it protect him?"

Hana smiled wryly. "I think not. He came back in ashes, in a small wooden box. Though this was several years before I was born." She turned the *seninbari* over, examining the workmanship of the knots from beneath. "Is that what most people still make, then? Tigers?"

"People make lots of things," Yoshi said tentatively. "Tigers are popular. *Hinomaru* are too."

She broke off, nervous again as Hana moved the fabric closer to the lantern's flame. *She'll burn it,* she thought. *As if she hasn't ruined my life enough already.*

But her mother's hands remained steady. Not only did she not burn the belt, but she even nodded in something like approval. "You didn't do that, though. Use the coins."

"I was afraid that that would take more time and work than I had. I wanted to make sure it was finished."

"This is for that farmboy in Manchuria?"

Yoshi touched the hawk in her pocket. *"Nn."*

"The one your father likes so much."

"Yes. Shinagawa-*san.*"

"That young widow's son. The one who was married to Papa's foreman, before he died."

Her mother was gazing at her intently. *She knows,* Yoshi thought; and while it wasn't the first time she'd had the hunch, it left a faint tang of guilt anyways.

"Yes," she said, trying to keep her voice steady. "I'm seeing him tomorrow—well, actually, no. Today. He and the other officer candidates in his company are coming to Tokyo at three and leaving for Yokohama at five for some sort of special officers' test."

"Not much time to declare everlasting love, is it," said Hana tartly. "You'll have to try to get him on the way back, too. Will you kiss him?"

"*Mama.*" Yoshi flushed.

"Don't look so shocked," Hana said, smiling. "I'm not opposed to love, you know. In fact, I keep your famous phrase about it in my heart and mind whenever possible."

"Famous phrase?"

Hana leaned back and shut her eyes. Her slim fingertips traced the dotted tiger, like a blind woman's brushing over the word *tiger* in Braille.

"*L'amour conquiert tout,*" she said.

Love conquers all. Yoshi felt her flush deepen. She remembered all too well when she'd said this—if not the exact date. It must have been about five years earlier; before the Takarazuka Revue and the Western-style restaurants in the Ginza shut down out of respect for the national crisis.

It had been the first and only time that Hana agreed to take Yoshi to see the Takarazuka, at their glittering new Grand Theater on Ginza *Doori.* The performance, a dance-filled confection entitled *The Rose of Paris,* was set in pre-Revolutionary France. Like most Revue productions it featured high heels and feathered headdresses and elaborate period costumes, as well as rousing routines like "You've Mended My Broken Heart." Also like all Revue productions, it ended with the troupe's signature *ra-in dansu* (line dance), followed by an equally signature audience stampede towards the theater's exits. There, scores of young women formed a quivering wall awaiting the show's male-role star, Yukiko Ono.

But it was the hours after curtain that Yoshi treasured the most. Mother and daughter wandering the Ginza together, chatting (in French, since it was a Thursday). They'd paused at window displays and street musicians and tossed coins into the Kinokuniya Fountain. Yoshi had wished only that her whole life could be like this— that she could be a normal girl, going out with her almost-normal mother, doing things normal families did together.

Later on they went for tea at the American Café, which featured camp tables and fake palm trees and canvas director's chairs inscribed with names like Chaplin and Clara Bow. They talked about America a bit, about their plans to one day visit it after they'd seen London and Paris. About whether, when they did go, they'd visit New York first for the excitement of it, or Hollywood to try to see real movie stars. At Yoshi's request Hana did her impression of a Yankee accent for her daughter (*"Howwwdeee, y'awllll,"* nasal and flat). Then, reverting to French, she asked Yoshi what she thought the point of the play had been. And Yoshi—who had been pondering this herself for the past hour—proudly offered her insight: *"L'amour conquiert tout."*

Her mother had made a strange face at this, something halfway between laughing and crying. She'd said something typically caustic about love not being like that in real life. But Yoshi still thought of that day as the last truly happy time they spent in each other's company before Hana got taken away by the military police and, upon coming back, took to her couch.

"Love conquers all," her mother repeated now.

"I was just a girl when I said that," Yoshi muttered.

"And now, of course, you are an old woman. You are millions and millions of years old, Yosh-*chan*." Hana pressed her fingers against her temples. "How under heaven did you ever get so *old?*"

Yoshi looked down at her toes, poking grubbily through the thin synthetic fabric (*sufu*) of her socks as they always did after a day or two of wear. She could feel the dust and sweat of the past week coating her skin. They no longer had indoor plumbing since they'd "donated" all their steel pipes to the cause. And the bathhouse on their street hadn't opened for days due to the fuel shortage.

"I wish the all clear would sound," she said.

Hana was studying Masa's sash, her tongue pushed against her cheek. *"Nee,"* she said, "what's this here?"

She pointed to a small cluster of blue dots, ink marks to indicate where contributors should put their stitches, just in front of the tiger's roaring mouth.

"It's supposed to be a hawk," Yoshi said, unplugging the ceramic canteen she kept beneath the bench and sipping judiciously.

"A what?" Hana asked.

"A *hawk*." The water tasted the way the air down here smelled: close, musty. Steeped in sawdust. She held the canteen out to Hana, who shook her head. "Like on your cigarettes."

"The tiger is chasing a hawk?"

"The hawk is—leading the tiger. Or perhaps it's just keeping it company." She shrugged. "Masa likes hawks. So I tried to make one." Which of course wasn't the full truth. She'd never forgotten Masa's comment about her being beautiful, "like a hawk." She'd wanted to put herself on the belt with him. Now, though, it sounded absurd. Even to her own ears.

"Odd hawk, to want to fly with a tiger." Hana handed the belt back and pulled her own hawk-emblazoned cigarette packet from her coat pocket. "You know what they say about them, anyway. Hawks. Don't you?"

Yoshi shook her head. "No. What?"

Hana shook out a cigarette, lighting it. Smoke promptly filled

Yoshi's nose and mouth. "That the wise ones don't show their talons. To their prey."

"Oh, that's right." Yoshi nodded; she'd heard this somewhere.

"Does that mean," Hana said thoughtfully, "that our soldiers hide their bayonets when they fight, do you suppose? Do they simply kill the enemy with that sacred Yamato spirit the papers are always talking about?"

Yoshi thought of Rule Number 7 in the Civilian Defense Handbook: *During an air-raid, all citizens should refrain from unpatriotic, pessimistic or otherwise morale-damaging remarks and thoughts.* If someone were to open Hana's head and look inside, all they'd find would be *hikokuni shisoo*; unpatriotic thoughts.

Byoki da, she reminded herself. *She is sick.*

Hana had tilted her head back and was gazing at the sealed-off night sky, as though she'd magically acquired the power to see through steel, rock and wood. "I suppose you're hoping that if you give this boy his fancy belt, it will protect him from danger."

"I suppose you don't believe it will?"

"I don't believe anything can protect us now. Anyone who tells you otherwise is either a liar or a fool." Something else in her tone—bitterness, perhaps, but spiked through with a vein of real pain—made Yoshi look up at her sharply.

"Lots of things protect us," she said. "The Emperor protects us. And *Amaterasu*. And the Imperial Army. And Papa, too. You can't deny that he's protected you."

Hana raised an eyebrow. "Protected me from what?"

"Well, from the *kempei*. For instance."

Hana laughed so abruptly and harshly that it sounded like a small detonation.

"*Nan de?* He did get you out when they questioned you that last time."

Hana tightened her lips. "You have no idea what I went through before he did."

"You told me they just made you write an essay pledging your loyalty to the Emperor."

"That is what I told you, yes."

Another chill started somewhere at the top of Yoshi's spine. "That wasn't what happened?"

Hana gave her an intent look. "Do you really want to know what happened?"

Yoshi stared back at her. "Yes," she said.

If Hana heard the uncertainty in her tone she didn't heed it. Hands folded in her lap, she sat back. "First," she said, her voice almost without inflection, "they told me they knew I was an English spy. And that they knew there were others in my network. They wanted me to give them the names of those people."

It felt as though every movement in Yoshi's body stopped—blood congealing in its veins, heart ceasing its soft percussion. Nerves dropping their electrically charged game of tag.

"When I didn't have any to give them," Hana went on, "they beat me. First they beat me with my clothes on. Then they took off my clothes . . ."

"They *what?*"

"They stripped me. Looking for 'evidence,'" Hana said, smiling tightly. "Then they asked me again to give names. When I still couldn't answer they beat me on my arms, back and the backs of my legs. I passed out for a while. When I came to they'd pushed my head into a bucket of freezing, dirty water."

Yoshi felt her stomach contract, in something far more painful than a hunger pang. She shook her head, her eyes stinging with tears. "Why?" she whispered. "Why did they do that?"

"Because they *could.* Just like they could half suffocate me with a wet towel, taking it off of my face just long enough for me to speak a word or two, take one breath before putting it back over my mouth."

Yoshi felt the color drain from her face. "I can't believe that. That's—that's unthinkable . . ."

Hana shook her head. "No it's not. They could have done more. Much more. They could have killed me, disposed of me entirely, and hardly anyone besides you would have noticed."

"And Papa," Yoshi murmured.

Her mother leaned back and closed her eyes. "They'd done that with several people I'd known from abroad. People who'd studied in London and Paris. They read the names out loud to me and told me how they'd died. They told me I should prepare to join them."

"Did they . . . ?" Yoshi paused, barely knowing what she was even asking.

Hana shook her head. "No. In that, at least, I suppose I was lucky. He told me I was such a Westernized slut I disgusted him. That he couldn't even bear to touch me without his gloves on."

Trembling, Yoshi raked her hand through her hair. Her insides felt bruised and tender; as though she were the one who'd been beaten and abused. "But Papa knew the police," she managed at last. "He had an agreement with them."

Hana took out another cigarette, not lighting it right away but tapping it silently against her bony knee. "The Ministry of Agriculture's influence can only extend so far." A small smile. "And then, of course, your father left me. Everyone left me."

An image came: the barn in New Nagano. The unmistakable sounds that had come out of it. Yoshi tried to summon her voice. "I stayed."

"Stayed where?"

"Here. In Tokyo."

Her mother laughed. "Where else would you go?"

Yoshi suppressed a cry of frustration. Could she really not know?

Most of the city's children had already evacuated to the countryside. If not, they—like Satako and her five younger sisters—were hoping to go as soon as they found a host home big enough to accommodate their family. The exodus had started after the Education Ministry's declaration that *while the likelihood of real or extended damage from air attack remains viewed as remote, citizens up to the age of sixteen years are strongly recommended to be removed to rural areas, as an extra safety precaution.* Kenji had been in full agreement, urging his wife and daughter to leave the city even before the official warning came out. He'd even found them a borrowed cottage on land belonging to farming clients in Nagano. The prospect of it—siren-free nights, fresh air, no dreary school or factory work—had thrilled Yoshi. But Hana had ruled it out without a thought; just as she'd ruled out accompanying Yoshi to Manchuria. "Surely you're joking," she had scoffed. "*Move* there? To a *farmhouse*? What on earth would I *do*?"

"Yoshi-*chan*," she was saying, her tone more gentle than it had been in a long time, years maybe. "Yoshi."

Yoshi opened her eyes. The room seemed to spin briefly before coming to a standstill around them. "*Nn,*" she murmured.

"There is a reason I told you these things tonight. Something you need to know."

Yoshi shook her head. In her mind's eye she was still seeing it—her mother, stripped. Her mother, bruised, unconscious. How could her father have allowed these things to happen? How could the Emperor have allowed it? After all, they were all the Emperor's children, weren't they? But what father treats a child, or treats *anyone*, like that?

"*Yoshi-chan!* Are you listening?"

"*Hai,*" Yoshi murmured, feeling her eyelids prickle damply.

"There's something you must always remember."

Hana leaned in, close enough that Yoshi felt her slightly sour breath against her temple. Her mother's face gleamed in the lantern light, smooth and shining. Lacquered white; a pale mask against the dark. Five thin fingers grasped her wrist. "Nobody can protect you but yourself," Hana whispered. "In times like these, people you think you know can become strangers, or even monsters. From now on—from this *moment* on—you must only think, first and foremost, of protecting yourself. No one else matters—not even me. No matter what. *Wakaru?*"

"Hai," Yoshi repeated, barely breathing the word.

For an instant neither moved. Yoshi had the odd sensation of being briefly stopped in time, just like that: two images in one of Hana's sepia-toned photographs.

But then her mother's face softened; she released Yoshi's hand. Fumbling on the bench, she found *Lady Chatterley* and pulled the book into her lap. As usual, she didn't open it. She just sighed and leaned back against the wall, as though the exchange had thoroughly drained her.

Feeling drained as well, Yoshi leaned back against the wall too. Outside a truck rumbled past on the narrow street. She heard shouts, a shrill whistle. Then the echoing *crack* of something sharper—a burst tire? A firecracker? In the end she really didn't care. The only sound that mattered was the all clear whistle. Would it even come? Would they have to sleep here?

Sighing, she began rerolling Masa's sash in her lap.

"Don't put it away, *nee,*" her mother said.

Yoshi blinked at her. "Why not?"

"Don't you want me to put a stitch on for you?"

"Why put a stitch on it if you don't believe it works?"

"Because *you* clearly believe it works." Hana held out her hand. "And because perhaps, even if it doesn't protect him, it will help him feel a little less lonely out there."

Yoshi hesitated. Then she held out the belt, its silver embroidery needle stuck through in one corner. The latter still trailed a good length of red thread left there by the last woman who'd contributed a stitch—a nurse who'd just returned from leading a training course somewhere in the Korean colonies.

"Shall I put it on the hawk?" Hana asked.

"Put it—put it on the tiger's tail. Please."

Outside, the Army truck had either left or been abandoned. There were no other noises: Yoshi didn't even hear the barking dog. She had a sudden image of emerging from their little hole to find the whole world had simply disappeared. Shivering again, she pulled her sweater more tightly around her torso and took another sip of stale water. Hana crafted an expert-looking French knot, then nipped the thread with her small, stained teeth. Surveying her work, she nodded in satisfaction and handed it back to Yoshi. Then she cocked her head, seeming to remember something.

"Yoshi-*chan*. Hand me the emergency bag, *nee*. There's something in it I need."

Puzzled, Yoshi handed over the handkerchief-wrapped bundle. She had packed it carefully on Kenji's written instructions, choosing mostly items suggested by the Civilian Defense Handbook: the family's ancestral tablets. Real estate records. A few pieces of Hana's more valuable jewelry that they hadn't donated. And food: there was hard tack and dried seaweed. A can of precious stewed meat from a case some Army contact had given to Kenji. There was a small package of rice, two extra sets of threadbare clothes. So far as Yoshi knew her mother neither knew nor cared about any of it.

But now here was Hana, authoritatively loosening the knot.

"I was sure I put it in here," she said, fishing around inside. "How odd." Her face cleared: "Ah. *Atta*."

She held up her prize, and Yoshi made out a silken bag, its color vaguely familiar but indeterminate in the dark.

"What is it?"

"Something for which I have no use. But you may." Hana handed the little bag to her daughter, who turned it over in her hands with a vague feeling of recognition. "Something you brought me, actually. After going to visit your father in *Manshu*. Don't you remember? He gave it to you to give to me."

Yosh nodded slowly: the green ring. She hadn't thought about it in years. In fact, apart from that one sickening moment outside the barn, and of course her time with Masa, her memories from her Manchurian trip were a blur of sawdust and cold and rough-hewn shacks, all faintly tinged with nausea.

Holding the silk pouch now, she remembered the day her father had given it to her. *Put that somewhere safe . . . I want her to know I'm thinking of her.*

The knot was just as tight as Yoshi remembered it being; she split one of her already-ragged nails trying to pry it apart. But she succeeded, and the small square bloomed open against her knees to reveal in its center the ring, glinting and green. Wordlessly, she handed it over to Hana, who slipped it on her thin middle finger.

"When I first saw it it made me think of Scarlett O'Hara," Yoshi mused, as her mother turned her hand back and forth in the lantern-light.

Hana gave a short laugh. "Given how many times you made me take you to that movie, it's a wonder more things don't."

Yoshi found herself smiling as well. She had just turned eleven when *Gone With the Wind* first played at the Ikebukuro Cinema. Entranced with Vivien Leigh—those glass-green eyes; those rich green gowns—she'd forced her mother to take her four times. "The stone is the same color as Leigh-*san*'s eyes," she noted now, reaching her hand out to get it back. "Why didn't you ever wear it?"

"It's always been too big."

"You could have had it sized down."

"No, I couldn't have. You know what happens when we bring things to the jeweler."

Yoshi nodded. The last time she'd brought a watch of Hana's back from being repaired a *tonarigumi* representative showed up, politely inquiring whether the household had any "unneeded and luxurious" jewelry items they could donate to the cause.

"Besides," added Hana, "if I wore every piece of animal hide or jewelry your father gave me, I'd look like that awful Christmas tree Matsukaya Department Store used to put up every December. Do you remember the year they put a cross on the top—with Father Christmas nailed to it instead of Jesus?"

With a hoarse laugh she handed the ring back to Yoshi, who slipped it over her middle finger. It fit her better than it did her mother, though it was still a little loose. "Why did you put it in the emergency bag?"

"I'm not quite sure," replied Hana vaguely. "I'd honestly forgotten that I had, until just now. I suppose because it seemed to suit you."

Which of course made as little sense as anything else Hana had said tonight. Still, Yoshi decided to take the gift at face value. "It's—amazing," she said, meaning it. "*Arigato*, Mama."

She leaned back, studying the little accessory again, overcome by that awful one (or three) words she'd thought to herself earlier, back in the house: *Kirai?* What kind of a daughter hates her own mother? It struck her that perhaps she was sick herself; that these strange and violent thoughts were a symptom. Could one inherit melancholic confusion through birth and blood?

"You are a good girl." Her mother was looking down at her novel. "Do you know, Yoshi-*chan*," she said, her voice faintly singsong now, "that I had a dream last night. A strange but quite wonderful dream."

"You did?"

Hana nodded and then—for some reason—switched into English. "I dreamt that I was on the roof. In the sun, in my white swimsuit. Do you remember when I used to do that?"

Yoshi nodded. It had infuriated Kenji and outraged the neighbors, but Hana had done it for years all the same.

"It was a glorious day," Hana went on. "I went to the edge of the building, and looked out, and saw the sky and grass and, way out beyond them, the sea, twinkling in the sunlight. It was so green. And something inside me just told me . . ." Her mother laughed, a rare, real laugh. "I somehow knew that I could step off the roof, and that I'd be fine. Because in the dream, I somehow knew that I could fly. And do you know . . . I did. Yoshi. I *flew* . . ."

Hana's words were starting to slur the way they used to when she drank heavily, though Yoshi knew Hana hadn't had a real drink in over a year—less out of choice, of course, than because there was almost nothing alcoholic left to drink that wouldn't kill you.

Concerned, she looked over to see Hana had once more collapsed back against the soot-streaked wooden wall. Her chin dug into her sunken chest. Her fingers opened in her lap: petals on a white, night-blooming flower. On a sudden urge Yoshi covered one with her own. "Are you all right?"

"*Mo. Ii wa.* I'm just so *tired*, Yoshi-*chan*." Sighing again, she tipped her head back and shut her eyes. "This goddamn war," she said, in English.

"*Soo, nee,*" said Yoshi soothingly. She slipped the ring off again and was squinting down at the inside of the band, trying to see whether there was a name or a date, or perhaps a vow of love, inscribed somewhere on it. "Is it a wedding ring?" she asked. "Do *gaijin-san* exchange these when they're engaged, maybe?"

Her mother didn't answer, and looked up again. To her surprise, Hana's eyes were fully closed. Her chest rose and fell slowly.

"Mama?"

No answer. Yoshi shook her head, awestruck by the ease with which her mother could flit between consciousness and slumber. She remembered Masahiro all those years ago, laughing at the way his little sister had done the same. *She does that sometimes,* he'd told Yoshi. *Just drops where she stands . . .*

Then another emotion intruded: something cold and desperate. It was the same feeling she'd had when she'd seen Hana in her evening gown and makeup last week. The same feeling she'd had as a small child, watching her mother "make herself fancy" before one of her lunches or dinner parties, a sure sign she was going to be out for hours, or even the night. Yoshi had always feared that it would end up being even longer—that she'd reach for her mother one day, and find her gone.

For a flickering instant there was the urge to wake Hana up; to shake her. To lay her hooded head on Hana's lap. Instead, Yoshi picked up the cigarette pack Hana had left on the bench and withdrew one slim white stick. She held it limpidly in her right hand—just below where the ring glinted in tarnished opulence. "But if you go," she murmured, in English, "where will *I* go? What will *I* do?"

And then—as if in answer—it finally came: the all clear whistle.

Within moments there followed the relieved voices of neighbors and policemen, shouting out, checking in with one another: "That was a tough one, eh, Shimada-*san*?"

"*Soo, nee,* Haneda-*san!* Twice in one night! I wonder if the watch-towers made a mistake?"

"Mistake? Not them. They never make mistakes. Yanks probably just got cold feet and flew back to bed."

"Lucky Yanks. I could use some sleep."

"*Shikatta ga nai, nee?* We'll sleep when the war is good and won. Good night."

"*Oyasumi nasai.*"

The sound of doors sliding shut. An announcement floated over-head from the direction of the police box: "Citizens in shelters: please leave now. The drill is over. I repeat: the drill is over."

These last few words were half obscured by the system's usual sojourn from static into an ear-piercing squeal. It was a sound that set Yoshi's teeth on edge, even ten feet underground. But she remained in her seat, as reluctant to leave the small dark space—the bittersweet moment—as she had been to let Hana fall back asleep.

AT 7 A.M. the next morning her mother's ring—discreetly dangling from a chain around Yoshi's neck—still seemed to be working its tarnished magic. Yoshi left the house at seven without waking Hana—which, while not entirely unexpected, was nevertheless a relief. The things Hana had said the night before sat queasily in her stomach, like the acidic remnants of a bad dinner: *they took off my clothes. He told me I was such a Westernized slut I disgusted him. No one can protect you but yourself . . .* As Yoshi rushed through her toilette, ate a few mouthfuls of sorghum mixed with soybean skins and washed them down with weak barley tea, the words circled her head, tainting the bright, clear morning the way black ink taints clean water. She raced out the door as though fleeing her own doom.

The Asakusa-bound tram was running on schedule for once, and so she made it to school a full twenty minutes early. There she discovered that her least favorite teacher had inexplicably been assigned to a different classroom, and replaced by her most favorite, a youngish woman with a swelling belly and a kind face. Sasegawa-*sensei* not only added another stitch to Masa's belt, but she also gave Yoshi's class some of the extra rations she'd obtained after her husband took a trip to the country. It was only half a steamed sweet potato per girl, and like everyone else Yoshi was so sick of sweet potatoes she almost didn't want to eat it. But she'd forced it down, swallowing the yellow flesh with the same stoic efficiency with which the runners shuttled balloons from station to station at the factory. For once, whether it was the extra food or just her nerves, she felt that endless, grumbling gut-emptiness partially appeased.

After handing in her headband and bowing to the Emperor's picture, she raced down the block to the *sento*, the French soap she'd taken from Hana's lingerie drawer that morning tacky in her warm hand and a prayer resounding in her head: *please-be-open-please-be-open-please-be-open.* And astonishingly, for the first time in two weeks, it was. Black smoke spewed from the chimney into the blue sky, and the air smelled of clean laundry and the sea. The line was short, too. Yoshi only had to wait a half-hour. She used that time to secure three more stitches on Masa's belt.

She took her bath, soap-stung eyes fixed fiercely on her towel and clothes (people stole everything these days, even hairpins) and her hands busily washing everything—every inch of her bruised, thin body. As she hurried back into the dressing room and into her clothes she felt lighter than she had in months.

Her luck continued as she boarded the Tokyo Station bus, which while not on time was still just ten minutes late. As usual, it was crowded. But she secured the last seat in the car next to a young mother carrying a baby on her lap who was also clearly coming from the bathhouse. The baby, pink-cheeked and squeaky-clean, gurgled and beamed. He sat on Yoshi's lap while his mother stood up to put something up on the rack, and she quickly buried her nose in his thick black hair, wondering whether Hana had ever done this with her. Wondering if she, too, had smelled like talc and honey. When the mother sat down again she gave him back with reluctance, thinking *Maybe Masa and I will have a son.* The thought filled her with aching sweetness, and she pulled out Masa's belt to recount the stitches. There was only one left to do. Yoshi thought about asking the mother next to her, but the baby was fussing now: she had her hands full.

About ten minutes into the trip an Imperial Army officer pushed his way onto the bus. Seeing no seats, he launched into a tirade. "Someone must give up their seat," he ordered. "When encountering those who fight for your nation's honor and future, it is your duty to show them respect."

A year ago, this speech would have prompted a flurry of movement, resulting in several seats being evacuated and the officer sprawling across two or three to take a nap. Today, though, no one moved. Yoshi kept her eyes on Masa's *seninbari*, held below the seat back on her lap. The woman fed her baby from a ceramic bottle. Somewhere in the back, an old man coughed.

"Do you hear me?" the officer shouted. "The Emperor *orders* you up! Get up, damn you! All of you!"

Again, no response. The officer flushed, then turned and spat upon the clean-swept bus floor. "You are all traitors, do you hear?" he called, stomping back towards the door. "In the Army you'd all have been shot." He stormed off the bus, pausing only to rip an advertisement for Kao face soap (no longer available anywhere, as far as Yoshi knew) from its frame. Relief rippled through the car: there were murmurs, a few chuckles. The baby gave a soft burp.

"Do you need a stitch?" the young mother offered, indicating the belt. "Here. If you hold Taro-*kun* again for me I can help. Where is he?"

And as Taro-*kun* played with Yoshi's ear his mother placed the last, finishing French knot on the tip of the hawk's beak, and handed it back with both hands and her head bowed: *"Gonbatte kudasai."*

"Thank you," Yoshi said, and gave the ring a secret squeeze of thanks.

It was all going so well that even when the sirens started again a little bit before two o'clock Yoshi was only a little bit worried. They were at Ueno, just a short ways from Tokyo Station. After filing out with the other passengers, she huddled in a shallow city shelter, scanning the sky and smelling the old man next to her (tiger balm, garlic). Her pulse pounded, not at the thought of possible B-*sans* but of seeing Masahiro in his *Kantogun* uniform, in a matter of mere minutes.

The raid lasted just half an hour, once more with no signs of planes, and they all piled back onto the bus. Yoshi managed to get a seat again. But there at last her good luck ended; for after several minutes of grating sounds and belched smoke, the conductor stood up and bowed. The charcoal-burning engine seemed to be malfunctioning, he informed them apologetically. The bus would have to be taken out of service.

The rest of the car erupted in weary groans, but Yoshi felt her blood turn into ice. The dream came back—of Masa, calling. Masa, leaving. Masa a gleaming dot upon the horizon. Before even realizing she'd gotten up she was pushing her way down the narrow aisle and leaping down the back steps. She ran into the street, nearly stumbling into a sidewalk shelter and feeling the ring slam against her chest. Barely breathing in her panic, she tried to flag down a charcoal-propelled taxi, another tram, anything.

She ended up in a *jinricksha* pulled by a tattered boy who looked roughly half her age, but who nevertheless insisted on an outrageous, inflated price (twenty *sen*) before he'd so much as get back on his seat. True to his word, though, he was quick, his bony thighs pumping so fast they nearly blurred as he carried them past the buildings and ditchdiggers and a fife-and-drum band from a nearby middle school. Still, they didn't reach the station until almost 3:45, and Yoshi was panting before her feet hit the pavement. Flinging the boy his coins, she paused to take off her *geta*. Then she set off in a full sprint, pushing past housewives with shopping packages and farmers returning home from the city market and tea sellers hawking thrice-steeped tea. She heard disapproving *tsk*'s as she hurried past the donation posts and the Patriotic Housewives of Tokyo welcome desk, and somewhere by the *bento* stand (which now sold boxed lunches that were more box than lunch) she heard a *Hey! Slow down—that's dangerous!*

But she paused only briefly, and only long enough to confirm on the arrivals board that Masa's train had arrived: Track 19. Platform 6.

Track 19. Platform 6. Maybe he'd still be there. Of *course* he would. He'd have nowhere else to go. And his connecting train left in less than an hour, and from the same platform.

Collecting herself a little, Yoshi put her shoes back on and ran her shaking hands through her disheveled hair. Glancing around to ensure no policemen or Patriotic Housewives were near, she slipped Hana's ring on her finger. Then she turned and examined her reflection in one of the glass-mounted posters lining the station wall. This one showed scores of stern-faced citizens welding bamboo spears on a beachhead. *The Children of Yamato Shall Fight as One,* it asserted. Yoshi, however, ignored this prediction: she was interested in the more immediate future. Pulling out the lipstick she'd snuck from Hana's cosmetic bag—the same one she'd seen Hana holding by her vanity last week—she carefully unscrewed the cap. Then, sucking her cheeks in and pursing her lips, she painted her mouth Siren Red.

HER FIRST THOUGHT when she reached the platform was one of relief: *I didn't miss him.* Rather than the relatively quiet span of concrete she'd expected to see a half-hour after the train pulled into its berth, there was instead a hive of khaki-clothed confusion. Soldiers shouted and tossed duffels to one another. Stationmasters waved white-gloved hands and begged for order. Red-vested porters raced to and fro with wagons carrying the trunks of the more senior officers, who followed in their riding boots, with long, striding steps.

Shielding her eyes with her hand, Yoshi gazed at the bustling mass, searching for a tall boy with blackbird eyes and blackbird hair. Which car was he on? Which part of the platform would he be stepping onto? Which way would he turn to look for her? But even as she ran through these questions it began to dawn on her that they weren't the right ones.

For something was wrong—very wrong. The soldiers weren't getting out of the train. They were clambering *into* it. And the stationmasters weren't welcoming them home. They were helping them find cars that still had empty seats.

She ran forward, nearly tripping again as she fumbled with the buckle on her satchel. She stopped the first stationmaster she found, an elderly man with a limp who seemed to be overseeing the operation. "Excuse me," she panted. "Excuse me. I'm sorry. But is this the train carrying the officer candidates arriving from Manshu?"

The man looked at her, his grizzled jaw working. His eyes lingered on her red lips, her dirty feet.

"Yes," he said. "Yes, it is. But it isn't arriving anymore. It's leaving."

"Leaving?"

"The train they were supposed to take later was reassigned. Fuel embargo. Only way to get 'em out today was to get 'em out now."

"Now?" she repeated, barely feeling her lips move.

He nodded. "Of course, we had to kick all the civilians off of it. Let me tell you. That didn't make us very popular. All well and good to support the troops, until they make you miss your train. But that's war, isn't it. We've all got to sacrifice. Seventy million as one, and all that . . ."

Yoshi didn't stay to hear the rest. Pulling Masa's *seninbari* out from her bag, she ran up to the first car and peered into it. A hundred young faces peered back, some smiling, some expressionless. None of them belonged to Masa.

"Excuse me," she called in through the half-opened window. "Shinagawa Masahiro. Do you know which car? . . ."

But the men—who were breaking into a rousing version of "The Eagle That Had No Nest"—either didn't hear her or chose to ignore her. Forcing herself to stay calm, she gave the car one last glance and raced down to the next. Nothing. Nor was he inside the next.

The platform was almost clear now. Behind her Yoshi heard the stationmasters announcing the last call. "Doors will close shortly," they shouted into their bullhorns. "Please watch your hands and feet. Please be careful. Doors to Train 260, bound for Yokohama City, will close in a few moments. Please be careful."

"*No!*" Yoshi rushed down to the fourth car on the track. The men inside this one were already playing cards, but there was one who just sat and stared bleakly back at her. Wrapping the belt around her arm, she cupped her hands around her mouth, and shouted at him: "Please. Please—I'm looking for Shinagawa Masahiro-*san*. From Shin Nagano in *Manshu*. Do you know what car he's in?"

"Eh? Shinagawa? He's in the last car, I think." His eyes fell on the belt. "You trying to give that to him, sister? I can give it to him. Hand it over."

He reached a rough hand through the window. Yoshi stared at his callused fingers, then back at his face. What if he was lying? Or was thinking of the wrong person? Would all her hard work and stitches, and Hana's stitch, and the other nine hundred ninety-eight of them go to save a total stranger?

It wasn't worth the risk. "*Domo,*" she called back, and raced on.

At Car Six the train's whistle sounded. At Seven the doors juddered shut. At Eight and Nine the stationmasters paced the platform, scanning for exposed limbs, noses, bits of clothing as the soldiers inside began to push the windows closed. Feeling as though her lungs might burst, Yoshi sprinted to Car Ten—the last car—and then stopped short before it, staring up.

At first all of the passengers looked the same to her: just one shorn head after another. But then her eyes met with another pair of eyes staring out the window. They were black, black, blackbird eyes; sharp and wry and warm. When they saw her they widened in recognition.

"Masa!"

Still gasping for breath, Yoshi stepped as close as she could to the train's cold metal siding. *"Masa-kun!"* she called. "Masa! It's you, isn't it? Can you hear me?"

Masahiro pressed his face to the window, beaming. His face had filled out in three years since she had last seen him, his nose bigger, his chin stronger and stubble-covered. And yet, at the same time he seemed somehow hollower too; his eyes deeper in their sockets, duller than she'd remembered.

With a noise halfway between a laugh and a cry, Yoshi unwound the *seninbari* from her wrist and held it up to him through the glass. Masa nodded. He made as if to push the pane open, but an officer who'd been patrolling the aisles slapped his arm away and scolded him harshly. Masa bowed his head and then said something, pointing at Yoshi through the glass. The officer paused and looked straight at her. Her heart lifted slightly as, thin lips parted in a tight grin, he reached over towards the window himself. Rather than opening it, though, he merely slid the bolt into place.

Then, as Yoshi looked on in shock, he turned back to Masa. Taking off his visored cap, he beat the young soldier on the head and shoulders with it, shouting at him so violently his face glowed.

"Stop!" Yoshi called, horrified, as Masa covered his head with his arms. "Stop! He didn't do anything!"

But the officer kept on beating. And then the whistle blew again, and the train sighed a sad, steel sigh as it finally started to move; slowly at first, but gradually picking up steam. Yoshi ran alongside it, her eyes locked on Masahiro's, and to her relief the officer moved off again down the aisle. She tried to shout for Masa's attention: *"Masa-kun! Ganbatte . . .* good luck!"

But he had turned away from her. He was staring stoically at the ground, his sharp-boned face flushed in shame. Yoshi picked up her pace, gasping for air, waving the thousand-stitch belt like a white flag. Her thoughts were so jumbled and frantic that it actually occurred to her to try to leap onto the track and keep running. But then a white-gloved hand was clasping her elbow, pulling her back to safety.

"He's gone, miss," said the stationmaster. "Please be careful. He's gone."

At first she struggled, straining after the departing car, watching it through misting eyes. But as it pulled into the darkness of the tunnel she allowed herself to go limp, dropping her arm and letting the tiger belt fall in a white pile onto the dirty cement. She stared down at it a moment, feeling her pulse tap in her fingertips, the ring's green stone digging into her palm. Somehow over the course of the struggle it had twisted around on her finger. Her fists were both clenched, and the metal hurt enough to make her gasp. But she didn't release her grip.

"Miss," the stationmaster said. "Miss. Are you all right? You dropped this." Bending over, he picked up the white strip from the dusty platform. As he ran it through his gloved hands, comprehension and pity touched his features. "I see. Oh, a shame. You meant to give this to a young man."

Yoshi nodded numbly.

"Well," the man said comfortingly, "you can always send it to him via Imperial post. They're very good, you know."

"Will—will they be coming back after the test?" she asked, finally finding her voice. "From Yokohama?"

He sucked his teeth. "Ah, hard to say. The plans change so quickly, you see. It all depends on where they're needed. And we're down to so few trains these days . . . it's very hard to know these things." Rolling up the belt neatly, he handed it back to her with a small bow. "But you know what? Just having a pretty young girl like you thinking of him will protect him too. Don't worry yourself too much. Is there anything else I can help you with? Do you need help finding another train?"

She opened her mouth to say *No, thank you.* But what came out was something else: "What will become of me?"

The man frowned, leaned closer. "Excuse me?"

She'd spoken the sentence in English. "Nothing," she whispered, flushing. "I'm very sorry to have been such a bother."

She tucked the belt back into her satchel, carefully closing the flap so that the red-stitched tiger disappeared from sight.

"YOU MEAN YOU didn't even get to *talk* to him?" Sa-*chan* asked, incredulous.

Yoshi shook her head. "By the time I got there their train was already leaving. I waved at him. But they'd already shut and locked the window."

She didn't mention the part about the officer smiling at her as he beat Masa with his cap—it felt too raw. Still, pedaling behind her on her bike, Satako made a small sound of sympathy. The same late night breeze whipped her red hair ribbon against Yoshi's face.

"*Zan nen, nee,*" she said. "So you still have the belt. Even though you finally finished the stitches. Oh, it's too bad you got there so late . . ."

Yoshi brushed the fluttering grosgrain off her cheek and stared into the black distance. Though she'd scrubbed Hana's lipstick off in the station's W.C. her lips still tasted like stale wax. Back on its chain, she felt the ring against her chest, beating there in time with Satako's wobbly pedaling. She wanted to throw it into the river.

"You can send it to him by post," her friend offered.

"That's what the stationmaster said."

"Well, maybe that's what you should do then."

Satako tossed her head, and the ribbon made its tickling way back towards her cheekbones. "Oh, *really*, Sa-*chan*," snapped Yoshi, "can't you tie that thing better?"

"Sorry," said Satako mildly, though she didn't stop pedaling.

Yoshi sighed. Her whole body ached even more than it had during last night's air raids. Not just from the mad rush to the station, or from the afternoon at the balloon factory, or the past four hours she'd spent stooped over cardboard planes with a tiny paintbrush, meticulously copying out serial number after serial number onto boxy, white-painted bellies. It ached from disappointment, and an even deeper fear that she knew was irrational, but which was no less terrifying for that fact. For while it wasn't Masa's fault that his unit had had to leave the station early, it *was* her fault that she'd gotten there so late. She'd let her vanity and selfish desire for herself get in the way of duty. And now even if he passed his exams and got promoted to lieutenant he'd go into battle unprotected. *If he dies,* she thought bitterly, *it will be my fault.*

Her stomach, so briefly contented after its extra ration of sweet potato, now felt bloated and gassy. There was something else as well: for the first time in months, maybe years, she missed Hana. It wasn't the usual weary worry about whether her mother was behaving, or had gotten herself arrested again. It was more akin to a hunger; to that greedy, non-negotiable need of small children when they get lost or catch a fever or scrape a knee. It was a feeling she'd had all night, though at first it had been faint; a kind of nagging discomfort somewhere in her belly. Gradually, though, it had gotten stronger, and by 10:45 it had developed into a full-fledged stomachache. By that point there'd been one siren, but it had been called off almost immediately. The model planes were detailed and drying on old newspaper. Yoshi had stared at them, seeing not the painstaking numerals and round red suns but the tattered blue cover of her mother's Lawrence: *She was gone, she was not, and she was born: a woman.*

Finally at 11:15, as the rest of the girls unrolled their mats and blankets and claimed their sleeping spots in the gymnasium, Yoshi made her way up to the teacher and shyly requested permission to go home. When he asked her why, she lied, since she couldn't very well tell the truth. "My mother," she said. "She wasn't well this morning. I think she had a fever. I'm sorry. I really feel I should go home. You see, I'm the only one there to take care of her."

Aomori-*sensei* looked at her for a long moment, his eyebrows raised. *Your mother,* he seemed to be saying. *Ah yes—I know your mother.*

But all he'd said was, "Is that so. Well, you've done some very good work, Yoshi-*kun*. Why don't you go home now and come back first thing tomorrow."

He'd even granted Sa-*chan* permission to go with her, to give her a ride. And he'd given them both notes in case they were stopped for breaking curfew.

"HE'LL COME AGAIN," Sa-*chan* said, panting slightly in her effort to stay balanced as she propelled them both up a small incline on Asakusa *doori*. "He has to come back through Tokyo to redeploy, doesn't he? And then they still have more than one leave."

"The stationmaster wasn't sure. He said as long as they remain low on trains and fuel, the schedule will just keep changing."

"*Saaa,*" said Sa-*chan* thoughtfully. She paused a moment to fling a breeze-blown braid over her shoulder. "Well, anyway, the war will be won soon. Then you'll have lots of time to play and catch up."

The words were meant to be reassuring; Yoshi knew this. But for some reason they sounded more like mockery. "*Mo, ii wa,*" she said sulkily. "I don't want to talk about it."

"All right," said Sa-*chan* amiably.

They cycled on in silence; past the dark temples and shuttered shops, past the *miso* factory at the corner of Kototoi *doori*. They'd just crossed the Kototoi bridge when she heard in the wind an undefined, low, rumbling sound. *Thunder,* was her first reaction, though the sky was dark and clear. Or perhaps it was distant drumming from some festival—though most festivals had been banned out of respect for "the crisis."

A moment later the sound had both broadened and refined into the whines of individual engines. Satako stopped the bike, planting her feet on the ground, and in one smooth motion Yoshi slid off the handlebars.

"Zeros?" Satako asked.

"Maybe," Yoshi said. "But there must be a lot of them."

Satako released the handlebar with one hand. The bike wobbled and nearly fell; grasping the bars reflexively, Yoshi leaned it against her leg.

Around them on Kototoi Street others were stopping too; charcoal taxis, *jinricksha*s, a few more post-curfew cyclists illumined by pools of blackout-painted lamplight. People peered from nearby doorways, half-dressed and sleep-tousled. A Victrola jarred to a stop mid-verse of the "Nanjing Victory March." The night-soil man who had been placidly plodding along ahead of the two girls creaked his cart to a halt, his straw fedora tilted back on his balding head as he, too, stared into the sky. His cart horse—an aging chestnut who had somehow escaped being eaten (perhaps because there was no meat left on his bones)—stamped his big hooves uneasily.

From somewhere behind the heavy rhythm came a sharper *clip,* heels on asphalt. Yoshi turned to see a young woman in a faded fur-trimmed coat and a permanent wave she'd clearly put in her own hair.

"What *is* that?" she asked vaguely, stopping across the street from the girls and setting down her suitcase.

Yoshi scanned the sky once more, trying to locate the source of the growing din. This time it wasn't difficult.

They came flying in from the direction of Tokyo Bay, their pace surprisingly leisurely: gleaming planes. Scores and scores and scores of them. At first, in fact, Yoshi couldn't see an end. It was like standing beneath an infinite flock of silvery, blunt-nosed gulls. They were flying low, too; lower than Yoshi had ever seen planes fly before. Low enough that she *almost* thought, peering at those glinting glass windows, that she might make out the pale faces of their pilots. Instead what she saw after one plane dipped towards them—almost as though it was scrutinizing Yoshi as closely as she scrutinized it—was the half-naked blonde woman painted on its nose. Despite the darkness, she also made out the letters etched above the woman's head, a garish halo: *Blonde Bombshell.* The picture was of Jean Harlow, and the pulse of recognition this brought was quickly swallowed by the larger realization of what it meant.

"They're Americans," she shouted, over the now-thunderous engines.

"Yankees?" Satako's jaw dropped, her teeth releasing the braid tip. "Are you sure?"

Yoshi nodded. Masa had sent her detailed diagrams of the enemy planes he'd studied at his military academy. B-17's. B-24's. He'd indicated their weak points with small arrows and neatly printed footnotes: *three-finned propellers, flimsy in high headwinds; highly flammable engines due to extensive magnesium content.* Occasionally he'd also drawn a heavily bearded Yank pilot, his pale eyes bulging at the approach of a sleekly built Zero.

Looking up, though, Yoshi could see no connection whatsoever between these enormous birds of steel and those derisive little sketches. Nor did anyone around her appear to expect the American planes to fall apart or burst into flames. Most were already scurrying towards basements, schools and air raid dugouts.

"Why didn't the radar catch them?" the young woman with the suitcase was asking. "I didn't hear any sirens, did you? And where is the nearest shelter around here, anyway?"

She made both inquiries blandly, as though asking the location of the nearest tram stop. Yoshi didn't answer. She was thinking again of Hana, asleep on her settee. Her blue book lying unread on her chest . . .

As she touched the ring again she saw that her hands were shaking. But she reslung her satchel over her shoulder and propped the Fuji back up to remount.

"I need to get home," she said. Above, the silver flock wove almost playfully through the Army's searchlights and the first bright snaps of anti-aircraft fire.

Satako was covering her ears against the noise now. "Are you crazy?" she shrieked. "We need to get to a shelter."

The shelter, Yoshi thought, with a renewed surge of panic. Was there any way that Hana would—without Yoshi there to prompt her—get up, put on her own bomb hood and her boots, and remove herself to the backyard? *If I'm going to die, let me die in my own home . . .*

But even before that thought was finished it had started: small bright sticks were tumbling from the bomb bay doors. Igniting midair, they still seemed little more than flaming matchsticks, drifting onto the half-asleep city. So many small starbursts reflected back by steel bellies. The suitcase-woman even admired them at first: "*Ahhhh. De mo, kiree nee!* So pretty!"

Then a nearby house went up in gold and crimson, adding its crackle to the engines' screams. Squinting, Yoshi made out black figures fleeing through the front doorway. By then the adjacent houses were alight as well.

The largest blaze was several meters away down the street, but the air around them clogged immediately with smoke. It burned through Yoshi's nostrils, thickening her thoughts, making her body feel sluggish. *Think,* she ordered herself. *Move.*

The flickering road was filled with frantic people rushing back and forth, calling out for family members or friends. Yoshi watched as two men—one very old, one a teenager who must still be too young for the Army—beat frantically at their smoking roof with wet branches. But they quickly abandoned the effort, racing first towards one crowded shelter and then—turned away—towards another in the next yard.

Scanning the block, Yoshi realized she could only make out one shelter that still seemed to be letting people in. It was across the street and a bit down, near where the night-soil man had abandoned his terrified horse. As she strained to focus three middle-aged matrons ran towards it, towing four panicked children by the hand.

"Over there," she cried, pulling on Satako's wool sleeve. "We need to go where they're going. Get on." She nodded towards the handlebars—they had a better chance of beating others to the spot if they rode. Satako coughed, then nodded and began to clamber back on. But a sudden change—like a chord-shift in the nightmarish chorus—caused them both to glance skyward again.

It hardly seemed possible but there were new planes now, swooping through the still-falling incendiaries. They, too, were impossibly large; nothing at all like Masa's clever little diagrams. For all their bulk, though, they moved with weightless precision through the searchlights that scraped against the dark sky. Yoshi imagined a school of huge, shining whales, deftly evading a fisherman's net. Then they too opened their huge bellies, and gave birth.

The second round of bombs fell in much larger bundles, slow as dreams, bright as water. But when they landed—everywhere at once, it seemed; in a single smoking heartbeat—the ground shook. It felt like an earthquake. In an instant, both girls were on the ground. Yoshi felt her teeth slam together. She tasted blood and soot and, after that, something astringent. Pain burst out somewhere towards the back of her jawline. Hand to cheek, she disengaged herself from Satako and tried to scramble back to her feet. Then another cluster landed, this one directly across the street from them. She dropped back down, clutched at her ears.

This device, however, didn't explode right away. Watching it through the small shaking space between her elbows, Yoshi saw it spit something out; a thick wet jet. The air seemed silent in that moment; a hushed space of ash, the stench of gasoline and dread. After an absurdly long wait it came: a booming flash, a roar so deafening that the screaming world went quiet.

Yoshi's ears were still ringing when the heat hit her with the force of a flung boulder. It blistered her lips, sealed her eyes shut like melted wax. *I'm dead,* she thought. But she wasn't, she was still standing. Prying her eyelids apart with trembling fingers, she blinked: everything in her vision was in flames. As her sight adjusted she heard a loud crack, a hiss, a groan—as though some huge beast had just been dealt its death blow. The house directly behind them leaned drunkenly to the right, then collapsed, releasing a fountain-like spray of burning embers. A woman screamed, and Yoshi turned to see the suitcase-lady. Her fur collar and hair were in flames, which quickly spread to the synthetic stockings on her legs. Yoshi's last sight of her was like something she'd seen once in an old painting in a temple; something their teacher had called a "Hell Scroll." Entitled *The Gods of Heavenly Punishment,* it showed a huge, fiery demon consuming tiny people limb by limb, surrounded by more flames and staggering, fire-limned figures.

By now, everyone was running, colliding, falling. Satako was nearly knocked over by two children. Both were naked but for their fire hoods, which themselves had burst into flames on the small heads. Hard on their heels came their mother, a *furoshiki*-wrapped bundle held aloft, another strapped haphazardly onto her back. The second bundle was smoking, but as Yoshi stepped back it burst into flame as well. She saw a small arm stir: it was an infant. By the time she'd managed to make her cracked lips move, the group had disappeared into the smoke. Another woman emerged, pausing briefly to help her child when it stumbled—only, apparently, to realize it wasn't hers at all. The discovery made her drop the little girl's hand: *"Let go!"* she screamed. *"Let go of me! I'm not your mother!"*

Disengaging herself roughly, the woman dashed back towards the flames while the girl—no more than four or five—stared after her. Yoshi stepped towards her, her own hand extended. The child leapt as though Yoshi had brandished a sword. "You're not my mama," she hissed. "Where is my mama?" And she backed away into the smoke.

Sickened and sweating, Yoshi squinted back towards the shelter she'd seen. All she saw there was another wall of flame. A figure leaped jerkily against it, arms stretched skyward in pain or supplication. Behind it the night-soil man's horse screamed and pitched over, pulling its cart into charred pieces. "It *hurts*," she heard. "It *hurts . . .*"

For a single bizarre instant she thought the cry had come from the dying animal. Then she realized it was behind her. Whirling around, Yoshi saw Satako flailing her arms. The bundle on her back, her leather satchel, coat and skirt, even the wet braid she'd been chewing—they were all on fire.

She will die, was Yoshi's first thought. It came with an odd calmness; as though this were some inevitable, even uninteresting event. But then—to her own astonishment—she was suddenly in action. Stripping off Satako's wool coat, shaking it out like a blanket. She pushed her friend to the ground and rolled her, left-right-left-right, as they'd been taught. She stilled the jerking limbs. As the heat rose between them she felt the skin on her own chest start to blister. "Keep still, Sa-*chan*. Keep *still.*"

And then, miraculously, the flames between their bodies were gone. There was just Satako, sobbing weakly, and Yoshi panting and crying and coughing. There was just the smoke and the flames, the roaring heat behind them.

Panting heavily, Yoshi unpeeled the singed jacket from Satako's motionless form. Her friend's round face was half blistered, half completely charred. One braid was gone—singed off; the other smoking slightly, still tied in its bedraggled red hair tie. One eye was swollen shut. The other stared vacantly, its pupil dilated in shock.

"It hurts," she said, barely whispering.

"Can you stand?" Yoshi asked her. Then—because it didn't matter, she *had* to stand—"I'll help you. Here." She linked her arm through her friend's, pulling her heavily to her feet as to their right another building heaved a huge groan and collapsed. A laundry drying rack, its wooden limbs etched in flame, came flying at them at high speed. As Yoshi ducked, another item from the house dropped at their feet. At first Yoshi thought it was a beam of some sort, patched with red paint. Only as she stepped over it did Yoshi see that it was a body, charred and lifeless, wrapped in a scrap of torn red silk.

She forced herself to look away. With stinging eyes she surveyed Asakusa *doori*, fully a-dance in flames. It seemed hopeless; before her gaze another curving firewall sprang up, and then another. No matter what Nihon Hoso Kyokai or the *Mainichi* said, the Americans were not unskilled. They were as precise as any scroll artist, painting these fiery blossoms across the city.

The road was now littered with the corpses of entire families; men, women, babies. A dog or two. Behind her a woman wept on the road, arms extended helplessly towards her collapsed, fire-engulfted house. At first Yoshi didn't know what she was gesturing towards, but when she turned she heard a child's voice, crying out weakly from amid the roaring flames: *"Okaa-san. Okaa-san; tetsudate . . ."* Mother. Help me.

"I'm a terrible mother," the woman wailed. "I can't go there. I can't. I'm a terrible mother . . . I can't go in."

Turning away, Yoshi had a brief vision of giving up. Of just lying down where she stood. Sleeping or dying there. Then she noticed something she hadn't earlier: that the crowd was moving, more or less, in one direction. Staggering, jostling, falling down and only sometimes recovering, the blackened stream of people inched its way towards the west. Where could they be going?

The answer dawned like a mythical breath of fresh air: They were heading towards the river.

Of course.

"The Sumida," she shouted.

Satako just stared blankly, so Yoshi repeated it, mostly just to hear the words in her own ears: "Back to the river. The park. Lean on me."

Satako inclined her blackened head, and Yoshi took this as consent. She cast another glance behind them, barely remembering what she was looking for until she saw it: Satako's bicycle. It had somehow landed across the street, and now leaned against a stump that an hour earlier had been a lamppost. It was upside down, perched improbably on its broad seat the way Yoshi and Satako would sometimes position their tricycles as children together. Working the pedals with small hands, they'd watch with a strange sense of power as the trike wheels spun emptily against the air.

But both the pedals on the Fuji were gone, the basket a twisted mass of blackened wire. And the bike's tires were not just not spinning. They were actually melting, stretching and dripping from their bent frames like strings of thick black toffee. For some reason, the sight unleashed the first real stab of grief Yoshi had felt during this surreal and horrifying evening. A sob rose in her throat. Swallowing it back down, she tightened her grip on Sa-*chan*'s shoulders, gently pulling her in the direction of the crowd.

"Come on," she told her. "We'll have to walk."

WHEN SHE CAME to she was stiff, the burns and blisters left by the eternal and blistering night masked by a greater and duller ache. She recognized the cold wet weight pulling her shoulder as her school-bag, which somehow had remained slung over her chest. At first, she could not feel her hands. But as she tightened and flexed her fingers she realized that they were clasped onto a set of cold and wet shoulders.

Yoshi's first thought was that the shoulders were Hana's. She often woke to find herself bent like this, groggily shaking her mother awake before fully waking herself. What she couldn't understand, though, was why Hana was so very *wet*. And for that matter, why Yoshi herself was: for it came to her suddenly that she was drenched. Drenched, and thirsty. Cold, too. Her teeth were chattering.

Opening her eyes, she peered blearily at the gray light of the dawn; at the smoking riverbanks, the twisted black stubs of tree trunks. She began to remember then: the walls of fire. The streams of screaming, burnt people. Dazedly, she looked down to see that it was not Hana but Satako in her arms. Satako; propped against a charred piece of driftwood that Yoshi had found floating by them in the night. Satako, not moving. Was she unconscious? Or was she just sleeping? *Sleep would be good,* Yoshi thought hazily. *Sleep will help her heal* . . . Gingerly loosening one hand, Yoshi patted her chest unthinkingly, checking that the ring, too, had survived the night, and noting just as dispassionately that it had.

BIT BY BIT, it came back—the hours before she'd blacked out. By that time the planes had finally left, their thunderous roar replaced by crackling flames and the moaning of the wounded. But Satako had remained unconscious for almost an hour after Yoshi dragged her into the water. She was heavier than Yoshi, and to try to ease her weight Yoshi had finally held her just at the water's surface, half-floating. Even so, her blistered limbs had ached to the point where she contemplated letting go; of simply letting her friend drift beneath the debris-filled waves as she'd seen so many others do this past night, both here in the Sumida and in a smaller canal they'd passed before reaching it. The canal water, it had seemed, was too shallow to absorb the scorching heat. The one Yoshi had seen had actually been boiling, blistered corpses bubbling to the surface and then sinking down to the depths.

The Sumida itself was cooler. But amid the frantic press of the crowd Yoshi had seen children stumble, and seen some of them fall. She'd seen the fallen ones pressed under by the fleeing feet of people who may have been siblings, neighbors, perhaps even parents. Those who weren't pushed beneath the waves found themselves pushed far out into it. If they couldn't swim they sought to survive by climbing onto those in front of them; stepping on hips, backs, shoulders, even heads. The wet crowd had turned into a kind of sinking human staircase; a collective desperate surge towards the burning air.

Yoshi and Satako had survived only because they'd somehow ended up on the crowd's outskirts, where the press was weaker and where Yoshi had more control. She'd still had to wrest their way from the crowd. But she was nevertheless able to find them both spots where they risked neither being run over nor pushed under. For what had felt like a hellish eternity she'd half held Satako against her shoulder, her arm going numb with the effort. When something caught against her back Yoshi assumed it was another charred corpse; but when she turned to push it off she saw that it was something much more useful: a charred piece of wood. Heaving and groaning with the effort, she'd somehow propped Sa-*chan* atop it. Then she'd passed out herself.

"Sa-*chan*," she whispered now. Her friend didn't answer.

Yoshi thought of Hana again. She had to get out of the river; had to get them both out. She looked down, numbly trying to find her bearings. Satako's wristwatch had stopped somewhere after two o'clock—which must have been when they first ran into the water.

Now, though, the sun was weakly climbing in the east. From its trickle of light Yoshi made out a landscape as bleak and unfamiliar as the moon.

Gone were the manicured greens and curving footpaths of the park she'd known so well as a child. Every centimeter of the Sumida's riverbanks were now covered—as everything, it seemed, was now covered—by a smoldering carpet of ash and rubble. Gone, too, were the trees that had lined the river's banks for as long as Yoshi could remember. In the few cases where they hadn't been utterly destroyed they'd been transformed into charred black posts that sent smoke curling into the tired gray sky, pointless smoke signals in the wake of the apocalypse.

As for the Sumida itself, the only thing familiar about it was its width and its gentle curve towards the cooling horizon. Even the water looked less like water than a sluggish morass of trash and detritus, interspersed with endless bumping, blackened bodies. Those who, like Yoshi, had survived the night stood slumped in or near the water, their ash-streaked faces reflecting little more than numb disbelief. In some cases it was hard to tell who'd lived and who had died: Yoshi's gaze landed briefly on one woman sitting half-in, half-out of the lapping tide, a toddler cradled in her arms. As she watched, a filthy wave pushed the woman's unprotesting form on her side, so that her mouth was now covered by water. The movement dislodged the child, which—with equal passivity— washed out gently into the river's slow current. As it floated closer Yoshi saw it had no face at all. It had been completely burned away.

Her mouth tasted burnt, brackish, and she remembered that when she and Satako first waded away from the crowd in the river they'd both knelt and drank straight from the filthy water itself, the agony of their scorched mouths and throats outweighing the logic that told them that this, of course, had to be unsafe. Satako had vomited soon after.

Looking back down at her friend, Yoshi took a deep breath.

"Satako," she murmured, "Satako-*chan*. Can you hear me?"

Her voice sounded strange in her ears, which were at once almost deaf and yet still ringing with the roaring of planes. Something else felt strange as well, though it took a moment to label it: *silence*. In fifteen years in Tokyo, she'd never heard such chilling quiet. Even with the curfews and censors and blackout orders, the Tokyo of yesterday had been a place of continual noise; a place of temple bells and shouting salesmen; of barking dogs and honking cars. Of squealing children out on school trips, and blaring military marches. Now, all Yoshi heard was the quiet crackles of the fire's aftermath. That, and low moans of the wounded and dying.

She shook Satako again. Gently at first; then harder. After two or three shakes her friend still wasn't moving, and Yoshi forced back a sour surge of panic. "*Satako!*" she said, more loudly now. "Sa-*chan!* You have to wake up. We have to go home . . ."

But her movements did nothing more than push both the wood and her friend's still form further into the river. Shutting her eyes, Yoshi took a deep breath. For a moment there was a panicked impulse to stay that way: to slosh back to the shoreline and from there back to Honjo, her eyes sealed tight and yesterday's world alive in her head. But then she thought of Hana. *You have to protect yourself.*

Taking a ragged breath, she opened her eyes and pulled the wet wool shoulder up a little, so that Satako's right eye—undamaged but for the fact that all its lashes had singed off—came into view. The eye was her friend's eye: open. The color and sheen of buttered toast. It wasn't blinking.

"Satako," Yoshi whispered again, "you must wake up. We have to get home."

But Satako didn't move, and then somehow Yoshi was shouting at her: "We have to *go!* I have to go home and find my mother! Don't you *understand?*"

Nearby, an old woman in a singed housedress waist-deep in the water looked up vacantly. A blackbird startled from its smoking perch.

"It isn't fair," Yoshi screamed on. "It isn't *fair* to just—to just lie here like this. It's selfish. I saved you. Now you have to help me save Mama!"

Her arms shaking, she began pulling her friend's stiff form towards the shoreline, sobbing with each waterlogged step; pushing charred bits of wood and flesh and things that could have been either out of their way as she went. When the old woman reached a hand towards her, either to help or to ask for help, Yoshi ignored her. *Maybe I'm still sleeping,* she thought. *Maybe I just have to wake up and then wake up Mama, like I do every night . . .* Tremblingly, she pinched her right wrist with her free hand. She could barely feel the pain, but it was there. Nothing changed.

"*Oi.* Miss. Miss. Is she alive?"

A man's voice this time; it came from behind her. Turning, Yoshi saw the charred roof tiles, building fragments, burnt boughs, bodies, floating limbs—and amid them all a dory, painted vivid aqua blue. The boat was rowed by an old man with a face as black as coal and singed spots around his chin and gnarled ears. He also appeared—at least from the waist up—to be naked. The sight was so incongruous that at first Yoshi was tempted to take it as proof that she was, indeed, still sleeping.

The old man cocked his head. "Hey there!" he called again. "I said, is your friend alive or not?"

Yoshi hesitated for a moment, her parched mouth working wordlessly before she heard a small voice, her own voice, reply: "No."

The man studied her. He had a cigarette clamped between his blackened lips, and for an instant this struck her as the strangest part of all: the thought that anyone could ever, deliberately, allow flame or spark or smoke near them again.

"I'm going that way," he shouted, pointing downriver. "Towards the nearest hospital, if it's still standing. I can take you with me. But just you. Just those who are still breathing. I can't do anything for the dead."

"But . . ." Yoshi stared down at Satako's stiff, motionless form. "What do I—"

The man shrugged. "The Army'll be by in a day or so. They'll pick her up with all the others, lay her out for identification. You can come back then and claim her."

"Can't I at least bring her to the shore?"

"Won't do either of you much good, will it?" he asked. "You've barely moved her ten centimeters. The ten minutes it takes you to get her to the land and get back could be the difference between someone else's life and death."

Yoshi swallowed, the sensation knife-like against the smoke-swollen flesh of her throat. Then she shook her head. The man shrugged, then lifted his oars again, muttering something to himself. The blue boat nosed forward.

As she watched it, Yoshi felt her knees threaten to buckle. "Wait," she choked. "Wait. I'll—I'm coming."

The man stopped again. "Well, be quick about it. Lots of other folk need rides."

"*Hai.*"

Squeezing her eyes shut, Yoshi formed a silent prayer in her head: *nam amidabutsu nam amidabutsu nam amidabutsu . . .* She didn't know what the words meant, but it was what her father chanted when he made his morning offerings to their ancestors. Her father . . . where was her father? . . . *Nam amidabutsu nam amidabutsu . . .* She gave Sa-*chan*'s shoulders one last squeeze . . . *Nam amidabutsu nam amidabutsu . . .* She forced her stiff fists to unclench . . . *nam amidabutsu nam amidabutsu . . .*

"That's a good girl," the man said.

Yoshi opened her eyes. She saw the charred piece of driftwood floating off on its own downcurrent, Sa-*chan*'s motionless form following behind. She turned towards the dinghy quickly, but not before seeing the stricken flutter of a red ribbon, trailing away beneath the blackened water.

VII. *Buffalo, New York*

MARCH 1945

THE BABY SLEPT LIKE AN ANGEL. HE HAD FROM THE START, FROM the first night he came back from the hospital. Having been warned that the first year was hell on earth, Lacy had gone to check on him at least five or six times. Each time she had found him in the exact same position he was in now: flat on his back, arms flung out like wings. Rosebud lips releasing soft, even breaths. If he woke with gas or soiling he never howled or screamed. He'd just summon her with tentative, gentle whimpers. Most nights, though, he remained motionless, as he was right now.

When Lacy told people about little Cammy's sleeping they always acted as though she'd won some sort of prize. "Oh, you're so *lucky*," the woman behind her at the grocer's said yesterday. "Mine both woke up every two hours from birth until they were practically, well, *twenty*." And of course Lacy nodded, jostling her son on her hip even though (as usual) he showed no need of being soothed. She didn't tell the woman the truth because she knew it sounded crazy: that she sometimes *wished* the baby would wake up. Even with a nightmare. She was awake so often herself, and it got so lonely it scared her. Sometimes his silence just scared her more; to the point that she checked on him more often than she would have had he been a squaller. On some nights she even slept with him in her bed, her hand palm-down on his small chest. Monitoring its staccato heartbeat, its baby-blowfish rise and fall.

She reached out, gently tracing the toddler's warm, round cheek with her thumb. His lashes—as pale as a ghost's—twitched slightly at the disturbance, but otherwise it was as though she didn't exist. There was a faint twinge of disappointment, mixed in with raw adoration she sometimes felt as painfully as an open wound. Once again, she'd have to wait for morning to seep through the blackout curtains before she'd see those blue eyes—Cam's blue eyes—open.

Shivering a little, Lacy retied her robe around her waist and made her way over to the bedroom desk. Settling into the creaky arm-chair, she picked up the pen the bank had given her when she went in to buy her latest round of war bonds (*Keep your money fighting!* it read). *Well,* she wrote, *he's still sleeping, the most ridiculously calm and wonderful sleep you could ever imagine a "terrible two-year-old" having. I guess you must have given that to him—you always could sleep like a champion. Remember that time I drew a hamburger on your forehead while you slept and you didn't even notice until you went to shave?*

I hope you're still able to do that—get your rest, I mean. I'm sure you need it. Wherever you are.

She paused, chewing on her pen tip and staring at that last line. *Wherever.* The word had become a sort of prayer by this point, imply-ing logically as it did that Cam had to be *somewhere.* That he was still at least on the planet. Lacy had never been much good at praying for things—she'd always been the kind of person who preferred to sim-ply get to it, get them *done.* But this was one thing that was miserably, hopelessly beyond her scope of ability. She couldn't wish him into being alive, into coming back. She could only pray. *Wherever.*

She went on. *For my part, I'm having another "one of those nights." I was able to sleep a little between eleven and two, but at two-thirty I was as wide awake as though one of your dad's roosters had crowed in my ear, and I haven't been able to fall back asleep since. Which was a shame: for some reason I'd been dreaming about banana splits. I had a huge one right in front of me, with chocolate sauce and everything. My first thought when I woke up was,* What a waste—I should have at least slept long enough to eat it, *because there hasn't been a banana in sight anywhere since at least last June. Oh well. Hopefully by the time you get back the war will be over and we'll have all of our old treats back again. I can't wait.*

Well, I suppose I should try to sleep again. Mike's on home leave this week, and he's offered to take me to lunch. I don't want to fall asleep in the car like I did last time! I will send him your love, as you know you have mine.

She signed the note as she always signed them, *Love forever, your Lacy Lady,* spritzed it with perfume and tucked it into an envelope addressed with the APO box she'd been using for the last three years. Had it still been '42 or '43 she would have walked it to the post office in a few hours, pushing Cammy in his avocado-green Bilt-Rite. Back then handing the letters to a real person had seemed to increase the odds that they'd find their way into Cam's hands. By last year, though, it'd gotten to the point that she couldn't stand the pitying looks she got from the staff. These days she just walked them to the postbox.

Checking the clock (4 a.m.), she licked a stamp and affixed it to the upper right-hand corner, setting the letter atop some bills. Then she settled herself beneath her duvet, opened her bedstand drawer and pulled out the letter.

It was one of Cam's longer ones, as well as his last. By the date of it—April 17, 1942—she now knew that he'd written it the night before he took off, though when she first got it she'd spent hours studying the censor's stamp, trying to figure out where it had come from. Now she smoothed it on her lap, making sure that her fingers were clean and that no new folds or creases marked its yellowing surface or Cam's schoolboyish, block-letter handwriting.

Dear Lace (it began), *Well, I guess this is it—my last night aboard this floating hunk of metal. The mission starts tomorrow, and while I can't tell you anything about it in writing you can be sure I'm doing just that in my head, just as I am always telling you about everything here in my head. It's kind of strange, but I've kind of started to feel as though nothing really happens until I do that . . .*

She stopped here as she always did, shutting her eyes. Concentrating. As though she were a radio antenna tuning in to those long-promised thoughts. As usual, though, nothing came, and so she read on through the rest of it: the parts about Bob Eberly, and not swearing, and bringing her green ring back. All lines she knew now by heart if not better (by soul?), though she preferred to read them over and hear them in Cam's own soft, gentle voice in her head. When she was done she folded the flimsy sheet again and tucked it back in the envelope. After checking her lips for traces of lipstick, she planted a kiss on the address. Then she replaced it in the drawer, on top of the telegram that had arrived later that same day.

Having just read Cam's letter she had thought it was a joke at first. She'd even turned it over to scan the back, looking for some crackpot's postscript on the back: *Ha-ha, just kidding!* But of course, the back was blank. There were only those two lines in the front, curt, official and unpunctuated: *I regret to inform you report received states your husband Lieutenant Cameron Richards missing in action in the Pacific area since 19 April. If further details or other information of the status are received you will be promptly notified.*

There had been no further word from the adjunct general, though Lacy had received a surprise visit from James Doolittle himself. He'd strode up to her door in August, pausing just perceptibly at the sight of her belly, which by then was the size of a beach ball. As he introduced himself she thought she heard a faint catch to his voice. But he recovered himself quickly enough, congratulating her on the baby, telling her what a hero Cam was. Assuring her every effort was being made to find him.

That was three years ago. Then again, she reminded herself, three years was really nothing in the scheme of things. Her own parents would have been married for nearly thirty, come this August. Cam's parents for even longer than that; though how mild-mannered Martha Richards managed to stay tied to that man was something Lacy never understood.

Wherever, she murmured to herself one more time. Then she settled into the vast emptiness of her mattress to watch the dark sky brighten through the window.

WHEN SHE WOKE again it was to what felt like an indoor cold front and the cool blue gaze of her son. Cammy had pulled himself up in his crib and was just standing there watching her, with an intent, serious expression that looked so much like his father's that even this early in the morning it tightened her throat.

"How long have you been up?" she asked him, rubbing her arms to rid them of goosebumps.

"Bird," he replied, pointing at the Audubon Society print of a cardinal she kept over her bed. "Fly."

"You're too good, sweetie," she told him, groggily swinging her legs over the bed's edge. "It's not normal."

"Tweet," he said. "Tweet, tweet, tweet."

After changing his diaper she rinsed it carefully in the bathroom sink, wringing it out and hanging it to dry. Like everything else, flannel was in short supply these days. Lacy only had what she did because the assistant manager at Penney's had a crush on her and put a bolt aside whenever one came in.

After dressing Cammy in a fresh diaper and his little Sunday suit, Lacy pulled on a dress she'd made from old curtains last year and one of Cam's old cardigans for extra warmth. Then she carried her son downstairs for his morning cream of wheat. As she waved the spoon in the air she made the airplane sounds he loved, puttering the food to a landing between his pink lips.

"Mo," he crowed, waving his arms. "Mo, Mama."

"You want more? Well, all right then. *Vroooooommmmmm* . . . here it comes!"

His face glowed with pleasure at the game. He was as easygoing an eater as he was a sleeper; the only thing he'd ever refused was an experimental recipe she'd found in the *Pointers for Meat Points* pamphlet, which she'd tried on a piece of beef so dubious it hadn't even been given a grade but was all the butcher had left that day. The dish came out bluish and gloppy, and when Lacy put it on Cammy's tray he looked up in such consternation she doubled over with laughter, wishing for the first time in a long while that she had a working camera.

Other than that, he ate everything put in front of him. No fuss, no tantrums. He'd never once tossed a bowl of peas onto the floor. It almost made Lacy feel guilty sometimes; particularly when she saw what a hard time some of her friends had feeding their children, and with food choices so limited now, too.

"It was bad enough before rationing," her old college roommate Janice lamented the last time they'd met for lunch. "But now? You might as well forget all about it. They hate cottage cheese. They won't touch margarine. They eat up the sugar ration in two days." She shook her head. "Sometimes you really don't know how lucky you are, Lacy Richards."

"Lucky?" Lacy said, laughing.

Janice colored slightly and looked away. Her own husband was in the Coast Guard and was rarely farther away than Long Island Sound, watching for enemy submarines. He called home nearly every night, and managed to get home at least two weekends a month.

"Well, you know what I mean," Janice said. "And just imagine how proud of him Cam is going to be when he finally gets home!"

Lacy had imagined this, though usually it was in spite of herself. She'd laid down strict rules on the topic of dreaming: she would neither fear the worst nor hope for the best, lest the gods punish her more than they already had.

"Well, I'm proud of him right now," she said, and gave Cammy a kiss that left a splotchy red wreath across his little freckle-spattered nose. "Do you suppose they have ice cream today?"

"MO?" CAMMY ASKED now as she took his dishes to the sink. It was less a demand than a mild question.

"You can have more when you get to Grandma's," she told him over her shoulder.

"Gamma," he said happily. "Soupy."

"That's right, Soupy," she said, smiling at the way he associated "Gamma's house" with the dog, rather than with his own grandfather. Not, of course, that she blamed him.

Dishes done and dried, she set out breakfast for their sleeping tenant (toast, an egg and an empty cup; he'd help himself to the coffee) and bundled Cammy into his sweater and jacket. Opening the Bilt-Rite, she settled him into it and pulled her coat from the hook, noting as she did two more places where the cuffs had frayed. She felt like a hobo whenever she wore it in public, but with the temperatures still in the twenties some days and Cammy growing so fast, she really had no choice: most of her clothing points went for him. In her last letter to Cam she'd reminded him—only half joking—of his promise that they'd move to California when he got back. *It's just too goddamn cold here,* she'd written. *Or maybe I really was one of Manet's Tahitian ladies in a past life. Either way, I'm ready for some sun.*

When she reached the postbox she picked her son up again and let him toss the mail into the slot. It was an act that always made him shriek with joy and wonder, though she'd never quite figured out why. "That one's for Daddy," she said, as he tossed last night's letter down the chute. "Let's hope it gets to him soon."

"Dah-dee," he sang back, with a lack of comprehension that she expected but which broke her heart nonetheless. She shut her eyes for a moment, hugging him so tightly that he squealed and pushed her away.

"*Yowza*, Mama!" he said indignantly.

Lacy hid her smile in the fat fold of his neck. She had no idea where he'd picked that one up, but he seemed to be using it for *Ow* at the moment.

When she reached the Richardses' house she heard Soupy's hoarse, gruff bark, which he used to greet more or less everyone now that he was mostly blind and deaf. The bark was followed by Cameron Senior's curt "Now *stop* that, Mister Soup! Bad, bad dog!" As usual, the words had no effect.

Letting herself in, Lacy wheeled the Bilt-Rite into the front hallway and parked it by the closet, pushing the brake pedal down so it wouldn't roll on the uneven floor and pushing Soupy's hopeful nose away from her legs. Hanging her coat on the closet door, she picked Cammy up and began the painstaking process of unbuttoning his jacket, and then his cardigan. She was four buttons down the latter when she heard footsteps behind her and a strong male hand landed on her shoulder.

"Lemme take a look at my nephew," boomed a familiar male voice.

Lacy shut her eyes, bracing herself. It didn't matter, of course, because when she turned around the first thing she saw was her husband, beaming and arms outstretched. Her heart leapt before she could rope it back down. Because of course, it wasn't Cam.

"Mike," she said, trying to keep her voice steady, "it's so good to see you back home safely."

Though three years separated them, Cam and his younger brother looked alike enough to pass as twins. Now, grinning

Cam's grin, Mike Richards pulled both his sister-in-law and his nephew into his arms. As his lips brushed her cheek Lacy gave herself one moment (just one!) to pretend Cam really *had* come home. She breathed in his familiar scent (they both used Bay Rum and Brillo), felt his strong chest against her breasts and his muscled biceps against her shoulder blades. She closed her eyes, and thought *Oh, baby. How I've missed you* . . .

Then, as always, she stopped herself and stepped back. As she did Cam's uniform lost its wings and Air Corps patches and became that of the 7th Infantry Division. His features changed too; the face becoming slightly rounder, the eyes closer together. The nose just a little bit smaller and straighter. As usual, though, that one forbidden, fleeting moment had left its mark. Lacy's knees were watery; her pulse racing.

Thankfully, Mike—busy taking Cammy from her—didn't seem to notice. "Coffee?" he asked, his voice muffled by the baby's fine white-blond hair.

"Oh, I'd love some."

She trailed after him into the kitchen, letting him pour her a cup of Maxwell House before leading the way into the living room. Watching them from behind, she tried not to think about how perfect they looked together: a boy and his father. An apple off the old tree. On his last home leave—nearly a year ago—Mike had taken the two of them to lunch at Woolworth's. All the waitresses made eyes at him and coy comments about how the "little angel" was going to grow up looking just like his daddy. Mike just sat there beaming, as though it was all just another one of his jokes. Lacy, however, had finally had to excuse herself. She'd hurried to the ladies' room and squatted down in a stall, where she'd wept—out of frustration, out of sadness. Out of that ever-present ache that was Cam's impossible yet unarguable absence. If she was really honest with herself, there was also a tiny twinge of guilt; as though she really *had* slept with her brother-in-law. Which of course she hadn't, though it was something she'd let herself imagine once or twice. Very briefly. Before catching herself, and bringing down both her nightgown's hem and her mental blackout curtain.

It didn't help much that after she'd pulled herself together enough for a cigarette and a quick powder touch-up, one of the waitresses came in and gave her an envious smile. "My," she'd said, vigorously wiping down the sink, "you must be so happy today, having your handsome man back alive and unharmed. You're very lucky."

Lucky, she thought now. Why the hell did everyone insist on saying that? *Lucky* this. *Lucky* that. If this was luck, she'd prefer to take her chances with black cats and broken mirrors.

"He's gotten so big!" Mike was saying, swinging his nephew into the air so high that the baby's soft head just skimmed the doorjamb and Lacy fought back an instinctive yelp of warning.

As usual, the Richardses' living room was almost as cold as outside: her in-laws took the government mandate on fuel conservation to heart. Though they'd sealed the windows and taped the corners and lit a big fire in the fireplace, Lacy still wished she'd left her sweater on.

"Seriously," said Mike, seating himself in a nearby rocker and bouncing her son on his knee, "what are you feeding this guy?"

Lacy smiled, inching herself down the sofa towards the fire. "Everything but the kitchen sink, on most days. He's gaining almost two pounds a month."

"That's a Richards for you," boomed Cameron Senior, from his usual post in the Sleepy Hollow. "Good, solid stock, our men. We grow 'em right."

"Jeez, Dad," groaned Mike, "you make us sound like your cattle."

Lacy suppressed an urge to roll her eyes. As far as Cameron Senior was concerned, both his sons had been immaculately conceived—on their father's side. Although, Lacy thought (leaning back and taking a sip of the coffee—it needed sugar, but of course there was none), that was also interesting. Especially considering the tales Cam had shared that showed just how little regard his father had always had for him as a child.

Cam always told them the same way; in that calm, slow voice that held not a hint of rancor or recrimination. For Lacy's part, though, some of the stories made her so furious she'd have punched the old goat right now if she could have. For instance, there was the time Cameron Senior took his sons to a 4-H sheepshearing contest at the county fair. At one point a young ewe had struggled so hard that its owner's shears slipped, causing blood to spurt everywhere. Mike—four at the time—had been unfazed by the accident, even laughing at the sight of a "red sheep." But seven-year-old Cam was sick with worry. In his painful, stuttering way—which was always worse when he was distressed—he asked his father what would happen to the wounded animal.

"What did he say?" Lacy asked him.

Cam had paused for a moment. "He said," he said finally, "that what wasn't good for the loom would go into the stew pot. He looked right in my eyes as he said it, too."

It had taken her a moment to fully register what that must have felt like. "Surely—surely he didn't mean for it to sound like that?"

"Like what?"

"Well, that you were no good to anyone?"

"Sure he did," Cam said simply. "But it didn't matter."

"How on earth could that not matter?!"

Cam smiled at her indignation. "As he was talking I was looking over his shoulder, and it was then that I saw my first airplane in the sky. I think it was a Boeing Model 15. I remember thinking that I wanted to be in that plane. Just get pulled right up into it. Like I was a saved soul being sucked into the Rapture."

"I still don't see how that made it all right."

"It's kind of hard to explain," he said slowly. "It was sort of as if from that moment on, I had a purpose of my own. I wanted to work with planes. Maybe even fly them. Knowing that made everything easier—like I had an escape waiting."

All that had changed, of course. Cam's Distinguished Flying Cross and Purple Heart—neither of which he knew he'd received— hung front and center above the Richardses' fireplace mantel, flanking a framed note from FDR himself. *Your son is a hero*, it stated. *His actions and bravery have given solace to a nation that was sorely in need of hope. Whatever else may happen, please know that both he and you have my most sincere and heartfelt thanks, for life.*

"How was your night, darling?" Martha Richards was asking, searching Lacy's face with some concern. Her expression implied that she'd asked this question at least once already.

"What?" asked Lacy absently. "Oh, I'm sorry. Fine, thanks, Mom."

"We worry about you, you know. All the way over there, alone."

"I'm not alone. After all, we have Dr. Sullivan. I'm sure he'd put up a fierce fight if there was an intruder."

She laughed to show that this was a joke. Dr. Sullivan was close to seventy. Moreover, with all the wounded coming home from the war he was at the hospital most nights. These days, they barely passed each other in the hallway.

But Mrs. Richards just shook her head. Both she and Lacy's mother had been against her taking in a tenant, even an old one. They'd wanted her and Cammy to move in with one of them. But Lacy had known from the start that when Cam came home, it had to be to the house they'd bought together, with her and Cammy inside. The only way she could think of to keep the payments up, at least without taking on a war job, was to turn Cammy's nursery into a rental. So she'd moved Cammy in with her, put an ad in the *Gazette* and rejected the first two (young, male, military and single) applicants. After which the good doctor appeared. Much to her relief.

"Well," said Mrs. Richards, sighing, "at least the news from Japan is encouraging."

"Is it?"

Lacy gazed into her coffee cup. Between the lack of sleep and seeing Mike again she felt oddly brittle—as though even a hint of sympathy might cause her to break down in tears. It was a dangerous state to be in. Especially in this house, which was filled with Cam's pictures and model planes and bronzed baby booties. Then again, maybe she was just hungry. Only now did she realize that she'd forgotten her own breakfast again.

"You haven't heard?" barked Cameron Senior as Lacy reached for a piece of the dry, date-sweetened war-cake Mrs. Richards had put out. "Don't you ever turn on that expensive radio we gave you?"

"Of course I do," Lacy told him, though in fact she rarely did these days. In the beginning she'd hardly ever had it off. But as the months then years went by with no word on Cam's whereabouts, the news started to feel less like enlightenment than punishment. Tales of the ruthlessness of Japan's soldiers; of Bataan death marches and *banzai* charges could keep her awake for whole nights. As Cammy started talking she tuned in even less, afraid that someday a bulletin would break in with the worst news possible, just as his son grew old enough to understand it.

"Well, I don't see how you could've missed this one," said Cameron Senior, looking disgusted—as though her ignorance confirmed all his worst fears about her. "It's absolutely tremendous. Sounds like we bombed the hell out of Tokyo Friday night."

"We—as in America?"

"Sure did." Mike had Cammy slung over one shoulder, the baby's legs kicking gleefully, his diapered rump butting Mike's ear like a lumpy twill-covered pillow. "Hundreds of those Flying Fortresses. Flying in real low this time, I hear."

"Did they do a lot of damage?" Doolittle had told her during his visit that after his raid he'd fully expected to be court-martialed—both for losing so many planes and for failing to inflict any real destruction on his targets. Instead, he was given the National Medal of Honor and promoted two ranks, to brigadier general.

"And then some." Mike whistled, improvising a falling-bomb sound that made Cammy laugh and pound his uncle's back in delight. "Sixteen square miles of Tokyo, turned to toast. They don't know the casualty count yet, of course. But it's got to be in the thousands, if not tens of thousands. Probably worse even than Dresden."

"Worse than Dresden," repeated Lacy, staring into the fire. She was finally starting to warm up a bit, but a cold finger of fear crept up through her chest. "You don't think . . ."

Mike shook his head. "I've asked around with the folks who would know. It's pretty much confirmed that all American prisoners from the raid were shipped back to China."

"Oh." Lacy felt herself go slightly limp in relief. A month or so after Cam's disappearance she'd opened the morning paper to a picture of three other raiders blindfolded, in Tokyo, where they'd been brought to be tried for "crimes against humanity." Two of the men—a gunner and another pilot—were sentenced to death, but Lacy didn't recognize either name. She did recognize the one given a life sentence as Cam's copilot and best friend in the Corps. A tall, wisecracking Jew they all called Midge for some reason, but whose real name was Joshua Friedman. He'd been at their wedding: a strapping, handsome man with flashing eyes and a whip-quick tongue. He'd roasted Cam royally during his toast.

But the man in the grainy picture had looked nothing like that. Stooped and emaciated, he had a thick, tangled beard that made him look like some sort of wild bushman. After reading the article over twice, Lacy barely made it to the bathroom before heaving up the contents of her breakfast—something she was sure she would have done even if she hadn't been in the throes of morning sickness at the time.

For a minute or so no one spoke. The fire crackled congenially. "Well," Lacy said at last, "I guess it's good if we hit them hard. Maybe it'll end the war sooner."

"From your lips to the Lord's ears," said Mrs. Richards fervently. She stood up to clear away the coffee things. "Where are you two planning to go today, by the way?"

"I thought Niagara," said Mike, setting Cammy down on the rug and pulling a toy tank from one of his pockets for him. "Lunch in Little Italy first—there's a new place, supposed to be good. Then I'd like to pick up some souvenir stuff and postcards for the boys back at base. And of course wherever Lacy needs to go to do her shopping and whatnot. Maybe we'll even fit in a movie."

"A movie?" Lacy laughed. "All I'd do is fall asleep again." Though what she really wanted to avoid were the previews. The last film she'd seen had opened with an animated bomber, exploding violently in midair. The fact that it was an Axis bomber (the clip was an ad for war bonds) didn't make a whit of difference: for the next two hours, while Joan Fontaine roamed the moors and explored the ghostly recesses of Thornfield Hall, all Lacy saw was that one plane. Exploding. *Boom.*

"Will you go by way of Broadway?" her mother-in-law was asking. "I need to have someone drop off some fat at the butcher's."

"I'm sure we can," said Lacy, guiltily remembering her own stack of cans. Like everyone else she knew, she saved her waste fats from cooking. But she'd been far less conscientious than Mrs. Richards about getting it back to the butcher, who then shipped it off somewhere for conversion into glycerin. The glycerin could apparently be used in bombs and bullets, though whenever Lacy tried to picture this she ended up imagining a fleet of Boeings releasing a greasy shower of bacon fat onto confused civilians.

"Of course," said Mike, setting Cammy on the floor, standing up and pulling his service cap from his back pocket. "Everything's possible with a C-sticker."

"Now don't go driving around like a maniac," said Cameron Senior darkly. "That extra ration's supposed to be for official Army business."

"It *is* Army business, Dad," said Mike, clapping his father on the shoulder. "I've got the wife of a war hero here. Just doing my part."

WITH CAMMY AND Mrs. Richards waving from the front porch, they pulled out in the Richardses' old Ford Tudor Touring Sedan—a car in which Lacy had spent many nights necking and wrestling with Cam in the overstuffed backseat, back in the days when they were still courting. As they cruised down Sycamore Street she crossed her legs, flushing faintly at the memory. She caught Mike watching her sidelong. It made her feel oddly self-conscious.

"What? Do I really look that bad?"

"You look swell," he smiled. "Just like always."

"You're a liar," she said tartly; but she pulled out her compact to check her face. "I look like something the cat dragged in. Something dead. And maybe chewed on." She shivered.

Mike laughed; a high, strident laugh that sounded nothing like Cam's, though his face wore the same wide grin. Lacy blinked back into her compact, pretending to powder her temple while she dabbed at damp eyes.

"You still thinking of moving West when Cam finally gets back?"

"Absolutely." She smiled weakly. "California, here we come."

"The beach would suit you." He winked. "In fact, if you'd let me make a poster of you in a swimsuit this week—just for practice, say—I could bring it back to the boys. For morale, you know. We'd ace our next battle for sure."

"Stop it," she laughed. "You're such a stinker." Though she didn't mean it. Mike had always been much cockier than his brother, and once this had annoyed Lacy to no end. Now, though, she found she appreciated it. She appreciated anyone who gave her reason to laugh.

They'd reached Paisano's Butchery, and Mike hopped out and grabbed his mother's bag of greasy cans from the back. "Be right back," he said. And then: "Oh, I almost forgot. I've got something for you."

He patted his jacket pocket, then pulled out a paper-wrapped package. "Here," he said, handing it to her. "Thought this might come in handy."

"What is it?"

He winked. "Open it and see."

He jogged towards the shop, pausing to confirm the placard posted on the door (*Official Fat-Collecting Station Here*) before pushing it open and entering. Mystified, Lacy pulled off the string and peeled the paper off. Inside was a banner about the size of a table runner. When she unrolled it she found three cartoon faces in a row—Hitler's, Mussolini's and Hirohito's. The two Europeans looked unkempt but human, staring gravely off into the distance. Hirohito, by contrast, looked like a bucktoothed monkey, leering straight back in her face. A headline hovering over all three read *Keep 'Em Where They Belong—In the* Can!

"So what is it?" she asked, as Mike slid back into the driver's seat.

"You hang it over the toilet," Mike told her. "I figured it would be good motivation when you start to potty-train Cammy. Help teach him aim."

Lacy found herself laughing again. "You're awful. You know that?"

He grinned, starting the car. "Just doing my job as an uncle. Oh. And one more thing." Reaching inside his jacket, he pulled a small booklet from his breast pocket. "This one is just for you."

Taking it in her hand, Lacy saw that it was a book of clothing ration tickets. She looked up at him again. "Why are you giving me this?"

He shrugged. "I'm shipping out again in a couple of weeks. From the sound of things I'm not going to need any fancy suits where we're going."

Lacy hesitated, fingering the thin gray paper and thinking about her hobo trenchcoat. "Are you really sure you don't need them?"

He shook his head, his eyes firmly on the road ahead. "And I know Cam wouldn't want his wife walking around in a coat that had holes in its elbows."

"Oh," she said, folding her arms in embarrassment. "So you noticed those."

"I've learned to pay attention to things. It's something they teach you in Counter-Intelligence."

"When did you join Counter-Intelligence?" she asked, surprised.

He shrugged. "I took a test back in Hawaii. Believe it or not, they let me in."

"Well, congratulations, I guess." She hesitated, then slipped the ration book into her purse. "And thank you," she said, and touched his arm lightly.

They rumbled along the near-empty road, each lost in their thoughts. Lacy was remembering the first time Cam brought her home. How intent she'd been—for the first time ever, really—on making a good first impression on a beau's mother and father. Mike was only fifteen then, and while Cam was the oldest and had already made Dean's List at U of Buffalo, it was Mike who had the glow and confidence of favorite child.

By that point Lacy knew all about Cam's struggle with his stutter. How it had shaped his relationship with both his parents, keeping his father disdainfully at bay and his mother too close for comfort. Martha Richards had endlessly coddled and hounded her eldest, a helpless effort to—if not cure him—at least protect him from the cruel unstuttering masses. Knowing all this, Lacy had sat down in the Richardses' dining room that first night fully expecting to dislike them all—including Mike, who she blamed for Cameron Senior's biased affections. She'd expected to sit next to Cam, as his redeemer and defender, and was dismayed to find herself seated next to Mike instead.

Over the course of the meal, though, the boy she got to know was nothing at all like she'd expected. For one thing, Mike obviously worshipped his older brother. He defended Cam from several of Cameron Senior's slighting remarks throughout the meal, and told Lacy what a catch she'd landed herself. Later on, when Cam stepped out with Cameron Senior to check something on the car's engine and Mrs. Richards had bustled off to make coffee, he pulled Lacy aside in the living room.

"Listen," he said. "This will probably sound sappy, but I want you to know how happy you've made my big brother. And that means a lot to me."

He looked so serious as he said this, and so much like Cam himself, that Lacy was left momentarily speechless. "Well," she laughed self-consciously, when she found her voice again, "I haven't done anything for him that he hasn't done for me."

Mike shook his head. "Oh yes you have." He hesitated, then lowered his voice. "The thing is, most girls before you either made him too nervous to ask out, or else dropped him like a hot potato once they heard the way he talked. Having you means the world to him. I can tell. It's given him a whole new view on things."

Lacy had just smiled and said something dismissive. Watching them all later, though, it struck her that Mike was right: Cam *had* changed. He held himself with more confidence, spoke with greater assurance. He met people's gaze straight on when he talked to them, and if he disagreed with something or someone—even Cameron Senior—he didn't hesitate to say so. In short, he seemed to see himself

more as Lacy saw him now; as kind and smart and good. Not to mention handsome. The fact that Mike understood this impressed her.

Mike's loyalty impressed her too. In the years after that dinner
he followed Cam to the University of Buffalo, taking the same
major, pledging the same fraternity and even joining the track
team, though he wasn't very good at it. He tried to follow Cam
to the Army Air Corps as well, though he washed out of flight
school after two months. Undaunted, he'd offered his services to
the Army, where he'd aced basic and distinguished himself training in the Mojave.

The Mojave maneuvers were ahead of a planned posting in
Africa, but at the last minute his division was reassigned to the
Pacific. Some men in his regiment met this change with trepida-
tion, since it meant they'd be fighting the Japs head-on. But Mike
was thrilled. *I feel like God sent me a message,* he wrote Lacy on a postcard from Honalulu, where they'd been sent to practice amphibi-
ous warfare. *It's like he's saying* Your brother's alive, and I'm sending
you to go find him.

"When are you shipping out again?" she asked him, picking at
a stray thread on her coat cuff (which of course just unraveled it
further).

"A week or so. Rumor has it we're going to one of the Ryukyu
Islands. Okinawa."

"*Oh-kee-now-wa.*" Lacy shuddered. "Will that be like that other
one—where was it. Saipan?" She'd heard just one report of that
battle before switching off the Philco. Even so, it cost her two nights'
sleep.

"Who knows? Maybe it'll be easier."

"From your lips to the Lord's ears. Like your mom always says."

He shook his head. "Amen to that, sister."

———

THEY DROVE ON in silence until they reached the Rainbow Bridge, stopping as they always did on the New York side to take in the breathless drop, the tumbling foam and spray.

"It really is something," said Mike, as they leaned over the railing together. "All that water. And yet that's really all it is, isn't it. Just water. So what is it, do you suppose, that makes people come just to see it?"

Lacy shook her head. "I don't know. Something about the size of it, I guess. And the height. Whatever it is, it sure works." She laughed. "It worked on us, anyway." Like most Buffalo newlyweds, she and Cam had honeymooned here: one exorbitant but luxurious weekend at the General Brock (*The Only Fireproof Hotel in the City*, the brochure boasted). Their first day they spent naked in the king-size bed in their suite, doing things Lacy hadn't known were possible, much less so fully pleasurable. The next day they made it as far as the lounge downstairs, where they drank coffee, played checkers and read (Cam *The Keys to the Kingdom*, Lacy *Lady Chatterley's Lover*, which someone had recommended as good honeymoon material). That had more or less been the extent of their stay, though the day of their departure they darted out just long enough to buy souvenir paperweights for their families. Little glass worlds of tiny, tumbling falls and bobbing barrels. Tiny signs saying *Niagra Is for Lovers*. When people asked how their trip was later, where they'd gone and what they'd seen, they just looked at each other and laughed. Looking back on it later, though, it almost seemed to Lacy that they'd known what was coming down the pipes. That in just two months, without warning, their own small, snug world would splinter, and they'd be flung an ocean's width apart.

Squinting down at the churning depths now, Lacy's tired eyes started playing tricks upon her, carving fleeting shapes into the foam: a leaping rabbit. A white bird. A woman plunging from a cliff. For a moment it struck her just how easy it would be to go that route—to just push herself over. It was one way to escape it; the sleepless nights and uncertainty. The endless scrabbles for points and bad food. The midnight letters that she sometimes thought she wrote less out of faith than out of habit. The aching silence from the adjunct general's office. The sweet torture of looking into her son's face and seeing Cam there, but also not there.

But then she thought of Cammy, of his bright eyes and easy smile. His soft warm neck; its salt-sweet smell when she picked him up in the morning and buried her face there. And she knew, as she'd always known, that none of it really mattered. Nothing mattered but her baby—keeping him near her. Keeping him safe.

She felt a hand on her shoulder. "Lace?"

Turning around, she found herself staring straight into Mike's blue eyes. For once, they were entirely devoid of humor.

"Here," he said, and it was only after she'd taken his handkerchief that she realized she was finally crying for real.

Laughing a little, she wiped her eyes and handed it back to him. "I'm sorry," she said. "It's just . . ."

Mike held his hand up. "Please. You're family." He blinked himself a few times, wiped his eyes on his uniform sleeve. Then he put the handkerchief back in his pocket and looked back out at the freezing water.

"We'll have to throw him a hell of a party when he gets back, you know," he said, his voice tight. "Drinks, dancing. Maybe a band. The works."

"Sure we will." Lacy clasped her hands together over the railing, her left hand absently toying with the right's middle finger, the one where her mother's ring had been. "Maybe even a cake. A real one, if there's enough sugar by then. And ice cream. He loves cake and ice cream."

"Sounds like a plan."

They stood there a little longer. Then Mike looked at his watch. "Holy moley," he said. "It's nearly two. Let's go eat."

THAT NIGHT SHE wrote Cam his daily note on a postcard, one with a big picture of the General Brock on the front (*Remember this place?*). She wrote him about Mike and Okinawa, and the party they were planning for him, with a band and dancing and ice cream and cake. When she was finished, the card stamped and addressed and placed in the "to mail" pile on the desk, she lay on her back on her big empty bed and slowly unfolded the letter.

The mission starts tomorrow, and while I can't tell you anything about it in writing you can be sure I'm doing just that in my head, just as I am always telling you about everything here in my head . . .

She paused, shutting her eyes and silencing her thoughts. Straining to pick up a snatch of . . . something. Anything. Even a single, stuttered word. She listened so hard that her body trembled with the effort.

But all she heard was the quiet thudding of her own pulse, and behind that the measured whisper of Cammy's breath, drawing in, letting out. Drawing in, letting out. Keeping time with the vanishing night.

VIII. *Tokyo, Japan*

NOVEMBER 1945

HE AWOKE TO A SHARP-EDGED DARKNESS THAT WAS VIBRATING with such vengeance that at first he thought they must somehow be under fire; perhaps even hit. Perhaps they were spiraling towards an explosive and smoke-embellished death. Part of him even welcomed this possibility. But his overwhelming instinct, it seemed, still favored survival, because even as he thought *What the hell, it's probably for the best*, Billy Reynolds was already checking his seatbelt buckle; was already leaning forward and covering his head with his hands as the dour air hostess had shown them at takeoff. He shut his eyes and waited, his thin chest squeezed to his knees and his dry lips pursed in silent prayer—not to God nor the sun goddess nor his father nor Daniel (*oh Christ Daniel*) but to Anything Else he hadn't yet alienated or soiled or destroyed.

And then a hand was on his shoulder, and a woman's voice in his ear that at first sounded startlingly like his old high school English teacher back in New Hope. Saying: *Sir. Sir. Are you all right?*

Do you need a comfort sack? And he uncurled from himself and looked up, blinking into not Miss O'Leary's lined and bespectacled face but the wide blue eyes of the air hostess who'd replaced the dour one in Saipan. Her name tag read *Hannah Cortlandt*, and she had apple-pink cheeks and blond hair. She looked like a model for Coca-Cola advertisements.

"Sir?" she asked him again.

Billy rubbed his eyes with the heels of his hands, then looked around groggily. The other passengers—most of them fresh recruits like him—were all sitting upright in their stiff leather-padded seats. A few were eying him with open curiosity.

"Where are we?" he asked her. His mouth tasted like drying glue, with an after-tang of sour mash.

"Just beginning our descent into Tokyo," she said. "We had a little turbulence there for a bit. Headwinds off the Bay, I'll expect. You seemed to sleep through most of it."

"I did?" It hadn't felt like sleep. It had felt exactly like what his brain had told him it was: a plummeting fall towards a well-deserved end. Then again, it had been so long since he'd really, truly slept that perhaps he no longer knew what it felt like.

"Not surprising, really. That's pretty powerful stuff you've got there."

Hannah Cortlandt reached out, her white hand headed directly between his legs. Billy pulled back in alarm until he realized her target was the Four Roses bottle he'd been gripping there, between his knees. She held it aloft to the slanting sunlight that was pushing through the small, square windows, as though to illustrate its complete emptiness to the whole plane.

"You all right now, Lieutenant?" she asked, pointedly. "Can I get you anything before we land?"

"I don't suppose I could get another bourbon," he said, only half joking; and as she rolled her bright blue eyes his heart gave a sort of painful hiccup at the thought of finally landing in Tokyo. It was something he'd managed—with the booze's help—to keep himself from imagining over the past thirty hours. Would the MP's be waiting for him when he got out, right there on the tarmac? Or would they wait until he got to headquarters and descend on him there, in front of his fellow recruits and superiors and maybe even (God forbid) MacArthur himself? How long did it take, anyway, for a telegram to cross the sea and reach the various officers required to act on it? Longer than two days? Perhaps even a week? Yes, certainly a week. He had a week at least . . .

The hostess was studying him, her tongue a pink bud tucked in the corner of her mouth. Her eyes softened a little as they met his.

"You know," she said, "my son has red hair. Three years old. His isn't quite as bright as yours. More of a strawberry blondish. But still."

Billy gave a stiff smile, his standard response to such comments, which he got perhaps six times a week. In his twenty-two years, one thing he had learned was that his hair color made him a kind of communal property across the world. It was a ticket to a club at once exotic and profoundly familiar, and one to which only people with that elusive gene could lay claim. Though growing up in Tokyo his coloring had made him feel less like a club member than the center-ring act at a circus. Japanese caregivers, playmates, even policemen would stop short and finger his curls with a breathless *eeeeeeehhh?* of disbelief. Asking how many carrots he ate and whether his blood was orange too and (as he got older) whether *all* his hair was that color.

At the moment, however, it was clear that the air hostess had made the observation in the Western sense. Warmly: *Well aren't you special.* Rather than comforting him, though, this only made the pain well again. He felt it pooling, hot and liquid, behind his eyes.

"Seriously, though," he said, hearing his voice crack, beyond caring, "you don't happen to have any Anacin or anything, do you? And maybe some club soda? Or just water?"

"Well, technically we're not supposed to give anything out at any point during the approach," she said; then hesitated. "But I dare say you're looking pretty green around the gills there. Let me see what I can do."

As she bustled back down the aisle he stifled the urge to curl back into himself in despair. *One step at a time,* he told himself. *Maybe he hasn't even reported you yet. Maybe he won't report you at all . . .* Though he didn't really believe that. Of course Daniel would report him. From the look on his face two days earlier, Billy had known without a doubt that he would. Hell, had any of their superior officers been awake at 3 a.m. Saturday night he would have been turned in within the hour. He wouldn't even *be* here.

He turned and pressed his face against the cool, coated glass of the little plane's windowpane. The cloud cover was thick and unusually low-lying; he couldn't yet see what the city had become. On the other side of the pane, beads of condensation formed and rolled towards the plane's tailfins, like neatly aligned tears. *Don't cry,* he told himself, for the billionth time in his life. And then—perhaps for the millionth time in two days: *Christ almighty. What the fuck was I thinking.*

Though of course, he knew the answer to that one: he hadn't. He hadn't been thinking at all.

HE AND DANIEL McNEIL had first met three months earlier at the Army Intelligence Program at U Michigan. It was a program Billy's father had learned of through one of his Army Air Force contacts during Billy's second year at Princeton. At that point conscription had seemed inevitable, and Anton Reynolds was at the low ebb of his highly erratic financial fortunes. "It's the solution, William," he had said excitedly—or what for him passed as excited (tone very slightly higher, cadence marginally faster). "After Basic Training and intensive language training you'll enter as a service intelligence officer. Just as I did when I served in Switzerland. You'd like that, wouldn't you?"

What, Billy remembered thinking, *if I just said "no"? That we both know that I am nothing like you at all, and at this point I have no desire to change?*

Nor was he entirely sure that the city he'd largely grown up in even existed anymore. Going by the headlines, at least, it seemed as if that mild and tea-scented nexus of art and manners had gone through some vicious alchemical process, one that had turned it into a bastion of mass hysteria and mindless violence. Even after Pearl Harbor happened the headlines he saw stunned him—JAPS RAPE, LOOT IN NANKING; JAPS BEHEAD BURMESE WOMEN AND CHILDREN; JAPS MARCH ALLIED PRISONERS TO THEIR DEATHS IN BATAAN. When it came right down to it, he wasn't at all sure he even *wanted* to go back to that Japan. At least, not before the war ended.

As usual, though, he had said none of this. He said instead what came closest to what his father wanted to hear. "It sounds all right," he said, "but do you really think they'll take me? I mean, I've forgotten an awful lot of the language."

"Surely you are joking," said his father, in a tone belying no humor whatsoever. "You grew up there. And they're reluctant to take too many of the Nissei fellows from the camps, with the war still going on. In fact, my connection told me that some of the fellows they've taken have had no Japanese experience at all."

Well that's just swell, Billy thought, picturing a class full of football bullies who drank Pabst and dated girls with names like "Bunny" and who probably pictured Japan as some sort of cross between hell and *The Mikado.*

Despite his reservations, though, he'd applied that same week, sailing through the screening process without breaking a sweat. After the Christmas break at Princeton he'd departed for Ann Arbor, there to begin a course that was—apart from the living misery of Basic Training that would follow—ten times as vigorous as any program he'd ever lived through. They studied eight hours straight of Japanese daily. There were only Japanese papers and books in the program library. Japanese was to be spoken at all times, even in the dorms. Billy found himself one of a dozen-odd BIJ's, or "Born in Japans"; sons of missionaries, diplomats and expatriated businessmen who like him had either been born or partly raised in Japan. Like them, he found the language classes challenging but grounding. He had missed the language of the nation of his birth; its breathy sibilances and staccato cadences. And resuming his study of *kanji* characters was a bit like reuniting with old friends, which was a welcome feeling indeed, since at Michigan (as at Princeton and at New Hope High School and St. John's in Tokyo before that) he didn't seem to be making many.

That is, not until Daniel.

Billy had been sitting at Metzger's, the old German restaurant he patronized whenever a check came from his parents. He was consuming a plateful of Sauerbraten and studying *kanji* so intently that he didn't notice when the table next to his was taken. He did notice, however, when a sweating stein of beer (Belgian; the German stuff had long been banned) appeared in front of his notebook.

"Take a break, Looie," a deep voice boomed. "You're gonna strain your eyeballs."

Billy's first reaction was annoyance, as it usually was when anyone he didn't know spoke to him. *Can't he see I'm* working? But when he looked up that sentiment dissolved in a heartbeat. Or rather, a flurry of them, each one short and painfully sharp.

For staring back at him was a pair of the greenest eyes he'd ever seen. The speaker's nose was fine and pointed; his hair wavy and black. His lips were startlingly red. In fact, were it not for the Errol Flynnesque cleft in his chin, the guy would have made a rather fetching girl. But the truth was (and it was a hidden truth; a dark and libelous and criminal truth, if one Billy had long come to miserable terms with) if the guy *had* been a girl Billy wouldn't have been this excited. Or terrified.

"What do you know about it?" he said cautiously, hardly daring to move.

The other man—a first lieutenant, he saw from his epaulettes—smiled, exposing teeth as white as his mouth was red. "With the Japanese program, I see," he said, pointing at Billy's notebook.

"That's right. You?"

"German. Seems to make sense in this setting." He indicated his own book, which Billy saw was the first volume of *Der Zauberberg.* "And I guess you do too, given that together we form two-thirds of the Axis." He held up his own beer. *"Sieg Heil."*

And though the familiar warning signals were now screaming, silent sirens in his head (*Don't do this to yourself; don't set yourself up*), Billy found himself joining the toast. *He's a new friend,* he reassured himself. *That's all. And God only knows I need one.*

But of course, once again he was lying.

THE NEXT TWO months, in those few hours they weren't immersed in their respective programs, Billy Reynolds and Daniel McNeil spent almost exclusively together. They saw *Shadow of a Doubt* and *Frankenstein Meets the Wolfman* sitting side by side but never touching, Billy nevertheless feeling the warmth of Daniel's leg through his slacks and clenching his thigh muscles so tightly he once gave himself a charley horse. They wandered the art collection at Alumni

Hall, Billy with the new Contax his parents had given him and Daniel his sketch pad, rerendering Grecian nymphs and Egyptian cat gods. Daniel sketched Billy in profile once—a darkened silhouette standing by a windswept Homer seascape, in which he looked not gawky and freakish but almost handsome. Billy wanted desperately to take pictures of Daniel as well, if only to give him some rendition, some shape of the man to touch and hold, if only in miniature and in private. But it somehow felt too intimate, too forward, and in the end he never summoned the courage to ask.

They listened to Satie, who was Billy's favorite composer, and to Brahms, who happened to be Daniel's. They discussed photography and painting and took long walks along the Huron, smoking and tossing stones at the water. Beyond their complementary interests, they found they shared something else: childhoods in what was now enemy territory (Daniel's mother was Bavarian by birth). They also shared disapproving fathers.

"What does your pop disapprove of?" Billy asked, when it came up. "The women you date?"

It was one of several supposedly innocent questions he'd asked throughout that month. *Got a girl somewhere? Read much Wilde? Like Rachmaninoff?* All delivered lightly but with carefully hidden focus. Watching Daniel's face as he responded for some hint—even the slightest of movements—indicating his deeper inclinations. And in each of these answers (*Haven't found one I like yet; God yes, brilliantly funny; Well, I'm not wild about the rhinestones*) Billy, foolishly, thought he'd at last found hope.

"I'm not really his sort of guy," Daniel said this time. "He's more of a man's man. Likes to fight, likes to curse, has never shed a tear in his whole manly life."

"What, do you cry more than him?" Billy had asked, carefully. He'd cried all the time growing up. When they'd left Japan, in fact, he'd cried for two days, and not just because he'd had to leave his dog Rassy behind there. He'd cried because he somehow knew already that however odd and apart he felt in Tokyo, he would be a hundredfold more so in Pennsylvania. His mother had been all sympathy; knocking on the cabin door with a pot of hot tea and clean hankies. His father treated his grief with the same chill blend of bafflement and disgust with which he treated most of his son's so-called "peculiarities." Now, though, Daniel just laughed.

"Hell yeah," he said easily, "I cry like a girl sometimes."

"Me too," said Billy. And to his mortification realized he was almost in tears himself again, if only in relief.

Another time they talked about Japan, and Germany, and about a quarter-bottle of Four Roses into the evening Daniel leaned back against his well-stocked bookcase. He turned to look at Billy, and with real pain shading his unmarred face said: "I have to tell you, Will, I still don't understand it. What the hell happens to a place, do you think? When one thing or person goes bad, and instead of leaving them behind the whole damn country just goes after them, lock, stock and barrel?"

And what Billy thought was: *I love you*, because he realized—quite suddenly and simply—that it was true.

But he didn't put it into words; of course he didn't. He shrugged, and downed another shot. "Hell if I know, Dan," he said.

Even then, though, and even through his cool and carefully "normal" act, came the increasingly clamorous chords of his own conscience. The latter was whispering to him, over and over: *what are you doing. What the fuck are you doing.* Because of course he knew where this was all leading, both from past disastrous alliances and his imagination's terrifying meanderings. And yet, he couldn't seem to stop. It was like being forced to watch himself in a Passion play, knowing full well he'd end up nailed to his own perverse cross.

Then the war ended, with a suicide in a bunker and two bewilderingly brutal atomic clouds. There was confusion for a while, but in the end they both got assignments, to vanquished Tokyo and broken Berlin. Billy left first, and on the last night before his train (to San Francisco, to a Pan Am plane headed for Alaska, Hawaii, Taiwan, Saipan and what seemed like every urban center in the Pacific before reaching Japan) Daniel invited him for farewell drinks at Metzger's.

They met at their usual table and toasted two-thirds of the Axis, as had become their custom. New to their station, the waiter lifted a brow. Daniel just laughed and said, "Oh, don't look so sour, puss. We know the war is over. In fact, my boy here's shipping off to To-ki-yo tomorrow, to work with Arthur MacArthur Mac*Arthur*."

On the third *Arthur* he saluted, which resulted not only in a round of laughs but a bottle of Four Roses and two Cuban cigars sent over by the bartender as a token of appreciation for the uniformed men who'd won the war and would now win the peace. And though Billy knew that he shouldn't, he not only drank the bourbon with Daniel but moved across the table to sit next to him, on the pretense of needing a light. Then he stayed there, his legs close to Daniel's but not touching, his thigh muscles so tight they quivered. His nostrils picking up the scent of Daniel's hair cream, his sweetly pungent breath, his cologne.

They matched one another shot for shot, puff for puff, joke for bad, stupid joke in increasingly slurring Japanese and German, until finally the room was spinning and Billy's heart was pounding, not so much from all the booze but over the tender, child-like flush creeping up Daniel's white neck and onto his white cheeks. Billy wanted to touch it, that tiny tongue of pure color, but he knew better at that point and so he didn't let himself.

Meeting and misinterpreting his gaze, Daniel grinned his white grin, puffed out a smoke ring and said: "Well, Looie, I'll sure miss our beer hall nights together." He clapped his hand on Billy's shoulder.

"Me too," Billy said, his entire body pulsing with the connection. Cautiously—his heart knocking so hard he half thought it would give him away—he pressed his fingers against Daniel's fine-haired white hands.

And—here was the thing, here was the miracle—Daniel let him. Even as Billy blinked, held his breath, counting: *One . . . two . . . three . . .* his friend's warm hand *still* remained there, lightly curled against his starched dress shirt, fingers pressing down just slightly; *five . . . six . . . seven . . .*

What Billy felt then could only be described as jubilation, though the realization—that they were sitting together, and touching, and *holding* that touch—was so overwhelming that for a moment the room swooped out of focus. Billy put his hand to his forehead, blinking, and only then did he feel the warmth of Dan's hand leave his skin.

"You OK, buddy?" Daniel asked, pulling back. "You're looking a little toasted."

He was peering at Billy and smiling slightly, as though they were sharing some private boys-only joke. *And are we?* Billy wondered, trying to focus his gaze. By now hope was spreading and warming through him in a way that was far more delicious and dangerous than whiskey. But as he turned to look again at Daniel's glistening green eyes, it seemed to him—it really *seemed* to him—that Daniel felt the exact same thing he was feeling.

Don't trust it, said the small voice assigned to keeping his cover. But like a train whistle racing into an unknown distance, it came from farther and farther away.

"I am a little toasted," he admitted, ducking his head. Momentarily forgetting that it was a cigar and not a cigarette, he took a hefty drag on his smoke. Then he doubled over, coughing his head off.

"Oh man. Very smooth," Daniel laughed, whacking him on the back a few times before reaching for his water glass. Billy savored that sensation too: that firm, warm *slap* of his friend's hand on his back. At once painful and so long awaited.

"I think I need some air," he said tightly, when he'd found his voice again.

"Good idea. Let's bring this."

Winking in a way that made Billy's pulse skip another beat, Daniel picked up the Four Roses and hefted it in a silent toast. And though the last thing Billy needed was more liquor, he nodded.

"You're a genius, McNeil-*san.* You know that, right?"

"Hell yeah, *Herr* Reynolds."

And then, to Billy's utter shock and terror and delight, Daniel flung his arm right over his shoulder and hugged him close. In this way they half staggered, half swaggered to the street, accompanied by a scattering of patriotic applause and a few *Bon Voyage, boys!*

OUTSIDE, THEY LEANED unsteadily against the rain-dampened brick wall, lighting and splitting their last Lucky. For the first few puffs they just stood there, breath and smoke mingling whitely against the crisp October air. Then Daniel said: "You ready, brother?" and took another slug of booze before passing Billy the bottle.

"For what?" Billy accepted, thinking at first that he'd just feign a drink but thinking the better of it when he touched the bottle's mouth to his own, and felt it, still warm and damp from its last set of lips. "For Tokyo? Yeah."

But what he was really thinking was *no.* Because it struck him, as if for the first time, that not only would the city of his childhood not be there but Daniel—this man right here, whom he loved—wouldn't either.

So he drank, and then drank again. Strangely enough, it seemed to clear his head rather than cloud it further. The world stopped spinning, and when he fixed his gaze on Daniel's face Daniel returned it. This time Billy didn't look away or down as he usually did. He kept it there, steady, open, without reserve. He drank in the man's beauty, his pale skin and aquiline nose, his glistening lips. He tried, with only his eyesight, to take and preserve in memory the photograph he hadn't been brave enough to take over these past three months. And Daniel stared right back.

"What are you looking at?" he asked at last, not dismissively or suspiciously or jokingly as he might have, but seriously, his own gaze not wavering either.

Billy swallowed, his pulse roaring in his ears. "You," he said.

"Oh yeah? What do you see?"

"I see . . ."

Christ. Billy licked his lips.

And then before he knew what he was doing; before he even had time to *think* of what he was doing, much less prevent it—he was leaning towards that face, towards those glass-green eyes and red, red lips, registering even as he did so the shift in Daniel's expression with the hyper-clear focus of a driver spinning into a car crash. Registering the sleek black head turning away in shock, so that Billy's sad little kiss landed not on Daniel's lips but on his Old Spice-scented, shadow-stubbled cheek.

"*Fuck*, Will," said Daniel, in a tone that at first seemed to express more wonderment than dismay.

There was an instant of total silence, and Billy—barely breathing—dared to hope that maybe he'd been right after all. Then he watched Daniel's eyes flit towards the street and widen, and Billy followed his gaze to see that an elderly man and a woman had paused in their evening stroll and were staring at them both.

When he turned back he felt something hitting his arm with

bruising force, and it was Daniel, shoving him away, hard. With the other hand he was clapping his cheek as though it had been branded. *"Fuck,* Will," he said again, his tone turning ugly.

"Dan . . ." Billy said, reaching out for him instinctually. But Daniel only struck his hand away again even harder.

"Don't *touch* me," he snarled. "What the *fuck,* Will."

Billy felt the pit of his stomach drop away as sharply as though he'd just stepped into a deep ravine. *Oh god.* He pulled back against the wall, trying to make himself small; small enough to disappear, waves of self-loathing washing over him like filthy water. "I'm sorry," he whispered. "I'm so sorry, Dan . . ."

But this only seemed to infuriate Daniel more. "I mean, *what* the *fuck,*" he went on, in that same strangled, high-pitched voice. Behind him, the couple clasped arms and hurried away. "Are you really telling me this? That all this time you've been a fucking *homo?* A *pervert?* And they're about to send you over there—to goddamn Japan—to *represent* us?"

He was breathing hard now. The flush that had so catastrophically entranced Billy earlier saturated his entire face, making him look frenzied and abruptly crass. His lips were wet, flicking spittle into the air; his eyes bloodshot with rage. The sight was enough to not only quell Billy's ardor but make him feel nauseous. Then afraid. The fear was a new and more instinctive fear than he'd felt earlier; a fear not that he'd blow his cover (because of course he'd just done that) but that Daniel would attack him. As his own father so often pointed out, Billy wasn't of much use in a fight. Even after four years of *karate* classes in Yokohama.

"For fuck's sake, you pervert," Daniel went on. "Sodomy is a court-martial offense. You know that?"

"Danny," Billy said, thinking *Oh god, I'm going to be sick . . .*

"Don't you use my name. Don't use it ever again. To you, I'm

Lieutenant McNeil, and you just keep your fucking distance. Until tomorrow, at least. Because—because—you know what? Because I'm going to report you. First thing in the fucking morning."

"Please," Billy whispered. "Dan . . . I mean, Lieutenant . . ."

But by that point Daniel had turned on his heel and staggered away, leaving Billy staring after him, the bourbon clenched in his fist and the bile climbing his throat. He kept his eyes on the retreating back, silently, beseeching. But Daniel didn't turn back. He didn't even pause.

WHAT THE FUCK *was I thinking?* Billy thought again now, and looked once more at his fellow recruits. He searched their tired and apprehensive faces for signs that they'd heard the miserable story of his downfall; of his public denouncement as a deviant. But if they had they gave no signal, or else gave one so close to their normal disinterest in him that the two were virtually indistinguishable.

"Here you go, sir."

The hostess had returned, carrying two white tablets and a pink Dixie cup full of tepid water. "I doubt it'll do much good," she added, with a motherly wink. "But you can take stronger measures once we land."

Grimacing, Billy gulped down both the pills and the warmish liquid, crumbling the Dixie cup into a damp pink ball in his hand. He looked out the window, but while the cloud cover had now cleared the plane was banking in a way that obscured his view. What, he wondered wearily, would he see when they banked left again? The MPs? No, not yet. But what about the city itself? For an instant, and for the first time, he felt a tingle of fear. What if he didn't recognize *anything?* What if Curtis LeMay—with the help of Billy's own father, who had built the Japanese-style building LeMay's men had practiced on—had bombed the place right out of existence?

Don't worry about it, he told himself bitterly. *You're not staying here long anyway. It probably won't even affect you.*

And yet twenty minutes later, when he was standing at the plane's entrance and staring out over what had once been the serene green vista of the Tokyo Golf Club (another institution his father had built), Billy found that he was, in fact, very affected. That, in fact, he was stunned. For what he saw was not the burgeoning, erratic skyline of his memory, but a sweeping and charcoal-black plain, one studded with standing buildings, empty but for rubble piles and makeshift shanties.

"Good Lord," he murmured, too horrified to even take the shot he'd set his new Contax up for. "Good God," he whispered.

It was as if they had landed on the moon.

"Sir," said Hannah Cortlandt. "Is there something else I can help you with? Did you leave something in the cabin?"

She looked meaningfully over his shoulder, and for one paralyzed moment Billy thought maternal affection had abruptly heated up and she was now propositioning him. Then he realized that there were eight other officers right behind them, and she was simply asking him to get a move on.

"No," he'd said, picking up his duffel. "It's all here."

THE DEVASTATION WAS even clearer on the drive over to the Pyle. Gone were Shinjuku's hustling alleyways and second-floor girly joints. Gone the Ginza's glittering hostess bars, the bawdy burlesque of Asakusa, the aristocratic mansions of Omotesando. Gone too were the clean bright streetcars that had, a little over a decade before, shuttled him to and from club meetings and theater events and calligraphy classes, as well as (for those four unhappy summers) the *karate* classes his father had forced on him to give him "backbone."

Now from his backseat in the USOF truck all he saw were burnt-out shells of stranded buses and trams, dinosaur skeletons littering a strange and prehistoric wasteland. He saw pubescent girls dressed in cheap bright dresses and plastic high heels, slinking up and down the same streets they'd once walked in kneesocks and saddle shoes. He saw filthy children barely old enough to walk—much less to feed themselves—rummaging with dogs in garbage heaps for scraps of food. He saw it, and reminded himself that the Japanese had brought this on themselves; that before they'd suffered this they'd inflicted death and suffering on as great or a greater scale elsewhere. *It's not murder,* his father had said. *It is war.*

And of course, Billy believed this, just as he believed America's war had been a just one. If it caused destruction, it was to prevent greater destruction; if it caused death, it was to prevent more death.

And yet, staring at the wasted scenery—the bloated children, the scarecrow adults—he found that it didn't fit into an equation. The filth and illness and rubble seemed neither part of an action nor a consequence of one; neither a crime nor a punishment. It was simply what it was: a charred expanse of loss and nothingness. An end.

Shutting his eyes, he remembered an exchange he'd had on one of the last class days at Michigan. Their language instructor had been replaced by a pale and lean Army official, there (he said) to bring them "up to speed" on Japan's "current conditions." After showing them a slideshow composed mainly of blurry aerials, he'd gone through a list of the sixty-seven cities the U.S. Army Air Corps had firebombed in the war's final months—along with the percentage of each city that had been destroyed. *Yokohama, fifty-eight percent. Tokyo, fifty-one percent. Toyama, ninety-nine percent. Nagoya, forty percent . . .* The list went on and on and on.

"Jesus *Christ,*" Billy muttered as the lecturer, apparently parched by his fiery litany, stepped outside for a drink of water.

The guy sitting next to him—Colin Sanger, the son of a Fukuoka missionary and a student who'd be booted out for ties to Harvard's Young Marxists—snorted. "Let's at least hope the man gets what he wanted out of all this," he said.

Billy turned to look at him. "What man?"

Sanger leaned back in his seat, tenting his fingertips. "Who else? Bombs Away LeMay. You know this was all part of his lobbying effort to get the government to fund an independent Air Force."

"What?" Billy gaped. "That's bullshit. They did it to shorten the war."

"Like the London Blitz shortened the war for Germany?" Sanger lifted an eyebrow. "Don't believe it. What I heard is that the Army was getting ready to can the AAF altogether—too costly, too many accidents. And of course, all that money that could be going into the Army proper. This was LeMay's way of showing Truman that airpower is a military force to be reckoned with."

"That's just not possible," Billy told him.

Colin had looked at him almost pityingly. "It's war, buddy," he'd said. "Anything's possible."

AS THE TRUCK turned onto what had been 日比谷 通りin his last life here but was now *HIBIYA STREET* in English only, Billy repeated both phrases, comparing them. *It's not murder, it's war. It's war. Anything's possible.* A wave of inexplicable panic washed over him; a feeling that he might open his eyes and suddenly find himself on fire. When he did open them, though, he saw instead the inert body of an old woman by the road, a one-eyed cat licking a gash on her forehead.

By the time they reached GHQ all he wanted was to get inside, back to some semblance of undamaged civilization. To a clean and preferably Western-style toilet. But even the Pyle proved a shock. Before the surrender the building had been used as an Imperial

Army training base. Word had it that Douglas MacArthur had pegged it as one of the structures potentially useful to the victors, which LeMay's bombers should therefore avoid. What Billy hadn't realized was that he knew this imposing ediface from an even earlier incarnation. It had been Tokyo's Grand Takarazuka Theater, home to the all-women's singing and dancing troup with which he had once been briefly obsessed. In Billy's memory it was a gilded palace, draped with neon and hung with posters of popular actresses made-up, decked-out and coiffed to look like French counts and Italian princesses. Now it was as sober and worn-looking as any building that had survived the firebombings, its only adornment the red letters spelling out the name of the late journalist to whom it had been rededicated: E-R-N-I-E P-Y-L-E.

The other members of the Language Detachment grabbed their duffels and made their way towards the entrance. But Billy just stood there, his neck craned, his pained mind racing. He sensed something wrong—something that didn't fit. When it hit him it was this: when he'd thought about Tokyo these past months, in spite of everything he'd still thought of it as the city he'd always known. He'd thought of a clean skyline framed by the drape and tier of scalloped rooftops, interspersed with the occasional hard edge of a Western-style building. Its streets filled with rustling robes and the *pokpok* echo of wooden shoes, and the rich, mixed scents of *sencha*, incense and tea.

In short, he'd allowed himself to imagine he was coming home.

Inside, he left his duffel at what he vaguely recalled as the theater cloakroom and found his way upstairs to the Civil Intelligence offices. He gave his name, rank and serial number, then took a seat with his clipboard, his head still pounding despite the aspirin from the plane. But beneath the yellowish buzzing lights and the dutiful *taptaptap* of the typewriters the ballooning panic receded, and he found strange solace in filling out the mundane questions that the *Occupied Japan Intelligence Individualized Agent Record* put forth. Name? *William Anton Reynolds.* Date of birth? *5-26-1923.* City of birth? *Tokyo, Japan.* Areas of expertise? *Japanese language and culture, political science, French language and literature, architecture, photography (hobby) . . .*

"Is there a First Lieutenant William Reynolds present?"

Billy looked up to see a captain with a manila file standing in the doorway.

"Reynolds?" the man repeated. "William Anton Reynolds?"

Fuck, William thought. He stood up and saluted. "Yes, sir. Right here."

The speaker gave him the once-over, thin lips pursed. "Colonel Matthews wants you in his office, soldier. Pronto."

"Yes, sir."

So it didn't take a week. It took barely two days. Who knew the USOF was so fucking efficient?

Billy tucked the clipboard beneath his trembling arm and made his way past the other smirking recruits. "In hot water already, Reynolds?" someone snickered, sotto voce. But Billy's thoughts were so focused on putting one foot before the other that he barely heard the question. *What am I going to tell them?* he was asking himself frantically. *They'll be furious . . .*

He was thinking, of course, about his parents. But he was thinking too about the stockades they'd marched and jogged by dozens of times during Basic. Topped with rusted barbed wire, they were the threat that kept every soldier in line. But what really frightened him were the sounds he'd sometimes hear coming from their depths—howls and screams of what sounded like sheer pain.

"What the hell do they *do* to them in there?" he finally asked a bunkmate.

"In the slammer?" his SCO had replied. "The MPs beat the shit out of them." He said it as though it were obvious.

"That's part of their sentence?"

"Nah. That part's just for fun." He'd winked, though in a way not altogether unfriendly. "And for the real pansies they do worse. You can only imagine."

BILLY TRIED TO push that appalling thought from his head, and to collect those left in its wake. What the hell was he going to *say*? "*Sodomy*, sir? Not at all. It's true that I fell over. Perhaps even into Lieutenant McNeil a little bit. But you see, sir, we'd had quite a bit to drink . . ."

But again, it was still his word against Daniel's. And Daniel still outranked him. What was more, that elderly couple had witnessed the scene firsthand. What if Daniel somehow managed to track them down? In that case, the best course of action might merely be confession. "*Yes, sir*. It's true: I'm a pervert and an abomination. I don't know why I'm this way, but I would like to apologize for any inconvenience it might be causing."

They were inside the colonel's office now, a large and windowless room that in its first incarnation had been a dressing room for the Takarazuka chorus line, though Billy had no idea how he'd made that connection. Then he remembered: the playbills for the Takarazuka productions. For a year or so he'd collected them with a passion, and they always included (with typically Japanese attention to minutiae) a detailed diagram of the building's rehearsal stages and back rooms.

Billy had no idea what the room had looked like then, but it had clearly had a full-scale rehaul since. The walls were painted that uniquely oppressive military gray, and hung with a picture of Truman and an assortment of diplomas and medals. In the middle of it all sat Colonel Rory Matthews, at an enormous oakwood office desk that had probably belonged to an equally high-ranking Japanese officer in the Imperial Army's days here.

"Lieutenant Reynolds, sir," announced the captain, in a voice implying apology.

"Ah," said Matthews. "Good. Thank you, Captain. You can leave us."

The captain departed. Billy disliked him already but was sorry to see him go. He was suddenly aware of feeling very alone.

"First Lieutenant William Reynolds, sir," he said, saluting.

"At ease, Lieutenant Reynolds," said the colonel. "Have a seat." He waved a ringed hand towards a worn-looking leather chair. He was a large, florid man with a shaved head and an impeccably pressed collar. At first glance he looked a little like Daddy Warbucks.

"I've heard a good deal about you," Matthews went on as Billy settled into an armchair. "Got all the poop right here."

He tapped a thick letter that sat squarely before him on the desk, and Billy's first response was to cringe. Then he looked at the white envelope, with its triple row of airmail stamps, and thought *Hold the phone: it came by* mail? Because of course, that made no sense. Even assuming Daniel had sent his complaint off first thing Monday morning, there was no way it would have beat Billy here.

"Sir?" he asked hoarsely, barely daring to hope.

"Your father," said Matthews. "As you may know, he did some work with the Army Air Corps a few years back. Worked with a Colonel Jamison—friend of mine, it just so happens."

He tapped the letter again, and Billy felt as though he'd fall right off his chair in relief.

"I did hear that, sir," he said, realizing too late that he wasn't supposed to know about the Dugway project.

Happily, Matthews either didn't recognize or didn't care about the breach in security. "In fact," he continued, "I believe it was Colonel Jamison who told your father about our program there. He asked me to keep an eye out for you, son."

Son. Billy felt his eyes prickle. He couldn't remember the last time anyone had called him that. Not even his father. "Thank you, sir."

Matthews picked up the letter again, leafing through to a different page. "I'm also told," he said, "that you were among the highest performers back in Ann Arbor. That right?"

"So I was told, sir."

"So you speak fluent Jap."

Billy nodded, though he'd always hated that word. One of the things that had first impressed him about Daniel (apart, of course, from his disastrous goddamn beauty) was that he'd made a point of never using such terms. He called the Germans Germans, the Japanese Japanese. He'd called Negroes Negroes. "It's a matter of respect," he'd shrugged when Billy commented on it once. Though clearly even Daniel's respect had its limits . . . *All this time you've been a fucking homo? A pervert?*

"I'd say that's pretty impressive," Matthews was continuing.

"Well, to be fair, sir, I did grow up here."

"True. Strange, but true."

Matthews stretched his arms up in a muscular stretch, then reached the right one towards a sleek wooden box neatly positioned on the desk's corner. He lifted the lid, then showed Billy its contents. "Havanas. Nothing better. And worth a fair bit of green here, I might add." He winked.

Billy stared at the gold-banded log miserably, feeling Daniel's hand landing on his back. "No, thank you," he said thinly. "I've— never been much of a cigar man. Do you mind if I have a cigarette, though?"

"Be my guest."

Billy pulled his Luckies from his breast pocket. He lit one as the colonel puffed on his stogie. They sat in a companionable and smoky silence, until Matthews said: "So. Good to be back?"

Billy cleared his throat. "Well, I've only been here a couple of hours, sir. It seems an awful lot has—uh, changed."

The colonel's lips twisted. "That's a nice way of putting it. The truth is, we bombed the shit out of this city. Killed over a hundred thousand civilians in under four hours. Left nearly half the capital in cinders. The half that's still standing is overcrowded, disease-ridden, on the verge of starving to death. Oh—and full of rats."

Unsure of how he was expected to respond to this statement—with respectful silence? A round of applause?—Billy settled on a vague nod. He'd of course seen these statistics, both in the Intelligence reports they'd been assigned and in the scant newspaper coverage after the AAF launched its incendiary campaign. Though clearly, he still hadn't anticipated them . . . His head gave a surly throb.

"In short," the colonel went on, "this is not a cushy posting like some of your friends may now have in, say, Paris. The city is a goddamn wreck, and this office—quite frankly—has more work than it can possibly handle. If I were to be completely honest, I'd say we're desperate for help. But there aren't that many folks that speak Jap. So you'll be busy."

He puffed again on his cigar and eyed Billy thoughtfully. "But out of consideration for your father's excellent work for us, I'm going to give you one of the better jobs. You're a decent translator, I take it?"

"Decent enough, I suppose." Which was modest; he'd been the best in his class.

"Good. Then I'll likely have you do some transcript work—interviews, confessions, that sort of thing. But I'm going to put you mainly in with the press and public relations group. They're in charge of fielding the Japanese-language notes and letters General MacArthur gets here. You'll also work with our media specialist, Captain Frank Tuttledge, on vetting news articles before they hit the press, et cetera."

Billy frowned. *"Before* they hit the press, sir?"

The colonel gave a short nod. "Affirmative. We don't publicize this much, obviously—free speech and all that—but we keep about as tight a rein on the papers right now as Tojo did. Nothing can be published without SCAP approval. And nothing is approved that touches—even obliquely—on any subject deemed 'inimical to the objectives of the Occupation.'" He grinned. "That's a quote, by the way."

"Issues such as . . ."

"You'll get the list. But it includes anything negative about American GIs here, for example. Not surprisingly, our boys get up to some high jinks sometimes. During our first few weeks they maybe went a bit overboard."

"In what way, sir?"

The colonel shrugged. "Took some toys. Kissed some girls. One paper ran the crazy figure of thirteen hundred rapes in Kanagawa, in the first ten days alone. Needless to say, that's the sort of irresponsible reportage we need to avoid. Ditto with most stuff about Hirohito and Fat Boy."

Billy lifted a brow. "The papers can't write about the atomic bombings?" The American papers had been full of news about Hiroshima and Nagasaki—graphic descriptions and scientific quotes that somehow contributed not more but less to his understanding of what had happened to those cities. According to some reports there was almost nothing left of either—a concept that left him queasy even as his baffled brain refused to process it. Up until today he'd had no way at all to comprehend it.

Matthews was shaking his large head. "For now, it's on the blackout list. The Chief thinks it'll spread unrest and discontent. Don't want that at this early stage of the game."

He disappeared behind his papers again, his presence marked by an acrid cloud of smoke while Billy tried to digest what he was hearing. *There aren't that many folks that speak Jap?* he thought, incredulously. *How about the sixty-odd million Japanese citizens we left alive?*

Somewhat belatedly, he remembered his cigarette. But by the time he'd lifted it to his mouth the full first inch was already ash. He watched in horror as the tip crumbled off, floating gently towards the cream-toned carpet. Thankfully, Matthews was still hidden behind his folder. Billy covered the spot with his toe.

"May I ask, sir," he said, "what happens if an article does slip past us? Last-minute or something?"

"If we don't like it, the paper gets pulled. Every edition. They all get pulped and tossed, ASAP, and the papers have to reissue the damn whole thing right. Which, of course, costs them an arm and a leg, which none of them can afford. Last time it happened the paper at fault almost went under. God knows how these people got anything done before us." He shook his head, stubbed out the cigar. "Anyways. They're finally getting pretty good at vetting themselves at this point. Still, you'll have to read carefully. And if *you* let anything bad slip through, there will be consequences. My influence only extends so far. You understand?"

Billy nodded, momentarily forgetting that he wouldn't be here long enough for any consequences. Or at least, not consequences of that sort. For the first time, he felt a stab of regret. Despite himself, he very much liked this man. Even more surprisingly, he sensed the like was mutual—that Matthews neither knew nor cared if he liked girls or boys or goddamn cows but respected him based on his ability. If this was true, it was a rapport unlike any other he'd felt with supervising officers in his year of service. It was a real waste that he wouldn't get to explore it further.

"So I think that's it," Matthews was concluding. "I've got a five o'clock meeting to prep for, so I'll make my adieus. But if you need anything at all as you're settling in, don't hesitate to ask."

"Actually, sir, there is one thing. We have a house in the country—

Nagano prefecture. Karuizawa, specifically. I guess a lot of the foreigners who didn't get out before the war started were shipped over
there as a kind of exile, and the Japanese Army put them into various houses they commandeered for the purpose. My dad's a little
worried—he asked me to take a day to go out and check on it. See
if it sustained any damage."

"So you need a pass."

"Sooner the better, if that's not too much to ask." *While I'm still
here.* "Just one night ought to do it."

Matthews stood up, tucking the letters and reports back into the
folder on his desk. "How about you start work tomorrow and take
Friday off, along with the weekend?"

"Sounds great," said Billy, following suit. "Thank you, sir."

"Not at all." The colonel gave a short salute. "Be here by 0800.
Dismissed."

Billy saluted back and took several steps towards the door, trying
hard not to think about the fact that the next time he was in this
office it would probably be to collect his marching orders home.

BACK AT THE Nippon Yusen Kaisha (another building deliberately spared for them) Billy flopped onto his single cot and stared
glumly at the steely gray ceiling. For some reason he'd been given
the best room on the hall. It was the only single, sporting not one
but two window views and a fine old oak desk he imagined must
have belonged to a high-ranking company division leader. Luck? he
wondered. Or was it the colonel pulling strings for him again? Well,
luck or favoritism, it was too late, as usual.

Mostly to punish himself, he pictured setting his little alarm
clock and getting up every morning. Racing to the showers with
his Dopp kit. He tried to imagine how he'd have decorated his

bedside table, the stern white walls; perhaps putting his favorite photographs by the bed, his Bette Davis poster by the window, his old Noh masks and woodblock prints on the opposite wall. He had all these things with him, right there in his duffel. But as things stood he wasn't even sure if it was worth unpacking his clothes.

In the end, though, he did unpack a little. Just his underwear and socks. Doing so felt vaguely comforting. He hooked his *yukata* on the door, stacked his books and journals on the bedside desk. Hung his camera on a painted nail that stuck out of the wall. Then he collapsed on his bunk with the well-thumbed copy of *Finnegans Wake* he'd been too drunk to read on the plane ride over. He got about three pages in before his eyelids threatened closure on him again, and with a sense of almost hedonistic pleasure he let them. Still, when the sharp *rapraprap* came on the door he was on his feet before he was even fully awake, his heart in his mouth and one thought spinning through his mind: *At least I can sleep in the slammer.*

But when he opened the door it wasn't the MPs but three of the other recruits from down the hall. "Hey, Reynolds," one said, a wiry Jewish guy from New Jersey who Billy vaguely remembered standing in line behind for the airplane toilet, "we met on the plane. Frank Rosen, remember?"

"Oh, right."

Rosen beamed. "Word has it you're Matthews' new pet."

"Says who?"

"It's all over," said Marcus Sato, a Nissei Billy had known peripherally back at Michigan. He let out a low whistle. "Nice digs. Say, want to celebrate with us? We're heading to the American Club. They say there are a few pretty hot dames in the secretary pool. *If you're interested.*"

Someone in the group snickered. It was a sound that by this point Billy was as accustomed to as "Taps," though he'd never figured out if it meant they knew about him. Not, of course, as if there was very much to know. Shameful longings, hidden during the day and furtively fantasized over at night. A brief and euphoric exploration at a sleepover with a seventh-grade classmate who never acknowledged Billy again. That one morose night in Princeton when he'd wandered into a place called Barcy's where an older man bought him whiskey shots and showed him pictures of his grandchildren. Then he led Billy into the alley behind the bar. The guy had smelled of gin and tomato juice. The top of his bald head had a mole on it that had looked like Florida, moving back and forth. All Billy really remembered was that it took forever, and that he couldn't get away fast enough afterwards.

And then, of course, there was Daniel. *Daniel. Oh god . . .*

He was about to tell them all to go to hell when he happened to look back at the bed. There it was—waiting for him. The thin white pillow; the nondescript Army-issue blanket. The unopened Joyce lying atop it. The thought that this lonely tableau might be the last image of Tokyo for a long time—if not forever—made his throat tighten.

To his own surprise he turned back to the group and shrugged. "Sure," he said. "I mean, what the hell."

THE AMERICAN CLUB was located in what had once been Shibuya-*ku* in western Tokyo, but was now renamed "Washington Heights," with a fresh new Old Glory flying from the roof to drive the point home. Shooting it from the horseshoe driveway, Billy found himself framing a sprawling squat building that had been a Japanese gentlemen's club of some sort before being requisitioned by the

IJA as an officers' gymnasium. It was then handed over to the victors, who quickly set it up as a combination rec room, bar and dance hall.

Inside the main lounge area Japanese waiters in waistcoats glided silently through the space, trays of drinks and ashtrays held aloft. A scruffy group that looked as though it had just been flown in from Las Vegas played big band music on the stage. Apart from the waiters and Marcus Sato, everyone appeared to be white. Apart from a small bevy of rather rumpled-looking women sitting in a glum row at the bar, all of them also appeared to be men.

The women, of course, were the SCAP secretaries—or "sexataries," as the group dubbed them—for whom his new companions had such high hopes. Billy watched with amusement as Lieutenants Sato and Rosen torpedoed themselves into their midst, fueling up at the bar, zeroing in on their targets, drinks primed and ready in hand. They were roundly rebuffed, one right after another, practically before they'd finished their introductions. *Banzai*, Billy thought; and he smiled for what felt like the first time in a million years.

"Well," he said, when Rosen returned to their table, crestfallen, "at least she put you out of your misery quickly."

"You can laugh," Rosen griped, "when *you* get someone's number."

But he said it with a smile. And when Billy replied, "Don't count on it, I'm not known as much of a ladies' man," he got a round of genuine-sounding laughter.

Wanting to preserve the moment, he took a couple of goofy group photos, then one of the bartender setting an orange slice afire. He shot the crowd of sexataries lighting up in mechanical terror at the sight of the flame, and then an older white woman in a *Happy* jacket, with *geisha*-style combs in her hair. He set one up of the couple the next table over, clasping hands and murmuring sick-sweet whispers of endearments, but thought the better of it as the discussion turned into a slurred fight over fidelity.

When he turned his attention to his drink, Billy realized to his surprise it was almost empty already. At the same moment, a smooth-skinned young man materialized like a genii beside him. "Finish?" he asked. "New *du-link-u* for GI?"

"Thanks," Billy replied in Japanese. "I'll take another of those. Two lime slices, one ice cube. *Onegai.*"

The waiter's face lit up. "Your Japanese is so good!" he said, seeming genuinely thrilled by this fact.

"Thank you. I grew up here."

"How interesting," said the Japanese, fixing his liquid eyes on Billy with renewed interest. "Where did you live?"

"In Aoyama for most of the year. *Nichome.* You know the big police box that was at the corner of Azabu Doori?"

The waiter beamed, exposing most of his polished teeth, the front top two slightly and rather charmingly crooked. "How strange!" he exclaimed. "I worked right around there. Before . . ."

Billy waited, curious to hear how this soft-faced man had spent the war. But the waiter merely waved his hand, dismissing it as he might any other unpleasant and faintly distasteful subject. "Did you ever eat at the Harimoto Fruits Parlor?" he asked, instead.

Billy chuckled. "Every Wednesday, after school.

"Aha!" The waiter clapped his hands in delight. "Well, I probably served you then. Though I don't remember serving anyone with that interesting shade of hair. I'm *sure* I would have remembered that."

And then he smiled in a way that made Billy's heart skip—first in surprise, and then raw terror. *Don't fall for it,* he told himself. *Don't you ever learn, asshole?*

But he did allow himself to lift his camera again. "Say," he said cautiously, "do you mind if I take your picture?"

The waiter was immediately on guard. "Why?" he said. "Are you MP?"

"No—no, nothing like that," Billy hurried to assure him. "I just like taking pictures."

The waiter warily flashed a look towards the bartender. The latter, however, was busy wowing the sexataries with his flaming-orange technique.

"All right," he said. He posed grinning for Billy, his drinks tray held proudly aloft. Afterwards he bowed his thanks. "It's a very nice camera," he added. "Contax?" And when Billy nodded: "I had a Fuji . . . before."

With that he hurried off towards the bar, leaving Billy replacing his lens cap and pondering whether everyone here split their lives into those two clean sections: *before* and *after.*

When the waiter returned with Billy's gin and tonic, he set it down atop a napkin upon which he'd written a name and an address.

"What's this?" Billy asked, warily.

The man pointed at his nose. "That," he said, "is me. Tanaka Jiro. And that is where I live. I'd like to see your picture, maybe, when you develop it." He smiled in a way that made Billy do a double take. This time, though, he didn't think he was misreading it.

To cover his discomposure he took a sip of his drink, which was bitter and citric and bracing. *Good to be back?* he thought, testing out the idea. To his surprise it was. At least for this short-lived moment.

And so he smiled back at Jiro, and said "Of course," and gave him a hefty tip, even though he knew it wasn't required in this country. The napkin he slipped into his pocket. And even though he knew full well that he wouldn't act upon it—even if by some miracle he was here long enough to do so—the thought of it there left a warm glow. *Well, what do you know,* he thought. *Billy got someone's number after all.*

He'd certainly had more luck than his fellow translators, who soon followed Rosen back to their table in defeat. SCAP "sexa-taries," it seemed, were not much impressed by language skills, and in any case had their sights set well beyond low-rank rookies from Intelligence. By eleven they had all paired up with at least one officer, and the least-plain among them had three. Sato, Billy and Rosen were debating whether to call it a night when a tall first lieutenant Sato knew somehow showed up with a towheaded second in his wake. Billy didn't get the fair one's name, but the tall one called himself Stretch, or Legs, or maybe Lurch (service nicknames had never made much of an impression on him). When the other guys complained about the slim romantic pickings he offered to take them somewhere with a little more spark.

"Where's that?" asked Sato.

"The America Club."

"We're *at* the American Club," Billy pointed out.

"This is nothing," said Lurch. "This is beans. C'mon."

"ACTUALLY," HE CLARIFIED on the bumpy ride to their destination, "it's a whorehouse."

"Swell," said Billy glumly.

"A good one, though," the blond guy chimed in. "Doesn't have that assembly-line up thing going like at the Paramount and the Paradise. It's more like some kind of geisha house, I hear."

But when they reached their destination it took just one glance for Billy to establish that, in fact, this place was nothing of the sort. He knew very well what a true *ochaya* looked like, having walked by one every day on his way to middle school. That build-ing had been a place of shadowed elegance; of arching gateways and silvered gables.

"The America Club," by contrast, occupied the ground floor of a former factory dormitory not unlike the one his father had built for the Army Air Force to practice dropping their bombs on. Its entrance was bedecked with tinsel streamers and hand-drawn Old Faithfuls, but even from here it struck Billy as sad and shabby. The front door sagged on its hinges as though it, too, were lewdly drunk, and the sounds that escaped it were anything but refined: shouted insults, slurred jokes. Mingling squeals of female laughter, high in pitch and robotic in rhythm. Somewhere in the background a piano tinkled off-tune ragtime, lending the scene the surreal aspect of a cowboy bar.

Both appalled and intrigued, Billy hung back from the others in order to take a few photos of it as well. He was just lining up his third when a large red thumb pressed itself against the lens.

"For Christ's sake, Archie. In or out?"

Billy lowered the camera. Lurch was standing before him, thrusting forward a foil-packaged condom. His face wore an expression implying he'd been doing this for several hours.

"It's Billy," Billy reminded him. And—to the condom—"No, thanks."

"What, no tail? Are you saving it for someone special?"

Billy felt himself flush. "So what if I am?"

"Oh, no problem. None at all."

Lurch shot a look at his towheaded sidekick, and Billy fought hard not to blush. "C'mon in anyway, Carrot Top," he went on. "We got some hot mama-*sans* in here who'll just eat you up when they see that hair."

In his mind's eye, Billy framed a shot of himself turning away on his slippery-smooth dress shoe heel. Just striding off. But as was so often the case, his mind and his eye did not share the same vision. While his mind watched him return happily to his private bunk and

Finnegans Wake, his eyes saw him slowly screw his cap onto his lens. They saw his right foot step obediently forward, then his left. They saw Lurch and his white-blond friend beam at him like a long-lost war hero. They saw the smirking door widen into a leer.

INSIDE, HE DECLINED another condom offered up by the richly tattooed doorman. Perching uncomfortably upon a stained yellow two-seater, he looked around the darkened room. The air in it smelled of old gin and dried fish, of bad perfume and nail polish, but this didn't repel him as much as it might have. It even reminded him a little of the darkroom, which—with its quietly sloshing liquids and magically materializing images—was one of the few places he ever felt truly "normal" and safe.

As his eyes adjusted to the dark he saw that Sato, Rosen and the others already had their laps commandeered by skinny Japanese girls. Lurch was on a couch with an older-looking woman in a *kimono*, and of the other two men who'd shared the Ford ride here there was no sign at all. When asked, Lurch informed Billy that they'd already been ushered into the "hanky-panky" rooms in the back. The only other American was an obviously inebriated MP, leaning into the piano and drinking Suntory whiskey from a ridiculously small *sake* cup. He looked bombed enough to have been doing this for some time.

The music shifted, and Billy shifted his own focus with it from the drunk cop to the ragged little piano player. From the back it appeared to be a thin boy of twelve or thirteen, which surprised him. Now that he could hear it more clearly the music struck Billy as pretty good.

"*Mesurashii, naa!*"

The word breathed itself damply into his ear, sparking a shiver that turned into a shudder as he turned around. The girl who'd just slid in next to him had a nearly perfectly round face, framed by black hair so exceptionally frizzed it looked like a Negress's. Billy had seen other *pan-pan* girls in the streets sporting the same look: *kanibaru sutayiru*, the towhead had called it. "Cannibal style."

"OK I *tacchi*?" she asked, tentatively extending a finger towards his head.

"You may touch," he replied in Japanese. "But it'll cost you ten *yen*."

He watched her kohl-lined eyes widen, her chin drop down to her collarbone. Then, predictably, came the screech: *"Eeeeeh? Usou!* You are lying! How on earth do you speak so well?"

"I grew up here."

"Eeeeeh? You're lying!"

"No, it's true," he said. "My father built a lot of Tokyo's buildings."

"Ussou!" she crowed, leaning happily into him. "Which buildings?"

"I think the Owen Elevator Building was his last one," Billy said, gingerly sliding away. "And the Imperial Hotel was his first."

"The *Teikoku Hoteru? Ussou!* You're lying!"

It had been a long time since he'd conversed with a tipsy Japanese girl. He'd forgotten how annoying it could be.

"Hontoo da," he said, and inched his thigh away from hers a little more. Her stockings were baggy and puce-toned and laddered in four different places. Someone had daubed bright red blotches of nail polish at the top of each run; they looked like bloody dots finishing off lower-case *i*'s.

"What do you have to drink around here?" he asked.

"We have *fu-re-shu furutsu kakuteru*," she announced brightly. "Twenty *yen*. Fifteen for you."

"Only I get a discount?"

"As long as I can touch your hair." She extended her forefinger again and stroked a curl above his brow—very carefully. As though her touch might make his hair fall out. For some reason this struck Billy as a rather reasonable possibility.

"Do you eat many carrots?" she asked.

"Me and Rita Hayworth. Just carrots. What fruit is in the cocktail?"

"Whatever the bartender could find in the city."

"And the alcohol?"

She shrugged. "I don't know."

"Ah," he said, thinking *The hell with that.* They'd been warned during training that, faced with a shortage of potable liquor, many establishments were serving a noxious brew called *kasutori*: a potentially lethal combination of water and methyl alcohol that the medics had blamed for four servicemen deaths and one blinding incident on the very first week of the Occupation.

"I think I'll just have a beer," he said. "In a bottle, *onegai.*"

The girl turned in her seat. *"Biru i-pon,"* she called to the barman, dashing his hopes that she'd leave to get it herself. Instead she scooched closer and took his hand. *"Ano nee,"* she said. "Red-*do-san.*"

"Billy *da,*" he said curtly.

"My goodness, but that's hard to say. *Biii-riiii.*"

She squeezed his palm. Her nails were several different colors at once: pink, red, a darker pink. When he looked more closely he saw that like her stockings they had been painted over several times, with each chip in the top coat revealing the contrasting hue of its predecessor. For some reason, it made him think of how women in Sei Shonagon's era used to layer their dress *kimono* with multiple, brightly toned under*kimonos.*

"So what is your name?" he asked her, as the bartender delivered to their table one room-temperature Asahi and one bright orange drink, garnished with what looked like a cabbage leaf. Billy reached for his beer quickly, less out of thirst than as an excuse to drop her hand.

"You guess," she said, coyly.

"Ah—Tomiko." She shook her head. "Fumi." Another head-shake. "Hirohito."

"Usou," she giggled, and slapped his arm. "You're so bad!"

"I give up."

She pointed at her nose, Japanese-style. "I am Sarah."

"Sara?" he asked. The word meant "plate" in Japanese. "Like the kind you eat from?"

She slapped him again. "No, *baka.* Like Bernhardt-*san!*"

"I see." He took another long pull off his beer, wishing that she'd stop touching him.

"And that's Betty. And that's Joanne. And that's Shirley," she said, pointing at the other girls in turn. "And that"—she pointed at the *kimono*-clad matron—"is Koko. She's the *mama-san.*"

"Unusual names for Japanese girls," he observed.

"Oh, we're all Americans now," she returned gaily. "Like Billy, and *Leg-su.* And John *Su-mi-su* over there." She pointed a chipped fingertip at the MP by the piano, who was already beginning to look glazed.

"John Smith? That's his name?"

She nodded brightly. "He's a major general."

Which gave Billy his second real smile of the night. "Well," he told Sarah, "he doesn't look very happy about it. Perhaps you should try to cheer him up."

"I tried. He said he was here to drink all alone. Isn't that just so sad?"

"It is," Billy agreed, though it frankly sounded divine.

The skinny pianist transitioned to a dirge-like rendition of "I Get a Kick Out of You." Sarah Bernhardt crossed her thick legs.

"*Sore de ne,* Red-*do san?* What other buildings did your papa build here?"

"It's Billy," he repeated. "I guess embassies, mainly."

"*Usou!* Which ones?"

"French," he started, ticking them off. "English. Canadian. Belgian, too. Are those ones still standing, do you know?"

She pursed her lips thoughtfully. "*Saaaa.* The French one's still here, I'm pretty sure. The English one—damaged, I think?"

"How about Manchuria?" he asked, taking another swig and welcoming the responding lightness he felt in his head.

"*Eh? Manshu?* Where was that one?"

"Near the Chinese one, I believe," he said, the absurdity of it hitting him anew—he hadn't thought about it for several years.

"Hmmm . . . I don't know." She took a dainty sip of her drink. Her nose and cheeks were already beginning to flush, and it came back to him again: that one devastating lick of red he'd coveted (was it really just a few days ago?) as it crept its way up Daniel's white neck.

"But—*saa,*" she was continuing brightly, "I'll bet Yoshi-*chan* would. Her father worked on the continent."

"Yoshi-*chan?*"

"*So.*"

The last thing Billy wanted was to have to talk with another girl. But before he could stop her Sarah was waving and singing out across the room: "*Chotto . . . Yoshi-chan!*"

At first no one responded. But then the music stopped and he saw that she'd been waving at the boy playing piano, who then turned his head to reveal that he was not, in fact, a *he* at all, but a very slender young girl. Her hair was ragged and short, her face untouched by makeup. When she spoke her voice was deep and husky. Unlike the other women, she made no effort to pitch it higher.

"Nani?"

"Manchurian embassy," Sarah shouted, though she no longer had to. "Where was it?"

The pianist studied Billy with huge, pitch-dark eyes. He took another pull off his beer and studied her back, discovering that she had cheekbones rivaling Hepburn's; that she had thick and almost-mannish brows. Yet somehow, on her face they didn't look mannish at all. They looked—lovely. *She* was lovely. It struck him, in fact, that she was the first truly lovely thing he'd seen here.

I know you, he thought, and felt his breath catch like dry bone in his throat.

"What's her name again?"

"Her? That's just Yoshi."

Yoshi. Yoshi. He couldn't remember any Yoshis. And given their age difference she'd have been quite little when he'd last been here . . . *And yet.*

"Yosh-chan!" Sara was shrilling. "The embassy!"

"Which embassy?"

"Manchurian, you idiot! Didn't your father work there?"

"He works *in* Manchuria," the girl said, with perfect Tokyo diction and enough maturity that Billy revised her age upward, to fifteen or maybe even sixteen. "But," she went on, "I don't know where the Manchurian embassy is."

"Uso," huffed Sarah, the word now not flirtatious in the least. "If your father worked in Manchuria how could you not know the embassy?"

"He got my travel papers for me, so I never had any reason to go there." Yoshi yawned, not bothering to cover her mouth. Her teeth were small and white, and perfectly in line. *I know her, I know her,* Billy kept thinking.

"Well, you might as well go back to playing then," said Sarah

Bernhardt crossly. "But something lively this time. *If* that isn't too much trouble." She bowed facetiously. *"Sankyu."*

Yoshi gave a diffident nod and shut her huge eyes briefly. Her lashes might have belonged to a giraffe. Billy continued to watch, mesmerized and baffled as she launched into a rippling arpeggio, then another faintly sweet, faintly discordant tune he'd never heard.

Yoshi, he thought again. *Yoshi? Yoshiko?* Why the hell did she seem so familiar? It might be the hair. With its boyish length and her sharp features she looked a little bit like a Takarazuka male-role star he'd pined after as a boy. What had her name been? Yukiko . . . something. Was it Ono?

Beside him, Bernhardt belched in delicate disdain. "Do you want to know a secret?" she asked, conspiratorially.

"Not especially."

She leaned over anyway, looking smug. "They say her mother was a *spy.*"

A shimmering vision of Mata Hari (bejeweled, serpentine, shot) rose in his mind. "What kind of a spy?"

"An *enemy* spy."

"Which enemy?"

"The English. And now they are afraid to get rid of her, because the English—well, because *you* won." She waved at him vaguely in a gesture that reminded him of Jiro the waiter's *before.* He was starting to see it as a universal sign of polite dismissal here: a helpless, vague wave. A signal stand-in for *the War.*

"Wait. So we won and . . . I'm not following here."

"Baka nee!" She slapped his knee. "Because her *mother* was a *spy.* She learned it from her *mama.* You see?"

His thoughts were still churning around the girl at the piano. "What was her last name again?" he asked, though she hadn't yet said it.

Sarah shrugged, suddenly wary. "I—I'm not sure I remember."

"And no American name?"

"She hasn't earned it yet."

"What does she have to do to earn it?" he asked, and she said something about "work" but he didn't catch it all because he was watching the girl's thin back again, the way her shoulder blades spread slightly apart and then drew together again. The delicate underpinnings of hidden wings.

She'd shifted back to Satie, and Billy recognized the piece as *Gymnopédie* No. 3. He and Daniel had listened to it together—was it only last week? "There's something so sad and yet so . . . full about Satie," Daniel had said. "It's like . . . it's like . . ."

As was often the case by then, Billy completed the thought: "It's like he's composing something about sorrow, but not just the sadness of it. The beauty too," he'd said. "Like he's exploring where sorrow and beauty intersect."

It wasn't something he could have said to anyone else without feeling like a self-conscious pansy. But with Daniel he could, and as if to prove this Dan had smiled a beautiful, sad little smile at him. "That's it," he'd said fondly. "That's it on the nose. "

Sarah Bernhardt now had her full weight on him, leaving him with the awkward feeling that he couldn't move without causing her to fall. Rather the way his old dog Rasputin would lean against him when he wanted attention. The difference, of course, being that Billy had liked patting his dog.

"So, Red-*do san*," Sarah purred, and he knew from her tone that she was honing in. This was the part he always hated, though he'd never had to navigate it in Japanese.

"I have a very comfortable private room in the back," she went on softly.

Billy cleared his throat. "Listen," he began, "I think you're very nice. But I'm really not here for all this."

She stroked his ear, not getting it. "For all what?"

"For . . . doing it. You know. *That.*"

He waved artlessly towards the beaded curtain (a signal stand-in for *copulation*), and watched her absorb the phrase with dawning, wounded comprehension.

"You don't like me," she said, pouting. "You think I'm ugly."

"No I don't," he lied, hating both her and himself for how her face fell.

She locked looks with him, and in her dark eyes he thought he saw that same gleam he'd seen in Lurch's when he'd rejected the condom. With her, though, it came as a relief.

"I'm very sorry," she said formally; and to his horror her lower lip trembled. *Please don't cry,* he thought.

Happily, she did not. She merely bowed stiffly before making a dolorous retreat across the room. Billy watched her go, studying her frizzed hair and ugly dress; her sturdy legs as they shuffled back towards the bar. They were such very *Japanese* legs, he found himself thinking. The sort of legs that seemed plump and ungainly even though the girl who had them wasn't in the least bit fat. *Radish legs,* his Japanese friends had called them. *Piano legs,* one of the new NYK hallmates had said.

Oh for Christ's sake, he told himself, *don't be cruel. Give it a rest.*

Signaling for another beer, he leaned back, pulled out his Luckies and lit one. He wondered fleetingly whether there was any way to leave without drawing further notice. After all, at this point there were three other Americans in the room—Major General John Smith, the white-blond looie whose name he didn't know, and Lurch. The major general appeared to be sleeping, one long leg bowed up on the bench, the other dangling on the floor. The towhead was up at the bar with his back turned to the rest of the room. And Lurch—who now had Koko-*san* sitting fully on his lap—seemed entirely focused on prying open her *kimono* while she slapped at his hands and tittered maniacally.

As Billy watched, Sarah Bernhardt sidled up next to the couple and whispered something that made the madam stop smiling. She gave Billy a sharp glance, then turned around to hiss something into the American's hairy ear. The latter lifted an eyebrow and looked lazily over before pulling Sarah Bernhardt onto his lap as well. Throwing her plump arm around Lurch's neck, the prostitute shot Billy a sour look. He couldn't really blame her.

Looking away, Billy chain-lit another Lucky and thought again about leaving. What would happen if he just—ran away? Past the bar, out the door and through the ruined night until he found his way back to his bed, his book, his discreet miseries? Then again, the city now was devoid of half the navigational landmarks he'd known before. Chances were he'd just end up wandering until he ran into some MP who'd write him up. Or some disgruntled veteran who'd try to behead him.

So he stayed where he was, picking up his Contax, wiping a smudge off the lens. He set up an idle photograph of his own shoes, positioning them pigeon-toed, then in ballerina first position. Then, seeing another pair of black shoe tips edge into the frame, he looked up.

The white-blond second had left the bar and come over. He held a beer, which he offered to Billy with an easy smile. "You ordered this, I believe."

"I did," said Billy, slightly annoyed. He wasn't much in the mood for company. But he accepted the bottle, and the second sat down, settling into the spot where Sarah Bernhardt had just pouted.

"So you don't like our girls or something?" the looie asked.

Billy quirked a brow. "So you work here or something?"

"*Touché.*" The lieutenant gave him a wry smile. "Only work I do is behind that curtain." He nodded towards the back. "I'm just waiting for Lola—one of my faves—to become available. Seeing as you seem to be waiting too, I thought I'd help things along." He offered his hand. "Mike Richards."

"Billy Reynolds," said Billy, forcing a smile. "Nice to meet you." What the hell did the guy want? He sensed that it wasn't what that boy Jiro had wanted. Mike Richards didn't give off that feel. "You work in Military Intelligence with Lurch?" he asked him.

"Yup."

"What do you do there?"

"For the most part, try to track down war criminals for the tribunal."

"That sounds . . . interesting," Billy said, though it actually sounded depressing as all hell.

"You're in translation?" Richards asked, offering him a cigarette. And when Billy nodded (as of this moment, at least, it was true), "Where you from?"

"Here, I guess. My folks live outside Philly now. You?"

"Upstate New York."

"Nice up there, I've heard."

Mike Richards shrugged. "It's OK." He was watching Billy closely, his pale eyes intent in a way that was starting to make Billy feel uncomfortable.

"I hear you work right up with the big guys," Richards went on. "Colonel Matthews. Maybe MacArthur himself."

"That's the plan," said Billy, though he hadn't heard the MacArthur part.

"You must be pretty damn good, then," said Richards. He stroked his almost-hairless chin, then cast a quick glance around as though fearing an eavesdropper. "I wonder if I might ask you a favor."

"What sort of favor?" asked Billy, suddenly wary. He knew that there was a thriving black market in Tokyo now, and that a lot of soldiers used it to boost their pay on the side. That was the last thing he wanted to get caught up in. He was in enough hot water as it was.

"Don't worry. It's nothing illegal or anything." Mike leaned forward. "Only—will you keep an eye out for me for anything that comes across your desk on a certain topic?" His right knee bounced in a rapid but tightly controlled rhythm.

"What sort of topic?"

"POWs. Especially those that were kept in northern China. I heard all the Jap Army records they recovered were being sent over to your division before coming to us."

"Maybe," Billy said, trying to figure out where this was headed. "Though a lot of Army and government records were burned in the days before surrender."

Mike Richards nodded. "But—just on the off chance. If you hear anything about American prisoners . . ."

He was clearly trying to speak casually, yet it was also clear that he was speaking about something that meant a great deal to him. "Is there someone in particular you're looking for?"

Richards finished off his beer and wiped his mouth with his sleeve. "You remember the Doolittle Raids?" he asked. "Back in '42?"

Billy nodded. Of course he remembered. Jimmy Doolittle and his team had provided the first spark of real hope in those bleak days following the attack on Oahu. "Doolittle was awarded the Medal of Honor for those, wasn't he?"

"He was. The pilots all got the Distinguished Flying Cross for it." He rolled the empty Kirin bottle between his hands. "My brother was one of them."

"Your brother was a Raider?" Billy asked, impressed. "You must be very proud."

Richards nodded, but his lips tightened. "He wasn't one of the ones that came back."

"Oh." Whatever remaining irritation Billy had drained away. "He was taken prisoner?"

"No one knows. Of the three other crew members only two, the copilot and the bombadier, survived the crash. The Japs executed the bombadier. Put him on trial for crimes against human nature, or something. The copilot—a Jewish guy named Midge I'd met a couple of times—he made it back. But he was in bad shape for a while." He shook his head. "Fucking inhuman, what those Jap soldiers put them through."

He drifted off for a moment, his eyes simultaneously locked on the filthy floor and focused on something miles away. "Cam's wife had a baby," he said at last. "Just seven months after he disappeared. The kid looks just like him. It's goddamn uncanny. It's like seeing my own big brother as a two-year-old."

Billy thought of himself, all seventy-five inches of him, standing next to his diminutive father on their yearly holiday card. *I'd say it was the postman,* Anton liked to quip about Billy's hair. *But he was a short fellow with dark hair just like me.*

"That's got to be tough," he said now. "Not knowing, I mean."

Richards nodded. "Yeah. I think Lacy's starting to give up on him. She doesn't tell me or anything, but I'm pretty sure other guys are asking her out . . ." He cleared his throat. "Anyways. I told her after I managed to get this post that I'd do my best to find out what happened."

Billy studied him sympathetically. He'd always wanted an older brother—someone to ally himself with against the cool dismissive force that was his father . . . He rubbed his temples tiredly. "Sure, Mike," he said. "I'll keep a lookout."

Mike smiled at him, a broad, white-toothed grin. "That's swell. Thanks." Fumbling in his pocket, he pulled out his card. It had another small square of paper-clipped to it. As he picked it up, Billy saw a passport-sized photo.

"That's him," said Mike. "That's Cam. If you find him you can reach me in Intelligence—though if you can't for some reason, there's my parents' address. There's a phone number too."

Billy studied the picture. It showed a handsome young man roughly his age, with hair every bit as white-blond as his brother Mike's, and the same smooth chin and pale eyes. "Good-looking guy," he said absently.

Richards gave him a strange look. "His wife sure thought so."

Despite himself, Billy fought back a blush.

Mike Richards stood and stretched, just a bit too expansively. "Well," he half yawned, "guess I should go see if Lola's free yet. Nice talking to you."

"You too."

Ears burning, he watched the other officer slouch back towards the bar. Then he looked again at Lieutenant Cameron Richards. Richards gazed gravely back, his point of vision just slightly past the lens, as though staring down a fate he alone could see. Billy wondered how many other copies were floating around this singed city. It had to be like looking for a needle in a burnt-up haystack.

He put the photo and card safely in his pocket, then sat back to light a Lucky. It struck him that something had changed, though at first he didn't know what it was. Then he realized that the piano had stopped. Maybe, he mused, that poor little girl had finally gone home to bed. He hoped so . . .

Glancing around the dark room, though, he immediately saw that she had not. In fact, she was being marched right towards him, Koko-*san* on one side of her, Lurch on the other. The adults looked determined and slightly devious. The girl looked frightened.

"Hey, Reynolds," slurred Lurch, as they came to a swaying stop together, "I got something for you."

The madam hissed something into Yoshi's ear. The girl nodded, her dark eyes on the floor.

Billy stood up uncertainly. "Is she OK?" He indicated the girl.

"Clean as a whistle," Lurch grinned. "First-timer, you lucky dog."

"That's not what I meant."

"It's what you should know, though."

Billy felt his heart slow. "And why is that?"

"Because me and Koko-*san* here have been talking," Lurch answered, rocking back and forth on his heels. "I was explaining to her that you didn't mean any offense when you gave Sarah over there the send-off. That since you just got here you were just a little out of sorts. She kindly agreed to help me give you another little welcoming gift."

Shit, Billy thought, grasping where this was headed just as Lurch swept an arm towards the pale child. "Fresh gook tail! Nothing better to get you settled in." He sounded like a used car salesman.

"Listen, Lurch . . ." Billy was having trouble breathing.

"Don't lie, Red. We *saw* the way you were looking at her. And as it turns out, Yuki here is about due for her first customer."

Her name is Yoshi, Billy thought, just as the girl looked up sharply and said, in startlingly British-sounding English: "My name is *Yoshi.*"

Up close she was even lovelier. Her chin was sharp and chiseled, her skin flawless and almost translucent in its pallor. There were mauve half-moons beneath her eyes and a faint network of blue veins beneath her brows, yet somehow these signs of wear and exhaustion only added to her tragic appeal. She looked so oddly out of place here, Billy thought. A heroine from some Dickensian novel. A waif.

"A thousand pardons." Lurch, who had looked surprised as well for a moment, had recovered himself quickly. "*Yoshi-san,* it so turns out, is past due for her first customer. And Koko-*san* happens to have been saving her for someone very special. Turns out she thinks you fit the bill." He winked. "I told you they'd go for that hair."

"That's—that's very nice of her," Billy stammered. "But the truth is, I'm really not—"

Lurch cut him off. "Oh, knock it off. Didn't you say you grew up here, Red?"

"Yes, but—"

"Well, then you know how rude it is to refuse a gift. Especially a gift like this one. It's a great honor they're doing you."

He winked again, and Billy had a brief fantasy of gouging out that same eyeball.

"You know," Lurch went on, "that if you turn me and especially Koko-*san* down, you'll offend the both of us terribly. Not to mention poor Yoshi here. How do you think that'd make her feel? Her very first customer, saying she ain't up to snuff?"

This can't be happening. Billy looked from the big man's face to the small woman in the *kimono*. The woman held the girl's arm so tightly it hurt him just to see it. Behind her, Billy noted that Mike Richards had left the room. But Sarah Bernhardt was still there, smiling coolly at him. The barman and the tattooed doorman were also following the exchange. Even the drunken MP, perhaps woken by the lull in music, was looking blearily over. Billy wished he'd run when he'd had the chance.

"Look, Lurch," he began again, helplessly.

"It's *Legs*, Red," Lurch said, patiently.

"Legs. What if I told you that I've got a girl back home."

"I'd tell you that's swell." Legs reached out and tucked a condom into his shirt pocket. "And that we all do. And that you can think of her while you're in there."

God damn *him*, Billy thought, just as a third voice broke in from the bar. "Say, what's going on over there? Reynolds causing trouble again?"

And glancing over Billy saw that little Frank Rosen had just staggered out, his shirt untucked and his service cap askew.

"Well, guess what?" called Legs back. "Koko-*san* and I have offered Red here a welcome gift of fresh Jap pussy. I'm just trying to explain to him that if he refuses, he'll ruin it for all of us."

The New Yorker looked from Legs to Billy to Yoshi, and Billy thought about how they'd laughed together earlier. But that small spark of hope was pinched out by the little man's next words: "Well, what the hell's wrong with you, Reynolds? Bow or do whatever you're supposed to do when someone gives you a Japanese cherry. And then, get your skinny ass back there!" He grinned. "Or I will. Hell, someone's gotta man up."

"A-*men*, brother!" Legs gave the girl a small push so that she almost stumbled into Billy, her thin arms outstretched for balance. His first instinct was to shrink away. But then their eyes met and he saw in hers a look of such utter bleakness that he felt a lump of sympathy in his throat: she was clearly far more frightened than he was.

With that recognition there came a sudden surge of pity. He did not want to bed her. He didn't even want to touch her—not, at least, unless it would somehow calm or reassure her. But the thought of anyone *else* touching her was suddenly more abominable than any of his own unnatural urges. So before he could question it or overthink it or talk himself out of it he grabbed her hand, and said in a voice he hardly recognized: "Oh for Christ's sake, give her here."

Without any coherent plan and yet strangely energized by this fact, Billy took ahold of her thin wrist.

"*Oide,*" he said. *Please come with me.*

THE ROOMS WERE arranged off a single dim-lit passageway, each one obscured by a flimsy sheet. As Billy followed Yoshi past them, he tried to ignore the sounds that flowed unfiltered into the hallway; the rhythmic thumps and liquid rustles, the stifled cries and open grunts. His armpits were damp, his head ached. With each step he took on the *tatami* dread tightened his throat a little more. It occurred to him that it might feel something like this when the MPs led him to the stand.

Yoshi had been walking ahead, but now she stopped before a doorway at the end of the hall.

"*Dozo,*" she said, without expression, and indicated the room beyond. Ducking to avoid the low-hung curtain rod, Billy stepped in.

It was a small room, equipped with only a camp bed and a chair upon which was set the stump of a wavering candle. As she let the sheet fall back Billy hesitated, then sat down on the cot with his Contax next to him. Yoshi stepped over to the chair and sat just opposite him, so that their knees were barely touching. She looked so young and frightened that Billy was seized by the unfamiliar urge to take her into his arms. Just to reassure her. And maybe himself. But he knew that that move would be misinterpreted as him wanting the one thing he *didn't* want, so he just sat there, fingers tapping anxiously on his kneecaps.

Yoshi fidgeted with a button on her blouse. "How would you like to begin?" she asked at last, primly. Her language was as erudite as it had been outside, but he sensed a new note of barely contained panic.

He gave a hollow laugh. "Frankly, I haven't the faintest idea."

Her expression didn't change a whit. Unnerved, he let his eyes settle on her white fingers with their unpainted nails. Her hands were beautiful, but callused—as though she'd done hard work in some field. She was also wearing a ring that was a little large on her. As she continued fidgeting it slowly slipped around, until from where he sat he could only see a band of silver, like a wedding band. He wondered whether she'd ever thought about things like marriage. Before all this; back in that great *before.* Had there been boys? Puppy love? A girlish crush, on either gender?

As she leaned forward her shirt swung open, and he saw that she'd actually been unbuttoning it. He was struck dumb by the sight of her pink-tipped breasts; small, white, softly pronounced atop the rib-lined white of her torso. Something about their spare perfection stirred him deeply, though not at all in a sexual way. He felt his heart pound.

"Would you prefer to stand?" she asked, her voice shaking audibly now. "Koko-*san* said sometimes Americans like to stand. Or we can—we can also recline."

She sounded so much like that airplane hostess that Billy was afraid he'd burst out laughing. Instead, and to his dismay, he felt his eyes tearing up. In helplessness, in embarrassment. In pity. "I'm fine right here," he lied, struck by how steady his voice was compared to his emotions. "Listen. Yoshiko-*san* . . ."

"It's Yoshi. Just—Yoshi."

"Yoshi-*san*. We—we don't have to do this now."

The woman next door—was that Mike's favorite girl? Lola, was it?—was moaning, and while he couldn't tell if it was in sorrow or feigned pleasure he could still hear every goddamn sobbing note. The walls were that thin.

"Don't you like me?" Yoshi asked. Not plaintively or angrily, but with a removed, almost scientific-sounding interest.

"I do like you," Billy said, which was actually true. "I like you very much. But what I'd really like is just to—to talk a little. Is that OK?"

She shook her head in a way that might have meant *yes* or *no* or *who cares.*

"The piano," he said, grasping at the first subject to cross his mind, "where did you learn to play it like that?"

"In Tokyo. I learned it from an Austrian lady from Yokohama."

"You're very good," he told her. Across the hall a man's laughter boomed—it sounded like Mike Richards. A woman's protest underscored it; a discordant duet. Yoshi threw a tense glance at the doorway, but Billy pressed on.

"Do you enjoy it? The music, I mean? Satie is one of my favorite composers. I especially love his *Gymnopédies* . . . you played that last one with such feeling."

"What I usually am feeling," she said, in a small voice, "is that no one is listening."

"I was listening."

She seemed about to respond. But then, as if on cue, the cot next door launched into a series of rhythmic creaks, each underscored by a high-pitched female yelp. Yoshi raked a white hand through her short hair, her opulent ring catching the candlelight.

"That's a lovely ring you've got there," Billy said, lifting his voice slightly against the din.

She touched it distractedly. "My mother's."

"From Japan?"

"My father got it for her in Manchuria."

"Is that so."

Pulling out a cigarette, he offered her the pack. She shook her head. "Your English is very good."

"My mother taught me." (*Her mother is a spy.*)

"Your accent—it's very—English," he said, tentatively. "Have you been to England?"

"No. But my mother went to school there as a child."

"*So ka.*"

She nodded, not seeming to notice his Japanese response and continuing on in her high-tea Londonese. "She also taught me French."

"Really? *Sans blague, tu parles français?*"

"*Bien sûr.*"

"And yet you've never been abroad?"

"Only to *Manshu.*"

"Right. Your father was working there."

"He remains there still."

From beyond the wall a man's grunt, then a low laugh. Yoshi shot another frightened look in its direction. What was she afraid of? Losing her virginity? Or failing to do so? Would she be punished if she failed this assignment—beyond not getting her American name?

"So you've heard from him, then?" he asked. "Your father, I mean."

She shook her head. "But I'm sure I will quite soon."

He just nodded, though as far as he knew there was little to no chance of hearing from anyone in Japan's former colonies. With their communications systems destroyed, their settlements overrun and their Army dead, fled, imprisoned or in hiding, most Japanese foreign nationals might as well have been on Pluto. But if Yoshi knew this she gave no sign.

Next door Mike (if it was Mike) apparently finished his session and let loose a fart, then a loud sigh. Billy heard a woman's low voice ask a question. The man mumbled something back lazily.

"How about your mother?"

She just stared at him, her lower lip caught between her teeth.

Sensing that he'd veered onto a difficult subject, Billy wracked his brains for something else. Before he could find one, though, the girl stood up abruptly and took one step across, so she was standing over him.

"What are you doing?" he asked, startled.

"What I am supposed to be doing," she said, pushing the Contax over to make room. "What you're paying me to do."

She placed her hand on his knee. She had twisted her ring back into place, but it still struck him as fantastically out of place. An evil snake's eye following each absurd, *Kabuki*-esque move. Her palm felt warm through his khakis. It also seemed to be trembling, though it was possible that he was the one shaking.

Her face might have been carved out of marble.

"Listen," he said, shakily, "I—I'm not here for that."

"Why not?"

"I'm just . . . not."

Still not moving her hand, she looked at him skeptically. "Then why *are* you here?"

She sounded almost angry, but when he met her eyes he saw she was close to tears. Somehow this decided him. He reached for her hand and covered it gently with his own.

"Why are *you* here?" he asked her.

She shrugged. "For the same reason everyone is."

"I don't believe that."

"Why not?"

"You're nothing like the others."

"You know nothing about me."

Looking into her stone-still face, Billy pictured himself at the same age, clothed in blue serge and secret shame. Standing behind the St. John's dining hall, huddled together with Koji Jones and Roger Elgin and Franklin Stern who—for once—had allowed him to join their circle at recess. He didn't know why until Franklin produced from his knickers pocket a postcard of a white woman, naked but for a pair of lace-up boots and a boa constrictor. The others whooped and whistled, and said things like *crazy* and *holy-moly*, their faces reflected fear and quivering reverence. But Billy had felt—nothing. Nothing at all.

What's the matter, Reynolds? Franklin had jeered. *Don't like the photograph? I thought you* liked *photographs.*

Then he pictured himself fifteen years later, still freckled and red-faced but naked, hunched before the Army doctor and his grim-faced nurse. He'd been so afraid at that first physical exam, afraid of meeting anyone's eyes. He'd been so certain they would find him out—about the sleepover. About the bald man with the shaking state of Florida on his head. *All this time you've been a fucking homo? A pervert? . . .*

"So tell me," he said. "Tell me about yourself."

She returned his gaze unwaveringly. Then, removing her hand from beneath his, she folded it with its mate in her lap. She took a deep breath. He thought at first that she was going to ignore the request. But then she began to talk.

"I didn't know," she said. "I didn't know what this place was. When I read the advertisement in the *Mainichi* they said it was a government office job for . . ." She paused again, translating mentally. "For cultured and patriotic young ladies."

"That's how they advertised it?"

She continued on as though he hadn't spoken. "The others here—most of them knew what it was. Some have done this before. Koko-*san* ran a—how do you say it—a soldier comfort house in Korea. And Yumi-*san*—I mean, Sarah—worked there with her." She dropped her eyes. "But in the beginning I didn't know."

"When did you find out?"

"When I answered the advertisement they sent me in with a doctor. After he'd checked me I put my clothes back on, and Koko-*san* came in and told me what this . . . shop was for. She told me that if I worked here she could pay me, pay me very good money. Also, they could help me find my parents because she was working with the city government now."

It was a load of horse crap, though he didn't have the heart to tell her the truth: that the majority of the city's records had either burned in LeMay's fires or else been burned ahead of the Occupation. That half of the people who would know anything about anything would end up prisoners before the War Crimes Tribunal—including, he could only hope, those who lured young girls into prostitution. And that those who didn't wouldn't be able to piss without MacArthur's permission. That with all the other things that needed very direly to be done—mass reburials; vaccinations; water supply; *food*—finding two Japanese citizens who were surely dead wouldn't even make the bottom of the list.

"And then," she was continuing on obliviously, "I remembered that I'd once seen a lady playing piano for people in a fancy hotel.

So I showed Koko-*san* that I could play music and asked if I could only do that. And maybe translate for the other girls."

"You took control," Billy said, impressed. "That couldn't have been easy."

She shrugged. "My mother taught me that I must protect myself."

She watched the candle flicker, her delicate jaw working from side to side. "In the end, Koko said I could play the piano, but just for a little while. Just to see how I fit in. After that I would have to do"—she waved at the bed, at him—"that. If I wanted to get paid real money. And if I wanted them to find my parents."

She fell silent, eyes molten in the flickering dark. Billy looked away, tightening his jaw so hard his teeth hurt, though stories like this had to abound in this half-dead city, in all of Japan's half-dead cities. It struck him once more that it wasn't *about* whether you called it war or murder, crime or justice. You could call it goddamn Betty Lou if you wanted to. The bottom line was still human misery.

What do I do? he thought, feeling suddenly defeated. *What the fuck do I do?* There were the obvious and meaningless phrases he'd run through with Mike Richards: *I'm so sorry; that sounds awful; I can't imagine.* He finally decided he'd just take her hand again. If she would let him.

But when he looked up her hands were busy doing back up her buttons. "I don't remember your name," she asked him, before he could speak.

"William Reynolds. Second Lieutenant. United States Army." Out of habit he almost gave her his serial number, but stopped himself.

Yoshi Kobayashi bowed. "*Hajimemashite*, Lieutenant Reynolds. Mr. Legs said you work with General MacArthur?"

He nodded. "I'm a translator there." Which, technically at least, was still true.

She studied him, biting her lip, seeming torn. "I wonder if you might perhaps be able to help me."

"With what?"

"With . . ." She tightened her jaw. "I want to leave."

For a moment he didn't get it. "Leave . . . what? Leave Japan?"

"Leave the club. Koko-*san's*." She took a deep breath, as though this were costing significant effort. "I want to *leave*," she said again, more forcefully this time. "I want to find a new job. Maybe with the Americans, like you."

Her English was as impeccable as ever, but he still thought he must have misunderstood.

"*Mac-Ar-saa no tame ni hataraki-tai no?*" he repeated, just to be sure. "You want to work for General MacArthur?"

She nodded emphatically. "*So desu.*"

Christ. He rubbed the back of his neck. What the hell was he supposed to do? Break her out of Koko-*san's* like some *effete* Clyde breaking Bonnie out of jail? Drag her into Jamison's office and beg like a boy? "Look how *pretty* she is! Can't we keep her?"

And yet . . . and yet. His brain was suddenly working furiously. Matthews *had* said that they had more work than they could possibly handle. That they were, in fact, *desperate for help* . . .

His thoughts were interrupted by a new sound from outside: hoarse male whispers directly outside their hanging bedsheet. Someone snickered. Someone else pounded on the wall so heavily that Yoshi started, and the candle guttered on the floor.

"Hey, Red!" came Legs' voice, slurring. "*Awfullllll* quiet in there, baby. You sure you're getting my money's worth?"

"Well, he *does* seem the quiet type," someone—Rosen?—simpered.

"Quiet, my ass. I bet he screams like a little girl." And then to illustrate his point Legs let loose a high, hellish scream: "*Aiiiiiiiiiiiiii iiiiiiiiiiiiigggggggggghhhhhhh!*"

Yoshi leapt in surprise, gasping. *Assholes,* Billy thought, and felt his hands ball into fists. In another life he would have remained silent, or maybe even started to cry. Now, however, he did neither of those things.

"Get the *fuck* out of here," he yelled instead, utterly surprising himself. "Go fuck your own goddamn gooks!"

There was a brief span of hushed silence, then a chuckle of approval. "Yes, *sir*," Legs said, and the voices receded.

Billy turned back to Yoshi, who—if possible—looked even paler than before. "Sorry about that," he said quietly. "I couldn't figure out any other way to get them to leave."

She nodded, but her eyes were wide with terror and something else . . . supplication?

"I want to leave," she said again, in a small voice.

Billy stared at her. And then, all at once, it was all clear.

"OK," he said. "Let's go."

She blinked. "Go where?"

"Somewhere not here."

Her lips parted. "Right *now*? Leave the club?"

"In the dust," he said, though it occurred to him that she might not understand the expression. He grabbed his Contax and slung it messenger-style across his chest, feeling the exhaustion and gloom drift off like withered petals. "C'mon."

She hesitated. "But . . . what about my parents?"

Jesus. He put a hand firmly on each of her shoulders, resisting a sudden urge to shake her.

"Yoshi," he said sharply, "even if your parents are alive, no one here can help you find them. Even if they are working with the government. They have no connections. They have no *records*. They can't do a goddamn thing."

She digested this, her upper lip pearled with perspiration. "Do *you* have connections?"

Billy swallowed back a groan of frustration. "MacArthur's offices have a hell of a better shot at it than the Tokyo government," he told her, which was true. If he didn't get court-martialed. And *if* they went for his idea. And *if* she passed all the tests and clearances they would doubtlessly put her through . . . Overwhelmed by the enormity of the whole proposal, Billy found himself wavering too. But when he met her eyes again it was clear that she'd come to her own decision. For now she was reaching for his hand.

"Come," she said. "Let's make a run."

And then they were doing just that; running. Down the dark hallway, past the dark rooms with their white bedsheets, past the murmuring murmurs and grunting grunts and sighing sighs of the people whose legs and arms and heaving buttocks those white billows barely obscured. They ran past the beaded curtain and into the lounge area, which was now empty but for the bartender wiping down his counter.

"Oh! He came out!" the bartender called out jovially. "Another beer for the honored guest?"

Billy didn't bother to answer. He made for the main entrance, leapt through the sagging doorjamb, feeling Yoshi Kobayashi lightly following him step for step. As they passed the tattooed doorman he remained slumped on his stool at first. But then he gave a shout and leapt to his feet, his small eyes bleary with sleep and his hand ominously fumbling at his belt for whatever sword or gun or maybe ninja star he kept there.

"*Oi!*" he shouted. "Stop now! Where the hell are you going? You can't do that. *Oi!* Come back!"

But they just took the next turn and kept right on running. They leapt effortlessly over rock and rubble, barely touching the ground, neither of them slipping or stumbling even once. At some point their clasped hands pulled apart and he looked up to see that she had taken the lead, was leaping nimbly in her thin and flapping house slippers, soaring over charred iron and trash-filled ditches, half-buttoned blouse fluttering like a kite tail in the breeze.

She led him past the grotty bars and seedy teahouses and frizz-haired *pan-pan* girls on the prowl for the evening's last, lost GIs. She steered them over streams of open sewage and piles of feces and falling foundations, and behind what looked like a collapsed firewall. She skirted several low, shallow bomb shelters that had been dug along the roads (which, he couldn't help but notice, didn't look like they'd provide much shelter at all) and finally ducked behind a small shantytown constructed of corrugated tin and broken beams, where—on some unspoken agreement—they paused to catch their breath.

"Well," he huffed in Japanese, bending over as he gasped. He hadn't run that fast since Basic Training. "*Daijobukai? Are you all right?*"

She nodded, her thin chest heaving. When their eyes met again her lips parted, and he thought that perhaps now she would finally allow herself to cry. But instead of sobbing she broke into a jagged and husky laugh: first one peal, then another. Despite himself Billy laughed a little too, simply from the joy of seeing her smile for the first time.

The skyline was thawing; the sun had begun its glum climb for the day. Rosen and Legs and Mike and all the other Americans—except, presumably, for Major General John Smith—would soon make the bumpy drive together back to the YK building, there to snatch a couple of hours' rest before lining up at Douglas MacArthur's vastly understaffed offices. And unless something unexpected happened, he would be there with them. At least for today.

Turning back to Yoshi, he saw her touch her lip with her pinkie. "I must look a wreck," she said, as though they'd just come back from a casual jaunt by the Thames.

"You look better than you did back there at Koko's place," he told her, which—strangely enough—she did. "That's it, then. Right? You won't go back there?"

She cocked her head. "No," she said.

"I have to go talk to my boss. Can you wait for me until I get back tonight?"

She nodded.

"Where do you live?"

She pointed out past the shantytown. Following the gesture, he saw in the near distance the blackened shell of a bus. Its windows appeared to be boarded up with plywood.

"You live *there?*"

"It's near where my house was. I don't want to go too far, in case . . ." She drifted off, eyes on the rubbled distance.

Billy bit his lip, nodded.

The light was stronger, the first few rays breaking out from the concrete-colored cloud bank and shafting down to illumine the broken streets. Behind them, a gaunt woman emerged from a tin-walled shack in the shantytown with a basket of wet laundry, a baby on her back. Bowing to them, she turned and began to pin the wet clothes up on a clothesline.

"Mrs. Fujiwara," Yoshi said. "She was my best friend's mother . . . before." She hesitated, then added: "She—all her other children died. There were seven. Satako-*chan* was in my class," she said flatly, as though pointing out the price of rice in a market.

"Oh," said Billy.

"She was luckier than some, though. At least she found parts of them to bury."

Billy swallowed. "Parts?"

She nodded. "For lots of people there was nothing left to bury at all."

Billy looked back at Mrs. Fujiwara, who had finished hanging her things. Catching his eye, she bowed once more to him before retreating back into her shanty.

Jesus Christ, he thought. *Lucky.*

Suddenly, it was as if the exhaustion of the past two days had finally caught up with him. He was so tired he could have dropped and slept where he stood. *How the hell are they doing it?* he wondered. *Just getting through each day? How do they get up in the morning?* He thought of Yoshi, sleeping alone on her blackened bus, her house and neighborhood gone and her parents in all likelihood dead, probably without any "parts" to bury and return to for solace. If it were him he'd probably just want to die . . .

But Yoshi now looked very much alive. Her hair was windblown and feathery, her cheeks pink from their unprompted sprint. Her eyes seemed to have lost some of that adult, hallow look. She seemed . . . hopeful.

"Hey," he asked, on an impulse, "can I take your picture?"

"Now?" She gazed at him. "You are strange," she said, in a way that seemed to imply that this wasn't an insult. But she nodded, and smoothed and buttoned the rest of her blouse up, and ran her ringed hand through her hair.

Wondering slightly at his own nerve, Billy unscrewed the Contax's lens cap, his palms perspiring despite the autumn chill. Wiping them on his khakis, he wound the film forward, pondering where to put her, how to frame it. But when he looked up again, she had already chosen.

She was standing before the shantytown, between two charred telephone pole tops that were still swinging from tangled wire like gallows victims. It was a bit more of a dramatic and off-balance shot than he would have chosen, but Billy just nodded and put her into focus. Then, following some unclear but compelling instinct, he waited for her to give the go-ahead. As though she were the true photographer here, and he simply the machine following her vision.

IX. *Los Angeles*

Tadahiko Hayashi

AUGUST 1962

THE TITLE WAS *"BARAKU"*—THE JAPANESE TERM FOR "BARRACKS," or shantytowns like the one that had lined her old street in Tokyo for years after Surrender. Staring up at the framed photograph, Yoshi felt her throat tighten; not just at the blackened landscape she'd tried so hard to forget, but at the sight of herself. Sixteen years old. Erect and almost defiant; her cheeks still flushed from their wild escape. Her clothes were ragged, and like everyone else at that time she was drastically underweight. But there was a lightness about her that had nothing to do with body mass—a sharp determination jutting through the fear, exhaustion and hunger the way a bone pushes out against skin.

It took her a moment to think of the English word for it: *hope.*

A little shaky, she made her way to a nearby chair and sank down into it, surveying the crowd for a familiar face. But Billy wasn't here yet, and of course without Billy she recognized no one other than her own sixteen-year-old self.

"Are you all right, miss?"

Glancing up, Yoshi saw a young blond waiter hovering over her with his tray. His eyes were wide and blue, his face genially concerned. If he'd made the connection between Yoshi and the enormous picture of her behind his head he gave no sign.

"Yes," she said, taking out a handkerchief to dab her upper lip. "I'm sorry. I'm fine. I just—I only just arrived last night. I think I'm jet-lagged still."

"Where are you in from?"

"Tokyo."

He gave a wry grin. "And the first thing you do is come to an opening for a photography exhibit of the place?"

"I—" For a moment she felt mocked. Then she realized he was flirting with her. *They'll do that, you know,* her friend Kuniko had said, *now that you don't wear a wedding ring.*

Forcing herself to smile back, she waved at the large poster that had been propped up on an easel by the entrance. *AFTER,* it read; *Images from Tokyo, 1945.* "The photographer is a friend of mine. He had an interview with someone, but we're supposed to meet here at five."

"I see." The waiter looked at his watch. "Well, if he's in an interview it might be running over. Would you care for a glass of wine? Might help pass the time." He winked. "And the jet lag."

Yoshi hesitated. In general she wasn't much of a drinker, but his smile warmed her to the idea and she found herself taking one of his plastic cups. "Thank you."

"My pleasure." He gave a short bow. "Let me know if you need anything else."

As he wandered away, tray lifted high and his engaging smile flashing at other gallery-goers, Yoshi watched with a faint sense of regret. She'd never been particularly social. In Tokyo, even before her disastrous marriage (and certainly since) she'd eschewed parties and dinner dates and dance clubs. She went to the movies fairly often but often alone, and she ate out less than once a month. And yet it had been good, in this foreign place where she knew no one, to have someone to talk to. If only for a few moments.

Sighing, she sipped her wine. It was breathlessly bad—both sour and oversweet, thin yet viscous. Yet the waiter had been right; it eased away a little of her dry-eyed exhaustion, unknotted the anxiety in her gut. Taking another sip, she leaned her head back against the wall and gazed around again. Crowds in America were different, she decided. In part it was because the people were simply bigger. But it was also because their *movements* were bigger; swinging strides when walking. Wide open-armed pre-embraces. Wild and energetic waves at friends and acquaintances and even total strangers as they made their way around the little room. It was not unlike watching a flock of seagulls; everyone jostling and murmuring and subtly repositioning themselves to get the best view of whatever work they happened to be studying. Japanese crowds, by contrast, were more like sparrows. Flying in formation one way, then—on cue—all neatly, soundlessly changing direction.

SHE'D LANDED IN Los Angeles the evening before, her first glimpse of the victors' land a silvery tangle of traffic winding itself between doll-sized clay rooftops. The city seemed much less dense than Tokyo—not to mention far neater. The Japanese capital had been mostly rebuilt in the past two decades. But large patches of it still seemed perpetually under construction; functioning to the beat of jackhammers and pile drivers, the gruff ditties of construction workers on miles of bamboo scaffolding.

L.A., by contrast, seemed fully finished from the sky. Its houses were new and modern, its parks broad and green. Its swimming pools looked like winking blue eyes. It was only as they came in for their final approach that it dawned on Yoshi how *huge* it all was;

that these neat houses were also *large* houses, some significantly bigger than her favorite Shinjuku movie theater. Beyond them lay the metropolis itself—a steel-and-glass garden of buildings, a few of them so tall she imagined their top floors to be filled with clouds.

She'd had one thought as she'd stared down from her window seat: *No wonder. No wonder we lost.*

"IT'S REALLY SOMETHING, isn't it," someone near her was saying loudly. "I mean, some of these pictures make the place look as bad as *Hee-ro-shee-ma.*"

The voice was high, the syllables drawn out the way they were in *Gone With the Wind.* Startled, Yoshi looked up from her drink to see a stocky matron in a tight polyester shirtdress. She was addressing an aging man by her side.

"Think they're all of Tokyo," he said, waving towards the entranceway. "That's what the sign says, anyways."

"But I thought they didn't use the A-bomb on Tokyo."

"They didn't. This was just from plain old bombing, I guess." He leaned over towards the picture, squinting a little. "Maybe he made it look worse than it was."

The couple wandered off, Yoshi staring after them in disbelief. *Plain old bombing? Worse than it was?* She thought of the blackened moonscape that had greeted her that morning, from the soot-filled shores of the Sumida. Of the mountains of charred bodies compiled by the Army; many of them so calcified and disfigured that even family members couldn't recognize enough to claim them.

What kind of a people, she wondered, does what was done that day and then has no concept of the enormity of their act?

She tossed back more wine, too shaken for a moment to register its foul aftertaste. But as she reached to set the cup on the floor she caught a glimpse of her own hand, the green ring glinting in the fluorescent light. Staring at it, she felt the same uncomfortable mixture of fondness and doubt she'd had ever since getting Billy's letter last year. *Anyway,* she reminded herself, *you are not one to judge.*

She set the cup down, glancing around the space again. Billy still wasn't here, and it somehow seemed rude—sneaky, almost—to look at his other pictures without him. She hesitated for a moment, then opened her purse and pulled from it the paperback she'd brought with her. It was *Lady Chatterley's Lover,* a copy she'd picked up at the airport after landing. She'd covered the volume with plain brown paper from a shopping bag so she could read it without feeling self-conscious, but she didn't open the slim volume now. Instead she pulled out the letter, which she was using as a bookmark. Pale blue and aerogram-thin, it was creased from dozens of rereads. It was dated February 1961.

Dear Yoshi:

It was with much surprise and great joy that I received your letter yesterday. I have thought of you often in the years since I left Tokyo, wondering what you are doing and even (I'll admit) wondering whether you ever chanced to see any of my photos that made it into Tokyo papers. So I was truly delighted that you not only saw my shot of the Tokyo University protests, but used it to track me down here.

Yes, I am working for the L.A. Times these days, mainly as a photographer but increasingly contributing to stories, too. After leaving the Occupation I had a stint in San Francisco, building up my résumé and freelancing. After getting the offer from the Times I moved here in 1956, and have been fairly happy with the place ever since. I travel a fair amount on the job but last year's trip to Tokyo—covering the renewal of the U.S.-Japan Security Treaty—was the first time I'd been there since the war. You're right; the changes are extraordinary. And the demonstrations (!) I could hardly believe that these screaming kids were the same straitlaced students I saw on the subway going to school. Kishi certainly seems to have touched a nerve on this one.

I am sorry that I didn't take the time to look you up, either before or while I was in the city. But I was only there for three days—hardly enough time, it struck me, to track you down, much less spend any quality time together. Your letter answered many of the things I'd wanted to ask you, though, and I am pleased and very proud to hear about your success in the publishing world. As you may recall, I had the privilege of working with Frank Tuttledge in the Japanese Media division a few times. He's a solid guy, and I hear nothing but good things about his East-West publishing venture. It sounds like an exceptionally good fit for someone of your talents and background.

You asked about my family. My father died last year of a heart attack, though he worked up until the very end. He actually came to Tokyo often on architectural consulting jobs; he felt very strongly about his responsibility to help rebuild the city. My mother remains on the East Coast, where she has her clubs and crafts to keep her busy. I tried to convince her to come West with me, but the only thing that would bring her out here would be the prospect of grandchildren and so far, that's looking pretty dim.

Speaking of parents . . . Yoshi-san, there is something that's been weighing on my conscience over the years, and when I read your letter I realized it was time to come to terms with it. I'm not sure why I didn't before. In part I simply lacked courage, I guess. I was also afraid that the information would hurt you—and you'd already survived so much. But reading your words yesterday, hearing how you've survived and flourished in my absence, made me realize that you are more than strong enough to bear anything I might say.

So here goes:

When you first joined Civil back in November of '45 you asked me to help you find information on your parents. A year later, we had a conversation in which I told you they were almost certainly dead. That much was true: given the extremely high death toll in your neighborhood on the night of March 10th and the fact that your mother's name doesn't appear on any hospital rosters, there seemed little chance that she survived that first firebombing. Similarly, it is now known that the Japanese village of Shin Nagano suffered some of the most brutal casualties of Russia's August 9th invasion of Manchuria, which—as you know—claimed the lives of over 100,000 Japanese civilians. Those who survived tended to be the youngest members of those communities; toddlers and infants left with Chinese neighbors and friends who—to the best of our knowledge—are now being raised as Chinese children. A few men survived, either by fleeing or by being taken prisoner. But your father's name had not surfaced on any of those lists.

But there was something more that I'd learned by that point; something I decided—wrongly, I now realize—not to share with you. The truth is that when I first submitted your name to Personnel that November I was told that your background check had raised some "red flags." The main issue, it seemed, was that you were the daughter of a suspected war criminal.

War criminal. Over a year after first reading it, the term still made Yoshi catch her breath. She reached for her wineglass, took another sip and read on.

Needless to say, this information surprised me, as I'm sure it is surprising you. Nothing in our discussions had led me to believe that you were aware of wrongdoing on your father's part. Further research, however, yielded reports from confiscated North China Army records. These included the names of some two dozen Chinese civilians who had been executed. These men (and a few women) were mostly farmers in whose deaths your father is suspected of having colluded, after they protested the requisition of their land for the Japanese village built there.

But there was also the name of one American, a Lieutenant Cameron Richards of the United States Army Air Corps who was a pilot in the 1942 Doolittle Raid on Tokyo. Lieutenant Richards' plane was downed outside Harbin in April 1942. It is believed that your father not only found him after he'd bailed out, but delivered him to the North China Army officials. According to their own records, these officials executed Richards April 19th by means of beheading.

In the end, I was able to get you past your father's accused deeds with

the help of my own father, who had some fairly high-up connections in
MacArthur's offices. Between his help and the fact that there was no way
to prove your father's role in these murders, we were able to secure your
approval.

Yoshi-chan: I want you to know that I'm telling you these things not
because I believe your father's crimes—if they were such—reflect in any
way on you. I'm telling you simply because I believe that you have the right to
know, just as Lieutenant Richards' family had the right to know how he died.
It's possible, of course, that you've heard about these accusations already, as they
are probably still somewhere in the official records. I hope this is not the case,
but if you have, my apologies for not telling you sooner.

In closing: I, too, hope that we can continue to write one another. And
I would absolutely encourage you to come visit America as you mentioned.
If it's of any interest, sometime next summer I'm planning a small,
private exhibition of some of the photographs I took in Tokyo during the
Occupation—specific date and place to be determined. I know that you of all
people don't need instruction on what Tokyo was like when the war ended.
Still, you might find some of it to be of interest.

All my best,
Billy

Yoshi folded up the letter and slid it back within the pages of the
Lawrence. She closed the book, then clasped her hands together
atop it. *Suspected*, she reminded herself, as she'd done a thousand
times since first reading the letter. None of this information ever
made it to a courtroom or a tribunal. So it was still entirely possible that what Kenji had done was not just innocent but actually
honorable—at least, by the standards of the time. He'd found an
enemy and brought the man to the authorities, but there was no
evidence that he'd done anything unethical.

Looking down at her hands, she twisted the green ring. She thought
of the black lighter, the American pilot's lighter. *He gave it to you?*

More like left it.

He died of his injuries?

You could say that . . . That reminds me. This is for your mother.

It's probably not even the pilot's, she thought—also for the thousandth time since getting Billy's letter.

It was after the civilian travel ban had been lifted two months later that Yoshi wrote her old friend and colleague a second time. She wrote with congratulations on his civilian success, and thanks for the new information on Kenji. She wrote him that she'd been initially planning to try to visit Manchuria next summer in order to try to find her half-sisters Aki and Maki there; but that given the near impossibility of getting a visa into China she'd decided to come to America instead. She wrote him that she would visit the following summer, for his exhibit, and that she'd send him more details as they took shape.

The next day she went to the American Library and asked the curator for every scrap of media they had on the 1942 Doolittle Raid.

"KOBAYASHI-*SAN!*"

The voice echoed across the room, as joyous as a yodel. Dazedly, Yoshi looked up to see her savior and former supervisor.

"Captain!" she called back; and then both blushed and laughed at how little he now resembled an officer.

When she'd last seen him, William Reynolds had been impeccably clean-shaven, tightly buttoned. He'd worn the moss-toned jacket and triangular cap of the USOF over his close-cut hair. Now, as he grinned at her above a small crowd of well-wishers, Yoshi saw that he was as lean and tall and pale as she remembered. But his hair had changed, growing longer even as it receded from his freckled browline, a wavy and wiry red tide. His style had changed too: now he wore a gray turtleneck under a black woolen blazer, and on his chin he sported a small triangular beard of the sort Yoshi associated with French movie directors. The mere sight of him—of someone this known, this trusted—brought hot, unexpected tears to her eyes. For one very long moment she wanted nothing more than to hurl herself at him headlong.

Instead, she stood up, slipped the Lawrence back into her purse and forced herself to walk casually to meet him while he disentangled himself from his admirers and came to meet her halfway. There they stood, face-to-face in the middle of the room, until after a moment he opened his arms to her. And while they'd hardly touched beyond a handshake back at the Ernie Pyle, she stepped into his embrace without a moment's hesitation. He pulled her against his thin chest and held her there while in her mind a white bedsheet unfurled in a doorway from the past. She'd never been close enough to Captain William Reynolds to know what, exactly, he smelled like, but the civilian Billy Reynolds smelled like cigarette smoke and cologne and something sweetly minty, like Listerine. It struck her, as she buried her nose in his lapel, that she hadn't been enfolded this fully by a man since she'd left her husband for the last time.

When he finally stepped back he kept his hands on her shoulders, as though he feared she might run off.

"Sorry I'm late," he said. "That guy from *L.A. Arts* went on and on . . . Let me look at you." And then: "*Christ!* You haven't aged a day!"

"Oh no," she countered, ducking her head, "I'm just an ugly old woman now. A thirty-two-year-old spinster."

"Like hell you are," he said fondly, and gave her shoulders a small squeeze. "Just think of what that would make me. And I know *I'm* still a whippersnapper."

Whippersnapper, she thought, stuck for a moment before the translation came to her: *young*. The term made her smile, but it wasn't entirely inapt. True, William Reynolds hadn't gotten younger over the past decade; but it had clearly treated him better than the forties had. He'd never been a particularly handsome man; had been too thin and pale and hunched. Too perpetually—sometimes almost pathetically—apologetic, even in a place as apology-filled as Japan. Now, though, he held himself with a new ease and confidence which seemed to make him not just taller but somehow more substantial. The West Coast sun had colored his pale cheeks, coaxed forth a spattering of toast-toned freckles. When he smiled warm lines fanned from his eyes to his temples, indicating that this was something he now did often.

"California agrees with you," she said, smiling.

"It does," he agreed. "A hell of a lot more than those badly lit office buildings in Tokyo." He turned back towards the gallery. "So have you seen everything there is to see here already?"

She shook her head. "Hardly. I was waiting for you. I do have two questions, though."

"Fire away."

"First: why did you include that awful portrait of me over there?"

She pointed at *"Baraku."* Billy opened his mouth, then shut it. "I'm sorry. I should probably have asked your permission first. I guess I was afraid that you'd say no."

She thought about this a moment. "I wouldn't have. Said no, I mean. But it would have been helpful to have some . . . warning?"

"Well then, I have no excuse," he said, sheepishly. "I should probably have also asked whether you would like a copy."

"No," she said quickly, firmly. She hated seeing herself in photographs. "No, I would not."

Billy gave a wry smile. "You were always a woman who knew what she wanted."

"That's a bad thing?"

"Not in my book." He squeezed her arm. "Second question?"

"The exhibition title. Why *'After'*?"

He shrugged. "Hard to explain. But it has to do with how everyone talked about the war when I was there. How no one ever seemed to want to actually use the term *war*. It was always about 'before' and 'after.' "

"They don't do that here?"

He shook his head. "Not as much. Perhaps it would be different if you'd won and we'd lost."

Yoshi nodded slowly, thinking that it was the first time he'd talked about it that way; *you* versus *us*. The winning side, the losing side. And yet what he said was true. Her friends and coworkers all worked long hours and had big weddings and children and then more children. Away from home they spent their growing salaries on trips to Hokkaido and Kyushu and—once the travel ban was lifted—Hawaii; at home they spent them on National radios and TV sets and Mitsubishi appliances and Toyota cars. And at work-place and home alike, everyone seemed in a mad race to *build build build*. To build new kitchens and garages, roads and cars and business connections until the old, war-torn city was no longer visible—any more than were the broken people who had scraped out their lives there in the days following the Surrender. That Japan—defeated Japan—was now part of an unspeakable past; one its inhabitants saw in nearly as mythical terms as the Emperor's once-presumed "divinity." It was simply—*before*.

"Anyway," Billy was saying—he offered her his elbow—"shall we take the tour?"

Yoshi linked her arm through his. "Yes," she said. "Let's."

They started to the left of *"Baraku,"* with an image called "Home-coming". It was a large photograph of a young woman and a much older man, leaning on a cane. The woman knelt just before a pile of debris, hands outstretched as though she were about to plunge them in, elbow-deep. Given the context, Yoshi guessed she and her father were trying to salvage something usable or undestroyed from the rubble of their house. But from the way Billy had framed her— faintly angled, the focus less on her connection with the man than with the garbage—it looked as though she were kneeling at some demolished and trash-strewn altar, praying for help.

Staring up at the picture, Yoshi found herself thinking how familiar this tableau would have seemed to her as recently as a dozen years earlier. Then, the city had hovered in a strange and hybrid state: dry ash and drying asphalt. New buildings rising gleaming against decade-old rubble. A phoenix, half-risen from its cremation. On her own old street in Bunkyo Ku the government had torn down the flimsy shantytown in which Mrs. Fujiwara and her one remaining child had lived. In its place, seemingly overnight, rose rows and rows of modern *apato* buildings; square and neat and sterile-looking, one unit cloned from the next; all so sanitized that when she first saw them Yoshi had had the strange urge to weep.

The other photographs told similar stories: of loss and resilience, tragedy and hard-sought fortune. The young mother with the baby strapped to her back, wandering in a rubbled no-man's-land. The toothless old woman in rags who crouched on the road, her prized *kimono* laid out for sale on dirty blankets. The ten-year-old street urchins with grimy faces and shrewd smiles, shooting marbles and smoking cigarette stubs. The teenage *pan-pan* girls in cheap *sufu* dresses and bobby socks and plastic pumps, their hands on jutting hips and their smiles heartbreakingly sweet.

There were white-robed veterans standing motionlessly before a monument to the dead, rice bowls extended to oblivious passersby. A crowd of demonstrators marched and shouted outside the Imperial Palace, utilizing their newly granted freedom of speech to protest the national rice shortage. They were scenes she'd seen many times in person, though it was only upon viewing Billy's pictures now that she reflected how radical a change they represented. How, mere months earlier, these same people would have paused in that same spot by the Emperor's residence only to bow in wordless reverence.

She mused as well at a shot of American officers at a street fair of some sort, their arms slung around pretty Japanese girlfriends. The women were dressed up in clothing that was clearly PX-procured; their rouged smiles appeared to be genuine. But the profile that struck Yoshi the most strongly was that of a young man standing outside the group. His body was partially obscured by a bean cake vendor's cart. But his face was clearly visible to Billy's lens, and his eyes were trained on the American men and the Japanese women. His expression was of unmitigated loathing.

Throughout the tour Billy fielded compliments and questions from the other viewers in the gallery, and Yoshi fully expected to lose him eventually to his admirers. Instead, after they'd viewed the last image together he led her away from the crowd to a small table in the corner. There he signaled the waiter and procured them two more cups of the atrocious wine.

"*Kampei*," he said, lifting his glass. And then: "You've been very quiet."

Yoshi smiled as the wine made its faintly sewage-tinged way over her tongue.

He cocked his head. "So . . . do you hate them?"

He was serious, she saw. And looking in his eyes she saw something else as well: the man he'd been at the Pyle. A younger and far-less-confident version of William Reynolds; a stooped red-headed boy who carried his camera the way the MPs outside carried their guns. In self-defense.

"I think," she said truthfully, "they are *subarashii*, William-*san*. All of them. Incredible. You have done an amazing job capturing it."

He flushed, his pale skin mottling with pleasure.

"Your father would have been very proud," she added. "I was sorry to read about his passing."

"Don't be. He lived a full life." He paused, a troubled look lingering on his face before slipping away like a moving shadow. "Anyways, the doctors say it happened very quickly. He didn't suffer."

"Still, it must have come as a shock."

He shrugged. "There have been a lot of shocks over the years. It was just one more." He frowned for a moment, then changed the subject. "So. Are you still playing the piano?"

She nodded.

"And do you still have the old Yamaha I dug out of the Pyle basement for you?"

"I do. It's still amazingly in tune." She laughed. "Although every time I play it I imagine Takarazuka chorus-line members doing a *rinu-dansu*. To Satie."

He grinned. "I'll have to hear you play the next time I'm in Tokyo."

"Will you be back in Tokyo soon?"

He leaned back in his chair, absently patting first his right breast pocket, then his left before pulling out a pack of Camels. Just as he always had at the Pyle he offered her the pack, and just as Yoshi had (almost) always done she shook her head. She watched him as he cupped his hands around the cigarette's tip to light it.

"Up to my editors, I suppose."

He exhaled, surveying her over the smoke. "You really do look fantastic, by the way. If you really are a spinster, it agrees with you. Though I find it hard to believe that you are one."

Yoshi felt her cheeks heat. "Well, I suppose you could also use the term *divorcée* now. But that seems much more . . . glamorous than I feel."

"The gay divorcée," he said; but then seeing her face he sobered. "It's final, then? The separation?"

"As of last month." Yoshi toyed with her wine cup. She had labored through Japan's bureaucratic divorce proceedings for nearly five years. This was the first time she'd spoken the word—*divorce*—in English.

"You must be relieved," Billy was saying.

She shrugged. "And sad, of course. It is right, I think, to be sad too."

He nodded. "I don't think I ever met him, did I? Your ex-husband?"

Yoshi shook her head. "We were married the year you left Japan."

"How did you meet?"

Yoshi studied the Camels he'd set between them on the table. Then, surprising herself a little, she reached for the pack and took one. "We were old friends," she said now, leaning over as he extended his lighter to her. "I'd met him in Manchuria, when I went to visit my father."

"And you'd stayed in touch during the war."

"We wrote letters." She inhaled, enjoying the feeling of smoke easing its way in and out of her lungs. "He was still in *Manshu* when the Russians invaded—he'd been with the North China Army, the *Kantogun*. For the first three years I went to greet every train that came from the North carrying returnees. I wrote his name and my father's on a sign and held it up until my arms ached."

"But he didn't come back?"

"Not until 1952. Three months after you left."

She drifted off for a moment, remembering that night. How the knock had sounded on the door of the women's dormitory in which she was living, and she'd expected nothing more than a neighborly request: a teabag, some sugar. A pen. Instead she found a harsh-faced young man in a patched and filthy *Kantogun* uniform, arms clasped behind him, socked feet planted apart.

"KONBAN WA," HE said. *Good evening.*

At first she could barely breathe, let alone speak. He was taller than she'd remembered; she tipped her head back to look up at him now. She saw his black-winged hair had thinned, and that his dark eyes seemed flatter, somehow. Or perhaps it was just a trick of the light.

"Masa?" she whispered.

He nodded. *"Nn."*

"How—how did you find me?"

"Your neighbor Fujiwara-*san* sent me here."

Up and down the darkened hall other dorm doors were opening. Dark heads popped out, staring at them. Yoshi knew full well that the house rules forbade "gentlemen visitors" to the second floor; yet even as she heard the matron's dense tread upon the stairwell she wrapped her arms around Masa's neck. Feeling his quick pulse there; feeling his thin arms clasp her in turn. Peering over his narrow shoulder, she saw Mrs. Ito bustling towards them, her lavender hair in rollers, a fierce frown on her face.

But Yoshi didn't hesitate. She took Masa's hard hand in her own. She smiled at him, and drew him in.

In the hours that followed, over a borrowed bottle of Suntory whiskey and periodic rounds of door-rappings, Masahiro had laid out his life after the Surrender. How his unit—or at least the half of it that had survived the Russian onslaught—was packed into cattle cars and carried into the Ukraine. How at the prison camp in Kramtorsk they worked in the rock quarries, twelve hours daily, often in below-freezing temperatures. Many men died that first year, and many more the second and third. At one point, Masa said, he prayed to die as well. But the very next morning he learned that he and a thousand other Japanese prisoners were being transferred to an "Anti-Chinese Crimes" camp back in China, where they'd spend the next four years before being released.

When he was finished talking he dropped his gaze to his coat pocket. "I almost forgot," he said; and Yoshi waited as he rifled through it, eventually pulling out something small and soot-covered.

"No," she breathed, taking it into her hands; touching the curved

beak, the outstretched wings. The carving was as filthy as Masa's uniform; one of its delicate talons had chipped off. But it was clearly a hawk. Clearly more than a hawk; it was the mate to the one he'd carved her back in northern China.

"You made it," she murmured. "I can't believe you really made it."

"I did it after lights-out in our barrack," he told her. "It's what kept me sane, all those nights." He hesitated. "It's really all I had there. Except my dreams of you."

His voice cracked on the word *you*, and something in his tone seemed to scrape at her insides. "Masa," she said, gently.

When he didn't respond she moved over and knelt next to him, tentatively touching his shoulder. She meant simply to be near him, to soothe him with her presence. But he leaned into her with a groan, tears silently tracking down his thin face. Then—she wasn't sure how it happened—he was pushing her down onto the mat, his hands fumbling frantically with her robe while she held him feebly, too surprised to know how to respond. Then he was on top of her, yanking up her nightgown and pushing, and pushing, and then finally ripping something inside her. When she cried out—and even in retrospect she wasn't sure whether it was in protest or mere pain—there was another furious round of knocking on the door. Masa clapped his hand over her mouth, his palm pressing down and down while he gazed into her startled eyes. Then he shuddered and collapsed, lying so motionless above her that Yoshi half feared he'd come all this way simply to die. Eventually she realized he was sleeping, and for some reason this moved her so profoundly that she simply lay there beneath him, until her arms and legs went numb.

When she finally edged her body out from under him he rolled onto his side and slept. The knocking resumed, and then finally subsided. At one point in the night he reached out for her and pulled her close, shaping his body to hers.

The next morning an eviction note was slipped under her doorway. Within three months they were married.

IT SHOULD HAVE been a happy ending—like in *Singing in the Rain* or *The African Queen* or at very least *Gone With the Wind* before Rhett Butler ran off. The truth, though, was that they didn't flourish, and the marriage wasn't happy—not even after word came from a survivor of the Shin Nagano massacre that Aki and Maki had been seen alive in a Manchurian farm town. Not even after they found a new, small, modern flat that Yoshi's salary from her new, post-Occupation job could cover. For one thing, Masa had trouble finding work. His time in China as settler, soldier and PRC prisoner all now counted against him. No one wanted to be reminded of Japan's Lost Paradise or the doomed war that had won and lost it, and Masa's years in a Communist-run camp led to suspicions he was a spy. It took a year to find a company that would hire him. When he did find a position—as a runner at the newly-reopened stock market—he worked long hours, leaving the flat early in the morning and often going out with his colleagues after work, coming home smelling like vomit and urine. On the nights he did come home he drank heavily, thrusting his empty glass at Yoshi for refills, answering her questions in grunts and monosyllables. Complaining of a headache when she played piano or even listened to the radio. Eventually, his presence made the *apato* feel chokingly small, and she began looking forward to her many evenings alone in it.

By the end of the first year she'd come to dread their physical couplings as well. Their lovemaking—while infrequent—maintained the pattern they had set that first night in her dormitory: rushed, removed. Often verging on violent. Even just sleeping together— merely sharing the same bed—could feel menacing. On some nights he'd sweat enough to soak the sheets. On others he'd have nightmares that made him shout out odd words and phrases (*Get her! The well! The chair!*) and thrash so violently he sometimes bruised her.

Then one night Yoshi woke up and found that she couldn't breathe; there was a crushing weight on her chest and something wrapped around her neck. Bucking and flailing, she managed to claw at her attacker's face. When her nails finally scratched flesh she heard a slurred curse. Then, at last, the pressure lifted.

Afterwards they sat at the tiny counter in their tiny kitchen, her throat bruised and aching, his scratched cheek still beading with blood. Masa didn't apologize. For the first ten minutes he didn't even speak. He poured himself some whiskey, lit one of his Mild Sevens and daubed his cheek with a white handkerchief she'd made him during their brief engagement.

"What is it?" Yoshi finally asked.

He looked at her dully. "What is what?"

"This thing that's happened to you."

"There's no way you'd understand."

"So explain it," she said, fighting to keep the shred of voice the attack had left her level. And when he didn't answer: "*Masa.* You might have killed me."

He looked out the window, a square glassed gap offering a view of new concrete. Outside a car rumbled by, tailed by wafts of Frank Sinatra. *Fly With Me.*

"I have dreams," he said finally.

"That much I understand."

"You can't," he said sharply. "They're dreams about things that happened—during the war."

Yoshi sat back in her chair, watching him. In the days when they talked more freely, she'd sometimes asked about the war—what it had been like for him in China. What he'd seen. She'd wanted to tell him about the night of the firebombing. But he'd end the conversation with a brusque "It was what you'd expect," or "It was tough."

He never even asked her about her experiences. It was as if he was pretending that the war had never happened, even while struggling over the fact that it had.

Now he met her gaze across the table. His eyes glittered blackly, opaque as ice. Staring into them, Yoshi was suddenly back in the Hongo-ku air raid shelter with her mother: *Do you really want to know what happened to me?*

She took a deep breath. "What sort of things?"

He finished off his whiskey, set the empty glass between them. With his eyes focused on it, he told her about life in the *Kantogun*. Not the honor and bravery implied in all his letters and all the news stories, but the misery of it. The meaningless cruelty and beatings that came with more frequency than food. The brutality of commanding officers and older soldiers towards new recruits. On his first night he'd been forced to play a game called *Ane-san*—"Big Sister." He had to perform a striptease, gesturing and pouting like a prostitute soliciting clients. When he wasn't convincing enough he was beaten and laughed at. On other nights he was beaten for no reason at all.

On his sixth day of service he was sent to bayonet practice in the fields, which was something they did each afternoon. On this particular day, though, the targets were not the usual scarecrow-like mannequins but two dozen live Chinese prisoners who'd been trucked in from another location. Many of them the same age or younger than Masa himself then. The first boy he was "assigned" begged for mercy, crying that he was the only child of his widowed mother. When Masa hesitated he felt the flat of his commander's sword on his shoulder and was told he'd lose his own head if he didn't obey orders.

"So you did it," Yoshi said.

Masa nodded, lighting another Mild Seven. "Turns out skin and bone are a lot tougher than stuffed straw. My first few thrusts were so inexperienced and ineffective that they did little more than poke holes in the poor kid's chest." He paused and refilled his glass. "After my seventh or eighth try the Chink finally died. Or at least, lost consciousness. Then I was given another. Then another after that."

She licked her lips. "How many . . . ?" She meant to ask *did you kill*, but the words died in her mouth.

"Four in total that day." His own words were starting to slur. Still, he refilled his glass and drank deeply. "It rained that night. I lay awake, listening to the water drip down into the tent. I was convinced that it was dripping blood."

"They were farm boys," she said, her voice shaking.

"We were told that they were insurgents."

"But you must have known they weren't. You *knew* they weren't."

"I knew what they told me," Masa snapped. "That's all any of us knew."

Yoshi closed her eyes, her lids squeezing so tightly she saw sparks against the fleeting darkness. She felt like a grenade that had had its pin pulled, and was just . . . waiting. All at once, she couldn't bear not to move.

Standing up, she stepped to the shelf where they kept their drinking glasses and pulled down another lowball. As she turned back, her attention was caught by two small wooden figures she and Masa had placed together on their first night here. There they were on the middle shelf, right above the sink: the female hawk he'd carved her back in Manchuria. The male hawk he'd carved in his prison camp. Standing proudly together on a little lacquer stand; a shrine to marital bliss.

She sat back down and poured herself a whiskey. The liquor felt like fire in her traumatized throat, but she also found it strangely bracing. Like that first ragged breath she'd drawn in after he'd released her, it told her that she was alive.

"Were there others?" she asked.

"Others?"

"Civilians."

Masahiro looked at her as though she'd asked if the sky was blue.

She had the urge to hurl herself across the table, at his own stubble-shadowed throat. She took another drink instead. "What about . . . what about the things you say in your sleep?"

He looked puzzled. "What things?"

"Like the well. You keep talking about a chair and a well."

He winced and looked away. "Why does it matter?"

"I need to know."

Masahiro rubbed a temple tiredly. When he looked up again he looked past her, his voice so low she could barely hear it.

"I'd had this order from my commanding officer," he told her. "He told me to dispose of an insurgent."

"An insurgent?"

He tightened his jaw. "All right, all right, probably not an insurgent. She was a woman, OK? A woman. Very pretty. We'd already killed her husband. Commander Yamazaki had taken her into a room. He did that with the pretty ones."

"Why?"

The question was out before she could stop herself. The look he gave her was pure disdain.

"Anyway," he went on, "I guess she wouldn't let him do it because he came out again in a huff. Scratch marks on his face and everything." Absently, he touched his cheek, where the blood from his own scratch was gradually congealing. "He was dragging her by the hair."

I'm going to be sick, Yoshi thought. But she couldn't move.

"Me and this buddy of mine," Masa went on, "Kanegawa-*kun*. He died later—dysentery. Anyways. Yamazaki had asked us to guard the door while he was in there with her. When he came out he dragged her to us and told us to take her out to this deep stone well in the backyard . . ."

Stop, she thought; *stop talking . . .*

"And to throw her down it."

She couldn't bear to look at him, so she stared down at her hands.

Hana's hands: long white fingers. Gently dimpled joints. The green "good luck" ring. She finally managed to part her lips. "What about the chair? You cry out about a chair sometimes."

He stayed silent for several seconds, turning his glass around in his hands. "The woman had a daughter," he said finally. "A little one—maybe three years old. She'd run after us when we dragged her mother outside. After we threw the woman down the girl circled the well a few times, then ran off. I thought she'd run away. I—I hoped she'd run away."

"But she hadn't."

Masa shook his head. "When she came back she was pushing this chair from the house. A pretty big one—I guess she was a strong kid for her age." He cleared his throat. "Anyway. As the three of us stood there watching she pushed that chair right up to the well's side."

A roaring silence seemed to fill Yoshi's ears. She almost choked trying to get the words out. "And then?"

He gave her an anguished look. "Do I really have to say it?"

The room seemed to be pulsing; pressing in on her. Suffocating. She shut her eyes against it, but that only made her see and feel it more clearly; the overwhelming panic. The bewildered child. The strange man dragging her mother by the hair. The well, with its gaping black mouth. Tears pricked at her lashes, but she was powerless to brush them off. She let them well, trace their wet pathways down her cheeks.

When she opened her eyes again, for the first time in months he was looking at her with concern. "Are you all right?" he asked softly.

It might have been the absurdity of the question, or the solicitous look on his face. Or the fact that whenever she breathed she was breathing him in; smelling and even tasting sweat and stale whiskey, exhaled tobacco, blood. Somehow, though, the spell broke, and she could move again.

"I'm going to be sick," she gasped; and ran from the room.

When she came back he'd fallen asleep, his thin arms cradling his touseled head on the table. Yoshi stood helplessly behind him, wanting to touch him, wanting to run. Knowing there was no one else left to run to. In the end she left him there, a pink shawl draped over his shoulders, a glass of water within reach of his limp hand.

"WE TRIED TO make it work," was all she told Billy now, quietly. "But we weren't children any longer. And it was as though something was . . . broken." She smiled ruefully. "I sometimes think it was my punishment for all the things I did wrong in my life."

He looked puzzled. "What things?"

The alcohol was affecting her again, warming her tongue, her cheeks, her thoughts. She decided to just say it: "I sometimes think I killed my mother."

"*What?*" It came out with enough force that a couple standing by the nearest photograph turned slightly to look down at them; reflexively, Yoshi lowered her own voice.

"I—I left her, you see. I left her alone that Friday night. I volunteered to spend the night at my school for a project, even though I didn't have to."

"But that doesn't make you a *killer*. How could you have known?"

"Because she wasn't well. She was ill. I knew she couldn't take care of herself if there was an air raid."

"Yoshi," he said. He looked genuinely stricken as he reached across the little table for her hand. "You didn't know there'd *be* an air raid. The bombers flew in under the radar. Even the Japanese Army didn't catch on—at least, not until it was much too late. That's why the sirens didn't go off."

"But there was always a chance. There had always been the chance. We'd been practicing for months, because we knew that. And I *knew* she wouldn't go into the shelter. I knew that. But even then—" Her voice caught; she shook her head.

"So you went," he said, gesturing dismissively. "You were a kid and you went to school."

"You don't understand. It wasn't just out of duty. The truth was that I couldn't *wait* to go. To get out of that awful house, if just for one night. Don't you see?"

He was about to answer when a voice interrupted them. *"There you are! I've been looking all over for you, Mr. Photographer-of-the-Evening!"*

Looking up, Yoshi saw a handsome, diminutive Oriental man wearing a black blazer and a beret. He had wine in each hand, and as he set the cups on the table he eyed Yoshi—or rather, *her* hand, the one Billy was now holding—with open curiosity and (it struck her) something else.

"Ah, *gomen*," Billy said, and stood up quickly. "I must have forgotten the time. I've been talking with my old friend here, Kobabayshi-*san*."

Billy pulled the man forward as Yoshi stood up as well. "Kobayashi-*san*," he told her. "This is my dear friend and roommate, Suminaga Akio."

The smaller man bowed gracefully. *"Hajimemashite,"* he said. *"Yoroshiku, onegai shimasu* . . . I've heard wonderful things from Will here. Though"—he winked—"he neglected to tell me how absolutely stunning you are."

His voice was easy and melodious, his wink and English as flawlessly West Coast as his Japanese accent was pure Tokyo. *Nissei*, Yoshi decided. Or schooled abroad for most of his life. Like her mother.

"I did *not* neglect to tell you," Billy was saying, with mock affront. "I told you that she looked like a Japanese Audrey Hepburn."

"You lie, Will," said Akio agreeably. "You lie like a rug." But he slapped Billy's arm affectionately, his slim fingers lingering on the black wool before reaching out to shake Yoshi's hand.

As Yoshi extended her own hand back, two things struck her. One was that she had never known William Reynolds to have any close male friends—or for that matter, any real friends beyond herself. The second was that for all their glaring physical differences these two men looked oddly . . . *right* together. Not just like flatmates, or even "dear friends" but almost like brothers, despite the obvious differences in height and build and skin tone.

As Yoshi retrieved her hand the third realization struck her: that they were more than friends. That they were, in fact, both friends *and* lovers. Perhaps oddly, the epiphany didn't bother, or even really surprise her, in the least. In fact, what she mostly felt was relief. First, that the question she'd unwittingly been asking herself these past years had been answered. And second, that whatever else he might be, at least Billy Reynolds wasn't as lonely as she was.

"You like the exhibition?" Akio was asking her in Japanese.

"More than like it," she replied. "It's—it's amazing. He really captured the feel of the city, hasn't he?"

Akio beamed with pride. "He's very talented, this *gaijin.*"

Billy gave his arm a push. "We're in America, my friend. You two are the 'outside people' here." To Yoshi, he added: "Akio's a photographer too. Though more on the magazine side. It was his idea for me to pull together my old photos and try to make something of them."

"It just took the idea," Akio said, shrugging. "You did all the rest of it yourself."

He stood up on his gleaming tiptoes to brush something from Billy's collar, and Yoshi felt a small stab of envy. Would she ever have someone feel such pride for her; or offer such tiny gestures of intimacy: brush lint from her coat sleeve, a stray lash from her cheek? Suddenly, she was aware of a nearly stupefying sense of exhaustion—as though she'd spent the last twenty minutes not sitting and drinking wine with a friend, but running at an all-out sprint. As it rolled its way over her a section of the Lawrence she'd read came back: *It's no good trying to get rid of your own aloneness. You've got to stick to it all your life. Only at times, at times, the gap will be filled in. At times! But you have to wait for the times . . .*

"How long are you in L.A. for?" Akio was asking.

"Until Wednesday." She forced a smile. "I leave for New York very early Thursday morning."

"Ah. And—what are your plans before then?"

"I want to see . . . Rodeo Drive, of course." She swayed a little on her feet. *Jet lag.* "And Grauman's Chinese Theatre. And of course, Disneyland. Other than that, I've left it fairly free."

"*Nee*, Billy," said Akio excitedly, "can we take her to Taylor's for lunch tomorrow?"

"Taylor's." Billy turned to Yoshi thoughtfully. "What do you say, Yoshi-*chan*? Feel like some good American steak?"

"I do, but not tomorrow."

"No?"

She shook her head. "I have—I have someone I have to see."

"For work?"

"Yes," she said, avoiding his eyes. "But I could go Monday, if that works."

The two men held a whispered conference, after which Billy nodded. "I believe we can steal ourselves away on a Monday. Let's talk tomorrow night." And then: "Are you all right? You're very pale all of a sudden."

"I think I'm just tired."

"Do you have energy to join us for a drink later? We're meeting some folks at around nine."

It wasn't even 6 p.m. yet, and the thought of spending three more hours on her feet was almost enough to make her topple over on the spot. Yoshi shook her head, pretending to be slightly embarrassed. "I think perhaps I should go sleep. I may have already had too much of your wine."

"Well, let's get you outside so you can get a cab."

Offering her his arm again, Billy murmured something more to Akio, who nodded and bowed.

"Yoroshiku onegai shimasu," he said. "I will look forward to seeing you again on Monday." And then to Billy: "You walk Kobayashi-*san* out. I'll wait by the bar, *nee?"*

When they reached the doorway Billy leaned over and gave her a quick kiss on the cheek. "You sure you'll be all right finding a cab? There should be several at the stand right across the street."

Yoshi rubbed her eyes, which suddenly felt as dry as sand pits. "I think so." She squeezed his hand, then turned back to the exit, offering a farewell glance at her sixteen-year-old self on the wall in the process. Before she could open the door, though, she felt his hand on her shoulder.

"Yoshi-*chan.*"

When she turned he was patting his pockets again. "There was one more thing I meant to give you . . ." He frowned, pulling something from the inside of his suit jacket. As she took it in her hands she saw that it was a white envelope, small and sealed but substantial-feeling.

"What is this?"

"Just some extra pictures I found when I was going through my old negatives."

"Surely not of me," she said in dismay, thinking back to numerous holiday parties and office lunches during which she was invariably caught with her eyes shut.

He laughed at her expression. "They're not that bad. Take a look when you have a moment." He gave her shoulder a squeeze. "I'll call you tomorrow night. *Oyasumi nasai.*"

"*Oyasumi.*"

Nodding sleepily, Yoshi slid the envelope between the pages of her Lawrence. Then, clicking her purse closed again, she stepped out into the warm California night.

———

THE DRIVE TO Sunset Park began as a wet blur of gray and silver and green, set to the comforting *clack* of windshield wipers.

"Not much of a beach day," the cabdriver noted, studying the address she'd handed him.

"I'm not going to the beach," she told him, and yawned. For all her exhaustion she'd spent much of the night tossing and turning on the king-size hotel bed, and then had almost slept through her 6 a.m. wake-up call. After setting the receiver down she'd lain there a moment in the dreary light, imagining it all over again: the American pilot on his knees. Yamazaki's sword flashing. *He died of his wounds? You could say that.* She imagined the widow's house as a tiny beach bungalow; as one of the Hearst-like mansions she'd seen from the air. She imagined ringing the doorbell and there being no answer; imagined the door opening and then slamming shut in her face. She imagined Bette Davis tears and Joan Crawford rage. A warm embrace. A slap on the cheek. The one thing she couldn't imagine was—for the first time in fifteen years—not having the ring's famil- iar weight and heft on her finger; not having a single thing in her life that her mother had touched. And yet somehow, if what she feared about the ring was also true, then holding on to it seemed far worse.

"So you're visiting friends?" the cabdriver said as they pulled onto the rain-silvered expressway.

"More of an acquaintance."

"Nice neighborhood."

She nodded, looked out the window. Even the highways in this country were absurdly oversized, fitting up to four or more lanes of enormous American cars: Chevrolets. Rumbling Buicks. Fords. The steady rain made the cars and the highway alike slick and shiny, as if they'd just emerged from their factories and cement mixers. Everything was so new here; so highly evolved. So *strong*. It struck her again how pathetic it was that anyone in her country had ever even mouthed the word *victory*.

"Where are you from?" the driver asked, as though hearing the thought.

"Tokyo." She said it a little warily; on the trip from the airport a similar answer had earned her an impassioned speech on the Day of Infamy. But this driver merely nodded. "Always wanted to go there. I ended up serving in France."

"I've always wanted to go to France," she said, which was true.

"I'm sure it's better now than it was when I was there."

"Tokyo is better too." They laughed together, which put her more at ease. Oddly, he reminded her a bit of Kenji: similarly stocky, with a pronounced nose and kind brown eyes. Like an older, heavier version of Cary Grant.

"Mind if I turn on some music?" he was asking.

"Of course," she said; and then immediately regretted it as the radio released a sad feminine croon about a soldier boy who left for war and never returned.

"This OK?" asked the driver. And while it wasn't, of course it wasn't, she didn't have the heart to tell him that.

They drove on for more miles, the pounding rain painting the cab windows with wetly shifting mosaics. Yoshi stared at the blurred, busy and yet strangely desolate highway landscape, trying to imagine what the pilot's widow would look like. Would her hair be fair, like her husband's had been? Would her face be round or long? How would she greet this strange Oriental woman appearing on her doorstep with no warning? And *should* there have been a warning? The Santa Monica listing Yoshi had found had included a phone number, but she hadn't been able to bring herself to call it. For what if Lacy Richards Murphy hung up on her, or refused to see her? Then the question would never be answered. And the pilot's ring (if it *was* the pilot's) would never get home.

He died of his wounds?

You could say that . . .

. . . And then she was asleep, the rain and the wet palm trees and the silver streak of the road blending into a muddled image of ruined homes and *pan-pan* girls and the old Yamaha piano Billy had found for her in the Pyle basement, until she woke to a heavy hand on her shoulder.

"Miss! Miss . . ."

Gasping, Yoshi opened her eyes.

"Miss, are you all right?"

He'd turned around in his seat to wake her. Yoshi slid up in her seat, touching her lips with her little finger. Her mouth felt dry and gummy, her throat oddly tender. "Yes," she murmured. "I'm sorry. I must have slept . . ."

"Out like a light," he commented cheerfully. "Wish I could fall asleep that easily."

He turned back towards his dashboard, set his emergency brake and then rolled down his window. Both the car and the rain had stopped, and she saw that they were in a small residential neighborhood full of stucco houses with neat yards and orderly gardens. The grass and flowers sparkled from their morning shower; a red-breasted robin hopped across a patch of green. Pausing, he picked a bit of string from the still-wet soil that turned out to be a writhing, terrified earthworm. As Yoshi watched, the bird yanked it out with ruthless efficacy, snapping it back with a single gulp.

"Is this Sunset Park?"

"Glenridge Way. That's the place."

He pointed to a small house across the street, a few feet in front of them. It didn't particularly look like a widow's house. It was painted bright yellow, with a green door. A bench swing with blue cushions stood on the little porch, moving slightly back and forth in the unseen breeze. There was a baseball glove lying half-open on the seat and a red bicycle leaning against the front wall.

"Mailbox says *Murphy* on it," he added. "That the name?"

Yoshi nodded, her palms prickling with sweat. *Lacy Richards Murphy.* That was the name she'd found in the *Doolittle Raiders Yearbook,* a publication the Air Corps put out in the Raiders' honor every year for their annual reunion. Last year's had been in Arkansas, and under the name *Cameron Richards (M.I.A.)* she had seen his wife and son's names for the first time: *Lacy Richards Murphy. Cameron Richards III.* She remembered blinking back unexpected tears: it hadn't occurred to her that the American pilot might have had a son.

"Pretty little place your friend has," the driver was saying, apparently forgetting their earlier conversation. "Her husband must be doing well."

She nodded, wiping her hands on her skirt, feeling the ring catch against the rough-weave cotton and then—for some reason—suffering a real wave of panic. Why had she thought she could do this? Now that she was here, the whole idea of it seemed idiotic. Showing up out of nowhere, still reeling under a different time zone. Holding out her mother's ring like a peace offering. As though one old trinket could undo the wrongs and hurts of two decades. As though it might even *mean* something . . .

Maybe they're not home, she thought; but even as she thought it the blue door was flung open from inside. She watched as a tall, long-limbed boy with golden hair leapt out and picked up the glove.

"I'm headed to the library, Ma," he called back through the door. Taking the mitt off, he tossed it into the air, caught it absently. "I'll be back by dinner."

From inside the house came a woman's voice: "Don't you forget, now. Tom and I are going to the movies later. I need you to babysit Joshy."

A shadow appeared behind the screen door. Yoshi leaned forward, but she couldn't make out any details beyond a full skirt and pale face.

"I'll be there." Setting the mitt down again, the boy turned and took the porch steps two at a time, his long legs as graceful as an elk's. He wheeled the bike to the curb, and as he swung himself onto it Yoshi felt a shiver go down her spine. He looked exactly like the yearbook picture of his father, and as his pale eyes met hers Yoshi had the juvenile urge to duck down below the window frame. But the boy didn't seem to register her at all. He simply pedaled off, disappearing down the next block.

The driver was opening the door. "Are you going to want me to wait here for you, miss?" he asked, stepping back politely, waiting.

Swallowing, Yoshi forced herself to step out. "If you could," she said, squinting a little in the sunlight. "I don't think I'll be long."

Pulling her compact from her purse, she surveyed her face bleakly. She looked decidedly *unlike* Audrey Hepburn; pale and drawn, with deep shadows beneath dark eyes that were still puffy from her back-seat sleep. She had a small smudge above her left eyebrow, possibly from the taxi window. Licking her handkerchief, Yoshi rubbed it off, then carefully repowdered her nose and cheeks. She applied a coat of Siren Red to her dry lips, then pulled out her business card holder and removed one of her Tuttledge cards. Finally, she went to remove the ring from her finger. But for the first time in her memory the accessory—which had always fit perfectly—actually seemed stuck on her middle finger; the tarnished metal biting into the pale flesh even after she twisted it fully around. Annoyed, Yoshi moistened her knuckle with her tongue and managed to get it off, leaving the skin beneath pink and irritated-looking.

Rubbing her palm against her skirt, she lodged her pocketbook under one arm. Then, ring in one hand and business card in the other, she began walking towards the house.

When she reached the door, she heard the sound of water running and porcelain clinking—someone washing up the breakfast dishes. She listened for a moment, marveling that anything could sound so mundane before—heart pounding—she rang the doorbell.

"Cam?" the woman's voice called. "That you? Did you forget something?"

The washing sounds stopped and a pair of heels clicked towards where she stood. Then the screen door was open again, and the woman she'd seen in shadow was standing before her, wiping her hands on her apron.

"Mrs. Murphy?" Yoshi asked, just to be sure.

"Yes," the woman replied pleasantly.

She had dark, shiny hair that was pulled back into a bun, and green eyes that narrowed uncertainly as they met Yoshi's. Lacy Richards Murphy was wearing just a touch of makeup. But her face was fresh and young-looking, not drawn and grim as Yoshi had imagined it in her restless hotel bed last night. She looked to be perhaps in her late thirties or early forties. She was, Yoshi realized (for some reason with a slight pang) exceptionally pretty.

"Can I help you?" she asked.

Yoshi found herself bowing out of reflex; then she caught herself and stood up straight again. "I—I am sorry to trouble you. I just . . ."

She stopped as a small boy with a dark thatch of hair came galloping out from the hallway on a hobbyhorse. With a shrill-sounding whinny he pulled up next to the woman, clutching her bare leg possessively, staring up at Yoshi with his mother's green eyes, as though she were a creature from the moon.

"Who's that?" he asked his mother. "Is it an Injun?"

"Shhh," said Lacy. "Don't be rude, Joshy. We must give the lady a chance to tell us her name."

She smiled apologetically at Yoshi. Biting her lip, Yoshi forced herself to start over. "My—my name is Yoshi Kobayashi." She held out her card. "I am from Tokyo, Japan."

The woman took the card. "E. E. Tuttledge?" she read, looking puzzled. "You're a translator?"

Yoshi nodded. "But that's not why I'm here."

Lacy cocked her head, waiting.

"You are . . . you were the wife of Cameron Richards?"

Something in the woman's green eyes seemed to shift. "Yes. He passed away in the war."

Yoshi nodded. "I know. I . . . I think this was his."

She held out the ring.

For a moment Lacy Richards didn't move; she didn't even blink. She just stared at the green stone, her green eyes widening.

She doesn't recognize it, Yoshi thought; but just as the relief began to register the pilot's wife reached out her hand.

"Where . . . where did you get this," she asked in a low voice, holding the small silver circle up to the sunlight. "Where . . ."

She shut her eyes for a moment, gripping the ring so tightly that Yoshi saw her knuckles turn white. Then she looked down at her son.

"Joshy," she said, in a tight voice, "go play in the kitchen."

"I don't want to," said the boy, still staring fixedly up at Yoshi.

"Joshua Francis Murphy," his mother said sharply, "you go right into that kitchen." Taking his small shoulders with both hands, she turned him around and gave him a gentle swat on the rear. The child let out a wail that seemed largely symbolic; a moment later he was galloping down the darkened hallway.

After he'd gone, Lacy turned back to Yoshi. All signs of welcome had disappeared from her face.

"Where did you get it?" Her voice had a new harshness to it.

"It—it was my mother's," Yoshi stammered. "My father gave it to her."

"Where did your father get it?"

For a moment her mind was blank; not just of answers, but of any language at all. No English; no French. There wasn't even Japanese. There was just an inchoate clump of sound lodged painfully in her throat; a jagged ball of harsh consonants and gentle vowels. She had no idea how to force the words through her lips.

"Well?" said Lacy Richards. She was still clutching the ring in her fist, and for some reason Yoshi took comfort in this; the idea that as long as the ring wasn't on the other woman's finger the thing she feared most might not be true.

"I—I'm not sure," Yoshi managed. "I was just a child at the time. But I—think he found your husband. After he . . ."

She drifted off, unable to finish. The American woman's face had gone ashen. Without a word, she stepped over to the bench swing and sank down onto its blue cushions. She sat there for a moment, pushing herself numbly back and forth before she cleared her throat and spoke again. Her eyes were still fixed on the ring.

"I've gotten letters," she said. "Reports. I got a map of where his grave was. I've got a Purple Heart. I've even got a goddamn Distinguished Flying Cross. I waited for years—for *years.* But it was only years later that we learned for sure that he was dead, and years after that that he didn't die in the jump."

"I'm sorry," whispered Yoshi; but Lacy ignored her.

"It would have been better," she went on, shaking her head, "it would have been better if he *had* died like that. In the fall. To hear that he was captured; that some goddamn Jap took a sword and . . . and . . ."

She lapsed into silence, still staring at her fist. Yoshi stood where she was, the word *Jap* ringing through her head, the image of Captain Yamazaki's sword flashing before her eyes. She shut her eyes from it but it remained there, glimmering . . .

From the unseen recesses of the kitchen came the sound of a television; a man's voice against tremulous violins.

"Jesus Christ," Lacy muttered.

Opening her eyes again, Yoshi saw Lacy turn her head towards the screen door in annoyance. "Hey! Joshy!" she called shrilly. "Turn it off, mister!"

"Awww, Mom!" the boy called back; but the music and the man's voice went away.

Yoshi bit her lip and stared down at her pumps, fighting back a hysterical giggle. When she looked back up Lacy was staring at her. Her expression was unreadable.

"So I suppose," she said in a carefully controlled voice, "my next question would be 'why?' "

"Why what?"

"Why this?" Lacy held the ring up again. She still hadn't put it on. "Why did you bring this to me? You certainly didn't have to. I wouldn't have known the difference."

I brought it to you because I had to know the truth, Yoshi thought. *About my father. About the war.* But of course she didn't say this.

"I brought it to you," she said instead, slowly, "because it belongs with you. It seemed . . . the right thing to do."

She felt Lacy Richards eyes on her, as green as seawater, as green as her ring. Assessing her; scanning her face for truth or for false-hood or the cool gray place in between.

"All right, then," she said, finally.

"All right then?" Yoshi repeated uncertainly.

"All right," Lacy Richards Murphy said. "You've done it. Mission accomplished. You can go."

She glanced meaningfully towards the taxi that was still waiting across the street. For a moment Yoshi just stared at her.

"Don't you understand?" Lacy repeated, her voice lifting in anger now. "You can go now."

Yoshi felt her face flood with color. Trembling, she turned away. But as she stepped from the porch Lacy spoke again: "Wait."

She turned back, bewildered. The pilot's wife was standing again, holding Yoshi's card before her eyes.

"Did you lose anyone in the war, Miss Kobayashi?"

Yoshi swallowed. "I lost my parents." She thought a moment, then added: "And . . . my husband."

It wasn't something she'd ever articulated before, but as the words came out she realized they were true. Lacy Richards Murphy seemed to ponder them too a moment. Then she dropped her gaze to the ring. As Yoshi watched, she slowly and deliberately slid it onto her middle finger.

"You know," she said, almost conversationally, "this belonged to my mother. She called it the 'come home to me safely' ring." She gave a sharp, grim laugh. "Cam always said that was a damn silly name."

For a moment, neither woman spoke. Then Lacy Richards Murphy slipped Yoshi's card in her apron pocket.

"Thank you," she said. "Goodbye, Miss Kobayashi." And with a vague wave of her ringed hand she disappeared into her house.

"NICE VISIT?" THE driver asked, opening the door for her.

Yoshi just shook her head and clambered in. Her breath was coming in short, sharp gasps; she felt as though she had a metal band around her chest.

"Where to?" the driver asked, restarting the engine and the meter. "Back to the Biltmore?"

She shook her head again; the idea of driving endless hours through empty highway and palm trees somehow made it even harder to breathe. "Somewhere—else, please. Someplace where I can just . . . sit."

"Sit, huh," said the driver, suppressing a smile. "Well, it's turned into a pretty nice day. How about the beach?"

Yoshi pressed her forehead against the cool glass of the window. "How far is it?"

"I know one about twenty minutes from here. Hidden gem. I'll bet you that after that rain there'll be hardly anyone on it."

"All right," she said; and leaning back against the seat, she stared down at her own hand, so bare now it seemed obscene.

FIFTEEN MINUTES LATER she was sitting on the shoreline, purse in her lap, sand-dusted pumps beside her. The beach was so small it didn't even have a name, but the driver had been right—apart from a flock of bickering seagulls, Yoshi had the little area to herself. Taking advantage of the solitude and the midday sun, she'd taken off her stockings, balling them up neatly inside her shoes so she could feel the sand between her toes.

Now she stared out at the Pacific, the flat blue line of sea and sky, as empty of emotion as space itself. *This is it*, she thought. *This is what started it all.* This was what they'd all been fighting over: a silk-smooth stretch of ocean between California and Yokohama. It seemed strange that something so serene, so intrinsically peaceful could have incited so much bloodlust; could cause fathers to kill husbands and pilots to kill mothers and young men to let babies fall down wells. *Why does it happen?* she asked herself. *Why do we do it? What have we learned when it is done?*

Overwhelmed, she looked down at her pale hands; the left stripped of the simple band Masa had placed on it at the Imperial; the right now stripped of the pilot's ring. The irritation on her right ring finger had subsided, but in its place was a new emptiness—a sense that her hands were so light and unanchored now that they might fly right off her wrists.

Shaking away the thought, she pulled out the *Chatterley*, thinking to lose herself in Lawrence's fluid narrative. But as she opened the volume something slid from between the pages—not Billy's letter, but the envelope he'd given her last night at the gallery. She'd been so exhausted that she'd forgotten to open it before going to bed, and then so rushed this morning she'd forgotten again. Now, curious and a little reluctant too (she really did photograph badly), she slid her finger beneath the flap and pulled out the small stack of photographs.

Immediately, she saw that they weren't from the Pyle. They were emptier-looking, and older: age had yellowed the whites and browned the blacks. At first glance the one on top seemed to show little more than a small black blot against a sky. Looking more closely, though, Yoshi saw it was a hawk, its wings spread as though to embrace the entire horizon, its curved beak defined against a cloud. She studied it, puzzled by an elusive sense of familiarity. As though she'd seen this exact image somewhere before, possibly in a dream.

She moved on to the next image, which showed a pair of plump, childish feet with chipped polish on the toes, and beyond them a very unusual house. The house had a stage-like patio with six small, blurred people sitting in chairs on it and (she had to look closely to confirm it) a *waterfall*, of all things. Tumbling from its tiled roof. She felt that same strange sense of déjà-vu: as though this were a picture from one of her old storybooks or a photo album she'd once had on her bookcase.

The next photograph was a closer shot of the patio, tightening in on a Japanese man holding a little girl in his lap. As she looked at it more closely Yoshi gasped again, wondering whether the lack of sleep and unaccustomed drinking and smoking were finally taking their toll. But even after she blinked there was still no doubt about it: the man was her father. Even more astonishingly, the child was Yoshi.

Kenji Kobayashi was leaning back in a deck chair, his stocky frame trimmer and his hair darker than Yoshi remembered it being. But the gold tooth—the one he'd sometimes let her touch for good luck—was right there, twinkling in the evening sunlight. He had a glass of beer in one hand. His face was split in a familiar grin, probably over something Yoshi had done or was about to do. Her own face was half-obscured, but it was clear that she was laughing—a delirious, love-laden little-girl laugh.

Yoshi stared down at the image, her breath caught and her

thoughts churning. Then she looked back at the empty envelope, which wasn't empty after all. Inside was a note. Hands shaking, she unfolded the single sheet of paper.

Yoshi:

I found these photographs on my last visit to see my mother, when I helped her clean out her attic. I've held on to them for months, but I've come to realize that they rightfully belong to you.

 All my love,

 Billy

Stunned, Yoshi looked up. It had occurred to her, of course, that her father's path might have crossed Anton Reynolds' during Tokyo's prewar building boom. She'd even asked Billy once, when they still worked together: "Did your father ever mention meeting mine? It seems likely they might have known one another."

"I believe they met once or twice," he'd replied, and that was all. Yoshi had assumed his curtness stemmed from the discomfort Billy felt about his father in general; she knew their relationship had been difficult. Staring down at Kenji's photo now, though, she realized that he must have also been trying to protect her—for of course he would have known about Kenji's role in Cameron Richards' death by that point.

For a moment, Lacy Richards' lovely, hurt face floated before her again. *The come-home-to-me-safely ring . . . Cam always said that was a damn silly name.*

Biting her lip, Yoshi shuffled Kenji's image to the back of the stack, half-wondering whether she'd ever be able to look at it again without this complicated mesh of guilt and grief. Then she glanced down at the last photograph, and all other thoughts fled.

For there, in the same doorway of the waterfall house, stood her mother.

Hana Kobayashi posed in the summer house's doorway, wearing an elegant but snug-fitting white sundress. She had on high-heeled pumps, and her lips and fingertips were dark with lipstick and varnish. Her hair was slightly mussed, and fell across her cheekbone in a way that partially obscured her face. But it was definitely *her* hair, with its chic trademark bob and the cold-pressed double wave that had so outraged the neighbors and the police. In her hand she held an ivory cigarette holder Yoshi had forgotten, but now looked at with a jolt of recognition. It held a Winston, its tip newly lit and sending up a faint scribble of smoke.

Yoshi flipped the picture over, her hand trembling. On it, in a childish hand, someone had written *Karuizawa, 1935.*

Mama, Yoshi thought.

Overwhelmed, she lay back slowly in the warm sand, pressing the photograph to her chest. The noon sun kissed her cheeks and her eyelids and her nose, and like a gift the memory descended:

She was small—very small. She'd been running down a hill; her feet were very dirty. Someone had painted her toenails red. She'd been trying to reach her mother, with that inarguable, ravenous need that small children can have for their mothers, and a teasing fear that Hana would not be there. But she was, and Yoshi had reached her, and was now held tightly in her lap.

Hana smelled of lavender and Winston cigarettes and the bite of some liquor, and Yoshi felt safe and sheltered in the pale nimbus of her arms. There were other people around them, but neither mother nor child paid them any attention. For that one moment they were alone; a single unit. Yoshi curled into Hana's body, and Hana hugged her so tightly back that Yoshi felt her mother's heartbeat against her cheek. Its rhythm tapped out a special message just for her:

You are loved. You are loved.

A Note on Sources

IN RESEARCHING THIS NOVEL I MUST HAVE CONSULTED DOZENS of sources, but several stand out as being particularly helpful. Max Hasting's *Retribution* is both an extraordinarily thorough account of the Pacific War and exceptionally compelling. *The Year of the Wild Boar*—a memoir of *New York Times* reporter Helen Meirs' year in 1935 Tokyo— was of great help in reconstructing the general mood in Tokyo in the years leading up to the Pacific War, and also inspired the conflicted character of Hana Kobayashi. Louise Young's *Japan's Total Empire: Manchuria and the Culture of Wartime Imperialism* provided a fascinating perspective on Japan's colonization of northern China. *Thirty Seconds Over Tokyo*, Captain Ted Dawson's classic memoir about the Doolittle Raid, was of enormous help in trying to re-create that extraordinary attack fictionally and lent inspiration to many of Cam Richard's experiences. *So Sad to Fall in Battle*, Kumiko Kakehashi's mesmerizing account of the battle of Iwo Jima based on General Tadamichi Kuribayashi's collected letters, provided tremendous insight into what it was like to be a Japanese soldier fighting a desperate and hopeless battle, and *Since You Went Away: World War II Letters from American Women on the Home Front* supplied both engaging and informative voices of wives waiting on the American side for their men to come home. *My Queer War* by James Lord provided insight into the lives of gay servicemen during World War II. Finally, the documentary *Riben Guizi* (*Japanese Devils*) offered profoundly affecting (if often disturbing) personal accounts by former Japanese soldiers who committed atrocities in China.

Acknowledgments

MANY PEOPLE HAVE OFFERED ADVICE, AID OR ENCOURAGEMENT to me in the writing of this novel. I'd like in particular to thank the Tokyo Air Raids and War Damages Center and its extraordinary staff for their support, and firebombing survivors Yoshiko Hashimoto, Toshiko Kameya and Shizuyo Takeuchi for their candid and detailed recollections of the night of March 10, 1945. Tadashi Okazoe and Masayoshi Ozaki shared both their time and their memories of life in the Japanese armed forces during the Pacific War, and Sei-Ichi Nakata provided a gold mine of information on both Japan's wartime past and Occupation. Thanks to Maurice Brill for sharing both memories and photographs of his time as a young intelligence officer in Occupied Japan. Retired USAF Colonel Marcy Atwood was invaluable in both directing me to American air history resources and teaching me what actually goes into flying a bomber, and former U.S. Navy flier Tom Cody read and corrected at least a dozen drafts of my U.S.S. *Hornet* section to make sure I got all the aeronautic details right (though I may still have missed a few—sorry, Dad!).

Yuko Sakata has to be the world's best researcher and translator, and I cannot possibly thank her enough for the time and attention she has given this project. I'd also like to thank Doug Shinsato and Tad Urabe for helping me find my way and many sources in Tokyo, as well as Chihiro Sato and Jonathan Hall for their most excellent interpretation services. Sam Morse of the Amherst College Asian Studies Department provided many missing links in terms of books and relevant photographs and where to find them. I'd like to thank my agent Elizabeth Sheinkman for feedback and support, editorial assistants Alison Liss and Rebecca Schultz for troubleshooting and input, and editor Jill Bialosky for (as always) inspired editorial guidance. Readers Hillary Jordan, Joanna Hershon, Lizzie Simon, Sarah Saffian, Ellen Umansky and Andrea LaFleur invested many hours of reading, rereading, discussion, challenge and encouragement, for which I am deeply indebted. And Scott Atkins and the Brooklyn Writers Space provided that rarest of New York commodities (at least for distractible writers like myself): quiet, distraction-free environments in which to lose myself to my work. Thanks also go out to the surviving members of the 1942 Doolittle Raids, both for their heroic service and for their inspiring presence and continuing spirit at the annual Doolittle Raider reunions, one of which I had the honor of attending.

Last but not in the least least, I'd like to thank my family. My husband Michael Epstein not only inspired this project but was both its biggest champion and its toughest critic—not to mention taking care of the home front for countless hours so I could actually write it. And daughters Katie and Hannah sustain me on a steady diet of love and humor while teaching me more every day about the things that really matter.

Photograph Credits